# BRIMSTONE

## CHERIE PRIEST

ACE
NEW YORK

ACE
Published by Berkley
An imprint of Penguin Random House LLC
375 Hudson Street, New York, New York 10014

Copyright © 2017 by Cherie Priest
Penguin Random House supports copyright. Copyright fuels creativity, encourages
diverse voices, promotes free speech, and creates a vibrant culture. Thank you for
buying an authorized edition of this book and for complying with copyright laws
by not reproducing, scanning, or distributing any part of it in any form without
permission. You are supporting writers and allowing Penguin Random House
to continue to publish books for every reader.

ACE is a registered trademark and the A colophon is a
trademark of Penguin Random House LLC.

Library of Congress Cataloging-in-Publication Data

Names: Priest, Cherie, author.
Title: Brimstone/Cherie Priest.
Description: First edition. | New York: Ace, 2017.
Identifiers: LCCN 2016046116 (print) | LCCN 2016054058 (ebook) | ISBN
9781101990735 (softcover) | ISBN 9781101990742 (ebook)
Subjects: | BISAC: FICTION/Fantasy/Historical. | FICTION/Horror. | GSAFD:
Fantasy fiction. | Horror fiction. | Occult fiction.
Classification: LCC PS3616.R537 B75 2017 (print) | LCC PS3616.R537 (ebook) |
DDC 813/.6—dc23
LC record available at https://lccn.loc.gov/2016046116

First Edition: April 2017

Printed in the United States of America
1  3  5  7  9  10  8  6  4  2

Cover art by Rovina Cai
Cover design by Katie Anderson
Title page art deco frame © maximmmmum / Shutterstock Images
Book design by Tiffany Estreicher

*This is dedicated to everyone in Cassadaga, Florida—*
*for you were all so unfailingly gracious and kind to this nosy writer*
*who wanted to tell a weird little story about your hometown.*
*Thank you for your thoughts, suggestions, and encouragement.*

*I'm glad your lake is coming back.*

# BRIMSTONE

## ALICE DARTLE

Aboard the Seaboard Express,
bound for Saint Augustine, Florida

JANUARY 1, 1920

LAST NIGHT, SOMEONE dreamed of fire.

Ordinarily I wouldn't make note of such a thing in my journal—after all, there's no subject half so tedious as someone else's dream. One's *own* dream might be fascinating, at least until it's described aloud—at which point one is inevitably forced to admit how ridiculous it sounds. But someone else's? Please, bore me with the weather instead.

However, this is a long train ride, and I have finished reading the newspaper, my book, and both of the magazines I put in my bag for the trip. Truly, I underestimated my appetite for the printed word.

It's a circular thing, this tedium, this nuisance of rolling wheels on a rumbling track and scenery whipping past the window, because my options are miserably limited. Once I'm out of reading material, there's nothing to do but sit and stare, unless I want to sit and write something to sit and stare at later on. So with that in mind, here I go—nattering to these pages with a pencil that needs sharpening and an unexpected subject on my mind: There was a man, and he dreamed of fire, and I could smell it as if my own hair were alight.

Whoever he was, this man was lying on a bed with an iron frame, listening to the foggy notes of a phonograph playing elsewhere in his house. Did he forget to turn it off? Did he leave it running on purpose, in order to soothe himself to sleep? I didn't recognize the song, but popular music is a mystery to me, so my failure to identify the title means nothing.

This man (and I'm sure it was a man) was drifting in that nebulous space between awake and a nap, and he smelled the dream smoke so he followed it into something that wasn't quite a nightmare. I must say it wasn't quite a nightmare, because at first he was not at all afraid. He followed the smoke eagerly, chasing it like a lifeline, like bread crumbs, or, no—like a ball of yarn unspooled through a labyrinth. He clutched it with his whole soul and followed it into the darkness. He tracked it through halls and corridors and trenches . . . yes, I'm confident that there were trenches, like the kind men dug during the war. He didn't like the trenches. He saw them, and that's when the dream tilted into nightmare territory. That's when he felt the first pangs of uncertainty.

Whatever the man thought he was following, he did not expect it to lead him there.

HE'D seen those trenches before. He'd hidden and hunkered, a helmet on his head and a mask on his face, crouched in a trough of wet dirt while shells exploded around him.

YES, the more I consider it—the more I pore over the details of that man's dream, at least as I can still recall them—the more confident I am: Whoever he is, he must be a soldier. He fought in Europe, but he isn't there anymore. I do not think he's European. I think he's an American, and I think our paths shall cross. Sooner rather than later.

I don't have any good basis for this string of hunches, but that's never stopped me before, and my hunches are usually right. So I'll go ahead and record them here, in case the particulars become important later.

Here are a few more: When I heard his dream, I heard seabirds and I felt a warm breeze through an open window. I smelled the ocean. Maybe this man is in Florida. I suspect that I'll meet him in Cassadaga.

How far is Cassadaga from the Atlantic? I wonder.

I looked at a map before I left Norfolk, but I'm not very good at maps. Well, my daddy said there's no place in Florida that's terribly far from the water, so I'll cross my fingers and hope there's water nearby. I'll miss the ocean if I'm ever too far away from it.

I already miss Norfolk a bit, and I've been gone only a few hours. But I've made my choice, and I'm on my way. Soon enough, I'll be in Saint Augustine, and from there, I'll change trains and tracks— I'll climb aboard the Sunshine Express, which will take me the rest of the way. It will drop me off right in front of the hotel. Daddy made sure of it before he took me to the station.

Mother refused to come along to see me off. She says I'm making an awful mistake and I'm bound to regret it one of these days. Well, so what if I do? I know for a fact I'd regret staying home forever, never giving Cassadaga a try.

She's the real reason I need to go, but she doesn't like it when I point that out. It's *her* family with the gift—or the curse, as she'd rather call it. She'd prefer to hide behind her Bible and pretend it's just some old story we use to scare ourselves on Halloween, but I wrote to the library in Marblehead, and a man there wrote me back with the truth. No witches were ever staked and torched in Salem— most of them were hanged instead—but my aunts in the town next door were not so lucky.

The Dartle women have always taken refuge by the water, and they have always burned anyway.

Supposedly, that's why my family left Germany ages ago—and why they moved from town to town, to rural middles of nowhere for so long: They were fleeing the pitchforks and torches. How we eventually ended up in Norfolk, I don't know. You'd think my ancestors might have had the good sense to run farther away from people who worried about witches, but that was where they finally stopped, right on the coast, where a few miles north the preachers and judges were still calling for our heads. They were hanging us up by our necks.

Even so, Virginia has been our home for years, but I, for one, can't stay there. I can't pretend I'm not different, and our neighbors are getting weird about it.

I bet that when I'm good and gone, my mother will tell everyone I've headed down to Chattahoochee for a spell, to clear my head and get right with God. As if that's what they do to you in those kinds of places.

Mother can tell them whatever she wants. Daddy knows the truth, and he's wished me well.

Besides, what else should I do? I've finished with my schooling, and I'm not interested in marrying Harvey Wheaton, because he says I have too many books. Mother said it was proof enough right there that I was crazy, if I'd turn down a good-looking boy with a fortune and a fondness for a girl with some meat on her bones, but Daddy shrugged and told me there's a lid for every pot, so if Harvey isn't mine, I ought to look elsewhere. The world is full of lids.

Harvey *did* offer me a very pretty ring, though.

I'm not saying I've had any second thoughts about telling him no, because I haven't—but Mother's right about one thing: All the girls you see in magazines and in the pictures . . . they're so *skinny*. All bound-up breasts and knock-knees, with necks like twigs. *Those* are the kinds of women who marry, she says. *Those* women are pretty.

Nonsense. I've seen plenty of happily married women who are fatter than I am.

So I'm not married. Who cares? I'm pretty, and I'm never hungry. There's no good reason to starve to fit in your clothes when you can simply ask the seamstress to adjust them. That's what *I* say. Still, I do hope Daddy's right about lids and pots. I'm happy to be on my own for now, but someday I might like a family of my own.

And a husband.

But not Harvey.

If I ever find myself so low that I think of him fondly (apart from that ring; he said it was his grandmother's), I'll remind myself how he turned up his nose at my shelves full of dreadfuls and mysteries. Then I'll feel better about being an old maid, because there are worse things than spinsterhood, I'm quite certain. Old maids don't have to put up with snotty boys who think they're special because they can read Latin, as if that's good for anything these days.

I'm not a spinster yet, no matter what Mother says. I'm twenty-two years old today, and just because *she* got married at seventeen, there's no good reason for me to do likewise.

SHE'S such an incurious woman, I almost feel sorry for her—much as I'm sure she almost feels sorry for me. I wish she wouldn't bother.

I have some money, some education, and some very unusual skills— and I intend to learn more about them before I wear anybody's ring. If nothing else, I need to know how to explain myself. Any true love of mine would have questions. Why do I see other people's dreams? How do I listen to ghosts? By what means do I know which card will turn up next in a pack—which suit and which number will land faceup upon a table? How do I use those cards to read such precise and peculiar futures? And pasts?

I don't know, but I am determined to find out.

So now I'm bound for Cassadaga, where there are wonderful esoteric books, or so I'm told. It's not a big town, but there's a bookstore. There's also a hotel and a theater, and I don't know what else. I'll have to wait and see.

I am not good at waiting and seeing.

Patience. That's one more thing I need to learn. Maybe I'll acquire some, with the help of these spiritualists . . . these men and women who practice their faith and explore their abilities out in the open as if no one anywhere ever struck a match and watched a witch burn.

ARE the residents of Cassadaga witches? That's what they would've been called back when my however-many-great-great-aunts Sophia and Mary were killed. So am I a witch? I might as well be, for if I'd been alive in the time of my doomed relations, the puritans at Marblehead would've killed me, too.

It's not my fault I know things. I often wish that I didn't.

Sometimes—though of course I'd never tell him so—I tire of Daddy thrusting the newspaper before me, asking which stocks will rise or fall in the coming days. It's ungenerous of me, considering, and I ought to have a better attitude about it. (That's what my sister says.) My stock suggestions helped my parents purchase our house, and that's how I came by the money for this trip, too. Daddy could hardly refuse me when I told him I wanted to learn more about how to best make use of my secret but profitable abilities.

I went ahead and let him think I'll be concentrating on the clairvoyant side of my talents, for he's squeamish about the ghosts. Whenever I mention them, he gently changes the subject in favor of something less gruesome and more productive . . . like the stock sheets.

Or once, when I was very small, he brought up the horses at a racetrack. I don't think he knows I remember, but I *do*, and vividly:

They were great black and brown things, kicking in their stalls, snorting with anticipation or snuffling their faces in canvas feed bags. The barn reeked of manure and hay and the sweaty musk of big animals. It smelled like leather and wood, and soot from the lanterns. It smelled like money.

He asked me which horse would win the next race, and I picked a tea-colored bay. I think she won us some money, but for some reason, Daddy was embarrassed by it. He asked me to keep our little adventure from my mother. He made me promise. I don't know what he did with our winnings.

We never went to the races again, and more's the pity. I liked the horses better than I like the stock sheets.

I hear there are horse tracks in Florida, too. Maybe I'll find one.

IF there's any manual or course of instruction for my strange abilities, I hope to find that in Florida, too. I hope I find answers, and I hope to find people who will understand what I'm talking about when I say that I was startled to receive a dream that didn't belong to me.

So I'll close this entry in my once rarely used (and now excessively scribbled upon) journal precisely the way I began it—with that poor man, dreaming of fire. That sad soldier, alone in a house with his music, and the ocean air drifting through the windows. He's bothered by something, or reaching out toward something he doesn't understand. He's seeking sympathy or comfort from a world that either can't hear him or won't listen.

I hear him. I'll listen.

Mother says that an unmarried woman over twenty is a useless thing, but I am nowhere near useless, as I've proved time and time again—in the stock sheets and (just the once) on the racetracks. Well, I'll prove it in Cassadaga, too, when I learn how to help the man who dreams of fire.

# 2

# TOMÁS CORDERO

Ybor City, Florida

JANUARY 1, 1920

The police must have called Emilio. Perhaps some policy requires them to seek out a friend or family member in situations like this—when a man's sanity and honesty are called into question, and public safety is at risk. I understand why the authorities might have their doubts, but no one was harmed. No real damage was done. I remain as I have always been since my return: rational, nervous, and deeply unhappy. But that's nothing to do with the fire.

My friend and right-hand fellow—the young and handsome Emilio Casales—sat in my parlor regardless, wearing a worried frown and the green flannel suit he'd finished crafting for himself last week. His waistcoat was a very soft gray with white pinstripes, and his neck scarf was navy blue silk. Bold choices, as usual, but well within the bounds of taste.

Emilio is not a tall man, but he's slender and finely shaped. He wears his new suit well. He wears everything well. That's why he has the run of my front counter.

Alas, he had not come to talk about clothes or the shop. He was there because the police had questions and they weren't satisfied with my answers. I'd told them all the truth—from sharply uniformed beat officer to sloppily geared fire chief. But any fool could tell they did not believe me.

Emilio did not believe me, either.

"It was only a *little* fire," I assured him. "It was discovered swiftly, then the truck came, and now it's finished. You know, I'd been meaning to repaint the stucco for quite some time. Now I am graced by a marvelous soot and water stain on my eastern wall . . . and that's a good excuse, don't you think?"

He was so earnest, so sweet, when he asked me for the hundredth time, "But, Tomás, how did it *begin*? The chief said the fire began in a palmetto beside the back door. I've never heard of one simply . . . bursting into flames."

We were speaking English, out of respect for the Anglo fireman who lingered nearby with his paperwork. The chief and the cops were gone, but they'd left this man behind—and he was listening, but he was polite enough to pretend otherwise.

"It must have been my own doing, somehow. Or maybe it was Mrs. Vasquez from the house behind me. Either one of us could have tossed a cigarette without thinking. It's been so dry these last few weeks." The winter weather had been a surprise—we've seen little rain since November, and it's been so warm, even for the coast. "There are leaves and brush, and . . . it wouldn't take much. Apparently, it *didn't* take much."

Emilio lifted a sharp black eyebrow at me. "A cigarette? That's your excuse?"

He was right. It wasn't a very good one. I rattled off some others, equally unlikely, but ultimately plausible. "Ashes from the stove—do you like that better? A spark from a lantern? Trouble with the fixtures? God knows I have no idea how those electrical lines work, or where they're located. It might as well be magic, running through the house unseen."

"Tomás." He leaned forward, his fingers threaded together. "It's your third fire in a month."

I lifted a finger. "My third *harmless* fire. They're silly things, aren't they? One in the trash bin, one in the washroom. Now this one, outside. It scorched the wall, and nothing else. You worry too much, my friend."

The fireman cleared his throat. "You should have a man from the electric company check the fuses. If only to rule them out, or diagnose the problem—and fix it before the house comes down around your ears."

"Yes!" I agreed. I was too merry and swift about it, I'm sure. "That's a wonderful suggestion. One can never be too cautious when dealing with electrical power; the technology is too new, and sometimes I worry for how little I understand its mechanisms. But it's too late to call upon the office this afternoon. I'll do it tomorrow."

"Good plan." He nodded, closing his notebook. "I'd hate to come out here a fourth time. My father would never forgive me if I let you go up in smoke."

"I'm sorry, come again?"

He tucked a pen into his front breast pocket. "He wore one of your suits to my wedding. He says you're an artist."

I'm sure I blushed. "Why, thank you. And thank your father, as well. Could I ask his name?"

"Robert Hunt. You made him a gray wool three-piece, with four buttons and doubled flap pockets, back before . . . before you went to war. I doubt you'd remember it. He could only afford the one suit," he added bashfully. "A simple model, but one for the ages; that's what he'll tell you. He still pulls it out for special occasions."

I turned the name over in my head. "Was he a brown-eyed man with gold hair, fading to white? I believe he had a tattoo . . ."

Now the fireman was surprised. "Good God, that's him!"

I warmed to the memory of wool between my fingers. The fabric was thicker back then, even a few years ago. The styles, the material . . . it's all gone lighter now, and more comfortable for men like us, near the tropics. "I never forget a suit, though my grasp of names is not so good. You reminded me with the details and the bit about the wedding. Your father, he had been in the service. Yes?"

"Yes, Mr. Cordero. Back in 'ninety-eight. The tattoo . . . it was a flag, on his right arm." He tapped his own forearm to show me where he meant.

"I saw it when I measured him." I nodded. Then, to Emilio, I said, "This was before you and your brother joined me. Back then, I had my Evelyn to help with the cutting and sewing."

IT never gets easier to say her name, but with practice and habit I can make it sound effortless. I can make it sound like I've fully recovered, scarcely a year since I came home from the front and they told me she was dead from the flu. She was buried in a grave with a dozen others, on the outside of town. Perhaps it was *this* grave, in *this* place—or maybe it was *that* grave, in some other quarter. No one was certain. So many graves had been dug, you see. So many bodies had filled them up, as fast as the shovels could dig. The whole world was crisscrossed with trenches and pits, at home and abroad. If the dead were not felled by guns, then they were swept away by illness.

It was just as well that I went to war. There was no safety in staying behind.

"MY Evelyn," I repeated softly, testing the sound of it. My voice hadn't broken at all this time. Hers could have been any name, fondly recalled but no longer painful.

What a pretty lie.

She and I said our good-byes when I went to Europe, but those farewells were in no way adequate for her absolute departure; and now, I cannot even lay claim to her mortal remains. I can only pray toward her ephemeral, lost spirit. I don't have so much as a tedious, cold headstone in a proper garden of the remembered dead. Not even that.

"TOMÁS?" Emilio placed a hand upon my knee.

I didn't realize I'd gone so silent. "I'm sorry. My head is aching, that's all. I'm very tired."

"Are you feeling well? Can I get you your pills?"

"It's not so bad. Only the same old thing . . . the war strain." I chose a term I liked better than "shell shock." "Sometimes it makes my head feel full, and foggy. Or it might only be the smell of the smoke, you know. There was so much smoke in the war."

Both Emilio and the fireman, whose name I never caught, finally accepted this explanation—at least in part. I settled for this small victory. I declined the pills, which were only French aspirin anyway, and wouldn't have helped at all. I urged them both to leave me, that I might settle in and make myself dinner.

I wasn't hungry, and I didn't plan to make dinner. But Emilio wouldn't depart until I'd assured him otherwise. He is worried, I know. He brings me candies and fruit empanadas with guava and cheese, like he wishes to fatten me up.

I do confess that I've lost a few pounds. Or more than that. I know my own measurements, and my clothes droop from my shoulders as they would from a wooden hanger. I'd rather not admit it, but there it is.

BY the time they were gone, the shadows had stretched out long enough to leave the house darkened, so I turned on some lights. Despite what I'd told my visitors, I wasn't really afraid of the electricity or the bulbous glass fuses in the wall. Oh, I'd keep my promise and visit the office downtown, and I'd ask for a man to test them all; it would keep Emilio and his brother appeased (as well as the fireman and anyone else who might have an interest) . . . but whatever was happening, it had little to do with that impressive technology.

I couldn't share my true suspicions about the fires.

God in heaven, they'd put me away.

# ALICE DARTLE

Cassadaga, Florida

I CAME LAST night to the village of Cassadaga, in the wake of a tense, peculiar exchange with a nearly silent Spaniard who must've understood more English than he let on—for he crossed himself and began praying loudly when he loaded up my trunk and prepared to chuck it from the train. Then he demanded an enormous tip for the trouble of carrying it to the hotel, an attempt at extortion that I flatly refused.

At first. Eventually, out of pure desperation, I offered him whatever was at the bottom of my bag.

Having pocketed his excessive fee, the coward then tossed my trunk into the middle of the road—and ducked back onto the train, taking my money with him. The bastard left me stranded in front of the hotel beside my trunk, which was now scuffed, dented, and toppled onto its side. It was also too heavy for me to wrangle alone, so I wasn't entirely sure what to do with myself.

But I *did arrive*. Safely, and in one piece, with a little less money than I'd planned—but all of my belongings. So what if the sun was freshly set, the town was dark, and I was alone in an unfamiliar place?

Who cared that I did not yet have a room at the hotel and had only assumed I'd find one upon applying?

I was thrilled to have arrived.

As I stood there marveling at my good fortune (obnoxious porter aside), I heard the settling mutters of songbirds, the awakening hoots of owls, and the rising calls of frogs and insects I might not recognize even if I held them in my hand for some up close and personal inspection. Overhead, the large, lacy leaves of palms filtered a few lights, and down along the streets I saw great fluffy plants with leaves like swords. Scraggly beards of moss dangled from trees, and beside my feet rested fist-sized magnolia pods, as hard as old leather.

This did not feel like a jungle, as I'd been warned it might . . . but it definitely felt different from Norfolk. In my narrow, nighttime opinion it also *looked* quite different from Norfolk, but I reserved that full judgment for morning, as the daylight might tell me something else.

FLORIDA is only another state, not another universe.

I am only a long way from home, not lost to it forever.

I lingered beside my trunk, my initial marveling completed.

Before me stood probably the largest building in town, and they called it simply the Cassadaga Hotel. It's a lovely wood structure with three stories and a marvelous porch that runs the full length of the front, and then some. I took my carpetbag, left the trunk behind, and climbed three short steps to take a deep breath at the front door.

I opened it and let myself inside.

Indoors, the place was bright, with a warm, friendly feeling to it. The windows were tall and pretty, and electric lights shined right through them—and through the lacy curtains, which were mostly for show. One of these windows was open to let in the evening air, which was stirred slowly by three high ceiling fans all in a row, their long brown blades shaped like leaves. The rest of the windows were shut, because apparently in Florida, this glorious evening air is considered just a touch too chilly for comfort.

Inside the lobby there was a beautiful wood desk with a glass-shade lamp atop it, its light glowing down on an open register . . . and upon the hands of a colored man who might have been old enough to be my grandfather. His eyes were sweet, his hair was salt-and-pepper, and his white cotton shirt was crisply ironed.

"Good evening."

"Good evening," I replied in kind. "I was hoping you could offer me a room, and I want to thank you in advance for any effort you might make to accommodate me on such short notice. I wrote letters to Pastor Floyd and Mr. Colby, but I should've written the hotel, too, I suppose, or perhaps found a phone and called first. Now that I consider it," I rambled, "this expedition has been conducted largely by instinct and enthusiasm, without much in the way of good planning."

"There are worse ways to go about having an adventure," said the man with a smile. "Besides, you've come to a community of clairvoyants. You might have known we'd have a room waiting."

I giggled, which isn't something I often do. But he was just so *nice.* "I am so grateful, sir—and so relieved." I took the pen and signed myself in to the hotel, and he handed me a key. "Thank you so much," I told him, noting that the number on the key was 14. "And one more thing, if you could, please—do you think it's too late to call upon Pastor Floyd?"

He shook his head. "Not at all. I'm sure the pastor will be pleased to learn that you've arrived."

"I have an address . . . ," I said, mumbling the last syllable or two of my declaration, because I was trying to dig the paper out of my carpetbag. "If you can point me to Stevens Street, I'm sure I can find it— Oh no!" I cut myself off, exclaiming like an idiot. "My trunk! I left it in the road."

"Were you dropped off by the gate pillars? In a hasty, impolite fashion?"

"Does it happen often?"

"Often enough. I'll ring for Timothy. He can see the trunk to your room."

Eagerly, I began to describe it. "It's oversized, steamer-style with a rounded top, and—"

"Dear, is it alone? Or might it be mistaken for someone else's luggage?" he asked.

"Yes, oh yes. Don't I feel silly . . ." My cheeks were going pink— I could feel it. I hated the feeling of pink.

"Now, now, Miss Dartle, I was only teasing. Let me summon our bellhop to help you right away. Poor Timothy needs to head on home for supper. If he dallies here too much longer, his mother will wonder what's keeping him, but yours was the last train into town, so he's almost free to leave."

When Poor Timothy arrived to go fetch my bag, he didn't appear to care one way or another about supper or his mother, either, but I surely wouldn't have expected that kindly older man—whose name turned out to be Evan Rowe—to tote the heavy trunk on my behalf. While Timothy attended to my belongings, Mr. Rowe led me to the front windows. "This is Stevens Street, right out here—see? Follow it two blocks that way." He indicated left. "Pastor Floyd's home is the big blue house on the corner."

Holding these directions in mind, I set off for the minister's place, down sidewalks that were still warm enough to feel toasty through my shoes, despite the season. Where there were no sidewalks, I saw sand so white and soft that it should've come with a powder puff. In the distance I heard soft splashings, like a waterbird wading or a hungry frog chasing flies.

Or chasing mosquitoes.

I hoped those frogs were chasing—and catching and eating—a great quantity of these odd winter mosquitoes. I slapped one on my wrist, stunning the insect and stinging myself in the process. We hadn't seen mosquitoes in Virginia since the season's first freeze. I'd blissfully forgotten they existed.

Not quite two blocks down the way I found the correct number displayed upon a two-storied house. It was a clean affair, with azalea bushes flanking the front steps and dark-painted storm shutters on either side of each window. Inside, the lights were on.

I took a deep breath, scaled the steps, and knocked firmly upon the door. I shuffled from foot to foot, on the verge of knocking a second time when I heard footsteps, and then the squeaking turn of the knob. The door opened, revealing a tall, distinguished woman with silver hair tied up in a great Gibson bun. She wore a light green dress. Its sleeves ended at her elbows, and its hem stopped before it reached her ankles.

"Hello," I said, with my bravest face forward. *Confident and calm,* I reminded myself. "My name is Alice Ellen Dartle, and I'm looking for Mr. J. A. Floyd."

"No you're not," the woman said. She wasn't cruel about it at all, but it took some of the wind out of my sails.

"I beg your pardon?"

"You're looking for *Dr.* J. A. Floyd. Or pastor, if you like. And you've found her."

"Come again? Oh dear, I'm sorry. I didn't mean . . . I should've *begun* with Pastor Floyd and saved myself the embarrassment . . ."

She took no offense. "It's all right, Miss Dartle. I'm glad to see you've accepted our invitation to visit. Please, won't you come inside?" The light caught her eyes so they almost twinkled. They were very blue, I have to say. Or maybe they only looked that way because her hair was so very pale. She did not seem nearly old enough to have such hair, and I almost said so out loud—but I caught myself before I could be so very rude.

I also didn't ask aloud how she'd known it was me, the sender of passionate, fraught letters, in search of a true home down south among these gentle mystics.

"Have you eaten?" she asked.

"No, ma'am, I have not."

"I was just pulling together a light meal when you knocked, so I'll add enough finger sandwiches and orange slices for two. I can't leave a guest hungry, now, can I?"

I was only too happy to agree to her hospitality. I was tired from the road, half starved, and uncomfortably warm from my walk. Also, to my great embarrassment, I was sweating under my shawl. I held my arms loosely and hoped my dress would dry swiftly. This wasn't quite how I'd intended to make my first impression—a damsel in distress with damp clothes and wisps of hair stuck to her face.

Fortunately, by the time Dr. Floyd brought out the lemonade and the cucumber sandwiches, my heart had quit banging around and I was ready to resume the composure that I'd promised myself I would present in the first place. I didn't do a wonderful job of it. I settled for (what I hope came across as) road weary but optimistic. Cheerful, if somewhat . . . minimally refined.

At first our chatter was the light sort, the kind made as part of introductions. She asked about my trip, and I told her about the train ride and my exhausted reading supply. She asked after my favorite authors, and I asked after hers. I complimented her fare and her beautiful home.

"This house? Yes, it's not really to my taste; I'm still rather proud of how it came together. My brother, Andrew, had it built, you see. We'd intended to live here together, but he fell ill last year and passed to the spirit world. That said, we still speak regularly. I often ask his advice with regards to the church and the camp meetings."

"The work must keep you busy."

"Mostly it's research, and education, and healing. Though often there's the added task of reassuring our neighbors that we neither ride brooms nor capture children." Her wry smile suggested she was only halfway joking. She took the last bite of the last sandwich and chewed it quietly. She swallowed. "Sometimes, I think they might believe me."

I took a sip of lemonade. "There was nothing in your letter about brooms or babies, so I'm prepared to believe that all children and domestic supplies are safe and secure. But I want you to understand, I'm intrigued by the *idea* of this place. It's so forward thinking, and it offers me so much hope." I was being too earnest again; the dam was cracking but there was nothing mere lemonade could do about it, so I babbled onward. "Over the years, my family has picked up house and moved a number of times to escape unwanted attention; I'm sure you know what I mean. I lost two great-aunts to the flames—over accusations of things so minor that it makes my skin crawl. They interpreted dreams? They foretold the weather, or the births of babies? Good heavens, if I'd been born a hundred years ago, I'd be a pile of ashes myself by now."

If I was annoying the woman, she was too sweet to say so. "More like two hundred years, I should think. If that's any assurance to you."

I nodded as if it were. "Two hundred, then. But even with all that time and distance between my tragic aunts and me, the fears are still too close for comfort. I've come here to learn how to use my gifts to help others. Preferably without the stares and complaints of neighbors, or threats wrapped around bricks and tossed through windows."

Her eyebrows made the most perfect V, turned upside down. "Did that actually happen?"

"Only the once." A few years back, and I knew good and well who'd written the note and who had thrown it. Both of the bastards were boys I'd known since grade school. We were never friends, but until the brick came, I did not know we were enemies.

"What did the threat say?"

I already wished I hadn't brought it up. I didn't like thinking about it. "Only that they knew what I was, and God would see me in hell. That's just what a girl wants to hear at fifteen, let me tell you."

"I can imagine. Furthermore, I can sympathize. You should see the contents of our general delivery box: a number of letters from people like yourself, and plenty more from those like your neighbors. I wonder if Lily Dale sees half so many notes—or twice so many, if it goes the other way," she mused. "They're better established and respected, but also better known outside the community. I suppose it evens out, in some awful way."

I hoped I hadn't dampened the mood too badly. Awkwardly, I fear, I attempted to steer it another way. "On the bright side, the hateful doubters drive away at top speed—and the hopeful learners like myself arrive to stay!"

She nodded approvingly, but something about the set of her face told me I might not like whatever she had to say next. I could feel it all the way down to my toes: I'd assumed too much. I'd said too much, and now she would be forced to disappoint me.

Unless I was being a worrywart, like Daddy always says. Well, when you see things coming, you worry about them. And I was worried about what Dr. Floyd was about to tell me.

"My dear," she began, those cool blue eyes crinkling with reassurance, but not nearly enough to steady my pulse. "It's a good thing you've come here, for we have much to teach you. However, you should understand . . . we are approached each year by far more people than we could reasonably accommodate—and among those visitors we find many keen occult enthusiasts, but few real talents who can make a contribution to the community. Mind you," she added with a somewhat darker tone, "we also find a few charlatans, and a few overzealous puritans who wish to expose us as frauds. Not that I suspect you of any such thing," she added just barely fast enough to keep me from bursting into tears. "But we have procedures in place, and we must apply them uniformly, to all interested parties."

"Procedures?"

"Tests, if you like that better."

"You can test me if you like—I'm good at tests! Please, ma'am . . . I'm really very good at doing . . . whatever it is I do." I said it desperately, and I hated myself for it. "Ask me anything. Give me cards, or ask me about a dream. I can do anything my aunts could do, and probably better than they ever did. Not that I would know, really, since they kept all that to themselves and carried it to their graves. Or to wherever their ashes went."

She held out her hands to stop me and then took one of mine in hers. She pressed it warmly, but it only served to squeeze the first damp tears up into my eyes. "Your family connection is promising, Miss Dartle, and please, I did not mean to upset you; I only wished to explain, so you understand why we must witness your abilities."

"I do." I sniffled. "I understand."

"Excellent." She released my hand. "Then I'll see you back to the hotel, for you need your rest. Tomorrow I'll round up the council, and we'll get to work."

"The council?"

"I use the term loosely. Our organizational structure is informal, to say the least—but there are a handful of elders, ministers, and healers who make decisions for the camp's well-being. Technically Oscar Fine is the camp's president, but he's in Orlando on business; so Mr. Colby will be present instead. Together, we assess potential residents in a private, controlled setting. I will tell you the truth, Miss Dartle: I expect that you will perform admirably."

I swallowed hard but didn't manage to retract any of those tears. Two or three had already escaped down my cheeks, and my nose was stuffed up beyond all decency. "You do? You aren't merely saying that to make me feel better?"

"I do, and also, yes—I *am* trying to make you feel better. Is it working?" she asked, one of those pointed eyebrows lifted again, as if pulled by a thread.

"Yes?"

"Good enough. Please don't worry, dear. If you were a hopeless case or a nasty fraud, I would surely know it. The whole town would know it," she said with a slight toss of her head toward the community beyond her doors. "*Please* do not worry. Tomorrow around lunchtime, I'll come get you—and we can walk together to the trials."

The phrase "witch trials" sprang to mind, but I kept myself from blurting it out. "I'd like that," I agreed instead, lying and telling the truth all in one sentence. "I would appreciate the support, but I don't wish to be any trouble."

"Oh, it's no trouble at all. And this is no trial by fire." Her left eye sparked—I saw the bright little pop in a glimpse, and wasn't sure I'd seen anything at all. But I *did*. I know I did. "And it's certainly no witch trial, so you can put those fears to rest right now."

"I . . . all right. I will."

She let go of my hand and gave it a pat. Then she stood up—two or three seconds before a telephone rang. "That will be Mr. Rowe. He wants to know if you've taken supper or if he ought to bring you some."

"You have a telephone? Here in your house?" It was a stupid question, and I wanted to kick myself. The machine rang like hell's own bells in the very next room.

"It's one of three in town. The other two are in the hotel and in Harmony Hall, respectively. Times are changing, Miss Dartle. We must change with them if we are to survive." She stopped and put her hands on the back of her chair. She changed her mind and gestured with one hand toward the phone—which immediately silenced itself.

I swallowed my next round of questions. They stuck in my throat like a lump of butter.

Thoughtfully and slowly, she paced behind the table, dragging her finger along a selection of books as she did so. Some titles I could read from where I was sitting. *The Burning Times. On the Persecution of Women by God and His Ministers.* There was one in Latin, something with too many "M's." Another one declared itself a treatise on *Heinrich Kramer's War on Evil.*

She asked me, "Do you know why witches burn? Why they're so often hanged?"

I had an answer for that one. I dredged it up from the bottom of my heart. "Because people are afraid of them."

"Yes, that's the root of it. But people have feared tyrants and kings for thousands of years, and precious few of *them* have ever been murdered by the masses. They haven't died in the tens of thousands. Not like *we* have, because we are mostly poor old women, orphaned children, the disabled, the disfigured. We are easy targets. Innocent targets, as often as not, but with no one to defend us, who would give a damn about our innocence?"

"No one?" I squeaked.

"No one who could help us," she said grimly. "No one with the resources to mount a proper response. So here at Cassadaga, we recruit and train the young, the modern, the educated . . . the monied and the wise—or even the poor and silly if their powers are valuable enough. That's how we arm ourselves against ignorance and fear. It's the *only* way," she added for emphasis, "and I hope that you can join us."

I bobbed my head too fast to agree with any dignity. "Yes, ma'am, me, too. Tomorrow, you'll see. Tomorrow, I will show you that I can help."

"I believe you," she said brightly. "Now, let me return that phone call before dear Mr. Rowe wonders what on earth has become of us."

# 4

## TOMÁS CORDERO

### Ybor City, Florida

#### 1920

I LIT A lantern, for we do not have any streetlights yet. The city makes promises, but the military also made promises, and I made promises, too. The point is, we do not have any streetlights.

I took my lantern outside to survey the damage created by the burning bush—or flaming palmetto, if I want to sound less biblical. Down the back stairs I stepped, and each one creaked beneath my foot. A cool breeze blew in from the gulf, cooler than anything I'd felt so far this winter.

It was either refreshing or ominous. I'm not sure which.

The late palmetto, now a charred stump of ashes, sat up against the rear of the house, flanked by several others of its kind. I didn't plant any of them, and neither did Evelyn; they were here when I bought the house in 1913.

When I held the lantern aloft, the light it offered was far more white and intense than the pinkish stuff that still rippled along the far west horizon. It gave me a better look at what I'd only glimpsed before, upon arriving home to the scene of minor mayhem.

Now, in the aftermath of the firemen, and Emilio, and the palmetto fire, I found fully a third of the wall covered in thick black soot. I swept a fingertip through the enormous stain, and in its wake I saw the butter-colored stucco beneath. Evelyn had preferred it that way, bright and sunny, but I was never so fond of it. If it'd been up to me alone, I might've chosen something darker and softer—something that contrasted less sharply with the red clay tiles on the roof. A light gray, perhaps.

As I'd said to Emilio, I might take this opportunity to pick something else.

The ruined plant at my feet no longer smoldered. It'd been soaked to mush by the firemen with their buckets, and then soaked again with the rubber hose for good measure—or perhaps to justify the elaborate trouble of unspooling it.

I tapped at the wet ashes with the toe of my shoe, and they crumbled, though the stump held together, more or less. Its fibrous, swordlike leaves had been reduced to blackened strips as frail as old paper. No, I did not love the palmettos that lined the back wall of my house, but this was not how I would have chosen to remove them.

I sighed and wiped my shoe on the grass, then returned my attention to the ominous shadow painted in streaked, smudged ash.

As I stood there, staring at my house and pondering the possibilities, I detected a strange smell. It was not the odor of burned vegetation. It was not the tang of ashes or the cracked-pepper notes of cooked stucco. I sniffed deeply and detected the same odd note I'd caught at the first two fires: a faint hint of sulfur. Yes, that's what it was.

Mind you, sulfur is a common enough stink. At times the Florida water reeks of it, and you can scarcely make coffee or lemonade that's good enough to drink. But this was . . . different. It had an element of sharpness, of darkness to it. A nasty bite, with a faint taste of metal that lingered in the back of my throat. I'd suspected its presence in the wastebin, I was fairly sure of it in the washroom, and I now was confident of it outside—as I looked at a broad black stain on the side of my otherwise yellow wall. Burning sulfur, and charcoal, and the dusty tickle of ashes. All of it stirred together in a tin can. It smelled like hell.

The soot stain sprawled and crept beneath the eaves to darken the underside of the roof's edge. It left its mark on the nearest storm shutters, rendering the red paint muted and cloudy. When I stepped back, still holding the lantern high—no, it was not my imagination: There was a pattern to this terrible shadow. It appeared to be the rough shape and broadly drawn angles of a face.

It was not a demonic face, for all that I prattle of sulfur and hell. It was softer and more feminine, if evil is not allowed that saving grace of loveliness. It appeared almost in profile, at a three-quarters turn, so I could see the smudged line of a cheekbone, a jaw, and a nose. Where the eyes should be there was only a shadow, but lower— down toward the ruined palmetto stump—I detected the suggestion of a shoulder and a hint of collarbone.

This was no mere stain. This was a mural.

"The fire made quite a mess, didn't it?" That was how Mrs. Vasquez announced she was watching me.

She leaned over the bottom half of a blue Dutch door. She leaves it closed to keep her small white dog from running loose and assaulting the neighborhood cats—or more likely, being vanquished by them, one by one, in turn. It is not an impressive little beast, but it has a great deal of idiotic spirit.

"Yes, Mrs. Vasquez. Thank you for bringing the firemen around. If you had not been so alert, it could have been much worse."

She nodded, folding her arms on the ledge. I heard a scrape and a scuffle by her feet; our houses are not more than a few yards apart. Sound travels as easily as smoke. "Felipe sounded the alarm before I ever saw the flames." The dog's name is Felipe, because (as Mrs. Vasquez told me once) he likes to eat horseshit.

"I must bring him a treat from the grocery next time I go."

"He's not so useless *now*, is he?" she did not ask so much as declare.

"I never said he was useless." Certainly not aloud, and not to his proud mama.

"No, not you," she granted. "But others. And Javier always said so, God rest his soul." She crossed herself. Her husband was lost neither to the flu nor to the war. He'd been too old to serve. He'd dropped dead of something else instead.

So Mrs. Vasquez and I are both alone in this world, except that she has her small companion, Felipe. I try to be kind. "Not everyone can appreciate such a fine and steadfast companion."

"You should take a dog for yourself. I know a man with puppies . . . you could buy one for the shop, to keep you company while you work."

I shuddered to think of the damage a dog might do, running loose among the bolts of cloth. I knew from watching Felipe how much piss a single small thing could hold, and I have silk to consider, linen to preserve. "A pet in the shop would be too much distraction, and a dog would be lonely during the day—should I leave him here at home."

"Then a kitten," she pressed. "Something to chase mice." When I only stared at the wall without responding, she sighed at me. "Tomás, you are alone too much. You should have some other heartbeat around the house, to keep you company."

"But imagine if the fire had spread. What if I should suffer another blaze, and the place should burn while I'm away? Any poor creature of mine could meet its end, all because you thought I was lonely."

"You *are* lonely."

My lantern fizzed and popped. It sputtered; then the light held steady again. "Yes, but that's not the end of the world. Now, tell me," I said quickly, to divert her from any further talk of pets. "The stain here, left by the fire . . . does it look odd to you?"

She shrugged. "It looks like smoke and ash. It looks like your house was almost destroyed, but the saints smiled upon you."

"Don't you think it looks . . . like a drawing?"

She squinted back and forth, from me to the wall. "From a certain angle, I suppose it might. But it surely isn't *art*. If anything, it looks like the scribbles of that mad Spaniard, with his paintings that make no sense." She flapped her hand disdainfully. I supposed she meant Picasso, because she is terribly traditional. She probably does not care for the moderns.

Besides, she wasn't wrong. The face was loosely sketched, and the forms were implied more than strictly pronounced. "I think it looks like a face," I insisted.

"So what if it does?" She flapped her hand again and shifted her weight on the sturdy old door. Felipe gave a little yap of impatience, but she did not yet release him.

"So what if it does," I repeated. I did not have an answer.

I bid her good night, and I retreated inside. A few minutes later I heard Felipe shoot free from the house like a tiny white firecracker—barking his foolish little head off, rather than pissing outside and returning immediately to his mother's loving bosom as intended.

I didn't mind the noise. It was not late, and Mrs. Vasquez would collect him before he made too much trouble. Maybe he'd scare off a snake or two. Maybe he'd get bitten by one. Life is a terrible gamble for all of us, two-footed and four-footed alike.

I made myself a cup of tea from water that smelled only faintly yellow, and I flipped through my collection in the Edison cabinet. It's a new model, a phonograph and radio receiver combined—but there's very little broadcasting for me to tune it to. There's talk of a station coming to Tampa any day now, and I hope it's true. Living voices would be better company than my records, and far less trouble than a house pet.

My collection of music is diverse but not expansive. I dismissed the albums one by one. I didn't want a waltz or a foxtrot, for I had no partner and the music would only remind me. The Latin dances and Spanish crooners were too dramatic for my mood, and as far as I can tell, the European composers either are all excessively bombastic or aim to bore the listener to sleep. I only wished for relaxing distraction and something unrelated to wartime patriotism. Was that asking so much?

I made my selection based upon a single song—"Love's Dream After the Ball," by Elizabeth Spencer, for it is sentimental but not overly maudlin. I placed it upon the player and set the needle down.

I took my tea to the couch by the large west-facing window and pushed the curtain back so I could see outside. The last of the sunset pink, as soft as the inside of a shell, had fallen into the water of the bay. The sky was dark, but electric lights were popping on inside houses all over the neighborhood. The city may not pay to light the streets, but we see to our own abodes.

EVELYN made no effort to resist progress, and as soon as electrical service was offered, she saw to the wiring in our house. It happened while I was away, and she wrote to tell me all about it. She described the new fixtures with wonder and delight: They were so vivid, and not nearly so hot as an open flame. (Just like the phonograph, the glass bulbs were also by Edison, who must have invented everything new, for the entire generation.)

Electricity and Edison and Evelyn. God, every train of thought comes back around to her. Someday, perhaps, it won't. But no day soon, I fear.

As vowed, I would visit the electricians in the morning, but I was not at all confident that the wires in the walls had caused the fires.

The first little blaze had occurred in the trash, and I'd discovered it almost immediately. The smell had wafted to my nose from the kitchen, where the tall wicker bin held mostly butcher's paper and fish bones, inedible bits of fruit and greenery, and some rice I'd regrettably overcooked. There was nothing within it that might spark any flame—no matches, no cigarillos or anything else. It was easily ten feet away from the stove, my only source of fabricated heat, and at that time, the stove had not been in use for hours.

Then came the fire in the washroom, sparked on a towel and my drying socks, which had fallen off the shower bar and into the tub. The towels and the socks had all been damp, last I'd seen them. How they'd caught fire remains a mystery, but in that fire I noticed what looked like . . . Well, not a face, no. But neither was it some random streak of wayward ash.

There was a distinct symmetry to the greasy mess of soot left behind.

HERE is my secret, which I have told no one (for whom would I tell?): I thought it was a handprint, left behind on the tub's white enamel. I would happily swear with one hand on a Bible and the other on a cross that it looked like someone had tried to climb out of the basin. Some hand had reached up and grasped.

Out from the ashes. Out of . . . who can say?

AND now there has been this third fire, because things come so nicely in threes. This one was larger than the previous two and much more dramatic. This one left me a face splashed upon the wall in its wake. It is a woman's face, smeared and dragged and staring at nothing—but as true and clear as the work of one of the modern painters for whom Mrs. Vasquez has no fondness. I tried not to think about it. I could not think of anything else.

I listened to Miss Spencer sing her heart out, and I sipped my tea. I cracked the window open and let the gulf breeze wash into the parlor, where I never entertained anymore.

Since coming back from England I'd had no guests at all, except for the dark-haired ladies with their condolences and cakes, and their husbands shifting nervously back and forth beside them as they murmured how sorry they were to hear about my Evelyn—and how glad they were to know that I'd returned home safely.

There's etiquette to grief, and I was glad for it. Old manners gave me appropriate things to say and proper responses to the scripted sorrows and sad eyes. I do not know what I would've done with myself if I'd never had the rituals to guide me.

Probably, left to my own devices, I would have drunk myself to death or drowned in the tub upstairs, long before the fire had any chance to blossom there.

I closed my eyes and thought of my wife, with her lovely profile and copper brown eyes, her high cheeks and smooth brow. I surrendered and indulged the ridiculous possibility: The image outside might represent any woman, and therefore, it might represent Evelyn.

What a peculiar hope it gave me—the notion that the fires might be some unnatural missive from her very own soul. She might remember me, in whatever far-off realm she'd found herself upon closing her eyes that final time. But if these harmless flames bore messages, then where did they bear them *from*? Surely it was no celestial place with saints and clouds and a choir of angels. Surely if she makes such an effort to reach me, she does so from nowhere safe and pleasant.

Yet still, I hope it's her. Even if she calls me from the flames of hell.

And that's a terrible, black hope indeed.

# 5

## ALICE DARTLE

### Cassadaga, Florida

MY HANDS WOULDN'T stop quivering and I couldn't keep my feet from fretting back and forth across the floor of my pretty, modest hotel room. I was hungry, for one thing. I was impossibly nervous, for another—and the cup of stiff, unsweetened coffee provided by Mr. Rowe did nothing to make me feel less like I was about to explode from pure terror.

A second nip of brandy might've done the job—or better yet, a third. I hoped nobody could smell the first nip, the one I took on the way out the door.

But as I stood in the lobby of the Cassadaga Hotel and trembled, beside me, a woman in a long, plain, dark dress looked me up and down while she waited to use the telephone. Her hair was red, fading to silver, and her eyes were the color of cinnamon. She gave me a wink and said, "I can only smell it a little, and only because I know what I'm sniffing for."

I was too appalled to respond. I sputtered, flailed, and tried to guess her accent.

"Dublin," she said, even though I hadn't managed to ask. "That's what you hear. Good heavens, child. Get a grip on yourself. You've only just arrived, and you're already falling to pieces."

"I need to brush my teeth."

"You've already brushed them twice."

"Stop telling me about the things I've done!"

"I'm trying to tell you something *else*." She gave me a gentle elbow, so she must've been halfway joking with me. "If I know what you've already done, you can trust that I know what you're *going* to do. And you're going to do just fine."

I did my best to obey her and compose myself, but I was afraid— of the tests, and of this tiny Irish woman with her pretty voice and trickster smile. God, what if everybody knew as much as she did? All the time?

A man who was using the telephone finished up and moved along. The woman smiled at me. She said, "Dr. Floyd is coming. She's right on time, as always. Buck up, girl. Pass your tests and come join us. There's work to be done. You, my dear . . . oh, I think you're going to be *very* helpful." Then she took the receiver and asked for Daytona Beach.

"Miss Dartle!"

Well, Dr. Floyd had found me. The odd little woman had been right about that, too.

The pastor was smiling brightly beneath a fine hat with a brim I would've found too wide for my own round face, but it suited her gloriously. She wore white gloves with tiny pearl buttons, and close-toed shoes with a modest heel. They matched her dress, a lavender-gray affair that made her eyes look even more stunningly blue than they'd seemed the night before.

"Good"—she checked the clock on the wall behind me—"*morning*, technically. I hope you slept well and you're ready for your tests."

"I am as ready as I'll ever be," I said, the words running together in my mouth. "I wish I knew what these tests were like. I wish perhaps you'd given me some hint last night."

"I deliberately elected not to, because you would have only obsessed, and worried, and fretted." To the woman at the phone, she offered a quiet "Good morning, Francine." Francine nodded in response but kept most of her attention on the call.

"Yes, ma'am—but you might as well know, I obsessed, and worried, and fretted anyway." I fell into step beside her. "At least you might've left me some way to prepare."

She put a friendly hand on my shoulder and saw me through the door first. "Oh, there's no preparing for tests like these—and all that fretting was for naught, my dear. Think of it . . ." She closed up behind us both and led the way out onto the sidewalk. "Think of it as a confirmation instead. Is your family the religious sort? A number of our residents are practicing Christians."

"My mother's a Methodist, and my father is a Methodist because my mother says he is. As for me . . . I don't suppose I have any idea what to believe. If I did, maybe I wouldn't have come here."

Soon we arrived at Harmony Hall, an older two-story building in a more traditional style than most of the houses I'd seen so far. I counted six rooms (or living spaces?) on the first floor, and the same on the second—with an open-air corridor between them.

Dr. Floyd and I approached together, and I didn't falter, pause, or otherwise stall my entry. I refused to behave like a coward.

Inside the corridor I found shade, which was a relief—and I spotted only the fourth telephone I'd ever personally set eyes upon in my whole life. It was mounted into the wall with some semblance of a booth around it, to guard it from the weather; above it was a great red fire bell, and beside it a gaslamp was hung with a sign that read, "Please Speak with Mrs. Handley Before Using Telephone." Naturally, the sign made me itch to grab the thing and start chatting, but I successfully restrained myself. I didn't know how to use one, so it was just as well.

Almost immediately, we arrived at the office of Mr. Colby.

Or I thought it must be his office. He was sitting in it, anyway—and several other people were keeping him company in the little flat. There were four other people, to be more precise: three women and a man. They all smiled in welcome, greeting me with a soft chorus of hellos.

"Ladies and gentlemen, this is Alice Dartle," Dr. Floyd introduced me. The rest she gestured toward, from left to right. "Alice, this is Sidney Holligoss, our resident physician; his wife, Edella, who you'll likewise find there as often as not; Mabel Dimmick, one of our most expert and widely known clairvoyants; and Dolores Brigham, a truly outstanding medium who's been with us since the community first began." She took a deep breath, to catch herself up. "And finally, of course, this is our founder, Mr. George Colby. Together, he and I will serve as administrators during these three tests."

"Three tests?"

"Three is a perfect number. It protects, it collects, and it informs." She sounded so formal, so official . . . like a school principal who genuinely likes you but still is forced to keep you in detention for some silly transgression—like using the telephone without speaking to Mrs. Handley first.

I swallowed hard and tried to look friendly, prepared, and exceedingly clairvoyant. I probably looked like a maniac.

"Come sit over here," she said, directing me to a round, three-legged table draped with a purple cloth. Upon this table sat several objects: a pendulum on a chain, a folded envelope, a pack of cards, and a bowl that was mostly full of water.

This wasn't a trial, certainly not a witch trial; that's what she'd said—but that wasn't true, was it? For I was a witch, in an approximated courtroom, waiting and praying for a verdict in my favor. I started sweating. My breathing went all shallow and I felt so light-headed, I just didn't know what to do. I wanted to stand up and run, and I wanted to lie down and die.

"Alice." The pastor said my name. She put a hand on my shoulder, and I tried to draw some comfort from it. "Relax. Everything will be fine."

The jurors regarded me kindly, but I felt well and truly wretched. Surely I wasn't giving them enough credit. They wanted me to succeed—wasn't that right? I had to trust Dr. Floyd. If I couldn't trust her, then I couldn't trust any of them.

I swallowed again. I sat down in the chair and scooted forward until the table's offerings were within easy reach, and I held my hands over them—waving slowly back and forth between the cards, the water, the crystal.

Here was my first test, and here were four objects. They were loaded, each and every one. I don't know how to say it other than that. They were loaded, as surely as any gun—each with some peculiar energy or history.

I lingered over the pack of cards. "I heard somewhere," I said quietly, "that the spiritualist church doesn't approve of the tarot."

The pastor shrugged. "You mentioned last night that you were good with them. I don't use them myself, and I've seen clairvoyants who are more dependent upon them than they ought to be . . . but there are many paths to the truth. Go on, in whatever manner makes you most comfortable. Take the items and read them."

Deep breath. Hard swallow.

I held my vibrating hands over the table. "Yes, ma'am, all right. I'll do my best."

For no particular reason, I started with the envelope. The paper was good quality; it'd come from a nice stationery set, a lady's set. I picked it up. I rubbed it between my fingers and held it up to my face to give it a good sniff.

Then I started talking.

"This didn't come from a girl, but an older woman, in her forties or fifties. I think I can see her, but . . . I'm not very good at guessing how old people are. I'm absolute garbage at it." Clumsily, I unfolded the envelope. There was an address, but no name. "It says 3234 South Orange Blossom. That's not a local street . . . it's to the west of here. In a larger town." I saw a flat expanse of sandy dirt, with streets laid out on a grid. Trains churning along tracks. A few brick buildings, a few stone buildings. All with flat roofs. "This was a love letter, and an apology. She took a train, to clear her head. She couldn't make up her mind between . . . between her lover and his brother." I felt the paper, its soft grain, its lingering odor of perfume—long gone, but I could still sense it. "Something with lilies," I muttered.

I looked up, gazing from face to face, hoping to see some acknowledgment that I was doing well. They all remained mildly impassive, except for Mr. Colby. He bobbed his head, but that might've meant anything. "And?"

"And?" I looked back down at the table and decided to try the pendulum next. I picked it up by its chain and let it dangle, unsure of how to proceed. I'd only ever used one to ask for yeses or nos, with little silly questions. Would it rain before sundown? Could my father's favorite boxer survive more than three rounds in the ring?

I held the crystal as still as I possibly could. It swayed back and forth, then into a soft clockwise circle. There was something about the energy it made, the gentle swirling that summoned a hum, or a buzz. I closed my eyes and listened. "The woman who wrote the letter . . . she was too late. By the time she'd made her choice, he'd chosen someone else. It broke her heart."

The pendulum stopped moving, and the ambient tone in my ears went away—so I turned my attention to the bowl of water. I touched the surface and let the ripples wobble in shaky circles. I saw tears, and bubbles. I heard the rush of a faucet. "She took to drinking, and within a year or two, she drowned in a bathtub. It wasn't . . ." I frowned, wondering how much I ought to say. But this was my test, and the more information, the better. Or so I hoped! "It wasn't exactly an accident."

Dr. Floyd had taken a seat to watch me, but now she rose to her feet. She did it suddenly; the motion surprised me, and I sat up straight. "Ma'am?"

"My turn," she announced.

"I beg your pardon? Did I do something wrong? Oh God, I did something wrong . . ."

She approached the table and took the cards before I had a chance to open them. "No, no, you didn't. I've just seen enough, and now it's my turn to read."

"Read . . . read what?"

Everyone else looked almost as confused as I felt, but nobody stopped her.

She shook the cards out of the pack and shuffled them loosely. I watched them with fascination, feeling the hum come back at the edge of my hearing. I imagined that they glowed, but of course they didn't. I imagined that they sparked, but that didn't happen, either. They only combined and recombined between her fingers. I was transfixed by her hands, even when she stopped to lay down a small spread—a modified cross layout that I didn't recognize.

She turned the cards over quickly, one after another, talking all the while—*rat-a-tat-tat*—like she was afraid someone would interrupt her with questions or commentary.

The Knight of Cups. "Alice, my dear. You've been courted recently, and rather seriously, by a romantic young man with a soft spot for soft women." Five of Wands. "But you sent him away. He did not understand you, and you weren't prepared to live with that. It was the right decision, I'll have you know. He would've never come around, and before long, you would've wanted to kill him." Three of Swords, reversed. "Your refusal hurt his feelings but did not break his heart. He will carry a torch for a while, but he'll find someone else. There's a better match for him somewhere, and he'll find it eventually." The Emperor. "Your father has been quite a force in your life, largely for good." She paused over this card, tapping it gently. "In this position, the card suggests a subversive figure. He's working in opposition to something . . . someone . . ." She turned the last one over, revealing the Empress, reversed. "Ah, it's your mother. He's the supportive and understanding one . . . No," she said, correcting herself, "tolerant. He's quite tolerant. Your mother looks away; she buries her head in the sand. She pretends she can't see. She cares, but she doesn't know what to do. You must forgive her. Or you might as well forgive her. It'll do you no good to stay angry."

"I'm not . . ." *Angry,* I wanted to say. But I didn't.

Dr. Floyd scooped up the cards and slipped them back into the deck. She smiled, a little tense. She smiled to the room at large, and to Mr. Colby in particular she said, "I've seen enough, and I'm prepared to waive the other tests. The objects were mine. I'll verify her reading and—unless anyone has any objections?—I'd like to see her join us here and begin tutelage."

She turned her back to me and rested her rear end on the edge of the table. She braced one hand on either side, like she was prepared for resistance . . . or even a fight.

No one fought her, but the elderly Mr. Colby asked, "Who would you recommend to tutor her? You hardly have the time for a new pupil."

"When Oscar returns from Orlando, he might make a most excellent teacher. Until then, Mabel? If you could be persuaded . . . I think you two might be a good match."

Mabel regarded me kindly, but with curiosity and uncertainty. She might've been in her thirties, with blond hair knotted up in a ribbon and a fine lace shawl across her shoulders. She was terribly thin, and I wondered if there wasn't something wrong with her.

Maybe she was sick. I would do my best to keep from asking. She said, "As you like, Dr. Floyd."

It was not the most ringing declaration of acceptance I'd ever received, but it was better than hearing, "Pack your bags and hit the road." I nodded slowly, stoically, and without so much as a sniffle I said to my new mentor, "Thank you, ma'am."

She shook her head. "No, no. It will be *Mabel*, not ma'am. Nor miss, or missus, or anything of the sort."

"Mabel," I whispered. "Yes, thank you."

"Then it's settled!" Dr. Floyd said cheerfully. To me, she added, "Alice, I'm afraid you'll have to stay in the hotel for another week or two, or perhaps longer—until the first wave of snowbirds goes home to roost."

"Snowbirds?" I squeaked.

"The northern guests, who come for the seasonal sermons and lessons. They'll be cycling through town quite a lot over the next month or two—until the weather warms up for them back in New York, or Vermont, or wherever they hail from. They come in droves in the fall, especially since the influenza has taken so many to the other side. But as soon as something becomes available, we'll get you settled in."

"You mean it?" I was overwhelmed, and relieved, and still not quite convinced that everything would be all right and that I was going to stay.

Dr. Floyd left her seat on the table's edge and came around to stand beside me. She put a hand on my shoulder. "Would you like a tissue, dear?"

"No, because I'm not crying. Not yet."

All the same, she passed me a handkerchief, just in time to catch the first of my happy sobs. "Come along, I'll take you to lunch. Mabel, would you care to join us?"

"I'd be happy to. Alice and I should get to know one another, shouldn't we?"

Outside through the open-air corridor the pastor guided me, while the rest of the council members murmured among themselves. Mabel paused for a word with Mr. Colby but assured us that she'd be along momentarily. We left without her.

"Thank you, Dr. Floyd," I said, in case I hadn't said it enough. "Thank you, a thousand times and then some."

She grinned and squeezed me around the shoulders. "On the contrary, I should thank *you* for stopping when you did. I had no idea you'd read so clearly on your very first test."

"Was the reading really that good? I felt like it wasn't specific enough, like I wasn't clear enough. I never got a good look at the woman's face, so I couldn't describe her. I couldn't figure out which city I meant, or the name of the train she took. Are you *sure* it was all right? I couldn't tell anything about either of the men . . ."

"Darling, in another ninety seconds, you'd have blurted my sister-in-law's name, and Dr. Holligoss would've been very embarrassed indeed."

"Oh. Oh *dear*, oh, Dr. Floyd, I am so sorry."

"For what? Rising to the challenge? I'm the one who picked the items on the table. I should've chosen something less closely connected to the town and its . . . oh, let's call it 'confirmed gossip.'"

"I *still* feel sorry. I am seized with the compulsion to tell you so, repeatedly, until I get it out of my system."

"Please do not. Young women apologize too much already. It's an awful habit, and I'll break you of it if I can."

"Yes, ma'am. I'm sorry, ma'am. I'm sorry for saying I'm sorry."

"Are you joking with me?"

"Yes, ma'am," I halfway lied.

She sighed—at me, or about me, or because of me. "That'll do for now. Now, come along, we'll eat in the hotel's restaurant, downstairs. The food is good and the prices are reasonable. You have a bit of money to live on, I believe?"

"An allowance from my father. You were right about him," I told her. "You were right about my mother, too."

"Lolli's cards were always on point. Or maybe Lolli was always on point, and she guides the hand that holds them, even now," Dr. Floyd said modestly. "But I'm glad you're not pressed for money just yet. It'll buy you a bit of time to learn before you take on clients of your own."

"I cannot *wait* to learn." It was the most truthful thing I'd ever said in my whole life, and I believe that Dr. Floyd knew it. After all, she knew everything else. I walked beside her, and I walked on air.

At long last, the world was opening up before me!

# TOMÁS CORDERO

### Ybor City, Florida

#### 1920

I CALLED UPON the electricity man, as I'd promised the fireman, and my shopman, too. He shook his head, and he put away his instruments. I sent him back to his office with my money, my thanks, and my apologies. Cautious, perfunctory measures thusly performed, I returned to Cordero's to see how Emilio and his brother, Silvio, were doing in my absence.

I opened the door to find Emilio behind the counter. He smiled at me, those picket-white teeth as pristine as his choice of suit—a crisp linen design of his own, with a three-button jacket that boasts lapels a little lower than I usually cut them. He'd chosen an ivory fabric with flecks of brown, and beneath it, he wore a buttercream yellow shirt.

"I hope you don't mind," he said before I could speak. He meant the suit. He had seen the way I was looking at it, gauging it from seam to seam. "I'm only trying this one out. What do you think?"

I held up a finger and twisted it, suggesting that he should spin around. "Let me see the whole thing."

Merrily, he performed a pirouette that would've done any dancer proud. Then he cocked his head. "Well?"

"I like the length; it hits your thigh just right. But the leg seems a little loose."

He shrugged. "It's an experiment. A looser fit will be the cut of the future, I think. It's very comfortable, and it's not so warm."

"It's not so . . . sleek, either."

"But it does not look *bad*, does it?" His warm brown eyes went tight with worry. "I left off one set of flap pockets to compensate for the lines. That's sleek, isn't it?"

"My friend, you would look sleek in a thin coat of dirt and gravel. The suit is not to my taste, but you make it look smart. An experiment, you called it?"

"I've been looking at magazines from New York and England."

"England?" I frowned. "Shop for ideas in Paris if you'd look across the ocean."

"I could not get my hands on anything from Paris, or Madrid, either. This city is a *backwater*, Tomás," he informed me with a dramatic sigh. "Therefore, I take my inspiration where I can find it. And," he added more brightly, "I've already had someone ask me about it. So I must be doing something right!"

I joined him behind the counter but ceased to argue with him. "Really? Someone wants you to make one?"

"A fellow named Ruiz; he manages one of the cigar plants. He's new."

"To town?"

"To country. But he knows a clever cut when he sees one. If I make him something like this, a custom piece based on my own . . . do you think . . . is there any chance . . . ?"

"You can take twenty percent," I quoted him. "Your usual salary, and twenty percent, since the style is yours."

His smile stretched wide, and his lips slipped down to cover his teeth. His cheeks were so tight, I thought they might burst. "You're very kind."

"You're very talented, and I'm very fortunate to have you. But tell me. *This* shirt." I changed the subject to a garment spread out for inspection. "Who is it for?"

"It's the Saladin order from last week. He'll come to collect it this afternoon. This shirt goes with the light gray flannel . . . over here. The medium-weight, not the more tropical stuff, because he's headed back to Pennsylvania next month. Speaking of which—in a round-about way—what would you say if I tried making suits with cotton?"

"I'd ask who on earth would want them."

"*Good* cotton, Tomás. Fine-grade Egyptian, not the rolls they send to Britain. We already use it for some of these shirts."

I sighed at him and folded the shirt into a tight, flat square. "For a shirt, cotton is fine. For a suit . . . it looks cheap."

"I could make it look *not* cheap."

"Not this year, please. We're still getting back on our feet. I love you and I trust you, my friend, but let's not take too many risks. Linen and wool for now. Cotton for the future. Good heavens," I groaned, not as serious as I pretended. "A future of loose cotton clothes. How I fear for the generations to come."

"You fear what? That they'll have cooler legs than we do? You're a silly man sometimes. Fashion changes, that's all. It moves in a great circle, but it comes and it goes. Today it all is fitted and slim; tomorrow it will be flowing and light. Or something else. Really, there's no telling." Still grinning with pride, he took the shirt and collected the four-button, two-flap-pocket, traditional gray suit with which it belonged. "But with your approval, I'll set these pieces aside for Mr. Saladin. When he arrives, I will dress him like a doll for one last check of the details, and I promise you, he will never want to take this off."

"You know, the greatest compliment I ever received came from

Carlos Gallego, who told me he wished to be buried in something of mine."

"*Is* that a compliment, though?" Emilio leaned forward on the counter, planting his elbows on the wood and his chin in his hands. "To hide your works of art from the world? Forever? Or until some grisly unearthing, in a distant future where everyone wears cotton . . . ," he teased.

I rolled my eyes in return. "It was a selfish compliment, then. But I took it in the spirit he intended." Then, while I checked the list of new fabric samples, I told Emilio about the man from the electricity company. I assured him that all was well with my house and its mysterious hidden wires that ran through the walls.

He was not much appeased. "If it's not the wires, then where do the fires come from?"

"That's a question for the ages," I murmured. I retreated to the workshop at the rear of the store.

He followed behind me. "So answer it. For the sake of my sanity."

"You know I can't. Not for that sake, or any other." The ensuing silence was full of accusations, and the smell of blood from the tongue he was biting. So I said, "I beg you to quit worrying. If I have been careless, then I shall endeavor to be more careful. If I have been thoughtless and clumsy, then I will keep my eyes open and exercise greater caution."

"Is that all?"

I threw up my hands. "What else would you have me do?"

"Perhaps Padre Valero might have some ideas."

It wasn't the worst idea I'd ever heard, though I didn't want to admit it, and I am not sure why. "I suppose fire safety is part of his job description," I joked weakly. "Keeping the faithful away from the inferno, as it were."

Emilio wasn't smiling anymore. He was knotting his lovely hands together. "I did not know you had such a blasphemous streak. It's never good to make light of the devil."

"You're right, you're right." I was happy for the excuse to withdraw from my ill-thought jest. "I'm only tired, and my head has been hurting again. I don't know what's wrong with me. If it will make you feel better, I'll see if he can make some time for me."

"Will you seek him for confession?"

Flatly, I told him, "I have nothing to confess." Since the war, I have not been so devout. Nor so forthcoming, to priests or anyone else.

So as promised (because I always keep my promises, I *always* do), I went to Our Lady of Mercy. Even the name of the place a promise, isn't it? Promises all around. Maybe there are patterns, and at least there are promises.

That's what I told myself. I don't know why I was feeling so optimistic, but my moods come and go in a circle, like the fashions.

No, not like that—not a circle. I believe it's more like the tide. The quiet misery comes, and the quiet misery goes. When it's here, I wallow in it. When it's gone, there's nothing in its place but a dull sense of numbness and an idle desire to listen to music.

When it's gone, I almost miss it.

At the edge of the neighborhood I reached the grand church on the corner of Tenth and Seventeenth. Our Lady is long and made of wood, with windows that curve on top and a rounded bell tower mounted front and center. The style is usually called mission, thanks to the Jesuits of yesteryear, though more traditional mission structures are usually erected in stucco or coquina. I don't know why Our Lady is different. Wood might've been cheaper, or easier, or someone might've liked the look of it better—I can't imagine why.

With all those candles . . . and all those old hymnals and Bibles . . . so much kindling. It tempts fate. Or God. Or nobody.

It tempts *me*, just a little . . . in the back of my head, some awful and strange dark spot that wonders what I'd find in the ashes. Not that I would consider taking a torch to the place, even for a moment. I involuntarily imagined it, and that's not the same thing.

Up the steps I walked, and the great door creaked loudly on heavy black hinges. I stepped inside and drew it shut, producing another great squeal to announce my arrival. But no one turned to look. The sanctuary was empty except for three old ladies, an old man with an open Bible draped across his knees, and two altar boys who were busy polishing the brass down front. Winter meant the sun was sinking early—or it felt early, though I hadn't even taken supper yet—so the light through the colored glass was as warm as honey. Before me, on the altar, were more candles than I could count. Most of them were lit.

*I should light a candle for Evelyn,* I thought. Next I thought, *What good would it do?*

I'd lit a thousand already. What a stupid sacrifice of wax.

"Tomás?"

I hadn't heard him approach. He was a few feet away, to my right. "Hello, Father. I am sorry. I know it's been too long. But could we talk? I need some advice, and I don't know if there's anyone else . . ." My voice and my thoughts trailed off. I didn't know what else to say.

"I am always happy to be your conversationalist of last resort, my friend. Come, this way," he said, and we retreated to the office he keeps behind the dark closet of the confessional.

Mateo Valero is a very tall man with a shock of white hair and very soft hands. He stands with a little hunch, like he means to reassure the world that he is gentle, despite his size. His nails are always as clean and tidy as Emilio's, and that's saying something. His desk is always spotless, too. His robes, and his handwriting . . . everything precise, but somehow none of it seems cold. He is warm and friendly and efficient.

"Tomás . . . in these last few weeks, I've heard your name a time or two," he began.

"Is that so?"

"Yes. Something about a fire. Or two."

"Word has a way of getting around." Especially when Mrs. Vasquez carries it.

"No one was hurt, I trust?"

"No. The fires were small and harmless. But they were strange," I admitted. "And I know what people think. I know what they say."

"About the fires?"

"About *me*."

He shook his head to dispel that line of concern. "Everyone knows you've had your troubles. No one speaks ill."

"Yes, it's all loving concern, I'm certain." It came out with more bitter bite than I meant to give it. But I know how easily *loving concern* can disguise salacious curiosity.

The padre is a Jesuit and therefore no fool. He didn't argue with my tone. "Yes, yes. Loving concern, and the other sort of concern, too. That's not why you're here."

Well, what could it hurt?

I took a deep breath and flattened my hands on the tops of my knees, smoothing the creases I'd pressed into my slacks. I rubbed them with my thumbs. "No, that's not why I'm here. But I *do* want to talk about the fires. The first ones were strange because I could find no source—but they were not dangerous, and I thought little of them. Only later did I wonder if I'd missed something, some clue or hint that I'd scrubbed away when I washed the ashes down the drain."

"A clue or hint . . . of what?"

I didn't answer him right away. "Of design. Purpose. *Intent*, you might even say. If I had looked closer, I might have seen signs that the fires were not accidental, and not ordinary. As in the case of the most recent fire."

His eyebrows rose. His fingers templed. He sat back in his chair, and it squeaked. "There's been another?"

"You didn't hear about yesterday?"

"The congregational grapevine has failed me."

"Well then, *yesterday*," I began, almost annoyed and not sure why. It isn't his fault that Mrs. Vasquez has a big mouth but slow feet and no telephone. "Yesterday there was a bigger fire, and there's been some slight damage to the house. This one occurred outside, against the back wall. It began in a palmetto, or so the fireman told me."

"A palmetto? Caught fire?"

"It's been very dry as of late, and it went up like a torch. It went up like a witch on a stake."

I don't know why I said that. I hated the words as soon as they were out of my mouth, but I could hardly cram them back in.

Evelyn was no witch. Evelyn did not burn then, and she does not burn now.

"Was there a cigarette? A match?"

"None that I know of, though that's not the matter for concern. I wish I had a camera," I said, and he thought I was changing the subject, but I wasn't. Quickly, I added, "If I had a camera, I could've taken a photograph. Then I could simply show you what I mean—without asking you to rely upon my memory and my opinion. And

Mrs. Vasquez's opinion, a bit," I added. "She saw it, too, and she agreed with me." It was an exaggeration, but she would likely go along with it. It would make her story more sensational when she inevitably passed it along.

"She saw what, Tomás?"

"The *face*." I quit fiddling with my clothes and folded my hands. Then I squeezed them together, like Emilio had when he was worried for me.

"The . . . face?"

Slowly, and with much trepidation, I said, "A woman's face, in three-quarters profile like an artist's sketch. It was left behind in the soot, where the fire had scarred the stucco. Mrs. Vasquez said it made her think of Picasso." I referenced my best and most likely witness again and summed up her assessment. "She was right—it was a thing of broad strokes and vague lines. But it *was* a face. There's no doubt in my mind."

"Did you think it was Evelyn's face?"

Her name felt like a blow to the chest. I gasped, softly enough that Padre Valero might not have noticed it. I could muster nothing louder than a whisper, a staggering breath with a few syllables to prop it up. It was a feeble response. "The face . . . belonged to a woman. It *could* have been Evelyn."

"But do you *think* it was?"

My throat closed up. There were no more words, no more vague grunts of possibility. I nodded. That was all.

Valero nodded, too, but more thoughtfully. He stared at me, and past me—undoubtedly wondering how shell-shocked a man could become yet still be permitted to roam the city at large. He untempled his fingers and selected a freshly sharpened pencil from a cup. He tapped it against the desk's edge. "You know, this reminds me of something."

"It does?"

"Mm-hmm. Several somethings." He pushed the chair back and climbed to his feet, strolling to a bookcase that spanned the full length of his office wall. He used the pencil as a pointer, tapping this spine, then that tome, with its blunted end. "There was a Frenchman, a priest . . . He died a few years ago. In a fire, I think."

I was confused. "I'm sorry, come again?"

"He was very interested in fires and the images they leave behind." He settled on a book, picked it from the shelf, and dropped it onto the desk—then began flipping through the pages. "Victor somebody. There's a museum in Rome dedicated to his findings. The Vatican . . ." He stopped at a chapter heading. The page flipping slowed. "Acknowledged his research, and his relics."

"Relics? There are relics?"

The pencil settled on a paragraph. Valero turned it over so the leaded point could underline a sentence and then circle a segment. (I was oddly surprised by his willingness to scribble in his books, but said nothing about it.)

He continued without looking up at me. "Yes, there are relics. He collected them from all over Europe," he partly read and partly paraphrased. "Victor Jouet; that was his name. It all began when a fire broke out at the Chiesa del Sacro Cuore del Suffragio, in 1897. In the wake of this fire, Victor found the scorched image of a face left behind."

"On a wall?" Like the fire at my own house?

"This does not say. He found it somewhere, and he never doubted that it was a face. Furthermore, he believed that it was a message from a departed soul." He leaned back in his seat, away from the open book that was splayed across his desk. "Victor theorized that the face was that of someone who'd died in a fire—so it's funny that you'd mention burning witches. At any rate, he traveled for many years, collecting his charred images—mostly handprints, fingerprints, and the like. He brought them back to Rome and put them in a little museum."

"Do you mean . . . it isn't utter madness, to see a face in the ashes?"

"Listen, my friend: I can't say whether or not there is a face on your wall, much less whether or not it's Evelyn. She was lost to the influenza, wasn't she? Not to fire, if that ever made a difference."

"And if it didn't?"

"Then it didn't. My friend, if you believe there's a message drawn in soot on the side of your house, the church grants the possibility that you're right. Who am I to argue with the church?"

My eyes welled with tears, and I dabbed at each corner with the back of my hand. "This is such a relief, you have no idea. I was afraid . . . I was so afraid . . ." I hunted for the words to match what I meant. I stumbled and came up empty-handed, empty-mouthed.

"Afraid of the signs in the fire? That's a reasonable thing. But do not forget, fear is a gift from God. Like all of His gifts, we should respect it, and examine it. Do not be ashamed of your fear, and do not hide from it. You must address it with your prayers. Confront it and see what it can teach you."

My elation wavered.

Address it? Confront it? See what it could teach me?

I've had too many dreams of fire being flung from a nozzle, too many restless nights of tossing and turning and waking in a cold sweat, remembering the trenches. *Some* fear might be a gift, and *some* might come loaded with helpful lessons. But I know from hard experience that some is pure cruelty, and nothing more.

My elation wobbled, but I nurtured it. I needed it.

My hands trembled. I touched my eyes again and wiped the dampness on the top of my pants. "For too long, I've been afraid of fire."

"You've known the flames too closely." He smiled at me, all glorious compassion without pity. He fiddled with the pencil. With a jaunty little toss, he restored it to its cup. "So remember Isaiah, the forty-first chapter. Remember that you passed through hell on earth, and you came out the other side for a purpose."

As if I needed reminding. "I will." I nodded, though I didn't know what verse he was urging me to recall. I swallowed and cleared my throat. "But what do I do if there is someone in some place beyond my reach . . . reaching out for me?"

He did not wish to appear stumped, because it would not do for a man of God—so he opted instead to appear mysterious. I appreciated the effort, if not the substitution. "That is a question you must answer for yourself, with help from the Divine. For to tell the truth, neither you nor I can know the true nature of these images. They could be the result of a tremendous coincidence; or they could be a heaven-sent message."

"Or elsewhere-sent, which is more my concern."

"There is no hell without heaven, and no purgatory without heaven's mercy. Do not let your fear overcome your curiosity or close your heart to the possibilities."

I left his office and left his church, and returned to the shop. This time, I found Silvio at the counter.

The younger Casales brother is short and lean like the elder—though he wears his hair with a different part, and his hazel eyes are handsome but weak. He wears spectacles with lenses so thick they distort the lines of his face.

Mind you, he is still a good-looking man with a fine sense of style, but his head for business is sharper than his brother's, much to my personal gain—for Silvio would rather keep the books than sketch patterns any day of the week. His preferences suit my needs nicely, for I would rather do almost anything than calculate lines of numbers.

Numbers were never my strong suit, even before the headaches and the dreams. Without my two able-bodied and strong-minded companions, Cordero's would surely close in a month.

I asked Silvio how he was doing this fine afternoon. My hands weren't shaking anymore, and my eyes were dry (I'm fairly certain). He greeted me in return, and said, "I'm glad you're back."

"You are?"

"Emilio said you might be gone for the day, but I wanted to tell you: December was an excellent month, Tomás. Your best yet!" He stopped himself and retreated. "Since . . . since you've opened again, you understand my meaning."

"I do," I assured him. I approached the oversized book, and he turned it around so I could see the figures. I looked only at the bottom line, which showed a slim but respectable profit for the previous month. Back before the war, I would've considered it a weak holiday season, but since my return, sales have been slow to pick up. Not all of my customers have returned to me.

MANY of my customers went to war, like me. Some of them didn't come back. Some of them returned from the front and found difficulties like mine: loved ones deceased, businesses failed or closed, families fractured. Money is uncertain for many, and suits like mine have always been a luxury. My customers' pennies have come in dribs and drabs since the bombs and the influenza.

OR, perhaps, my customers died and were buried in my suits, so no one else might ever see them again. I, perhaps, was flattered. Their children, perhaps, found my wares a little old-fashioned, and shopped elsewhere. Perhaps I have a good reason to let Emilio experiment with my fabrics while he is on my payroll. I am not old, but I have lost touch. With something? With someone? With the tastes of the upper crust?

"THESE are *good* numbers," Silvio assured me, taking my silence for disappointment. "They are better every month. Before long, we'll need to hire a new tailor to help with the overflowing orders."

"You're getting ahead of yourself." On second thought, I asked, "Aren't you? Or has your workload become unreasonable?"

"Oh no, not yet. But by June? If the trend continues, absolutely. I shall require an assistant."

"All right, then. Six months until you can have an assistant. Let's see if we can hang on for that long."

"You're too modest, and I have the utmost faith."

"Do you?"

Vigorously he nodded. "I *do*. And so does Emilio."

"I thank you for the confidence. Speaking of your brother . . . ?"

"Oh! Yes, he left twenty minutes ago. Devereaux sent a boy around to say he'd somehow come by two bolts of that flannel you asked about in October."

"The ivory, with blue flecks?"

"Exactly that." He grinned.

"What grand summer suits the stuff could make," I mused afresh. "I thought the manufacturer discontinued it."

"Then the Frenchman either lied or misjudged his own negotiating skills. Two bolts, he said, if one of us could come collect them."

"On credit? Or did you take his fee from the petty cash?"

"A combination of the two," he said lightly, as if this were not an embarrassment. "I've made a note here, and—since I didn't know when you'd be back—there's also a note on your office door making mention of it."

"That will be fine. I trust Emilio will bring a receipt."

"I'll take it off his hands when he gets back and send it directly to the magic envelope," he promised. The envelope is magic because slips of paper go inside, and rent, paychecks, and supplies come out—courtesy of Silvio's skills. "Everything is fine." He made another promise that was partly spun from fantasy. "We will be fine. You will be fine. And the clothes will be finer than that."

I hoped and I prayed, and in my head I lit a thousand candles.

Let him be right. Dear God, if you hear me—sweet Mother Mary, if you are listening—let him be right. He *has* to be right.

I have nothing else.

# 7

## ALICE DARTLE

### Cassadaga, Florida

LUNCH WITH DR. Floyd and Mabel Dimmick occurred around one o'clock at the Conservatory—the little restaurant in the hotel. I had scallops in a citrus drizzle and a rich chicken salad with grapes and walnuts that tasted almost like candy, with a glass of orange juice on the side. Then I had some macaroons for dessert, but I shared those with my companions so I wouldn't look too greedy. If I could've topped it all off with a bit of bourbon it would've been one of the more perfect meals of my life, but I learned (with a touch of embarrassment and awkwardness) that most of the spiritualists are teetotalers who do not partake of any spirits.

I made a poor joke about this being ironic. It received strained, polite chuckles. I was mortified. I apologized. I turned pink.

My companions were gentle in response. Mabel said she could take me to town—to nearby DeLand, that is—and there were places there where I could find wine and other such necessities. I mean luxuries. For me, personally.

"But I certainly can't. I shouldn't. It's illegal, anyway," I said, hoping this was the end of my mortifying foray into humor. "I should obey the law, and I should formally join the church—and obey its tenets, too."

Dr. Floyd laughed lightly. "Darling, Volstead is weak in places like these. There's less 'prohibition' than 'idle dissuasion.' We're too close to the islands for that, and the rum flows too freely. In some places, it's easier to find alcohol than freshwater."

Mabel nodded. "Or drinking water that doesn't smell like boiled eggs."

I'd heard of the rumrunners, and in my head they looked like pirates—with gold rings and parrots and peg legs to boot. "I've never been too interested in rum. Virginia is bourbon country. Bourbon and sometimes brandy. Or gin. But . . . Never mind. I can live without it, for the sake of the community."

Mabel leaned forward and put her hand on top of mine. "It's sweet of you to say that, but if you prefer a nip before bedtime, there's nothing in the church that would stop you. In fact, when Oscar's son returns from his trip to Gainesville, he'll probably initiate you into all the town's *real* secrets."

"The *real* ones?"

"Not so much spirits and tarot cards, but liquor and playing cards," Mabel supplied. "Popular pursuits among the younger folks, and frowned upon quite sternly by the older ones—which only means that Cassadaga isn't remarkably different from anyplace else. You can drink if you want to, and you can play cards or read cards, too, if you like. No one in the church will stop you."

"No?" I was suddenly quite aware that I knew very little about the church, except that it was graciously accepting of odd birds like me.

"Not as such," Dr. Floyd confirmed. "They'll gossip like old men on a dime-store porch, and someone will probably suggest that you show some restraint, but you can take that advice or leave it."

"There are no . . . commandments?"

"Do unto others as you'd have them do unto you. But we borrowed that one."

After a long pause, during which I stared wide-eyed and expectant, Mabel added, "That's it: Do unto others. Everything else follows from that. Keep an open heart and mind. Appeal to the Highest Good. Elevate yourself with love. Only use any gifts you possess for good. Respect the beliefs and autonomy of others."

Dr. Floyd explained, "We aren't very keen on rules, or organization, either. We prefer to leave people to their own consciences."

I absorbed this, and brewed up a thousand fresh queries with which to pepper these nice women. It was only fair to warn them. "I have so many questions—a million, at least."

Dr. Floyd signaled the hostess for our check, which she said she'd bill to the camp meeting. "Everyone in every faith has more questions than answers. Including us."

"If you really want to learn about the church," Mabel said, "you must attend the week's seminars and sermons. You'll learn some aspects of Spirit more deeply than others, but I'm confident you'll fill in the gaps soon enough. You're bright and eager, with a brain like a sponge."

"How do you know that?" I asked.

"I've spent fully an hour in your company, that's how."

So you can see why I'm absolutely in love with them both, and in love with this place.

I am in love with the friendly people who wave and tip hats on the sidewalks during the day, coming to and from the community hall. I'm in love with the two small lakes—one named simply Spirit and the other named after our founder, Colby—and their long-legged birds and tall grasses, and the boys from Lake Helen and DeLand who come fishing there.

I'm in love, I'm in love—with the winter blossoms that smell like oranges and jasmine, and the brilliant green trees with all their leaves, and the snow-white paths of sand that go up and down the rolling hills. I'm in love with all seven hills, small, nubby things though they may be.

(I'm told they're positively mountainous for Florida, and highly unusual. They're molehills, but I don't care. I love them.)

I love the men and women who come to speak, well dressed, with arms raised and hearts open, down by the lakes, in the amphitheater, the pavilion, whatever you'd call it. The church. It is open to the warm, humid air, and I love it—even with the bugs and uneven stairs, and the soft sand that eats my feet and lingers in my shoes. I love the whoosh of the ladies' fans, and the murmurs of people agreeing, and the little sobs of happiness when Spirit speaks to a soul who needs to hear it.

Most of all, I love this *awakening*. I am finally surrounded by supportive people who wish me well, and wish for me to learn and grow and find my footing in a world that has always either ignored me or told me to hush up, for my own good.

I am finding hope. I am finding faith. I am finding Spirit.

I am finding my way to a Higher Good that has room for me in it, and would not set me on fire given half a chance.

LAST night, Mr. Colby invited me to come down front at the vespers meeting. It wasn't an introduction or a prayer call. It was an opportunity to serve. I was flattered and terrified in equal measure, but Mr. Colby is such a patient, loving gentleman that it's difficult to tell him no, regardless of how petrified I was by the prospect.

But as he explained to me at great length, this is an important part of participating in the church at Cassadaga.

"We are here to help those who seek us out for comfort or consultation," he said gravely. "We must not hide our lights under a bushel, whether those lights are clairvoyance or mediumship—we must let them shine. We must contribute to the good of the world, Miss Dartle. If we cannot do that, then we do not deserve to be here."

"You mean . . . the church? Cassadaga?"

"All of it, dear. All of *us*."

IN time, I will become more comfortable and confident in my abilities, and in my audience. That's what he told me before I left his flat in the big three-story house across the way from Harmony Hall. I hope he's right. I hope it's not much time at all.

It's one frightening thing to read objects in front of half a dozen wizened witnesses, and another thing to speak for the spirits in front of the whole congregation—and all its seasonal visitors, who greatly swell the ranks.

WAIT. I should explain.

As I recorded above, I'm learning a great deal about the church, and some of the most exciting day-to-day bits (or week-to-week bits) are the open readings that occur as part of the vespers ceremonies. I'm told that during the slow season, when attendance is down, these happen only once per week, on Friday or Saturday nights. But in the busy season, when the camp is crawling with out-of-towners, they're held more frequently.

In the week and a half since I arrived, I've seen only two open readings for myself.

(I missed a third, as I was taking a trip to town with Mabel. I needed some things. I did not collect any rum, though I was sorely tempted—even though it's not my preference.)

The open readings are a simple affair, conducted without much ceremony. The vespers service begins, Dr. Floyd (or a guest speaker) will offer a few words, a hymn or two is sung . . . and then whichever mediums are called and willing go down front beside the pulpit and begin to share messages from the other side.

BABY steps. Good practice. A kind and receptive audience.

I kept these promises in mind while I waited for the hymn to wind down. I held the hymnal and moved my lips along in a vaguely melodic mumble, not because I cannot sing (I can sing quite nicely, I'd like for the record to reflect), but because I was fiercely anxious. It was almost as bad as my test on that first day.

And here I'd thought nothing could ever rival that event.

The book in my hands was red and stamped on the front with gold leaf. It was a Presbyterian hymnal, if the copyright page could be believed. Maybe all of the songbooks were Presbyterian hymnals. Maybe a Presbyterian had donated them. Maybe there'd been a big sale.

The final bars of "He's Able" tinkled out from the piano down to the left of the pulpit, and everyone sat down. For a few seconds, the fumble of heavy songbooks being slotted into pews made a silly rumble. Ever so briefly, it drowned out the chirp and chatter of fauna that always rose from the lake just beyond the pavilion—even though the din was rising as the sun was setting.

Dr. Floyd thanked everyone for the music. "It's raised the energy in a most delightful fashion, wouldn't you say?"

The audience mumbled appreciation and agreement in return. So did I, but it mostly came out in a series of feeble squeaks.

"Before we get to the open readings, I see a number of new faces in the crowd. Last night's train brought a fresh group of the faithful, I see." She smiled across the audience, and the audience smiled back. "So I wanted to mention the potluck. Immediately following the open session, we'll close the service with hymn number 314—and then we'll withdraw to the fellowship hall behind the library and bookshop for supper. There's plenty of food for everyone, and there's no need to bring anything if you've only just arrived. Please, make yourselves at home and know that you are all welcome, to the last man, woman, and child."

She was torturing me on purpose; I was sure of it—dragging out my debut for as long as she could, just to get me all worked up and flustered.

It was too warm already. Too warm for January in anyplace reasonable, despite the waning light of day. My thighs were getting sticky. Probably, when I stood up, everyone would see a thin seam of sweat running from my behind to my knees. I should've worn a darker dress. I should've worn a thicker slip.

Oh God.

"Now I'd like to introduce you all to one of our newest residents, Miss Alice Dartle, from Virginia. This evening's open reading belongs to her, and it will be her very first. I trust you will all treat her with respect and patience. Alice? Would you please come down and join me?"

I rose to my feet. My legs stuck together even though I was wearing a garter and very high stockings that were supposed to keep things from sticking together. I think they might have made the problem worse, because adding a layer of fabric to anything in January in Florida is a terrible idea.

"Thank you, Dr. Floyd," I said. I was still holding my hymnal. I put it down on the seat on the damp spot where my rear end had been.

The congregation had gone quiet, except for a soft fussing noise from a nursing infant somewhere off to my left, and the snuffling of a runny nose from an old man down on my right. I felt the whole world watching me, even if it was only a hundred people or so. Or closer to two hundred, now that I had time to look around and do a little math. Math was never my strong suit, but as I walked down the sandy floor of the aisle, I counted the rows of pews and I counted the people sitting on them, and the pavilion was rather full, so perhaps there were a hundred and seventy people. That is my best and final guess.

I thought of the gallows, and the stake.

I knew it was stupid. I knew these earnest, eager listeners would treat me nicely despite any flubs or foibles on my part. But oh, I did not want to disappoint them.

At the bottom of it all, I think that's the thing that scared me most. What if I could not help? What if I did not connect to anything, or anyone—flesh and blood or spirit?

What if I did not deserve to be here?

But it was too late to change my mind. I halfway prayed for a broken ankle as I went down the grade, interrupted by steps made from railroad ties. The heels of my shoes were not too high and rather square; they made the clop-clop sound of a horse's hooves, and this noise echoed through the space, or I imagined it did. What would it echo from? The tent canvas ceiling, which draped over our heads like a bed's canopy? The stout columns that held the whole thing up? The lake beyond?

No broken ankle rose to save me, and Dr. Floyd put out her arm to gesture me onto the stage. I followed her lead.

"Everyone, please welcome Miss Dartle."

A soft pattering of applause filled the air, and when it stopped I heard only the Florida evening buzzing, humming, splashing, and croaking. Gaslamps came on as I appeared, lighting the space as the sun dropped low behind the trees, lending the whole thing an air of spectacle I hadn't quite anticipated.

But like Mabel told me the other day, Spirit is drawn to Light.

The lamps gave the stage an eerie glow and probably made my skin look nice. There's something about candlelight and gaslight; they're good for a girl's complexion. I took comfort from that. I might be lost and bumbling, but my cheeks were surely as smooth as alabaster.

I cleared my throat and stood up straight.

"Hello, everyone. It's a pleasure to be here, and thank you so much, Dr. Floyd—and Mr. Colby." I scanned the crowd, but I did not see him. "Wherever he is. Um. Yes, thank you all."

Dr. Floyd withdrew to a seat on a bench behind the pulpit while I wished this was a proper stage and that I could not see the audience for the lights in my face. No, the lights were off to the side—giving everyone a great view of everyone else. No blessed blindness for me, only paralyzing clarity.

Breathe, just breathe . . . that's what Mabel had told me to do. She said to breathe, and listen, and keep my heart and mind clear, so that any interested spirits might make use of me. So I closed my eyes, since it seemed like the thing to do. One can always listen better when one's eyes are closed—it's a scientific fact. I'm sure of it.

And yes, once I'd blocked out the rest of the world, somewhere in the back of my head I sensed a tug of light. I can't think of a better way to describe it, but this tug of light came with a whisper, and a nudge. I heard a name, but I couldn't catch it.

Here he was. My first spirit, at my first open reading.

"I see a man," I began in the most vague and incontrovertible fashion possible. "He's an older man with great muttonchops, *vigorous* muttonchops," I emphasized. "He's very near." I heard the name again, but barely. "His name is several syllables, and it begins with an 'N,' I think." I felt a hand on my arm and blinked myself aware, looking back over my shoulder at Dr. Floyd. She was the only one onstage with me, and she was still seated ten feet behind me.

I left my eyes open now. I could see the man in my head and feel him beside me. "He's here for someone in particular. Does he . . . does he sound familiar to anyone?"

"My father, perhaps?" Someone spoke from the crowd. "He passed when I was very small, back during the war."

I found her and fixed on her face. She was Dr. Floyd's age, give or take, so that meant she was speaking of the War Between the States. Or as my aunt Phyllis always put it, "The Late Unpleasantness."

In my mind, I asked this spirit to speak up. I needed his name, and I didn't want the woman to provide it. I needed to prove myself. *Nathaniel,* he whispered louder this time, and I almost jumped out of my skin. It was the clearest word I'd ever been blessed with—my first direct response that didn't take the form of an image or a feeling. This spirit had spoken directly! To me!

"His name is Nathaniel," I said, more triumphantly than was probably polite.

"That's true!" called the woman in the crowd. She didn't nod back and forth to her neighbors on the pew. "It's him. He's here to talk to me."

THIS was not a performance. This was not a stage show, conducted by mirrors and mischief. This was family and truth, life and death, and everything that comes before and after. The weight of it humbled me and squeezed my chest.

Now he gave me images: the too-loud percussions of cannons; the shouts of men; the smell of blood and soot; the flap of a tent, opening and closing. "Did he die *in* the war? In battle, I mean?"

"Yes."

*On the hill,* he said, his voice the rustle of autumn leaves. His eyes were very green, very bright when he looked at me now. They were intense, intelligent eyes. *Don't leave the paths, they say. You'll break an ankle.*

I'd only just been hoping for a broken ankle. It must've been a coincidence, not that I understood what he meant, or why he'd say that. "On the hill? Don't leave the paths?" I repeated it out loud, in case I'd misheard—or in case the words meant something to his daughter.

"We know he died at Chickamauga," she answered, a catch in her throat. "But on the hill? Did he die on a hill? Is that where they buried him?"

The spirit nodded. *On the horseshoe.*

"A horseshoe?"

A man blurted out, "Snodgrass Hill. It's shaped like a horseshoe. My uncle fought there, too, at Chickamauga," he explained, seeming suddenly bashful about having spoken.

"Oh thank God." I was so relieved at the confirmation that I forgave myself the lapse in manners. "I mean . . . thank *you*, spirit. Is that right? Snodgrass Hill?"

He nodded.

"And you're buried there?" Another nod, so I said, "Yes, he says that's where he's buried." *I am sorry I broke my promise.* "He says he's sorry he broke his promise." *Her children are beautiful, and she raised them well. I am proud of her. I am proud of them all.* "Your children are beautiful, and he's very proud of them—and you."

Tears moistened her face, and probably mine, too. She clutched a handkerchief to her mouth and nose.

The spirit shifted to stand in front of me, between me and the nice people in the hard pews in the soft sand. I could see through him, or rather, I could see past him—but I only wanted to look *at* him, so that's what I did. I'd never seen a dead man so clearly before. He was not gaunt or frightening. He was ordinary except for the magnificent facial hair. He wore a blue uniform and a sad smile.

*Do not tell her this, for she'll find out soon enough: Her mother is with me now. It will not be a surprise, but it will be a blow.*

"All right, I won't. If you don't . . . if you'd rather I didn't."

*Tell her instead that I am here, and all of my love is here, too. Tell her that she is never alone.*

So I did as he asked, and the woman openly wept. I wasn't sure if I'd helped or only made something worse. "I'm sorry, ma'am, please don't cry."

She shook her head and sniffled, and said something like, "No, no. It's beautiful," through the handkerchief. "It's so beautiful, thank you. I'm so glad I came."

I was pinking again, but I wasn't so upset as usual. This time, I was flushing because I was trying not to cry, too, and not doing such a good job of it. I didn't have a handkerchief handy, and I couldn't imagine asking to ruin somebody else's, so I couldn't afford to burst into tears; that was all.

The spirit of Nathaniel disappeared as quickly and thoroughly as if he'd never been there, and in his place I heard another faint tug of light—or I *felt* the faint tug of light, however it works—and then I was joined by a woman named Anna who had died in childbirth. Her husband was in the audience with the child in question, a little boy of half a dozen years and ears that stuck out like the open doors of a roadster. He wanted to talk to his momma, and I frankly lost all semblance of decency. Dr. Floyd arrived just in time with a handkerchief and I destroyed it in less than a minute.

When I'd finished passing along the absent mother's love, I turned to the good doctor and said, "It's never been so clear before. They've never been so . . . *present*."

"It's the music," she said with her ever-present reassurance. "And the fellowship, and this place. Cassadaga raises the energy and brings them nearer. You're doing very well, Alice. Don't fall apart now."

"Too late," I confessed, even as I turned back to face the audience again.

Every face watched me, just as before—with that same mix of nervous anticipation and hope. Now a few of them were damp faced like me and Nathaniel's daughter and Anna's husband, and a few others looked worried, and a few more had their mouths hanging open as if I'd done something magical. One or two in the back shook their heads like they did not believe this trickery, but Mabel and Dr. Floyd had warned me that there were often a few of those in the crowd. Several children grew restless. I wasn't talking with *their* mothers, and they were getting hungry. One old lady had fallen asleep, her head on her husband's shoulder.

I closed my eyes, trying to clear my head. Another tug, another pull of light. A very faint one, somewhere close by—but not very strong. I didn't understand.

I smelled smoke again and wondered if Nathaniel wasn't coming back. I called his name in my mind, but he did not respond.

The light did not respond. Whatever spirit was waiting in the wings did not respond to me, not exactly. I don't think it knew who I was, or what I was, or what I wanted. I can only compare it to a blind and deaf man standing in a room full of people who are trying to get his attention. It knew I was there, but it could not imagine how to respond.

(It was a man. I caught enough of its energy to know that much.)

"There's another man . . . ," I said aloud, in case the words had any power. "I can't see him well. Sir?" I tried. "Sir, can you hear me?"

The shape of it changed, and it wasn't light anymore but something else—something dark and swirling and smelling of ashes, charred bones, and hair burned down to curls of soot. It shifted and leaned toward me, and I felt the appalling scope and size of it. It was huge, and it dwarfed me. I had asked for its attention and gotten it. Now I wanted nothing more than to be rid of it, forever.

To be rid of *him*, whoever he used to be.

"Hello?" I tried, desperately standing my ground. "Who are you?"

I opened my eyes but saw nothing, save the audience. Then the audience went away and I couldn't see that, either—and when I looked around I could not see Dr. Floyd or the pulpit or the sun setting on the other side of Spirit Lake, which was scarcely larger than a pond, but it was *their* lake, and they could call it whatever they wanted.

I felt like I was falling asleep, dropping precipitously into some dream. No, some nightmare. Someone else's nightmare. I heard the *rat-a-tat-tat* of gunfire—not cannon fire, and not muskets or rifles, but something much faster—and I smelled chemicals that burned my nose and made my eyes water. Someone else's nightmare.

A man. This man.

No, some other man. (He dreams of fire.)

"Who are you?" I asked one last time. I scarcely had the wherewithal to form each short word, but I did, and he heard me—this huge dark thing, this terrible ash-covered beast, he heard me.

He responded in a voice that was made of a forest on fire, in a voice that was made of everyone on earth who ever lived, screaming and dying.

*I am the hammer.*

I sat down. Or I fell down. Either way, in a moment or two I felt hands grasping me by the armpits, holding me upright, and then letting me lie down. I was gasping, panting, short and sharp. He was gone, and in his wake I saw someone else, smaller and colder and shaking. He was speaking to himself, or else he was praying.

*"Dios mío. Está aquí . . . está aquí . . . está aquí."*

Dr. Floyd wrote down my words—the very last words I mustered before I passed out cold, in front of God and everybody. She showed them to me later.

I don't speak a lick of Spanish, but apparently the dreaming man does.

When I woke again it was dark outside, all-the-way dark and not the half-light of sunset with gaslamps. I was lying on a chaise in the hotel lobby, and Mr. Rowe was sitting beside me—a tea tray on the small table between us. I was startled to find myself in such entirely different surroundings; I was worried about how I must've been man-handled into the hotel; and I was relieved to see his friendly face when he smiled at me and said, "Hello there." Then, to someone back behind the counter he called, "I believe she's coming around."

Mabel appeared, and with her came a man whom I hadn't seen before. "Alice!" she exclaimed, and dashed to my side just a moment too late to help me upright.

"I'm all right, don't worry. I just . . ." I reached for one of the little sandwiches that accompanied the tea. They were made from pimento spread, smeared between the fluffiest, whitest bread I'd ever seen. "Overexerted."

Mr. Rowe excused himself and Mabel took his seat. She thanked the man as he left, and accused me: "That was no mere overexertion—you and I both know it."

"What else would you call it?"

"She has a point," said the newcomer. He was tall and angular, with salt-and-pepper hair and a light brown suit. "Sometimes our vocabulary for these things proves insufficient."

"I'm sorry, who are you?" I took a bite of sandwich before he could answer. I needed food more desperately than I needed a response.

"Oscar Fine, at your service, Miss Dartle. I'm the president of the camp meeting association."

That's right, I'd heard someone mention him at some point, in passing. When I finished chewing, I said, "Dr. Floyd tells me that spiritualists aren't much for hierarchies, or organization in general."

"Spiritualists are not, but our camp meeting is a business—as a matter of necessity. There is property to be owned and maintained, communal structures to be addressed, and programming to produce. Someone must also make arrangements for guest speakers and con-vince the county that we need camping permits for those who bring their own supplies and choose to skip the hotel."

I took another bite, finished chewing, and swallowed. "Then it's a good thing they have you, Mr. Fine. I had no idea there was so much involved in running a show like this one. Not that it's *for* show." There I went again, blushing to the roots of my hair. "You know what I mean, though. Don't you? I mean the camp and the town, and . . . People here are all so very understanding, and they know things before I can say them, so I hope that when I say them *wrong* . . ."

Mabel leaned forward and said into his ear, "Dr. Floyd says she's already met Francine."

He laughed. "Oh, that mad little nun. Her gifts are extraordinary, aren't they?" He settled down into a broad smile, all full, stretched lips and fluffy brows held aloft. "We don't all see as clearly as she does, but yes, I understood you perfectly. I do apologize for the belated greeting, and I wish we could've met under different circumstances . . . but it's a pleasure to make your acquaintance all the same. I trust you've been kindly received? Treated well?"

"Oh yes." I bobbed my chin up and down, then stuffed the rest of the finger sandwich into my mouth.

"And I'm pleased to introduce the pair of you, but hellos and how-are-yous are hardly the most pressing of things right now. Alice, I'm sorry you missed the potluck, but . . ." Mabel frowned sternly at me, as if this were no time to be noshing on sandwiches and tea—but she was wrong about that. There's no greater time to eat than when one has freshly awakened from a sudden faint at the hands of peculiar spirits. That's what I always say. Or that's what I'm going to say, from this day forward.

I swallowed again and took a cup of tea. A sip would do me good. It might steady my hands, which quivered embarrassingly, rattling the cup and saucer together. They chattered like teeth. "I'm sorry I missed the potluck, too, and I am eternally grateful for whoever put this fine little meal together. Mr. Rowe?" I looked past her but didn't see him at the desk. "Or whomever. And I don't know what you want me to say, Mabel."

"I want you to say that you'll be more careful next time!"

"How?" I asked, as plaintive as a child. "I don't know what I did right, and I don't know what I did wrong. I can't imagine how I might prevent it. Besides, it was only a little faint." I tried to shrug it off, but the smell of burning lingered in my nose, and that terrible fire-fire voice still rolled between my ears.

*I am the hammer.*

"It was more than that."

"Then *you* tell me what it was," I snapped. I did not mean to snap, but there it is. I snapped. More calmly I said, as I picked up another triangle of sandwich, "I'm new here. I thought the open reading was . . . was . . ." What had Mr. Colby called it? "'A harmless baby step.' An opportunity to serve, and nothing to be afraid of, certainly. Nobody mentioned any fainting, but if that's as bad as it gets, then I'm prepared to take it in stride."

"How big of you." Mabel's arms were crossed against her stomach, under her thick wool shawl. She wore it with a tremble of chill, as if this were Virginia in January, and not Florida. As if there weren't bog insects buzzing on the other side of the window to my right.

Mr. Fine did not yet know I was a hopeless case—a frazzled brat who was out of her depth—so he went easier on me than my erstwhile mentor. "Unfortunately, that's *not* as bad as it can get."

Mabel left her seat and took a spot beside me on the chaise, and Mr. Fine replaced her in the seat. "I don't wish to frighten you, so let me say this, first: Incidents like yours tonight are very rare, and you are not likely to have another one anytime soon."

"Good to hear."

"Good to say." He grinned. "You are young, and you are new to this. Sometimes a reading becomes overwhelming, and—"

"I was *definitely* overwhelmed," I said too fast.

"—and that's a chance you take, or a chance you choose not to take. But tonight I think you brushed up against something more dangerous than a fit of emotion. I could hear it in your voice, when you asked the man who he was and asked him to come closer. You were wandering too far away from yourself, trying to get his attention."

That was a good way of putting it, really. "He was right there, just outside my reach, and it seemed as though he couldn't see me or hear me."

"But you could see him and hear him?" Mabel asked.

I didn't want to tell her about the words. I don't know why. Maybe I just didn't want to say them out loud. "I saw something. I heard . . . something. Someone."

She pressed, "But nothing you could identify or describe?"

"It was more like a presence . . . something large and unhappy. I only wanted to help." It wasn't exactly a lie. I could live with it.

Mr. Fine nodded and crossed one leg up over his knee. "It's a noble impulse, Alice, but someone should've warned you before you attempted the open reading."

"*I* should've warned her. Honestly," she said to Mr. Fine. "I didn't realize she'd see so much. She's got quite a bit of talent."

"So Mr. Colby tells me."

Mabel continued to defend herself, and I continued to let her. "But in my defense, mediums so rarely meet anything like what she encountered up on that stage. When they do, it's usually much later in their careers. Most of us need a certain measure of experience for those things to notice us at all—no matter how loudly the foolhardy might try to summon them."

Oh boy. Here came my questions, buckling and folding on top

of one another like train cars forced from their track. "Wait, Mabel—was there something onstage with me? And what do you mean, things? What things? Was the man I contacted tonight a thing? One of the things you're talking about, I mean?" I paused to take a breath. "What are we talking about again?"

Mr. Fine said, in his soothing, pleasant voice, "I suppose we'll all find out eventually, but for now, all we can do is speculate. It might be as simple as . . . well, that the dark things beyond are the spirits of truly bad people. That's what our faith would generally have us believe—for we don't expect to find any angels or demons on the other side."

Mr. Colby and Dr. Floyd had already told me about how death was only a change of state, and that good people in life were good people in death—and so forth. You couldn't expect everyone on the other side to be a friendly, helpful presence. It simply wasn't logical. "Mabel, what did you think it was?"

She made a face that said she'd rather not say. "I felt something enormous and heavy. Very dark," was all I could get out of her.

"Evil?" I asked. I tried to keep the word from squeaking, but I didn't do a very good job. "People can be evil."

He said, "People can be cruel and misguided. They can be traumatized and scarred. They can be frightened into terrible thoughts and appalling behaviors. I don't believe that this requires any firmer label than simple human nature."

"That's . . . awful," I told him.

"And wonderful, too—for the good in humankind overwhelmingly outweighs the bad," he said, with a glance at Mabel. "Alice, Cassadaga is a safe place, protected by the strength and character of its citizens. Spirits like the one you met can only wreak so much havoc here. We are each of us a ward, of a kind. Our goodwill is our first defense against ill intent."

"Are you sure it's enough?"

Mabel shrugged. "It always has been. We may as well trust that it always will be."

MAYBE and maybe not, but I'd argued enough already. I was tired, hungry, and more than a little bit frightened. My hands were not shaking so badly, and I was completely awake—and clear, and free of any supernatural companionship as far as I could tell. I was getting my confidence back in slow degrees, but my patience wasn't returning along with it.

But I fervently hoped Mr. Fine was right. I came here to be with like-minded people who would understand and accept me. I jumped in feetfirst, and I assumed liked-mindedness and understanding from every individual in town, without qualification. But now I had met something truly, deeply, profoundly evil, and nobody seemed to believe me.

I really should've known better. It was simply not logical to expect immediate, unqualified acceptance and trust. But plenty of things aren't.

# TOMÁS CORDERO

Ybor City, Florida

LAST NIGHT I took my supper on the couch beside the Edison cabinet, because I was able to find a single station broadcasting across the airwaves. Its voices chattered between the fields of static, but they were faraway and soft—hardly any stronger than if I heard them through a tin can and a string. I could not tell what they were talking about. Still, they comforted me. I did not feel so alone.

I *am* alone, but I am fortunate. I have been welcomed by others: the handsome young men who keep my shop would have me over for lunch every day if I'd let them; Mrs. Vasquez, who has brought me food and offered me more gossip than I could consume in a lifetime; even my Evelyn's sister. Before she returned to the island . . . Carmina had said, "Come and stay with us, if you want." But I did not want to be father to her son (he was only my nephew by marriage), and I did not want to take her war-lost husband's place.

I did not want to go back to the island. My mother took me and left after the war for independence there took my father. Now I've been here for so long that I scarcely remember my birthplace, and that is fine. I am an American, naturalized in time to fight in America's war.

This is the country I fought for, and bled for, and burned down the world for.

"Isaiah, the forty-first chapter," I remembered suddenly, and said aloud.

My scriptural skills have grown rusty with lack of use, but I have a Bible on hand, and I put my plate aside to retrieve it. The legs of my coffee table scraped the floor as I pushed it back and aside—no longer needing it for a dining table.

I found the old family Bible with ease, because it is very hard to miss. The thing is nearly the size of a car's tire, and it weighs at least that much. I hauled it down from a shelf with other books, knocking down the photograph someone took of Evelyn and me on our wedding day. She was holding a bouquet of fresh flowers. I remember she brought them home and put them in a vase. Every Saturday ever after, she would buy fresh flowers at the market—dahlias if she could get them, sunflowers if she could not—and leave them in the kitchen on the windowsill. When I came home from the war I found the skeletal remains of whatever she'd purchased last, brittle and brown in an empty vase. Still tied together with a ribbon, bleached bone gray from sitting in the sun.

I did not set the photograph upright. I left it where it was.

Instead I hefted the enormous book to the table and let it fall beside my plate. In the front cover there were notes of births, deaths, and marriages. The Bible had been Evelyn's. Her family had not practiced the faith of Rome, but rather some American flavor of Protestantism.

(I do not remember which kind. She'd lost interest in the church long before we met. It seemed a sore subject—so I never asked her about it. She was content to attend services at Our Lady of Mercy, or not at all.)

Now that I think about it, it was odd that the mighty old book remained in her possession. It's in English, but that's not so strange— her father's family had hailed from some different set of islands, far across the ocean in a colder, rockier place than any I've ever seen. Her mother had come from Cuba, like me.

*King James Version*, the great book's cover said. A king from that same island, I believed. Surely he hadn't done the translating himself. It must have been a gift, for his vanity. He must have bought and paid for it.

I flipped through onionskin pages as fine and brittle as the stuff I use to cut patterns in my shop, until I found the book and chapter I sought. I scrolled down the columns, following the tip of my finger to the place the padre must have meant.

*Fear thou not; for I am with thee: be not dismayed; for I am thy God: I will strengthen thee; yea, I will help thee; yea, I will uphold thee with the right hand of my righteousness.*

I closed the book. It didn't have anything else to tell me, not right at that moment, and a sudden pop of a vacuum tube brought the Edison voices into sharper focus . . . if that's the right way to put it. They became louder and less foggy, with less interference from the fuzzy noise that bookended them on either side of the dial. Now I could understand them as surely as if they stood in the next room over.

They were talking about God. Even in their hoarse electric whispers, I must've gathered that much. That must have been why I thought of the padre and the verse in Isaiah. Something just below my hearing was heard regardless, and my brain filled in the rest.

It was a manufactured coincidence.

*  *  *

"THESE tent meetings are growing in popularity across the land—
not only in the southern states."

"*Revival* meetings, that's what they're called."

"Revival meetings, as you like. A town or a church plays host,
invites speakers, and might even pay for a guest or two, and—"

"And people pitch tents, you say?"

"Some of them must. There's always at least the one great tent, to
serve as a sanctuary."

TENTS aren't much, so far as sanctuary goes. I'd rather have Our
Lady, or Cordero's. Or the house I shared with Evelyn, even if it
burns itself to the ground with me inside it.

"DID you know, it's not just the Baptists and the Pentecostals who
are doing this sort of thing."

"Is that so?"

"Oh yes. In fact, right here in Florida we have one of the largest
camp meetings dedicated to the faith of the spiritualists."

"Largest where? In America?"

"In the world, I'd think. There's a little place called Cassadaga—"

"So it's a town? Not a camp?"

"A bit of both, from the sound of things."

THE cabinet fizzed and popped, and the volume went up another
notch. Now they were yelling at me. Or yelling *to* me—though their
voices remained low and steady, chatty and cordial.

"PEOPLE live there year-round, and sometimes they invite speakers
to hold workshops and studies."

"And they camp?"

"There's a hotel. But if the hotel is full, people can, yes—I think so. Set up tents and the like. I'm told that it's quite popular with the northerners during these winter months."

"I should think so. But what do they do? Hold séances? Talk to ghosts?"

"Something like that, I'm sure. They put out a bulletin once a month, articles and that sort of thing. It's called *The Sunflower*, and those who are curious about their faith can learn more about it that way."

"A faith, is that what they call it?"

"Well, that's what it is. A faith in life after death."

"That's one way to put it. So do you believe?"

"In what?"

"In ghosts?"

"In ghosts?"

"In ghosts?"

"In ghosts?"

"In ghosts?"

THE volume crept up, notch by notch, until it rang in my ears and I couldn't stand it another moment. I jumped from my seat and slapped at the cabinet, pushing all the buttons and turning all the knobs to no avail.

"IN ghosts?"

"In ghosts?"

"In ghosts?"

FRANTIC, I reached behind the cabinet, fishing about for the cord. I found the fat black plug, and I ripped it out of the wall.

"INNNNNN ghoooooooosssssstttsssss . . ."

*  *  *

THE last whistling note from the last word's last letters dragged through the parlor and was silent.

I stood there panting in my otherwise quiet parlor. The plug dangled from my hand like an anchor, or like a weapon, I don't know—but the cabinet was quiet, and that was all I'd wanted. A brief, thrifty thought flickered through my head (I hoped that I hadn't broken or ruined it) and was gone.

I smelled smoke.

I stared wildly around the room but saw nothing. I dropped the plug.

I checked the kitchen, the bedroom, the water closet. I checked the office, the hallway, the foyer. I smelled a bonfire, raging somewhere so close I could touch it—I could blister and burn myself if I put out my hands too far in one direction or another. An invisible fire, with invisible smoke, and a warm current of heat that went coursing through my little house.

The fireplace was empty even of ashes, for it saw almost no use at all—even in January. It was for emergency cooking and unexpected, unlikely weather conditions. It was for a curse or a miracle, and it was as cold as a tomb.

I ran my hands along the walls, feeling for some source of the warmth and the smell, and I found nothing, not anywhere.

I returned to the Edison cabinet. Under the wood, the tubes were cooling. The current was gone—my connection to the outside world, to the men and their voices—I'd cut it off on purpose, and I'd done the right thing.

I *knew* I'd done the right thing.

That one voice, the one asking about the ghosts . . . it'd changed, and warped, and become lower and slower; it'd stretched out longer and longer, into that single phrase. I did not believe for a moment that it had been a mere hiccup in the radio.

"Is this some kind of message?" I asked the parlor at large. "There is talk of ghosts, so I should make note of ghosts? Is that what's causing these fires? A ghost?" I gazed warily around the room and into the hall. I stared from corner to corner, daring each shadow to present me with something beyond the pale. "*Whose* ghost?" I asked, barely any louder than a whisper. I was afraid of the answer. Any answer.

So nothing answered, except for the fading smell of smoke. It drifted into the background of my awareness until there was hardly anything at all—just a memory, a tendril of something burning. I stalked the room, then stalked the house again, my nose in the air.

I found nothing.

I cleared my plate, leaving it in the sink. I put the Bible where it belonged. I plugged the Edison cabinet back into the wall and sat on the couch, my whole body as tight as an Italian seam.

But when I called up the radio again, the station featured only one man talking. He was reading the news of the region to people like me—people who were sitting alone in empty rooms, twenty or thirty or fifty miles away from the man in his little booth, with his little microphone, reading the headlines off a little sheet of paper.

I wasn't so much listening to him as letting him keep me company while a peculiar new thought rattled around in my skull. *Cassadaga.* That's what the man had called it—the Florida place where spiritualists met for their seminars and séances. That's where people go to talk to ghosts, isn't it? A darkened room, a round table, a series of clasped hands all in a circle . . . it's how they adjust the knobs, how they tune in to whatever weird station is broadcasting from beyond the grave.

Now that I thought about it like that, I wondered how I might find this place, or speak with someone who teaches there—in case what I have is not an electrical problem, or a religious problem, but a *spectral* problem (if that's not too silly to say, with regard to such a serious subject).

I can still smell the smoke, though. Do ghosts burn? Do they set fires?

Would Evelyn?

I can't imagine that she would. She loved this house, and she loved me. No, if this is Evelyn (and I am jumping to conclusions, oh, such terrible conclusions), I do not believe she'd try to harm me, or the house. If it *is* her (and I should pray for her soul to be beyond this), if it *is* her, then she would only be trying to communicate—only trying to divulge some message, or some warning.

Didn't Daniel see the letters of flame burned into the wall of Belshazzar's palace? I almost drew down the Bible again, that I might look up the story and refresh my memory, but I remembered the words closely enough: *You have been weighed in the balance and found in want.*

These fires of mine might be a warning. So a warning of *what*, I must ask myself.

Clearly, I required some assistance—and while Valero had made me feel infinitely better in the short term, I needed to seek counsel beyond his expertise.

So this morning, after stopping by the shop to warn Emilio that I'd be missing for an hour or two, I stopped by the local library, and with a bit of help from the periodicals lady, I found January's edition of *The Sunflower*.

AND I thought of the kitchen window. I thought maybe Evelyn's last bouquet was made of sunflowers. Another coincidence, unless it wasn't.

ACCORDING to the line below the title, "As the sunflower follows the light, so must we."

I took the slim document to a seat by the window. It was only twenty pages long, folded like a brochure more than bound like a magazine, and it mostly featured listings for speakers, workshops, and services. Some of the workshops sounded interesting: There was one on sharpening one's intuition with help from the spirits, one about the uses of crystals in healing and divination, and one related to physical mediumship. I gathered that this last lecture had something to do with producing physical evidence of spiritual visitation, a prospect I found both repulsive and compelling all at once. Was that what was happening in my house? Physical mediumship? Surely ashes and flame must count as physical evidence of *something*.

I found short articles on individual mediums and on guest speakers, a welcome notice for a new medium named Alice Dartle, and a note from the town's pastor—who is apparently a woman. Likewise, a number of their mediums are women as well, though for some reason that's not such a surprise. I wonder why that is . . . unless it's quite simple. Everyone has heard of the Fox sisters and their uncanny abilities. Everyone knows that women have talked to the dead.

What a peculiar faith. What a peculiar church.

What a peculiar name, Alice Dartle. I'm not sure why it stood out to me, but it did—veritably leaping off the page, as if it was trying to attract my attention.

On the last page there were advertisements for a hotel, a theater, and a bookshop, as well as an address for general delivery. I made note of the address, thanked the periodicals lady, and went back to the shop, with Alice Dartle's name occupying my thoughts the entire time. So while Emilio measured a client and Silvio ran an errand, I sat down in the little back office, which was scarcely the size of a closet. I took a piece of paper and I began to write.

*Dear Miss Dartle,*

*First, it would seem that congratulations are in order. I saw the announcement in* The Sunflower, *declaring that you had been added to the community of mediums at Cassadaga. I hope you will be happy there, and that you will find the work you do fulfilling. And I hope that perhaps you can help me.*

*Please allow me to explain. My name is Tomás Cordero, and I have a strange situation that might benefit from your insight. I do not know where else to turn—I have tried the church of my fathers, and found some measure of comfort there, but little in the way of practical suggestion.*

*For you see, I am being haunted. That's the only way I can describe it, though it's not the kind of haunting one reads about in the dreadfuls and magazines. On the contrary, I am being haunted by fires. Small fires, except for the most recent one, which very nearly consumed my home (and perhaps a neighbor's, too). They appear in unlikely places with no source or cause to be found, and I've come to notice a pattern: These fires leave behind images, drawn in soot. These images are fingerprints and handprints, and once, a woman's face.*

*I lost my wife to the influenza while I was away at war. If this is her, struggling to communicate with me from beyond, it is imperative that I understand her before some irreparable damage is done, or lives are lost to these unusual infernos.*

*I am afraid she might be in hell, and I do not know how to help her. I do not know if I can help her. I do not know if I should.*

I sat back, pencil trembling in my hand. Well, this was the meat of it, wasn't it?

*I do not know if spiritualists believe in such a place, and I am not sure why I have chosen to write to you—only I saw your name and it spoke to me, in some strange way. Perhaps it is a sign from the saints or the dead, that I should approach you with my questions. Or else it is a ridiculous coincidence, and I am seeing patterns where there are none, and assigning significance to meaningless happenstance.*

*But your name spoke to me, and now I am asking to speak with you. I do not know if I am able to leave my business long enough to come visit you, but we could exchange letters, or even a phone call if the stars align correctly. In all honesty I do not know where Cassadaga is, or how far away—though I intend to find out. If it's near enough for a day trip, or a brief visit on a weekend, by train, I might be able to see you in person. Does that matter? I do not know how mediums work. I do not know what you need from me, in order to give me guidance. I have a bit of money, and can pay you for your trouble.*

*Please, Miss Dartle, respond to this letter if you are willing or able.*

*Thank you for your time, and your consideration.*

> *Signed, Tomás Cordero*
> *Ybor City, Florida*
> *(Very near to the Tampa*
> *Bay, and Saint Petersburg)*

I looked the letter over a time or two, or three, or four, and before I could talk myself out of it, I folded it up and stuffed it into an envelope. I addressed my message to the mysterious Miss Dartle, care of Cassadaga's general delivery, and I left it for the postman.

I hope I did not choose poorly when I chose Miss Dartle. She is new, and maybe young, or untrained, or untested. I hope I did not choose poorly when I chose to write the town at all, for I'm sure Padre Valero would look askance at me asking for assistance in a camp of witches. I'm sure that's what he would call them, and he might bring up an anecdote about Endor and Saul.

I remember more of those Bible stories than I thought.

Well, the padre made me feel something close to glory when he told me about the Frenchman and his flames . . . but I must be realistic with myself. Even if the notes by fire have happened before to others, and will happen again one day to someone else, they are happening to me *right now*—and they are a danger to me. They might be a danger to everyone close to me, by friendly companionship or mere proximity.

I hope I chose as well as I think I did, when I picked Miss Dartle's name off the page. I hope I'm not daft and delusional to think that she's the one to help me—if anyone in that town is able to do so.

LISTEN to me. I am grasping at straws.

BEYOND the office I heard Emilio cooing over the single-breasted day suit he'd freshly applied to Mr. Sadre. I looked around the corner and saw him stretching the measuring tape tight between his fingers. He crouched and fussed at the hem of the pants. "Maybe just half an inch . . ."

I left him to it.

I retreated to the workshop and the new fabric, pristine and stacked in tidy bolts. For irrational and nonsensical reasons, they comforted me. I liked the feel of them, the fine fabric beneath my hands, so smooth and blank. I closed my eyes and thought of what might be made from them, considering what cuts, what lines, what styles, might best be suited to each ream. I breathed the soft, clean scent of linen freshly washed and pressed, the faint odor of detergents.

I opened my eyes and saw that the newest bolts had been placed atop the Egyptian cotton order, the one that will turn out at least ten good shirts before I'm finished with it. The fabric was crushed beneath the stacks of linen and wool, and thoroughly rumpled.

I frowned, sighed, and plugged the small tailor's goose into the wall. Ironing has never been my favorite activity, but Emilio was busy, and the fabric was unusable until it was smooth. I'd take care of it myself.

When the goose was cooked, I brought it to the cotton. The fabric was off-white with gray pinstripes, something nice for fall—or what passes for fall in the bay. I let the weight do the work, pressing the wrinkles loose with a burst of heat that wafted up into my face. It was relatively cool in the workshop, and I didn't mind—not like I minded in the dead of summer, when you could almost press fabric by laying it flat on the sidewalk. The heat was dry and comfortable; it was pleasant on my palm, where I held the handle curve that gives the thing its name.

DID Evelyn have something precious that she often wore? There was a hair comb that came from her father's home, on that other island; it was tortoiseshell with a very fine carved edge. She wore it often, and always out of the house—never on days when there was no reason to run an errand. The ring I gave her when I proposed . . . that would not count. It was a diamond, but a very small one. She said it was perfect. Yes, but it was small. She was always beautiful. I saw how men looked at her, and I saw how the women looked, too. Her hair was the color of the espresso they sell in tiny white cups at the stands downtown—and her eyes were precisely two shades lighter, so that they looked nearly amber when the sun caught them.

And her smile . . . it was enough to light up the world. Never mind what she used to say about the one crooked tooth (on the top, a little left of the middle). I never understood why she held her hand over her mouth when she laughed. It was such a tiny thing. I wonder who ever told her it was ugly, or a shame. It was neither of these things. It was divine. It gave her character.

She smiled quite often. At children, at animals. She never met Felipe, the horseshit enthusiast, but she knew and loved his predecessor—Amelie. She was always slipping the old dog bites of banana or cheese, fattening the little thing up one slice at a time.

It was inconceivable to me that Evelyn might be in hell.

I was told there had been a priest, and that she confessed what meager sins she might have offered before the end came, despite not truly sharing his faith . . . But it could've been a kind lie, told to soothe my feelings. (Who would lie about such a thing?)

I smelled smoke.

I jerked the goose up, almost flinging it aside—almost hurting myself, or setting something else ablaze—and I patted frantically at the cotton, as if there were something I could do to save it.

I swore and sputtered, furious with myself. My mind had wandered too long, and my hand had lingered too slowly.

Emilio appeared in the doorway. "Tomás?"

"It's nothing, it's nothing. I wasn't paying attention. Everything is fine."

"Is that the cotton for the—"

"Yes." I stopped him right there. "I thought I'd press it; the linen and the wool . . ." I gestured toward the bolts, the goose still in my hand. I was afraid to put it anywhere. "I made a mistake. I gave it too much heat. Leave me to it. Go see to Mr. Sadre."

"He's paid and left." Emilio came to the board to look for himself. "Oh dear . . . well, it's not so bad. It's not much lost."

"No, only a foot or so. The rest will be fine." I reached for my shears and sliced the ruined portion loose, wadding it up and throwing it toward a bin we use to collect scraps. I missed. It tumbled to the floor. I stomped over to the bin, picked up the loose ball of cotton, and squeezed it, over and over again.

"Tomás, are you all right?"

"I'm fine. I'm stupid, but I'm fine." Before he could ask another well-intentioned question that would only aggravate me, I announced, "I'm not feeling well today, but it's only a headache. What time is it?"

"Nearly one o'clock."

"Do we have any more appointments scheduled?"

"Nothing I cannot handle myself. Go home, if it's only a headache," he urged. "The shop is quiet on Tuesdays, and if there's some great matter that needs your attention, I'll send for you."

"Yes. Yes, that's what I'll do. I'm sorry," I mumbled over my shoulder. I worked the fabric into a ball until it was small enough to hold with one hand—but this time, I did not throw it away. "I'm sorry, my friend, it's just not a good day."

"We all have those. Go on, and I'll see to Cordero's. I'll come around after close, all right? I'll bring you some supper from Antonio's."

"No, you don't need to do that."

He shrugged. "I'm doing it anyway. The less you cook in that house, the better."

I gave up and left, the singed cotton still wadded in my fist and still warm from the iron—or from my own body heat, I don't know which. I felt like *I* was the one on fire, pressed by the goose until I was flat and steaming. I sweated until my collar was sticky, and I pulled it looser at my throat, only to feel the slime-slick yellow that would stain it if I wasn't careful. I smelled salt and sulfur, and the sharp stink of burned fabric. I smelled the ocean to my west, and the azaleas that lined the street.

I unwadded the material. I held it up like a letter I was trying to read.

Was there an image? Was it sorrow that told me I could see the line of her brow, the lift of her cheekbone? Was it madness or a sign from God, that if I held it at an angle, I could see the corner of her mouth?

It was abstract, and much darker than the picture left behind on the wall of the house. It was smaller, tighter, and somehow more refined. It made me think of an illusion I once saw, where an image is an old woman when viewed one way—but a change of perspective reveals a young woman in the lines.

There she was. My Evelyn, coming to me in heat, in destruction. In flame.

Once I saw it, I could see nothing else.

## ALICE DARTLE

Cassadaga, Florida

I NEED TO write something down, but I don't want to. I ought to, so I will. But I'm not sure how to come around to it, so this might take a minute. I can always tear out my first few pages and toss them in the garbage, if it comes to that.

AFTER my first open reading, I cried myself to sleep. Well, first I asked for (and received) another sandwich and a glass of orange juice, even though orange juice doesn't taste very good before or after bourbon—and that was all I had in my trunk.

My supply is dwindling. I've been nipping just a small swig in the evenings, before bed.

I know that rum is the easy thing to get, here in the tropics, but I don't want any. I want the burning, smoky comfort of something from Kentucky or Tennessee. And now one bottle is empty, and the other is more empty than full. I shall have to write to my father to ask for more. Prohibition is about as effective in Virginia as it is in Florida, and the postman won't look, I'm confident.

But yes, I cried myself to sleep, smelling like orange juice and bourbon. I woke up smelling like sour orange juice and stale bourbon, and I thanked God that I lived alone. Heaven forbid anyone should see me like that. Christ forfend that they should get a whiff of me.

I freshened up, washed my face, smoothed my hair, and put on something nice to pretend that I was not afraid, and not embarrassed, and everything was just fine, goddammit.

Well, everything *was* fine. I dressed myself and fed myself and headed down to Mr. Schumacher's seminar on aural coloration as an indicator of overall health, and I didn't fall asleep once—even though I'm not sure I believe there's any such thing as an aura, really, and I didn't understand most of what he was saying.

It sounded silly. It sounded like the flimflam that my mother warned me I was signing up for when I started packing my things to come here.

I sure do hope no one ever reads this, because I sound like a terrible person.

I should *definitely* yank these pages and burn them. Absolutely. Just as soon as I'm finished. But then what would be the point of writing them in the first place?

I guess this is why Catholics have priests. I know it's supposed to be about cleansing yourself of sin, but I bet it's partly the relief of having a diary no one can ever read. That's how it works, isn't it? The priests aren't allowed to tell anyone anything they've heard.

If that's *not* how it works, I can't imagine why anybody tells them a damn thing.

WE aren't supposed to tell, either—if we have clients or cases, or meetings with people. A medium should be a perfect confidant and an unimpeachable fortress of discretion. That's what Mr. Fine said, and that's a lot of five-dollar words that add up to "We'd better keep our mouths shut."

I think there's more to it than discretion for the benefit of our clients, for an agreed-upon silence works for our benefit, too. I think we are safest when we hold other people's secrets. Just think of it: If my dearly departed great-aunts had held more secrets, they might not have burned. They could've used those secrets, cast them like spells, and summoned help. Someone would have spoken up on their behalf and not left them to face a court or a stake alone.

Help is help, even if you have to buy it with blackmail.

Dr. Floyd knows this. That's why she wants to build up this little community, and why she nurtures its reputation and its residents so enthusiastically, and with such eagerness. She's building up the town's defenses, shoring us up against a time of trouble. (And oh, but there will be another time of trouble. There always is for people like us.)

She's trying to make us strong enough that we don't resort to secrets, or blackmail, or trickery to survive when the torches come. But we'll have them if we need them.

BUT speaking of fire. I'm trying to, I swear.

Here I go.

I'VE been very anxious about my dreams, ever since the public reading. I've been afraid I might see that man again, the terrifying man made of soot and smoke, who appeared in my vision when I was finished with the old soldier.

The stranger had turned to regard me before I'd fainted. He'd looked at me—looked into me, *through* me—and I'd heard the gunfire, *rat-a-tat-tat*. Also, I'd gotten a whiff of something that smelled like alcohol, but not the kind you drink—the rubbing kind you get from a chemist. Something that burns fast and hot and leaves behind nothing. Something you'd use to start a fire, or feed it.

I didn't remember this astringent, chemical smell right away; it didn't come to me until I was almost asleep last night. I was lying there, trying not to think about the smoldering man who called himself a "hammer" . . . and thinking about him anyway. (I did not want to call him "the hammer." It felt too much like giving him what he wanted.)

So here's what happened this morning.

It was very early, so early that I want to say it happened last night, but the wee hours count for today—and I'm trying to record this accurately. I've been talking around it ever since I picked up my pencil and opened this little book and started my rambling.

It was dark, and I thought I was asleep. I thought I was dreaming, and it was something about my father and the horse races and a tea-colored bay. I was wearing a bonnet and carrying a little white purse, so it was Easter time, give or take. I was asking the horses which one of them was going to win, and they were making their best guesses. The bay told me that she wasn't feeling quite herself that day and that I should probably put my money on the white stallion with the gray spots. He looked a little small to me.

Then my father asked me where the lantern went. I didn't know what he was talking about. I asked him what lantern. In return he said, "Keep it close. Don't set it down, not here in the barn. It'll start a fire."

I heard something crackle and pop, and I caught a thin tendril of smoke, right up one nostril, and I wanted to sneeze. The horses started to clamor, kicking the stall doors and whinnying, crying, demanding to be let out. My father took my arm, but I yanked myself free and ran to the doors—opening them one by one, all in a row, and telling the horses to go, find someplace safe. They stampeded past me, huge and leggy and full of horror as flames caught on the hay bales and climbed the walls.

My father was shouting. I couldn't understand him. The smell of the smoke was more than I could bear; it stung my throat and burned my eyes, and I could hardly see without squinting and rubbing them. I couldn't find my father. I turned around but didn't see him—not even a silhouette. All I saw were flames and smoke, and the barn was burning down around me until it wasn't.

You know how dreams are. As random and boring as hell to hear about, each and every one of them. But I'm only talking to myself, so I need to finish this.

I need to remember the flames at my feet, and the smoke pouring up my nose, into my mouth. I was standing upright, my back pressed flat against some pole, my arms tied down at my sides. There were no horses. There was no barn. My father was dead. (I don't know how I knew this.) I was alone and I was dying, the pain from the heat beyond bearable, and I was fading, my head drooping until my chin lay flat on my chest.

And then, *rat-a-tat-tat*.

But now it was someone else's dream. These weren't my boots, and that wasn't my uniform. That wasn't my gun.

No, it wasn't a gun. It couldn't be a gun—there's no such gun like that one, or none that I've ever heard of. It did not shoot bullets, though there were bullets all around me. It did not shoot shells, though they fell and crashed and blew caverns into the trenches beside me. It shot *fire*, in a huge long stream. The man holding this gun could've stood on one side of Colby Lake and blasted a stream of liquid flame right into the worship pavilion.

I stood there, my mouth hanging open, hardly noticing the men wailing and dying around me—hardly hearing the screams of horses (yes, the horses were screaming here, too, and running from the fire) and the *rat-a-tat-tat* that never stopped for more than a moment.

The man with the gun was wearing a mask.

"You're the man who dreamed of fire," I said to him, although the war around us was so deafening that I could not hear myself speak.

He turned to look at me. Bright flashing infernos reflected off his lenses. I could not see his face. I could not see his lips move when he spoke in return. But I heard him over the impossible din, and what he said was, *"Alice?"*

FINALLY, mercifully, I shot awake. I sat up in bed and clutched my throat, patted my mouth and face, and coughed like it was consumption. "Oh my God," I wheezed. "Oh my God . . . it was so real . . ." And I was so glad there was no one to hear me, for I know it's ridiculous for a grown woman to be shocked awake by a nightmare. I could still see the man in the mask, with his cannon of fire. I could still smell the smoke.

I could really and truly smell the smoke.

I wrinkled my nose and took a big sniff. No, it wasn't my imagination—and it wasn't some tricky leftover from sharing the dream of another person. There was smoke, and it was close by.

I didn't hear any fire. No telltale cracklings or sizzling sounds.

I swung my feet over the side of the bed and wormed them into a pair of slippers I'd left there for just such a purpose. I heaved myself up and tottered, still woozy from the dream and worried about the smoke. I know you're supposed to stay down low if there might be a fire, for smoke rises and chokes . . . but this was no room filled with toxic haze, and when I felt my doorknob, it was as cool as the edge of my bathtub.

I held up my nose. The bathtub. The washroom.

That's where it was coming from.

The door was ajar, and when I pushed it open, pulling the chain to turn on the light, I let out a squeak of dismay. There it was, in the sink: a pile of cinders still spitting tiny red crinkles of char. It was the pamphlet and notes from Mr. Schumacher's seminar, piled there and set ablaze.

Lucky for me, the pamphlet wasn't long and I'd scarcely taken any notes. There was not enough fuel to make the blaze more noteworthy, and it was wholly contained by the bowl of the sink. I turned the faucet handle anyway, whipping it clockwise until a stream of cold water doused the whole mess to a runny muck of ashes and paper.

I shuddered and hugged myself, and looked into the mirror. You can sometimes use mirrors to see into the beyond, I've learned. That's one of the things they taught me in the seminar called "Seeing the Other Side: Scrying in Glass, Water, or Stone." According to the speaker, they'll tell you things if you look the right way or ask the right question. But I didn't see anything in this one except my own wild-eyed, teary reflection.

I was not at my best.

But as Mabel would say, "In my defense . . ." it had been one miserable night. Something (not someone, I am confident of this) came into my room, chose some tinder, and set a blaze. What a sinister invasion of privacy! What a horrible thing to contemplate, that I might have been there sleeping all the while, as something crept, flittered, or oozed about the place, picking and choosing what to burn and what to leave.

I took a washcloth and wiped out the sink, sending everything either down the drain or into the wastebin beside the toilet. I tried to breathe in and breathe out, and count, one-two-three, all those things you're supposed to do when your heart is beating so hard that it'll probably break clean out of your ribs.

It kept pounding anyway, a drumbeat in my ears, riling up a headache back behind my eyes.

I asked my reflection, "What the hell was that?" but it didn't have a good answer, or any answer at all. I had runny red eyes and pupils as big as poker chips. I had a breakfast meeting in another hour with Mr. Colby and Dr. Floyd, and we were supposed to talk about my progress and catch up after the whole awful business with the fainting and the open reading.

I didn't want to see either of them. I wanted to curl up in bed with what was left of my bourbon, and finish crying.

But that's not how the world works, not even in the magical fairyland of Cassadaga.

I reached for a clean washcloth and turned the water back on. I picked up the bar of soap and closed my eyes. The soap smelled like lavender. It wasn't enough. It didn't mask the glum, damp odor of drowned ashes.

I washed my face anyway.

I opened the curtains and let in the sun.

## TOMÁS CORDERO

Ybor City, Florida

I AM TAKING a few days to myself.

I told Emilio and Silvio that I would see a doctor for the head-aches, and get some French aspirin, and have some rest. I strictly forbade them when they asked about bringing me a meal or two. I assured them that Mrs. Vasquez was feeding me and that it was no concern of theirs. When Mrs. Vasquez realized that I was home for a few days, I told her exactly the opposite—that the fellows from the shop were taking care of me. "Emilio is taking very good care of me," I lied through my teeth. "I needed a few days to rest and to hire someone to clean up the back wall and the bushes. I might just get rid of those palmettos altogether."

"Good luck, if you try. But don't do it yourself."

"No, no. Of course not. I will see if Mr. Swinton and his son are free."

She kept her arms crossed and eyed me warily. She did not believe me, but I did not care. "I'll see his son tonight, when he brings his mother to prayers. I'll mention it to him, that you need some help with the house."

"You do that," I urged. I could hardly afford it, but I couldn't just leave my house looking half burned down from the rear, either. Even if I had the stamina to tackle the job myself, it would be ill-advised. Too many snakes. Too many sandspurs. Too many headaches.

Mrs. Vasquez took Felipe inside and closed the Dutch door. "If you need anything . . . ," she began her combined offer and admonishment.

"Yours will be the first name that springs to mind. I only need some rest. I only need some time."

She nodded, her eyes still narrowed. "If you say so."

I went inside my own house and put my packages down on the divan. I hadn't come home empty-handed. Some of it was work—small tailoring jobs, a hem here and a seam to be let out there—but mostly it was scrap fabric and newspapers, plus some old towels. And five boxes of matches.

Safely home, indoors, with no one watching, I sorted these things into piles. The work pieces I put in the parlor, on the table next to the Edison cabinet. The rest I toted into the kitchen.

I'd thought about using the bathroom, for the cast-iron tub seems like the safest, most fireproof object in the building; but the kitchen is bigger and the sink is also iron. It would also be safe enough for experiments, and I would not have to kneel.

First, I soaked the towels and set them aside in a large bucket. Then I dried the sink, closed the stopper, and prepared the small hot-press I keep at home for personal use. It isn't as fancy as the tailor's goose, but it would suffice. I turned on the stove and put the iron on the closest burner.

Finally, I selected another scrap of cotton, very similar to the one I'd burned at the store, and I examined it while the iron collected all the warmth my little range could produce.

I felt like I should say a prayer.

I am not good at prayers, but for Evelyn's sake, I gave it a try.

"Dear God, or dear . . . anyone who might be listening . . . I know that this must look ridiculous. It's a fool's errand, and a task that is bound to do more harm than good, or that's what I'm afraid of. But if she is trying to speak to me, if my Evelyn needs me . . . I will do what I can. Please, forgive me—if this is something for which I need to be forgiven. Our oath said 'until death do us part,' but I do not think that any loving God would force a man's fidelity to end on such a grim note of mourning."

I checked the iron and checked my instruments of destruction. I fiddled with the first box of matches, sliding it open and testing the contents. I struck one match, watched it blaze, and shook it out immediately.

I went to the nook in the wall and released the latch to lower the ironing board.

I kept praying. "It isn't a command, is it? At death you part, and all is finished. What if a man's devotion proves greater, and stronger, than even the hand of death? What if, from the other side of that veil, his bride should demonstrate a willingness to continue? What then?"

The kitchen was warm enough without the stove to heat it. I could feel a faint wave of heat radiating from that standing appliance. I checked the iron again. Not yet.

"Then a dutiful man should extend his very best efforts to reach her," I concluded.

When the iron was finally ready, I set the scrap of cotton on the board and pressed it. Out of habit I counted to five while slowly sweeping the iron back and forth, never quite stopping; but I forced myself past the norm, fighting against my every instinct, and I scorched the fabric in a great oval—filling almost all of the scrap with a terrible brown stain that would never, ever come out.

I held it up to the light. Was there a pattern? A message?

I saw only brown streaks.

I tossed the scrap into the sink and reached for another swatch of fabric—this one a nice strip of linen. It was more than enough to make a tie, but who makes ties from linen? Emilio, when I'm not watching, that's who—when he feels like dabbling in new things that sound ridiculous.

The iron was still plenty hot, so I set it down and let it stay on the cream-colored piece. I drummed my fingers along the board and chewed on my bottom lip. When the sample started to smoke, I lifted the iron and found . . . the imprint of an iron.

I hesitated. This wasn't working.

Next in the pile was a fine wool flannel that I liked quite a lot. It was good quality, a soft gray that wasn't too dark and wasn't too light. It would make no difference if I destroyed it, never mind how soft it was to touch, or how nice a pocket it might have made otherwise.

Or a collar lining. Or a decorative cuff.

I cringed to press the iron down upon it, but then I thrilled to lift it away! This time, I found prints, as clear as day!

They came from a woman's hand, with long, slender fingers. If I looked closely—if I grabbed the magnifying glass I sometimes use for the tiniest stitches—I could see a gap on the fourth finger, where a wedding band ought to go.

"It's you, isn't it?" I asked the flattened sheet. I said her name.

I prayed it. "Evelyn?"

Then I felt . . . whatever the opposite is of when a shiver runs down your spine. It was a radiant buzz of warmth, traveling from my head to my heels and back again—and in the wake of this strange, hot hum, I felt sweaty and shaky. It was not a chill but a fever.

* * *

I wondered what other offerings I might burn.

I did not sweep out the remains of the flannel; I just threw everything else I'd brought from the shop on top. "Evelyn, if this is you, give me a sign." I prayed her name again. It was a *delicious* blasphemy.

I dropped the match.

When there was nothing left but ashes and a few stubborn scraps of wool, I checked my sink with all the rigor of a policeman investigating a crime. I used a pencil to move the ashes around and lift aside the last of the flannel, and I blew gently downward, to chase away the lighter debris.

There it was.

The face. Again, a woman in three-quarters profile. It was a smaller version of the one that had been on the wall outside—reproduced so meticulously that they could have come from the same photograph.

Did I have such a photograph of Evelyn?

No, I did not think so. I would've remembered it. I would've kept it forever, even if it hadn't shown her full beauty, but only this slim portion of her cheek, the line of her nose, and the curve of her lips and chin. I had only a handful of photographs; all but two were of her.

Three are from our wedding, two of those posed after the fact in a studio. One is from our honeymoon, standing on the boardwalk at the Saint Petersburg pier. (We had no money. We did not go far.) One is from the day we bought the house, and she is standing in front of it with a smile on her face that is all love and potential and life. She is holding a basket of fresh bread and a bouquet of flowers that Mrs. Vasquez gave us as a welcoming present. I still remember the smell of them.

As for the other two photographs, one is a picture of my parents.

The other is a portrait of myself, modeling one of my suits. It is not here at home, but framed in Cordero's with a plaque beneath it, identifying me as the proprietor. I think it's a little silly, but Emilio loves it. On the day the photograph was taken, he said that I looked very handsome and that I should be my own best advertisement. I was flattered, and I told him that he and his brother were better ambassadors than I could ever be, but he wouldn't hear it. He sent me down to the studio that afternoon. I went. It was easier than arguing with him.

I wish yet again that I had a camera of my own. I wish that I could aim the lens into the sink and capture the face, with the remnants of the rough handprints (now smeared and partly obscured), so that I could keep it and remember it. I would not show it to anyone as proof of what had occurred. I did not want anyone to know what I was doing, and besides, any skeptic could claim that I'd made the marks myself.

I only wanted another photo of Evelyn. I would settle even for a preternatural portrait made of soot in the bottom of my kitchen sink.

But I couldn't stop there.

What else could I burn? I was vibrating with the thrill of it all, this sudden knowledge that she was listening and trying to speak. It could be no one else. No one else on earth or below it cared enough about me to go to these lengths, to defy both the grave and the flames of hell.

I darted from room to room, considering hand towels and curtains, swiping a pillowcase from the linen closet. Into the sink it went, all of it, and on top of it I added the flames . . . I threw down match after match until the sink was filled with ashes and the hardier corners of wool, and whatever edges of anything else that had not quite been consumed.

The ashes told me nothing.

The sink was black, and my arms were black all the way to my elbows. My fingertips were tender from striking too many matches too closely.

I turned on the faucet and washed away what I could, scraping out the rest. I scrubbed down the sink with a rag and some soap. I didn't get it clean so much as I got it ready for another round of fiery experiments.

If these were offerings, and if I expected a response, I needed to find something precious. I needed to make a true sacrifice.

I went to the parlor and looked at the bookshelves. I had some detective dreadfuls, some books on astronomy, and one or two on gardening. I also had my little book of photos. It was mostly empty, except for the aforementioned handful.

Maybe one of those would work.

I took the album down and opened it up. On the first page were photographs from our wedding. Two of them were identical. I could part with one, couldn't I? I slipped one out from the glued-on corners and looked at it closely.

When I flipped it over, I realized it was only the photographer's proof—and I could live without that, couldn't I? Just the proof, not the picture where I wore a suit of my own brand, and Evelyn wore a gown that her sister made, with a veil that her mother had worn on her own wedding day some twenty years earlier.

Now I wasn't vibrating so much as trembling. I carried the proof back to the sink. I stood there holding it by two fingers on one hand, and I struck a match with the other. I connected the two, and once the destruction was ensured by a tall, vigorous flame, I dropped the photo and let it burn.

"Evelyn, if this is you . . . *please*. I must know."

This time, yes.

This time when the last of the light was gone and the final seam of char had cooled to gray, I was rewarded with incontrovertible proof—for in the little shadow that was hardly any larger than a playing card, I was given the initials EMC.

Evelyn Maria Cordero.

I clasped my hands up over my mouth to keep myself from shrieking with joy.

THE smoky room went dark, then bright. I felt that same terrible tingle of heat course from crown to foot once more, and I squinted, my eyes red and stinging. The smoke clustered around me, closing in and smothering me, unless this was another one of those flashes—something from the war strain. I flinched, blinked, and shook my head hard. It didn't help. The darkness didn't go away, but I wiped my eyes and thought it was my imagination, probably. The room was no darker, no warmer. There was smoke. But that was all.

I looked down in the sink, at the remnants of the proof. What else could I offer?

I would not burn the wedding photo, the proper one of the pair of us. That one is sacrosanct, and Evelyn would not want me to destroy it. (I feel this in something deeper than my bones.) So I did not choose the wedding photo or the other photos of her. I would not trade the real thing for an uncertain copy. Not yet.

Instead, I thought of something that would have been irreplaceable to *her* . . . but something I could part with in good conscience. I pulled her family Bible off the shelf. I toted it back to the kitchen and dropped it on the counter. I put the book in the sink and opened it up to a random spot in the middle, so that half of the pages (give or take) fell in each direction. I tried not to look. I looked anyway.

> *And he made his son pass through the fire, and observed times,*
> *and used enchantments, and dealt with familiar spirits and wiz-*
> *ards: he wrought much wickedness in the sight of the Lord.*
>
> 2 KINGS 21:6

I flipped a few more pages, to make the book lie more evenly. That's what I told myself. In truth, I wanted to look away from those words. There was no wickedness here, in a man's devotion to a woman. To his *wife*, married as such in front of God.

I lifted another match. The flame wobbled. I let it fall. The book caught fire, its onionskin pages lighting up as bright as a lamp, the flame digging a hole through the New Testament. The hole spread across the spine to the Old Testament and to the family histories in the front pages, drinking up the ink and the colored plate illustrations. Licking up the lineage of half a dozen generations, painstakingly recorded in the hand of my wife, her mother and grandmother, and other assorted relatives through the years.

It all burned, and burned, and burned.

And when it was gone, I blew away the ashes and read the remains like tea leaves.

My heart did not stop, though I thought it might. I opened the kitchen windows and let the smoke leave. I didn't care if Mrs. Vasquez saw it, and I didn't care if it worried anybody. I didn't care about anything, anywhere, except that my dead wife had sent me an unmistakable message, written in her very own handwriting.

Two small words, left behind, and my whole world was upended: *Help me.*

OH God, Evelyn. I *will*.

I don't know how, and I don't know what to do, or whom to ask, but I will find a way and I will be whatever you need. I will do whatever is required. I will chase you into the flames and drag you out myself, though it should cost me everything. I will take your place, if that is an option that heaven will offer me.

But *how*?

I wonder how far away Cassadaga is. How long would it take me to get there?

Where else can I go, except to this town that speaks to the dead? Who else should I ask, if not the enlightened clairvoyants at the camp meeting? They converse with the spirits, and they do not pretend otherwise.

I hope they will hear me out. I hope they will have some wisdom to enlighten me. I hope I am doing the right thing. If I'm not, I hope the church will have me back should I return, hat in hand, to the confessional with a tale to keep Padre Valero awake for days.

This is worth a try. I believe that, and I must take steps toward this peculiar town with its collection of mediums, its seminars, and its meetings. I may need more than a few days to undertake this task, so tomorrow I will go to the shop and ask the dear Casales brothers to indulge my absence for another week or more. I don't think they will mind. I've been gone for such a length of time before, and the store has run beautifully without me. I can always hand those men the keys and trust that all will be well.

I should draw up a will. I should leave the place to the pair of them in case I do not return from this trip—or in case I never successfully undertake it. The house might come down around me in the night, and I might never awaken. I could be hit by a trolley tomorrow.

I'll write something up tonight.

I cleaned my kitchen, reluctantly washing the message down the drain along with whatever ashes were not content to blow away or be dropped sopping wet into the garbage. I left the windows open because the day was warm but breezy. I hid the evidence that I'd been setting fires, indulging in the very behavior I'd been so wrongly accused of. I'd left footprints in the fallen ash that dusted my floors. I pulled out a broom and did my best to banish them all.

And when I put the broom away, a tiny scrap of unburned paper fluttered past me, settling on the floor. I picked it up and read.

*Is not my word like as a fire? saith the Lord; and like a hammer that breaketh the rock in pieces?*

# ALICE DARTLE

Cassadaga, Florida

MR. COLBY COULD not make the meeting over breakfast that he'd arranged with Dr. Floyd and me to discuss my "progress" and so forth. He wasn't feeling well, so he stayed home and Mr. Fine looked in on him. I hear that Mabel brought him groceries, so I'm glad to know that he's being looked after with such warmth and care. He's quite an elderly fellow, and he has some trouble taking care of himself these days.

"We do our best to see to his needs," said Dr. Floyd, after apologizing for the founder's absence. "He's in fair health for a man of his years, but he has his good days and bad. Especially since he lost his little house, late last year."

"What happened to it?"

She shrugged uncomfortably. "He . . . he *lost* it. The bank took it back, I mean. It isn't gossip because it's no great secret: He gave so much of his time and money to Cassadaga and to the church that he isn't secure in his old age."

"Oh dear . . ."

"Yes, well, he is always welcome here, and we always make a place for him. The house was outside of town, out in DeLand. So now he lives here, either in Harmony Hall or in the Brigham house, depending on the season. Sometimes he stays at other camps. He's still quite well regarded, you know. People still want to hear him speak. It just takes so much out of him . . . and he has a hard time telling people no when they ask him to travel."

"That's terrible," I said. "I mean, the part about him losing his house is terrible. Not the part about him doing so much to help the community."

"I know, dear. I know." She took a sip of tea, and her eyes flashed that weird little twinkle at me. "He provided the land for the town. Did I mention that? He donated it, years and years ago. As far as I'm concerned, Cassadaga will always belong to him, and he will always have a place here—until he crosses over, and after that fact, too."

"I suppose no one really leaves. Or no one *has* to leave," I corrected myself. "Since there will always be people here to listen to them."

She took another sip of tea. It was warm enough that I couldn't imagine doing likewise. I'd opted for juice instead. "I hope so." The twinkle flashed again. She frowned, then caught herself—like she didn't want me to see either the twinkle or the frown.

"Dr. Floyd, what do you mean? Is something wrong? Is the town in trouble? Do you think people will come and . . . and take it away? Like the bank took Mr. Colby's house?" A phrase leaped to mind, but I caught it before it could escape my mouth. I did not say, *Do you think someone will burn it down?* But I probably thought it really loud. She probably heard me.

Dr. Floyd shook her head. Her hair was piled up under a smallish hat, and the result was stunning—both in appearance and in curiosity. I didn't see any hatpins and wondered how she kept it in place. "Nothing like that, no."

"Then . . . like what? Are you afraid of something?" I asked bluntly. "I get the feeling you're afraid."

"Afraid? That's too strong a word. I'm cautious by nature, but I don't live in *fear*."

"Then what's bothering you?" I pushed.

"Nothing is bothering me," she said flatly. I didn't have to be clairvoyant to know she was lying. "I'm merely distracted, and concerned for Mr. Colby." Once again, the flicker in those baby-bright blue eyes. Once again, she looked down just a little too late to keep me from seeing it.

To hell with it. I went ahead and asked, "Why are your eyes doing that thing?"

She dug in. "My eyes aren't doing anything. Now, we're here to discuss you and your studies, and your progress here in the camp. So let's be productive, shall we? First, which of the meetings have you attended? I know you attended the visitors' seminar 'Auras, Lights, and Crystals,' and I wanted to hear what you thought of it."

"I thought it was strange and silly."

"That's unkind."

"I'm only being honest."

"Honesty is no excuse for unkindness." She chided me, but she was happy to have the change of subject (happier than I was, I believe). She chased it down and forced it forward. "If it wasn't to your taste, or you didn't find it accessible, or you weren't drawn to Mr. Schumacher's philosophy and findings . . . you can say so without being rude."

I was feeling rude, but she was right and I'd already done enough to irk her for one day. I took it down a notch. "Fine. I did not find his . . . his research plausible, and I'm not sure there's anything to this whole 'aura' business, but I'm sure he's a lovely man and I meant him no disrespect."

"That's a fib if ever I heard one, but you were able to put it pleasantly, so I'll take it—and call it an improvement in your attitude. Now, did you attend Dr. Mason's workshop on prayers and meditation?"

"I meditated so magnificently that I fell asleep."

"Oh, for Spirit's sake . . ."

*ATTITUDE.*

I hated that word. It made me want to sulk, but I didn't want to sulk in front of Dr. Floyd, so I hope that I hid it well enough to fool her. I probably didn't. I mostly concealed my irritation by stuffing the last half of a piece of toast into my mouth. Because two could play that game, that's why.

"DR. Floyd?" A short, stocky woman in her forties with thick black glasses approached the table with a stride of confidence.

"Imogene, yes? Can I help you?"

Imogene pulled up a chair as if she'd been invited to do so, and dropped herself into it. She opened her mouth to say something to the pastor, then changed her mind and spoke to me, instead. "Well, hello there. You're the girl who did the thing at the open reading—then pulled a straight-out faint, after a damn fine show."

I blushed and nodded, but I blushed a little coldly. I wasn't sure if I liked this woman, who strolled about as cocky as a man and made herself comfortable at someone else's table. Also, I didn't like being called a girl, and I was well aware that I had fainted. No need to bring it up.

"Imogene Cook," Dr. Floyd introduced the pair of us, "this is Alice Dartle. She's new, but she's learning. Mabel has taken her under her wing."

"Good for Mabel. I couldn't stand to do it myself. You look like

a dear, don't get me wrong. I'm just real shit for a teacher, that's all."
I couldn't place her accent, but it was from farther north than Georgia and farther south than Ohio.

"So far, I'm only a middling student," I said modestly, mostly to prove that I wouldn't flinch at her language (since Dr. Floyd hadn't).

"You'll come around. That's what everyone says."

"Everyone's talking about me?"

The pastor chose this moment to interrupt, heading her off. "Imogene, darling. *What* can I do for you today?"

"Oh, right. David's back from his *sabbatical*." She said the word like it was code for something else. "And Perry Riffle wanted a word with you before the day gets too much longer."

"What on earth for?"

She shrugged. "I'm only the messenger, Doc. But it's something to do with a council meeting, now that Oscar's back."

"Right. I have . . ." She used her fork to poke thoughtfully at the last of her salad. "I have . . . something I'd like to bring up for discussion, now that we're all back in town. So it's just as well. See if you can round everyone up for a three-o'clock session on the second floor of the Brigham house."

"Why not the Harmony Hall office?"

"We might need more room than that."

I was lost, and no one was on the verge of filling me in, so I asked, "Something to bring up for discussion? Do you mean me?"

Dr. Floyd veritably snapped back, "Not everything is about you"; then she softened it by adding, "darling."

I stopped talking and pulled my napkin up out of my lap, wadding it into a ball just to give my hands something to do. "I'm sorry. I wasn't trying to—"

"No, I'm sorry. What I should have said was simply, 'There's camp business to discuss, and it's nothing to do with you, or your progress, or your training—all of which is going smashingly. Mabel says you're a strong learner with a good deal of patience. You're fitting in nicely, and I'm concerned about something else. It's nothing that should worry you.'"

Imogene Cook looked like she couldn't decide whether to stay and watch the drama or excuse herself to escape it. She erred on the side of beating a retreat. "Three o'clock you said?" She stood up. "I'll go round up Oscar and the rest, and I'll see you then."

When she was gone, I fidgeted with the napkin a little and asked quietly, "Is she on the council, too?"

"Imogene? No, but she might as well be." She sighed heavily, and again she begged my pardon. It took every ounce of willpower I possessed to keep from apologizing right back at her, but since she'd told me I did it too much, I stayed quiet. "I didn't mean to be harsh with you. I have no excuse to be rude, and I'm setting a terrible example."

"You could talk to me about it, if you wanted. I'm a good listener," I fibbed. I was a much better talker than listener, but I didn't want our session to close on such a sour note.

"I don't wish to burden you with it, as there's nothing you can do to help."

I like Dr. Floyd a great deal, and I have tremendous respect for her, but neither one of us was in the mood for this talk anymore—so we ended the meal as soon as we were able, and went our separate ways.

She walked away from me a little too briskly, looking back once, then twice. She glanced up and down the street and looked up into the sky, checked her watch, and darted over to the bookstore. Before she let herself inside, she looked back and forth along the porch, and back down the avenue into what could best be described as "downtown." I don't know what she was looking for, but she was acting like she thought she was being watched.

All right, obviously *I* was watching her, but she wasn't worried about *me*. As she'd reluctantly confessed, she was bothered by something else.

So now I was in a mood, and now Dr. Floyd was off to fret in the bookstore or wherever—but the rest of the camp was bustling with a new trainload of sunlight seekers and seminar enthusiasts, some of them with tents rolled up and stored with their trunks. They were just in time for a rousing class called "Fears, Foes, and Familiars"— by Miss Theresa Gains of Albuquerque. Lucky them.

A dozen or more cars were parked in front of the hotel, each one laden down with so much luggage that the tires sagged. All along the wraparound porch, people occupied every rocking chair and every table. People played checkers and people sipped sweet tea, or else they read newspapers and discussed the weather—because the weather was something to behold if you came here all the way from New England. On my way down the steps I heard one man declare that there were two feet of snow back home, and I've seen two feet of snow before. It's miserable.

I've seen a hundred degrees for a week at a time as well, and that's miserable, too. January's muggy warmth suggested that I might see more than a week of that weather to come, maybe as early as spring. But I still had months, at least, before the subtropical sun came back with all its terrible vigor. I still had months to pretend that nothing would change, and I would live here in comfort and harmony for the rest of my days.

If you could really call this "harmony." I was happy to be in Cassadaga, and thrilled that I'd been accepted . . . but also frankly disappointed in how things had stalled since my arrival. I suppose I'd expected to be inducted into a world of arcane secrets and furtive ceremonies . . . when I'd mostly been attending meetings and snoozing through lectures that all had three equally dull elements in their titles.

I suppose that Dr. Floyd's irritable restlessness had rubbed off on me, and now I was fussy and bored.

I didn't want to attend another stupid seminar, as I'd done plenty of those over the last couple of weeks, and there wasn't anything on the hotel bulletin board that appealed to me. I knew, because I'd checked it first thing in the morning, like always.

I had no interest in "The Laughing Dead: Humor, Surprise, and Joy on the Other Side," or "Drawing Your Spirit Guide: Flattery, Mimicry, or Insult?," much less "Beyond Palmistry: The Lines of the Face, Feet, and Back."

But if I remembered correctly, there was a movie playing a block away, in the tiny one-screen theater named the Cassadaga Calliope. I couldn't recall what was showing, or what time it would be shown—so I went back inside to look at the bulletin board again.

"*The Mark of Zorro*," I read aloud, and to myself. The first show was at noon, and the clock on the wall behind me said that I still had an hour before I should bother to find a ticket and a seat. Rather than sit around the hotel and resume the sulk I'd worked up while talking to Dr. Floyd, I decided to walk down to Spirit Lake and perhaps visit a couple of the little gardens along the way.

The whole camp meeting isn't more than a couple of miles square, I don't think, and although the day was a little warmer than I would've liked, I had nothing better to do than get some fresh air and poke around.

Past Harmony Hall and the other grand old houses I strolled, parasol in one hand and fan in the other. As I walked, I bobbed my head in a friendly fashion to any hat that was tipped my way, and responded in kind to any of the ladies who said, "Spirit be with you." Down by the water I passed the pavilion with its enormous white shades rippling in the lazy breeze, and upon the stage I saw Mr. Fine and Edella Holligoss. They were sorting through hymnals and picking out numbers for the hymn boards.

Beyond the pavilion was the lake, or honestly a pond, I think—but I shouldn't call it that out loud. It has a name, and that name has a "lake" in it, so I should respect the designation. Never mind that it's hardly anything more than an extra-wet spot in a swampy marsh.

Swampy marsh or no, people were out there having a good time. Two boys were fishing from the end of a brief and narrow pier, and a set of young parents had brought their little one down to the water's edge to squish barefoot in the soggy sand. It looked like fun, but it also looked like a good way to get your toes nibbled on by snakes, so although I could see the appeal, I ruled against the impulse to whip off my shoes and go wading.

I turned back toward the pavilion just in time to collide with somebody. I jerked back, and my fan went flying. My parasol almost took off after it, but I grabbed the handle just in time to keep it from flinging itself into the road.

"Are you thinking about a dip?"

"Good God, no," I responded before I could think of anything nicer.

The somebody I'd greeted so roughly was a nice young man about my own age. He wore a seersucker suit with navy pinstripes and an apricot-colored pocket kerchief sticking out. His shoes were very shiny and his smile was very encouraging. He was an odd-looking fellow, with a face like a handsome foot—all funny angles and unexpected proportions, but nice details.

"Me, either," he confessed. "Not least of all because I can't swim."

"Oh, I can swim just fine. I just didn't bring . . . didn't bring anything to wear . . ." I took a step back and to the side and scanned the ground for my fan.

The nice young man found it first. He picked it up, shook off a dusting of sandy dirt, and handed it back to me with a flourish.

"Thank you."

"Please, allow me to introduce myself—I'm David Fine. My father is the president of the camp."

"How nice for him. And for you. I . . . um . . . I know your father. I met him a few nights ago. He seemed . . . pleasant." I sounded like an idiot. I could feel myself pinking up, from the warmth and from the conversation alike. "But we haven't met. You and I, I mean."

"No, that's why I introduced myself. And you are . . . ?"

I straightened up. "Alice Dartle. I'm a medium and a clairvoyant, and I've recently come to stay here."

He nodded smoothly. "I thought it might be you. You're making quite an impression."

"Oh dear. I mean, oh good. That's what I meant."

"I'm certain that you did. So tell me, if you aren't considering a dip in the lake, how are you planning to spend your afternoon? Will you catch one of the new speakers? I hear that Mrs. Campbell is a marvel to behold. Her physical phenomenon is unmatched in the field. Her seminar 'Manifesting Proof' is alleged to be superb."

His smile was so distracting, I just wanted to agree with everything he said. "Yes, she's grand. Or that's . . . that's what I've heard. Just now. From you. Because until ten seconds ago, I'd never heard of her—I'm so sorry, I'm not usually such a mess. It must be the heat, or something from breakfast just isn't agreeing with me."

"Then perhaps it's time for lunch?"

"No, no," I said, though my first thought had been, *Yes, yes.* "It's only been . . ." I didn't have a watch, so I didn't know for certain. "Fifteen minutes or so. It was a late breakfast."

"Coffee, then?"

"Never cared for it."

"Tea?"

"Hot or cold?"

"Which do you prefer?" he asked, with admirable determination.

"Whichever goes best with bourbon."

"Bourbon? Have you ever had ginger beer with rum?"

I shook my head. "Everything is rum around here, isn't it? That's never been my first choice. I've never had a rum drink that wouldn't be better with bourbon instead."

"Then, please, allow me the opportunity to surprise you." He held out his arm, elbow crooked, like I should just take it and walk alongside him.

So I did. I took it and walked alongside him, falling into step easily and a little more comfortably than I expected. He was quite tall, and he stooped a little to both dodge my parasol and keep me from standing on tippy-toes.

"Where are we going, to test this combination of peculiar ingredients in a glass?" I asked. It sounded more clever before it came out of my mouth. That's my only excuse.

"How do you feel about Candy's?"

"The lunch counter? I've been there once or twice, and Mrs. Pearson seemed lovely. I don't recall seeing anything with rum on the menu."

"Of course you didn't see it, because of course you wouldn't. The whole country's gone as dry as a bone, haven't you heard? And besides, spiritualists skip the bottle. Or they're supposed to, I think. But plenty of them *don't*—especially not the snowbirds. Most of those darling Yankees are here for sightseeing as much as spiritual communion. They want their drinks hard, and they want their ladies fighting for the vote."

"Is that true?" I asked. "Wait . . . do the spiritualist ladies want to vote?"

"Some do, some don't. Like so many other things, Cassadaga doesn't have a firm opinion on the matter. How long have you been here in town?"

"A couple of weeks, I think?"

"And you're not bored out of your mind yet?" He gestured at the pavilion as we passed it, asking, "Can you stand to sit through another workshop? Aren't you exhausted by the sermons and messages?"

"Not in the slightest."

"You're a filthy liar."

"We don't know one another well enough for you to call me that."

"All right, I'll save the name-calling for after your first drink."

"Splendid," I said. "But does it *have* to be rum?"

He laughed in reply. "We'll have to see what Mrs. Pearson has on the shelf. No promises, you hear?"

We arrived shortly enough at the lunch counter everyone called Candy's, presumably because the woman who ran it was named Candice Pearson. She was standing at the register when we came in, but she left it to come and sweep David up in a hug—squeezing him like she meant to break him.

"David, you monster. When did you get back into town?"

"This morning, and please release your grip, madam! For the world has but one of me."

She did not fully release her grip, though she let him hang at arm's reach so she could look at him. "Since this morning? And this is the first I'm seeing of you?"

"It's been a *busy* morning. Look, I've met someone new. Her name is Alice."

Mrs. Pearson wiped her hands on her apron and offered me one to shake. "I can't recall if we've formally met, or if you've only bought a snack or two—and rushed off to your next set of lessons. Mabel and Dr. Floyd have really been running you ragged."

I smiled and shook her hand. "This is our first proper introduction, and I'm here to learn, so the lessons are a welcome necessity. Speaking of, Mr. Fine has declared that I need to learn more than just seminar subjects. He says it's time I learned some *secrets*."

"About the rum and cards? Oh, honey—those are hardly secrets."

"Well, I didn't know about them until just now!" I exclaimed. "And until Mr. Fine—"

"David," he corrected me.

"Until *David* put forth his rather persistent invitation, no one else had mentioned it, either."

"You're new here, that's all." She shook her head and waved away any other explanation. "Also, you're the pastor and Mabel's new pet, and they probably wanted to keep you to themselves."

"I'm nobody's *pet*."

"I'm only teasing." She went to a back door that I'd assumed went to a stockroom, but I'd assumed incorrectly. "David, don't make too much of a mess. Don't let things get sloppy."

"Do I ever?"

"Never, dear boy. That's why I'm leaving you to it."

She ushered us through the door, then closed it behind us—saying in parting, "When you're ready to go, leave through the rear. I don't want to hear about this from your father, you understand?"

"Yes, ma'am, as always."

So it turns out, Cassadaga has a speakeasy.

THE speakeasy at Candy's is only big enough to hold three card tables and a bar, but that bar runs the full length of the short wall, and it's nothing to sneeze at. The lighting is low, the décor is suitably subdued for a quiet operation, and there's a jar on the bar's counter full of money. Beside it is a sign that reads, "Spirit is watching."

"Everything here works on the honor system," David explained. "You make and drink your own beverages, because there's no one on staff to serve you. But you'd better be fair about it, or everyone will know."

"How?" I asked. Jesus, God in heaven—I was full of stupid questions today.

He raised one eyebrow and squared off the other one. "Really?"

"No, not really. The town's full of clairvoyants. Kindly forget that I asked. Now, where's the bourbon?"

"You're sure I can't persuade you to have—"

"*No.* What else have you got on hand?"

"Very well." He went behind the bar with a heavy sigh and reached up to a shelf I could've never grabbed—not even with my tippy-fingers. Bless him forever, he pulled down a bottle of Maker's Mark.

"Be still my heart . . ."

"It's for medicinal purposes," he told me with a grin. "The government lets them distill—they have a contract with the military or something."

"This is . . . this is the greatest day of my life. Since I came here. Really, I've often thought that bourbon was the only thing missing, or Cassadaga would be heaven on earth."

"Just wait until July rolls around. You'll be cooking in your own juices, even after the sun goes down." He poured himself a big slug and then made one for me. "You're *sure* you don't want to try the rum drink? We've got more rum than you could shake a stick at. This stuff I have to smuggle in from up north."

"Maybe for the next round."

Behind me, someone laughed. "The next round? I knew I liked this girl." She was sitting at a table alone, nursing a mug full of something that probably wasn't coffee.

"Hey there, Sister." David beamed. "While I'm back here, can I set you up another one?"

"No, dear boy. I'm fine for now. I have to go lead a prayer group in another hour, so I'd best refrain. Hello again, Alice," she said to me.

"Hello . . . Francine? Is that right?"

"It is correct indeed! You can call me that, or call me Sister, or call me Miss Getty, whatever suits you best. Come on, join me over here. There are no cards, but we can toast what little I've left in my glass."

I saw only a few other people in the darkened room, but I didn't recognize any of them. David said a few more hellos, but I took the seat next to the Irishwoman, who seemed genuinely happy to see me. Maybe she was genuinely happy to see everyone, because she beamed at David, too, when he pulled out a chair and joined us.

Three little candles in the center of the table provided most of the lighting, so we really did look like three witches sitting around a cauldron. A tiny cauldron. One that smelled faintly of paraffin and lavender, for someone had mixed some herb oil into the wax.

"I had no idea this existed. Does everyone know about it?" I asked.

Francine nodded. "I'd be shocked if they didn't. Why? Did Mabel give you the old 'Oh, there's no real hooch any closer than DeLand' story?"

"She *did*," I said, and I hoped that the darkness of the place concealed some of my glowering.

"Oh, don't get too upset about it. They're only trying to protect you, and if they told you there was no liquor in Cassadaga, they're technically correct," David informed me. "We're on the far side of the railroad tracks, and therefore we're outside the campground boundaries. From a strictly pedantic standpoint."

The geographic boundary hadn't occurred to me. "So the camp is only"—I tried to picture it—"a handful of blocks, over that way?"

Francine nodded. "The camp property begins at the gates, beside the hotel. It includes everything from there to the lakes, and north along the hills—including the structures around the water. There's not much to the place, and it's especially noticeable in the dead of summer, when the snowbirds have all flown home. It only seems bigger right now because there must be a thousand visitors plumping up the population . . . but most of them will leave when the season turns."

David held up his glass, calling for a toast. "But here, now, we clandestine three . . ."

"I count eight." Francine cocked her head at the others—four men playing cards at the far table, and one woman alone, reading a book by candlelight and sipping a glass of wine.

"We clandestine *eight*," he corrected himself. "We must toast to something. What will it be?"

I couldn't think of anything, but Francine said, "To springtime!"

David declined to agree. "That's silly."

"Then . . . to new members of our little community!"

He nodded. "I like that one better." But then as he brought his glass forward for a clink, he lowered his voice and leaned in so that the small flames lit him up from beneath his chin. "To new friends, and to secrets shared, and to candles, and cards. To flames, and to fortunes." He tipped the glass forward so it knocked against mine.

Francine was game. She put hers up as well, and everyone clinked all around out of solidarity, except for the woman with the book. She only raised her glass in our general direction, without looking up from her reading.

I downed the bourbon happily and let it warm me from the throat down. I hadn't realized I was chilly—it was the first time I could recall being cold since I arrived—but the alcohol took care of it in short order.

Then I sat up, startled. I almost spilled the drink, but I have better manners than that.

"What is it?" Francine asked.

"I almost forgot: I was going to go see a movie."

"You were planning to skip Gwen Millard's 'Philosophy of Modern Mediumship'?" David asked with big, accusing eyes. He wasn't in the least bit serious.

"I was going to flee from it as though it were the devil." I grinned back at him, though the admission left a funny feeling in my stomach.

Francine leaned forward and patted my arm. "No, dear. Don't do that."

"Do what?"

"Feel guilty. You're not here out of charity, and this isn't a university—where your scholarship depends upon some grade or some continued performance. You're *in*, don't you see? You're in the greatest club of all—a club full of people who have no rules except to do no harm, and help when able. Any puritanical leanings are strictly social, not spiritual. This is only a card room, and these are only drinks. Run toward drunkenness and problematic behavior, and you'll get a talking-to, but mind your manners and take your vices in moderation, and even David's father will look the other way."

"Is he a stickler?" I asked.

David sighed dramatically. "Oh yes. He's the worst sort of teetotaler—the sort who thinks that abstinence works for him, so it must surely work for everyone."

Francine bobbed her head like she knew something I didn't. "Abstinence of any sort is good for some and bad for others. Everything is relative, at a certain point."

I must've frowned at her, not because I was upset, but because I was confused. "I thought you . . ."

She answered before I could ask: "Yes, you heard right, I'm sure. I was a nun, and I believed in absolutes. But now I am not, and now I don't. I'm still a Catholic, but what can you do?"

"How does that work?" I wanted to know. I didn't know much about Catholics, but I knew they must be sticklers. Probably the worst sort, like Oscar Fine (if his son could be believed).

"It's very simple," she said. "I believe there is truth to be found in the church of my fathers. But I do not believe it holds *all* of the truth—much less the *only* truth."

Before she could say more, David hoisted his glass again. "I can drink to *that*. To all of the truth, whatever it looks like, and wherever it leads us. May we follow it wherever it leads, like the sunflower follows the light."

Yes, yes, and yes again.

I could drink to that, too.

# 12

## TOMÁS CORDERO

### Ybor City, Florida

SOMETHING CHANGED YESTERDAY, and I don't know if it's my fault or not—but it probably is.

I've pursued this phenomenon, and welcomed it, and invited it into my life. I've called, and called, and chased after Evelyn, and she has responded. She is listening. But I'm beginning to fear that something else is listening, too.

I can't control this. (I was never meant to control this.)

YESTERDAY I went to the post office to collect some stamps, and I stopped by the market for fruit and jam, since I promised Emilio that I would treat myself. (I treated myself as promised this time. Sometimes I don't. Sometimes I lie.) I also visited the library to return a book, and paused to buy a newspaper before catching the trolley back to my neighborhood and walking the rest of the way home.

I was not gone more than ninety minutes.

In ninety minutes, something terrible happened.

I came home to find fire trucks again, with their hoses unspooling and their rubber-jacketed men shouting. My heart stopped, jolted, leaped up into my throat, and sat there choking me.

At first I could not see, for the smoke and the trucks blocked my way. I pushed forward and was stopped by a heavyset colored man wearing suspenders. He was holding his mask with one hand and using it to direct traffic away from the scene. With the other hand, he used a handkerchief to wipe sweat and ashes from his face.

(His mask looked like the mask I used to wear.)

"Please," I begged him. "You must let me pass—that's my home!"

"I'm sorry, sir—we can't let anyone near the fire."

"No, please, you must . . ." I craned my neck to see past him, around the trucks, through the smoke. "You don't understand how I understand fire. You must let me . . ." I did not finish. The sea breeze took a breath and blew upon my block—scattering the billowing blackness. Hot cinders fluttered in the currents, singeing my hair and the exposed skin of my neck. They settled on my clothes and left small holes I would not find for hours.

The house that so brightly and wildly burned was not mine—it was the one next door.

"Mrs. Vasquez . . . ," I breathed.

The fireman heard me over the bustle of men waging war against the flames. "I beg your pardon?"

"It's not . . . that's not my house. I thought it was, but that's my neighbor, Carmella Vasquez. Where is she? Is she safe?"

"I'm sorry, sir." He might as well have been reading it from a script. It didn't tell me anything. The fire and the trucks and the rushing men in the rubber clothes and the flapping smack of hoses being rolled, unrolled, and deployed—the spraying water, the barking of a spotted dog—there was too much noise for me to read his tone and decide if it meant anything. There was too much distraction. It looked too much like a battlefield.

IT felt too much like war.

My head. It was filling with smoke. My headache. My shell shock. War strain. Who cared what it was called? My senses were overwhelmed. I thought I might faint, only I didn't feel like fainting. I felt like exploding.

I took a step back, away from the fireman and to his right. I wasn't trying to push past him; he was only doing his job, and he was correct to keep presumed civilians like myself away from the danger. I was only trying to see my house and assure myself that it still stood.

I craned my neck to see.

Yes, it was upright.

My walls that faced the Vasquez residence were black with soot, so black there was no chance of any pattern presenting itself later, I didn't think. (How awful of me, that this was the first thing I wondered. What a horror I am.) The firemen had run a hose between our houses, and alongside the other one that was nearest. They were holding the blaze in check, doing their best to keep the damage to the single home.

"Mrs. Vasquez?" I called at the top of my lungs. "Mrs. Vasquez!"

I scanned the growing crowd for her face. I looked at the fire trucks, hoping to see her huddled under a blanket, wet and red-eyed but alive and well. Frightened and stunned, but present. Madly, I looked for her. I looked for Felipe, and every time the spotted fire dog barked, I jumped.

But through the noise, through the smoke, through the awful warmth of the fire and the din of battlefield memories in my head . . . I saw no sign of either one of them.

I stood amid the havoc (of the scene and of my own mind) until the fireman came back with his cohorts—and together they ushered everyone back, away, to the far side of the walkway where the smoldering cinders did not rain down so often. The police arrived, and there was more yelling, more instructions being hollered over the crackle and sizzle of a house collapsing into coals.

I stood amid the havoc, neither soldier nor victim. I was part of a crowd. An audience and nothing more.

We huddled and clustered together in fear and concern, and I recognized only a few faces. Many were unfamiliar to me. They must have been rushing past, heading home or elsewhere, when they saw the fire and heard the commotion. *Human curiosity is disgusting,* I thought, even as I could not look away.

I told myself that mine was a *pure* curiosity—a keen self-interest, since my home was only feet away from the Vasquez bonfire. *My* curiosity was virtuous. These other people were gawkers; they were the scavengers who pick through corpses when the front goes quiet. They are the ones who take wallets and buttons and photos from the dead, and pocket them, and sell them in the quiet stores where no one is shooting and no one is dying.

I hated them. Irrationally but forcefully, I hated them all.

IT was midafternoon, but the sky was darkened with the black, greasy haze I knew all too well. I remembered the taste of it in the back of my mouth. I remembered the sting of it, when I blinked and blinked and blinked. I could feel my eyes going crimson as I stood there, unable to leave and unable to look at anything else.

The police pushed us all back a little farther. They made us clear the street so that another truck could come through, and another police car, too. A jaunty little ambulance arrived, and that might be a good sign? Only the living require such services, or so I lied to myself. Even as I remembered how they brought the dead off the fields and loaded them up in those jaunty little ambulances—how they stacked the corpses like cordwood—I lied to myself, because it was so much easier than accepting the truth.

I did not (for a single honest moment) think that Mrs. Vasquez was alive.

"It's the end of the world," I said under my breath, for no real reason except to keep on lying.

My house was being saved. The block would not go up in smoke—only the house of Mrs. Vasquez, whom I searched for still, even as I was confident of the futility. There was no trace of her in the crowd. No chance of her face hiding away in some kind soul's shoulder, where she cried as the sky burned down around her.

I don't know how I knew, but I knew: She was inside her house.

And when the roof fell in, casting up sparks and flames a dozen feet higher—and hotter, and flush with the fresh air—I knew that was the last of her. I could only cross myself, like many others were doing. I could only offer up a little prayer that Mrs. Vasquez and her dog were long gone to some cool, breezy afterlife by the time the timbers came down and the walls cracked open like an overboiled egg.

FINALLY the worst was over.

Finally the audience wandered away, back to their own un-scorched homes, where the air did not smell like an apocalypse. When I moved from my spot on the sidewalk, I left light-colored footprints behind in the shape of my shoes. I didn't realize I'd been standing so still for so long. I hadn't thought about my suit and how it was probably ruined.

Well, if I couldn't clean it, I could always burn it.

THEY let me go home, so I went home.

I stepped over one limp hose, all of its water spent. I splashed in the black, oily puddles that were left behind, all around, on the sidewalks and in the grass. I went to my front door and let myself inside. I closed the door. I leaned my back against it.

The air inside was much fresher than the stuff beyond. Thank God I'd closed up all the windows before leaving to run my errands. Thank God it hadn't been me, and my house, and what was left of my life lying ruined in the ashes.

(It probably should have been me.)

My skin felt clammy and cold, even though I was sweating. I looked down at my arms, and yes, my suit had gone from a light blue-gray to something the color of death. I rubbed a thumb across the fabric and managed only to smear the residue of Mrs. Vasquez into a grimy streak.

I turned my hands over and saw how pale my palms were, compared to the backs of my fingers. I wiggled my wedding ring and saw the lighter skin beneath it. It was a line left by this filthy burning air that had come to rest upon everything. Heaven knew how far the soot would travel and how many houses would wear the evidence of that old woman's cremation.

The thought sickened me, but it sickened me in a distant way. By then I was mostly numb. I felt dirty, and I felt tired. And somewhere far away, in the far regions of what decency remained, yes, I felt sickened.

Mrs. Vasquez at her Dutch door, the smell of her cooking wafting across the little alley between our houses. The sound of her singing to herself as she dressed for mass.

I stood there in the foyer and I peeled off my clothes. First the jacket, then the buttoned shirt. I left them in a pile. It's never a dignified pursuit, pulling off one's pants—but who was watching? No one. One leg at a time until I stepped free and they were a heap on the floor. I used my toes to fling them backward. They smacked against the door and collapsed into a pile there. I removed my underthings and treated them likewise, then strolled as naked as the day I was born into the washroom.

ALL the curtains were open. A few people were still milling about, gossiping about what must have happened and wondering how much of Mrs. Vasquez would ever be found. Would there be enough to bury?

I did not care if they could see me.

I did not care what they would say about me if they did.

I turned on the faucet knobs, left and right, one hot and one cold. I let them both run, and I took the biggest bar of soap I could find.

In the mirror, I looked exactly as disgusting and distracted as I felt. There was a seam around my collar like the one around my wedding ring. Not a winter tan, but a place where the ashes had not quite touched me. But they'd infiltrated the divot at my throat and spilled down onto my chest.

I added some soap flakes to the bathwater to give myself some bubbles—using the harshest laundering detergent I could find. I did not think that a bar of Palmolive alone would do the job, but maybe I did not give it credit. Maybe I only wanted the best possible chance of getting clean.

For half a minute, I wished for a big bar of the ferocious lye soap the army used. It was terrible, and it left my skin cracked and dry, but it washed away every smoky sin. So there was that to recommend it. If nothing else.

The water reached close to the curled rim of the tub, and I stepped inside.

I sank down to my chin, and then lower still—keeping my eyes tightly shut. I held my breath, reached for the bar of inferior (if gentler) civilian soap, and wrapped my fingers around it. I submerged myself, letting small bubbles escape from my nose. I bobbed to the surface again. I scrubbed the bar of soap into my hair and scraped my fingernails along its surface to collect it there and scrub even those tiny crevices.

The water cooled. I drained it and then ran a fresh bath to rinse myself off. I smelled like cream and perfume, and I was sticky with the leftover bubbles until I washed the last of it away. I held my head under the tap and gave my hair one more pass.

You see, the hair is always the worst. You can wash your hands all day; you can stand in the showers until the sun sets, but if you do not scrub all the ashes from your hair, you will smell them in your sleep.

Or *I* would.

I hated the memory of it. I baptized myself of it.

I ran those terrible thoughts, and the hideous undreamed dreams, right down the drain where they belonged—into the sewers, where it is dark and wet, and where nothing will burn no matter how many matches are struck. Either here or in hell.

I hauled myself out of the tub and grabbed a nearby towel from the rod. I dried my face first, and swabbed down the rest of myself—then collected a house robe and put it on. It was warm inside. I wanted to open the windows, but I knew better. By now, it would smell like death out there. It would smell like Mrs. Vasquez, her skin baked and peeling like pork, her hair dissolved in flames.

But outside, I heard a foot on my stoop. Then another. Someone was walking toward the door. Someone was knocking. I would have to let the bad air in after all, goddammit.

I slid my feet into a pair of slippers and went to answer, still holding the towel and rustling it through my hair as if I needed an alibi.

I looked through the window and saw two policemen. One was holding something; the other was looking at the door—up at me, through the glass. "Mr. Cordero?"

I turned the knob and opened the door. "Yes, I'm sorry. I hope you haven't been knocking long. I needed to . . . to clean up." I dropped the towel over my shoulder. "Can you tell me, is there any word of Mrs. Vasquez? Do you know what happened?"

He shook his head. "We can't check the house until everything has cooled. We hope that she was not inside, but there's no evidence to the contrary. Perhaps she has left town, to visit family? You are her nearest neighbor; do you know if there's any chance she was not home?"

The other officer said, "Or if she's traveling, do you know how we might reach her?"

"No, I'm afraid to say that I cannot help or offer encouraging news. She was here just this morning. I saw her . . . it was around noon. I had errands to run. I waved at her as I left. Everything was fine."

"So you were not present when the fire began?"

"Of course not." I sounded defensive. I could hear my own protests ringing in my ears. "I was at the post office, then the market, then the library. I stopped at a newsstand," I added, as it occurred to me. "When I returned, the firemen would not let me come close to my house. There was a big man, a colored fellow in red suspenders. He said I had to stay clear."

"Sir," the second officer said, holding up one hand—and holding his peculiar bundle with the other. "I'm sure it was a terrible accident. This is no interrogation."

I sighed, not as a matter of dramatic display, but from exhaustion. "I'm sorry, I don't mean to be so strange—it's just that I had a fire here, the other day. It was . . ." I chose my next word carefully. There was no need to lie, and perhaps a good reason to tell the whole truth up front. "Unexplained. There were questions—most of them mine, but the authorities had their queries, as well. I'm on edge because of it. It might have been my own house. It might have been me inside. I apologize. Mrs. Vasquez was my friend, and I am shaken."

"Naturally." The first officer nodded. Then he gestured at his companion. "And we are sorry to bother you at a time like this, but it is as you said: Mrs. Vasquez was your friend. There may be more questions later, in case you can help the firemen determine what happened, or when it happened—you might be able to narrow things down—but that's not why we're here right now."

The other copper held up the bundle. It was wrapped in a rough wool blanket, no doubt pulled from one of the fire trucks. It was about the size of a large bread loaf. "We found this under a police car. Someone said it belonged to her."

I took the smelly offering and lifted the blanket's hem. Felipe's big black eyes looked up to me. He trembled all over; I could feel it through the cloth. He was not his customary white with brown ears and a brown blotch on his behind. He was almost entirely gray and black.

"Yes," I said. "This is Felipe."

The officer shuffled his feet. "I don't know if you like dogs, sir, but somebody ought to take him."

I do not like dogs, as a general rule. My instinct was to foist this one back into the policeman's arms, but I could not do it. I had never before been so happy to see the little fellow. I had never before been happy to see him at *all*, but now I clutched him against my chest. "I'll look after him. I'll clean him up and get him fed."

"Will you keep him?" he pressed. He was a young man, and he had a kind, earnest face.

"I'll either keep him or find someone to keep him. Someone good," I specified. "I'll . . . I'll hold on to him for a few days, at least. Until you're sure about Mrs. Vasquez. Just in case . . . in case she returns. If she comes back," I said, like I thought there was half a chance in hell, "she will be glad to see he survived."

Satisfied by this, the men took their leave. I closed the door and unwrapped Felipe, who must've been hot under all those layers, but he quivered like he'd been hiding in an icebox.

"It's all right, little fellow," I lied to man's best friend. If you can lie to yourself, you can lie to anyone. "Come. I've had my bath, and you must have one, too."

EXCEPT for the unceasing trembles, he held perfectly still and let me clean him off, from the tip of his nose to the end of his tail—even his belly and ears. He stared straight ahead all the while, not looking at me. Not looking at anything. It was the stare of a soldier who has seen awful things, and done awful things. It looked like shell shock, or war strain, or one of those words. I wondered if he would have headaches and smell smoke for the rest of his short, uncertain canine life.

I dried him with the same towel I'd used on myself, and I made him a little bed from a mango box and a spare pillow.

"It's all right, Felipe." He looked at me that time. Not accusing me of anything, but asking me what I meant. "One way or another, it's all right. I won't let you go hungry, and I won't let anyone hurt you. That's all I can offer. Is it enough?"

He blinked slowly, stood up, and turned around a couple of times before settling into the bed like he owned it. He put down his head and closed his eyes.

"So we settle for one another. We may as well."

I wanted to copy him, to lie down someplace soft and sleep. I also wanted to ask him what he'd seen and go outside to listen to the last of the officers—fire and police—as they finished their reports and speculations and surveyed the blackened rubble of Mrs. Vasquez's home.

I had babbled to the men on my doorstep about the coincidence of it all, and I did not know if they thought it was likely that these two fires had happened so close, one and then the other, and were not connected at all.

I, for one, did not think it was likely. The longer I thought about it, standing there naked except for my slippers and robe, drying in the somewhat clean air of my parlor, the less I believed in coincidence and the more I worried about what had happened and what was to come. I worried so hard that I didn't think I could sleep if I were to try.

A drink, I thought. Just one. Some rum and orange juice, and a light meal. I should make something for Felipe, too. He would be hungry eventually. Even in grief, a dog must eat.

I went to the kitchen and stared at my pantry, then stared at my stove. I stared into the sink where I'd been test-burning all sorts of things, hoping for more words from my wife. Evidence of my experimentation remained. Anyone who looked could see in a moment that something had been burning in my kitchen, and it wasn't anyone's supper.

Surely, no one would come looking.

Surely, it was a waste of effort to collect it all and throw it into the bin, and then scour the sink and the countertops until mine gave every appearance of being an ordinary kitchen, belonging to an ordinary bachelor. But I did it anyway. The very first fires had started themselves, in my absence or while I was not looking.

How far away could they light themselves? In another room, I knew for a fact.

In another house? Was that possible?

I asked myself these things aloud, in a rumbling mutter as I wiped down everything one last time and tossed the rags into the laundry bin. I'd wash them all, first thing in the morning. I'd do them myself in the bathtub, rather than send out for the service. No one else needed to see them.

From behind me, a scraping noise approached.

It was Felipe, dragging the mango box and pillow. He pulled them up beside my feet, under the kitchen table. Satisfied with this proximity, he climbed back inside and went back to sleep.

I sat down on the floor beside him. I stroked his head while he snuffled and snored, all stuffy nosed from the smoke. I felt the soft suede of his ears, and the damp, smooth fur of his back, but I was careful to avoid the round bulges of his tightly shut eyes. With a pathetic catch in my throat, I wondered when I'd last touched another living soul—apart from a handshake, a patted back, or the professional ministrations of a tailor to a client. I resisted the urge to awaken the small dog and pull him into my lap.

I sat there beside him instead, petting him just to feel him breathe.

# 13

## ALICE DARTLE

Cassadaga, Florida

SOMETHING TERRIBLE HAS happened, and I don't know if it's my fault or not—but it probably is.

I've indulged this phenomenon, and worried about it, even as I invited it and encouraged it. I've opened myself up to danger, and danger has responded. It is listening. It is looking for every opportunity to present itself. I feel like a specimen under a microscope, wriggling upon a slide while some terrifying eye observes my every move and waits for the best, most terrible chance to toy with me.

Everything is a sign, if you're looking for a sign.

I can't control this. (I was never meant to control this.)

AFTER I discovered the speakeasy with the help of David Fine, Sister Francine and I went to catch the next showing of *The Mark of Zorro*. (The Cassadaga Calliope—like Candy's—is also on the other side of the tracks, it should be noted.) She said it'd be all right, and no one would miss us except for her prayer group, and they could do without her. Frankly I'd had enough Maker's that I was too fizzy to concentrate on anything much more serious.

I shouldn't have been drinking—certainly not in the middle of the day. I shouldn't have skipped the seminar with Gwen Millard, because she's a talented medium and I have much to learn from her. But the nun told me God would forgive us, and Spirit didn't care in the first place.

Good heavens, I wonder what that woman actually believes—when it comes to the structure of the Great Beyond.

At any rate, we paid for our tickets at the glass booth and went inside to a small, bright lobby with posters hung up for the movies to come. A red popcorn cart rattled in the corner, overflowing its pan with the fluffy snack—and filling the lobby with the most wonderful scent of warm butter and salt and things that are simply beyond delicious when one has gotten herself a tiny bit drunk and it's not even suppertime. The man who'd taken our tickets gave us each a small bag, which I mostly finished before the newsreel was over. I don't remember which seat we sat in, and I don't remember what row. I fell asleep about ten minutes into the story, and I don't remember any of that, either.

But I remember coming around to the smell of smoke, and to Francine shaking me. "Get up, get up! There's something wrong in the theater, and we have to go!"

I shot awake, is what I did. The lights came on a few seconds after my eyes opened, which did nothing to help with my grogginess—I was still baffled and blinky. I was disoriented and confused, but Francine was firm. She was an inch or two shorter than me and sixty pounds lighter, but she had me up out of that seat and under her arm before I could get my feet in line with each other.

The film reel was rattling, and the picture had gone off the rails; the great screen down front showed blurry frames that were melting as I watched. The light from the projector passed everything along:

the celluloid losing its shape, the lens warping, and the flames catching hold of everything.

"What's . . . what's happening?" I asked, continuing my long and ignoble tradition of stupid questions presented at the worst of all possible times.

Francine answered by pulling me forward, and both of us shuffled with our feet one in front of the other, single file, because we'd been sitting in the center of the auditorium. The rows of chairs were narrow, and not all of the seats retreated upward, folding mostly flat— like they were supposed to do.

My guide knocked them up with her knees if they fell before her. They knocked my knees on the way back down as I followed behind her. I pushed them aside with my thighs and wrangled past them, twisting myself into all sorts of undignified shapes until we made it to the aisle. It was wider there. We could hold hands and run.

Run to where? The only way out was the way we'd entered— through the lobby (as far as I knew).

After a moment of scrambling and coughing, we followed the other audience members to that doubled door on the squeaky hinges. A man reached it before we did and gave it a shove. It swung open, and smoke billowed outward.

Someone screamed. Everyone ducked as the thick gray cloud filled the theater, collecting on the ceiling and gathering itself up to fill more and more and more of the space. It was collapsing toward us, sending all the breathable air somewhere else—devouring it, maybe, I don't know how these things work—and so we fell to our hands and knees.

Francine was praying in a language that didn't sound like Latin, but what would I know about that, either?

"This way!" I heard someone say, but I didn't see what way he meant.

Above us, the projection booth exploded—sending a rain of broken glass and molten celluloid down on our heads. I screamed, jerking away from my companion and covering my head with my hands. Something landed on my arm, dripping there onto my skin. It burned like lava must burn, if anyone ever lives to tell of it.

I screamed again, and this time it soared into a high-pitched howl when I looked at my fresh, bubbling injury. Something thick and goopy had seared itself into my skin, and there it smoldered. I was so shocked I couldn't do anything but stare at it, smelling my skin cooking like a Sunday roast.

Francine slapped me, hard, right across the face. "Come on, girl! Move, or stay here and die!"

I nodded hard and wiped at the simmering goo—burning my hand while I was at it. It must have been celluloid from the melted reels above. It hardened as it cooled, but it hurt like hell and I scraped into it with my fingers, digging it away. I couldn't stand the thought of leaving it there.

The sticky muck tugged on the fine hairs on my arm and I squealed some more, but I got it out—most of it—even as I struggled to crouch, hunker, and keep up with Francine. It stuck to my fingerprints and wedged under my nails. It was warm, but it couldn't hurt me now. It'd done all the damage it could.

Now it was the smoke's turn.

The hunch of Francine's folded back lumbered before me, stumbling onward, ducking lower as the poisonous black air sank lower. It was dark, and she was wearing a navy dress. She was hardly more than a rounded shape before me, and I thought I was going to lose her—but she grasped my hand again and pulled me forward.

A sliver of light opened up. I could see it, but I couldn't tell where it was. Were we still in the auditorium? Had we passed the doors and gone into the lobby? Were we somewhere else?

Glass was breaking everywhere, from the heat or from falling objects that had been shattered and consumed, clattering down from the ceiling. A narrow piece of wood toppled to the ground before me, along with the curling poster for next week's matinee. I kicked it aside and stumbled over myself, but Francine wouldn't let me stay down.

"Almost there, almost out," she wheezed.

How could she stand to speak? My throat was full of fire, coated in smoke, and even my screams were so hoarse that now they sounded like groans. How could she see where she was going? There was a sliver of light, yes, but between us and that sliver there were tumbling arms and legs of people crawling over one another to escape, and there was the ever-sinking ceiling of roiling smoke. My eyes were burning so hard I could scarcely keep them open. I gave up on keeping them open. I squinched them shut and trusted the nun and her prayers. I had to. The world was burning down and I couldn't move without her.

I trudged forward and then tripped forward—and felt fresh air on my face like the blast from a powerful fan. It wasn't particularly cool air, and it still smelled like the Second Coming, but it was enough to make me open my eyes and gasp. I sucked it in; I'd been drowning and hadn't known it.

Someone new took me by the arm. I let go of Francine. I didn't see where she went.

I gulped air like a guppy thrown free from its bowl. I panted like a dog on a summer day. I drank down the fresh atmosphere as I let this new person lead me away from the inferno that used to be called a calliope.

A towel was thrust into my hands. It was damp, and that was useful. I used it to wipe down my face and rub my eyes clean, and then I sat down on a bench on the far side of the tracks, beside the gate pillars and adjacent to the hotel. From there, I watched the grand little building come down.

The roof went first. It belly flopped into the middle, sending up a tower of smoke, cinders, and sparks. The walls went down one by one after that, and when there was only a single wall standing— teetering, wobbling on borrowed time—a fire truck finally showed up from Lake Helen. It arrived just in time to watch the whole thing come down in one final burp of coals and smoke.

In all seriousness, the firemen could not be blamed. They were miles away, on the other side of sandy roads that might or might not have been paved. They got there as quickly as they could. One of them, a strapping fellow with a mask of soot around his eyes, offered me some water. I took it and tried to thank him, but no words came out at all. He walked away, back to the truck. The hoses were un- spooled and the pump was cranking right along, and soon the ashes were soaked—and steam rose from the ruins in wispy, warm waves.

Mabel was standing beside me, watching the steam rise across the street. "I'm glad you're all right," she said, not taking her eyes off the trucks and the water and the men with their hoses and boots and suspenders. "But what were you doing in there?"

My voice was sandpaper and soot. "Watching *The Mark of Zorro.*"

"Wasn't there a—"

"Yes," I cut her off. "There was a seminar I should've been attend- ing instead. I needed to . . . I wanted to . . . I was tired of studying. Just for a little while, I wanted to do something else."

"So you went to Candy's and went to a movie."

"I wanted a sandwich."

"I just bet you did."

I couldn't tell if she was teasing me about being fat or signaling that she knew I'd had a drink. I was too tired and frightened and short of breath to care. "Where's Francine?"

"I don't know. I saw her, though. She got out just fine. Then she left."

"She led me out. I would've died in there." Something awful dawned on me. "Did anyone *not* get out? Was anyone left inside?"

She shook her head and said, "We don't know for sure. Mr. Alders couldn't recall how many tickets were sold. He took in an awful lot of smoke."

"Will he be—"

"One of the firemen is taking him to the hospital in DeLand."

"Are there any ambulances?"

"None that would get him there any faster than Stuart Kipper."

"That's the fireman?" I asked.

"He lives a few blocks away. He knows Mr. Alders." She offered to take my towel, so I handed it over—wet and filthy. She folded it up and held it anyway. Then she changed her mind, sat down by me on the bench, and put the towel beside her legs.

"Mabel, I—"

"I know. Or . . . to put it another way, I don't care. You didn't do anything wrong. You passed on one opportunity in favor of another, and it could have cost you dearly—but it didn't. I'm not going to feed you some morality fable. It could've just as easily been the Brigham house that went up in flames, with you in it. People die by meaningless happenstance every day, whether they're having a drink or sitting in church."

"Thank you. I think. I still feel like I've been caught at something, and I've been righteously punished for it."

"Nonsense. That isn't how the world works."

"You're not mad at me?"

She turned to look at me with astonishment written all over her face. "Alice, people may have died today. A building burned. A business was lost. People were hurt and badly sickened." She waved toward the hotel porch, where several folks were being addressed by Sidney Holligoss, who was a doctor, that's right. (I only remembered it when I saw him with his bag and stethoscope. I also saw Francine, sitting beside a woman lying on a cot, holding her hand and speaking gently.)

I swallowed. It didn't do anything at all. "But it could've been much worse."

"That's a miserable and lazy way to look at it," she admonished, but her heart wasn't really in it. "Things can always be worse; that's a universal truth. All I'm trying to say is that in the scheme of things, your sip of . . . whatever you sipped . . . and your decision to miss the rest of the afternoon's meetings . . . were choices you made of your own free will, and I'm in no position to judge you for them. Like all decisions, yours had repercussions. Like some decisions, those repercussions were unforeseen and cataclysmic when they should've been negligible. Your entire consequence of the afternoon should've been a two-hour headache and a missed opportunity for knowledge. Now you've got a cough, red eyes, and a badly burned arm."

"My arm?" Oh God, in all the excitement, I'd almost forgotten it. How on earth do you forget something like that? The moment she mentioned it, I felt the wound so keenly that I wanted to explode into sniffles and tears, but I only sucked in my breath and squeezed my hand over it, instead.

"No, don't do that."

"But it hurts."

"I know it does. But that won't help—you'll only get it dirty. Come on, let's go to see Dr. Holligoss. Your throat will clear and your eyes will sting until they stop, and that's all . . . but this burn needs attention."

So I joined the handful of ragged, smoke-stained men and women from the theater, most of whom had been brought to the hotel porch. I recognized some of them from the audience or from the ticket line. By and large, they looked like they'd be all right; they were sooty and coughing, and some were lying reclined on the lounge furniture, catching their breath and moaning softly. But they were alive, and they were breathing, and no one looked too much worse for wear.

"Doctor?" Mabel called.

Francine looked up and gave me a nod that said she saw me and she knew I was more or less fine. Dr. Holligoss himself seemed not to have heard.

"Doctor, please . . . ," she tried again to get his attention.

This time he paused and came to join us. "Mabel, Miss Dartle. Oh good heavens—what have you done to your arm?"

Before I could answer, Mabel scanned the scene and asked, "Is anyone else in need of more . . . critical attention?"

"Only Alders, and he's on his way to the hospital. He kept going back inside, trying to pull people out. If he hadn't opened that second door, more might have been trapped."

"But everyone *did* escape?"

"It appears so. God, I hope so," he added under his breath. "Is anybody missing? Has anyone said, one way or another?"

"Not to my knowledge, but . . ." Mabel's voice trailed off as she stared back across the street and the train tracks to the crackling rubble of the Calliope. People still stood around fretting, like that did any good—and asking questions, which didn't help, either. Only the efficient, burly firemen were really doing anything useful over there. They kept people away, soaked down the cinders, and poked around at the ashes.

One of the trucks started up, kicked into gear, and turned down Stevens Street.

"Where's it going?" I asked.

"Spirit Lake," said the doctor. He ushered me to a seat and took my arm in his hands. "The trucks are empty. They may as well refill them here."

IT was my private and carefully not-spoken-aloud opinion that Spirit Lake would be half drained by such an operation, but no one else seemed worried about it, and someone had told me it was filled by a spring . . . so perhaps it would naturally regain anything that was taken from it. Or perhaps it would dry up, and so would Colby Lake or Lake Colby or whatever the other one was, connected by that little channel. Those two big puddles, full of grass. How many tanks would it take to empty them forever?

I held very still and watched the truck recede; I couldn't see the lake from where I was sitting, and I wasn't meaning to watch it fill up again—but it was a cheap enough trick to keep myself from looking at my arm, which smarted something awful. When I did give in to temptation and sneak a peek, I saw the skin curled up pink around the edges of the burned-away flesh. The wound followed the track of the dripping celluloid, running from the back of my wrist almost to my elbow in a long, curly drizzle. Where it had landed, my skin was gone—simply removed, because I had smeared the molten celluloid off and away. Had it been the right thing to do or not? I do not know. But at the time, it was the *only* thing to do.

"This is a very bad burn, Miss Dartle."

"I know," I whispered, looking away again. The truck was out of sight, but I could still watch the bookstore, the rest of the hotel porch, and one wing of Harmony Hall from where I was sitting. There were a million things to look at that weren't the pale white underlayer of skin with tiny red lines, as if someone had taken a heated scalpel and scrawled a signature. I felt like I'd been branded, claimed by someone having stamped their initials upon me.

Maybe that was a silly thing to think, but the long, dragged-out injury did have a style to it. Rationally I knew that the style could be summed up as "random splashes of melted goop," but it almost . . . at a squint . . .

Well, it really did look like a scrawled capital "H" followed by a drawn-out "K."

I don't know why that thought flung itself forward. It wasn't a useful thought. It wasn't a sane or reasonable thought, so I kept it to myself. I might as well have nattered on about somebody else's dream. It would've been equally stupid and meaningless.

I hadn't yet told anyone about the man who dreamed of fire. I felt almost protective of him, whoever he was. I could see him, in his mask, in my vision. He knew my name.

His mask. My vision.

While Dr. Holligoss tended to my arm, I watched the firemen finishing their job. Their masks hanging on their belts. Their glossy eyes. Their rounded filters, hanging off their faces. Their hoses. Their masks were . . . not quite the same as the one my dream man wore. But they were very, very close. Very much the same idea.

Was the man in my vision a fireman? Did they have firemen on the battlefield?

Only if the definition of "fireman" is "the man who brings the fire."

THE doctor washed my arm and applied a weird ointment that smelled of camphor and lard, and it took the edge off the warm, itchy sting. Oh God, it itched. "You'll have to clean it," he warned. "It will weep, and tighten, and itch—yes, *stop that*. Stop picking at it. I'm going to give you some bandages and wraps. Keep it clean, and keep it covered. I won't lie to you; burns are difficult to heal. It will take time. It will be very uncomfortable."

"I understand," I said, fingers twitching, trying to obey. Even through the bandage I could feel it oozing, writhing around in the ointment. It hurt, and it was disgusting, and I wanted to cut my whole arm off to get away from it.

"This is the unguent I want you to use." He passed me a small jar with a worn label. "It's from my own assortment and it's half used up, so I apologize. Today has been . . ." He looked around at his charges.

"Well, it's been a bad day for burns. I'll pick up more this afternoon, when I go to town."

I went inside, wondering whether this was what the veterans' shell shock felt like: numb confusion, with its undercurrent of pain. I walked through the lobby like a ghost, silent and aimless, until Mr. Rowe called my name.

I stopped to answer him out of pure reflex. "Yes?"

"This came for you with the morning's post." He held out an envelope.

"It must be my father," I said, joining him at the concierge desk. "I haven't heard from him but once since I arrived."

He shook his head. "Postmark says it's from here in Florida."

I frowned down at the mark. "Why-bore? Is that how you say it?"

"EE-bore," he corrected me. "It's a Spanish name. Near Tampa and Saint Petersburg."

"I don't know anyone in Florida . . . not anybody who isn't right here." I took the envelope and saw that it'd been addressed by a "T. Cordero." I thought about opening it on the spot but decided to take it upstairs instead. "Thank you, Mr. Rowe. If anyone needs me for anything, I'll be in my room. I need a bath, and I need to get some rest."

"I hope you weren't too badly hurt, ma'am."

"No, sir. Just a little burn on my arm. Thank you again."

For a moment upon opening my door, I had the sickening feeling that something was aflame inside—I could smell it! I was convinced of it!—but for all my sniffing and searching, I turned up nothing except the ashes in the garbage. They didn't smell like anything anymore, except for gray dampness.

Eventually I figured out that the smell of smoke was coming from my clothes, so I took them off and stood in my underthings and bandages. I threw everything into the laundry bag and tied it off, but I still smelled the smoke, following me around like a cloud.

Even though I needed that bath, I threw myself down on the bed first. My hair fanned out on the pillow, and that's when I understood: The smoke was in my hair. I wouldn't be free of the odor until I'd washed everything, even my tresses.

I hate washing my tresses. I even hate the word "tresses." But that's what my mother always called them when they needed washing, so there you go. I was too tired—and marginally more curious about the letter—to begin with the bath. So I sighed and slipped my finger into the seam of the envelope to open it. I pulled out the letter, un-folded it, and began to read.

# 14

## TOMÁS CORDERO

### Ybor City, Florida

I AM ON a train, somewhere to the east of Ybor City. I have packed up everything I could save, everything I could carry. I do not think I will be back. I do not think I am long for this world, and worse than that—I am a danger to everyone I know and love. (I am a danger to all of those who are left, though they number but few.)

I have put Felipe on a little leash, and he sits on the seat beside me. We do not need the leash, for he will not leave his place; but it makes the conductor and porter more comfortable to see him like this—tethered to my hand. As if he is some kind of wolf, and not a shaking, sneezing beast who's barely the size of a house cat.

The two of us are headed for Cassadaga. I don't know where else to go. I don't know where else to look for help.

I think I am doing the right thing. I hope I am not merely spreading this . . . this horror . . . or whatever is attached to me besides this small dog. I hope I'm not carrying it around, sharing it with everyone I meet.

* * *

I'VE decided this much: If the spiritualists think I am a danger to them, and if they cannot help me, I will leave. I will find some kind soul to keep Felipe, and I will end this myself. My service revolver is packed in the bottom of my bag. I have more than enough bullets to bring a man down. I don't know why I brought the whole box. I only need one.

HERE is what happened. This is how it's come to this.

THEY found Carmella Vasquez in the remains of her bedroom yesterday morning. In the remains of her bed, to be more precise. They think she fell asleep while smoking a cigarette, because they know nothing about her. Mrs. Vasquez did not smoke. She did not drink. She did not do anything to worry Padre Valero except indulge in too much gossip, and I don't believe for a moment that she thought it was a vice worth mentioning in confession.

The chief said that the fire began there, in the bed with her . . . or possibly under it. "She dropped the cigarette," he surmised. "It rolled beneath her."

I shrugged, like this was a plausible solution to the mystery.

"By any chance, do you have the dog?"

"Yes, he's here, with me." I pointed toward the mango box. Felipe was there, hidden beneath a towel. Only his nose peered out. "Why? Did someone request him? Mrs. Vasquez was a widow, and she had no living children. But if someone wishes to claim him . . ."

"No, no. One of the men asked after him. He said a neighbor took him in, and told me to ask."

"The dog is safe and well. He coughs a little, but that should clear up."

"Yes, yes. It should."

*   *   *

THE chief had not come to my door unannounced. I'd encountered him in front of the Vasquez ruins, writing notes on a clipboard. We'd stopped to chat, and he'd asked to come inside to ask me some questions. I'd had no reason to turn him away.

He left, as satisfied by my answers as either of us could hope. There was nothing of substance that I could tell him, and nothing of substance that he could tell me. We were useless, the pair of us.

I told Felipe, "You're useless, too." Like he'd heard the mutterings that went on in my head, or gave a damn about them.

He coughed softly and settled down beneath the towel.

"I don't mean it personally. It's no rebuke or accusation. If anything . . ." I went to the box and crouched beside it. I patted his hidden head, a lump the size of a peach. "It makes us two of a kind. Besides, I expect that you could do a much better job of"—I stood up straight and thought about it—"catching rats. Small dogs do that, don't they? That's what they're for, isn't it?"

He didn't answer.

"And your nose is much, much better than mine. Your eyes are, too, for all I know." Then, very suddenly, I wondered what he'd seen—and I felt sorry for him. "Well, you aren't useless. Not at all. I'm sorry. I shouldn't have said it. You are a very helpful and pleasant companion."

He didn't agree or disagree, one way or another.

He did not ask me to feel sorry for him, either.

YESTERDAY, I took him to work. I'd become nervous about leaving him alone; what if my house burned down, too? The poor creature. He'd survived one cataclysm, and I could not in good conscience subject him to another. At least, not alone. If the little beast must face down another inferno, he should do so with me beside him.

So I took him to Cordero's, despite the fact that I'd long sworn to Mrs. Vasquez that I would absolutely not entertain any dog in my shop, and despite the *other* fact that I'd resolved to take time to myself—and I'd been planning to take even more. A week, that's what I'd decided. A week would give me time to visit Cassadaga and return.

This was my excuse to check on the store: I would tell Emilio or Silvio about the week I needed and make certain that all would be well in my absence.

The truth was that I needed to leave the house. I'd burned everything worth burning on purpose, and in doing so I'd turned up two more decent images of Evelyn and what looked like the mark of her lips. She'd sent me one such mark with every letter she ever mailed to the front—every envelope was marked on the back with her favorite red lipstick, pressed in a kiss.

Also, I burned Evelyn's wedding veil. That's how I got the lip print in soot. It was the most precious of the things I'd burned, and the most intensely difficult to set alight. But by that point, to be honest with myself and Felipe, I would've burned her dress, too, if I'd had it.

I am told she was buried in it.

If that is true, then someone must have dressed her after she died. She wouldn't have been wearing it around the house, waiting to pass and feeling pretty. Had it been her sister? She'd come into town, I think. Or was it Mrs. Vasquez? I'd never thought to ask her, and now the time had passed. She had certainly never mentioned it.

What if no one had dressed her? What if she was thrown in the group grave wearing nothing but the clothes she'd died in?

If that was the case, what happened to the dress? I cannot stand to think that someone stole it, though I do suspect that things were stolen from the house before I returned from the war. (It was vacant for several months after she died.) Little things were missing, here and there. The glass goblets we'd used to toast our nuptials. A small mantel clock that had belonged to my father. A watch chain made of gold, which I'd left behind in the nightstand drawer.

Who would've taken them? What kind of terrible person steals from the dead and from the deployed?

WELL, the world is a terrible place—and maybe the afterworld is, too. Because I am on a train, keeping to myself, petting my small dog. (He is *my* small dog now. He is mine, and no one else's.) I am headed to either my salvation or my doom, and I don't know which.

I'm not certain that I care. I am so tired.

So very tired.

BUT. Earlier. Before the train.

I arrived at Cordero's with Felipe under my arm. I was worried about his coughing, and I didn't want to overexert him. He is a small thing, and he'd been through quite a lot. I know all too well how it feels to breathe smoke and fire, when the mask is out of reach or grasped too slowly. I wanted to give his lungs a chance to recover. One of us deserved to recover.

Emilio positively squealed when he saw the dog.

He darted forward to pet him. He collected him from under my arm and held him up—then clasped him close and cooed, "Oh, he's a handsome thing. What's his name?"

"Felipe."

"What a handsome little fellow you are, Felipe . . ." He rubbed his face on the dog's nose.

Felipe offered a short tail wag in response.

Then Emilio tucked the dog under his own arm, cradling his belly with one hand and stroking Felipe's head with the other. "He's very handsome . . . but I heard about your fire next door yesterday, and I was going to come by after the shop is closed. Are you all right?"

"I'm fine." I waved away his concerns. "The firemen kept the flames from spreading. The neighborhood smells like ashes and damp, and one wall of my house is filthy with soot. And now I have this dog because there's no one else to keep him. I believe that means you're all caught up."

He scrunched his forehead at me. He bounced Felipe forward. "What does *he* have to do with this?"

"He belonged to the woman whose house burned. She died in the fire."

"She *died*?" He sounded scandalized.

"They found her an hour or two ago. She was . . . she was smoking in bed and fell asleep. *Whoosh*," I added, miming an explosion.

"That's terrible!" He turned Felipe about and held him up so that they were nose to nose. "I'm so sorry, little fellow!" Then he asked me, "Is the dog hurt?" Before I had time to answer, he was spinning the Chihuahua gently around, checking him from ears to tail.

"He's unharmed except for the cough."

"He has a cough?"

"It'll go away." Probably. "He's mine now. He has no one else."

"Oh . . ." He was cooing again, snuggling Felipe with enough vigorous affection that the dog began to look uncomfortable. I suppose he was accustomed to his momma's more straightforward form of spoiling, with roasted chicken bits and cheese. I was afraid he might bite. (I had no idea if he'd ever bitten anyone. Even if not, there's a first time for everything.)

"Here, let me . . ." I held out my hands, and Emilio reluctantly gave Felipe back.

"He's lucky to have you."

"So I'm told."

"You're lucky to have *him*, too."

"So Mrs. Vasquez would have said. She'd been bothering me to take a pet for quite some time."

He nodded as if this were the deepest possible wisdom. "It is a pity for him, but a good thing for you. You've lived alone too long."

"Yes, you sound just like her."

"She must have been a wise woman. The world is a lesser place in her absence."

Then we chatted about the shop, and which articles of clothing needed to be cut and sewn, and who was expecting which suit and when. It wasn't more than a minute or two; business is slow but sufficient, and the brothers are on top of things. It couldn't have been more than ninety seconds, now that I recall it more concretely. It was less time than that, maybe.

Felipe began to wiggle in my grip. I shifted my hold on him, thinking he might be uncomfortable. He whined. He wrestled. He wanted to be set down on the floor, but I did not have his leash, and I didn't want him roaming unattended. I squeezed him tighter. Not so tightly that I'd hurt him.

"What's the matter?" asked Emilio.

"I don't know." But as soon as the words were out of my mouth, I knew—as quickly as that—what the matter surely was. I smelled it: the insidious creep of warm smoke. "Tell me: Is the iron on?"

"It shouldn't be. What is it? Why would you ask?"

"I can smell smoke. From somewhere. Don't you smell it, too?"

He frowned hard, concentrating, trying to confirm or deny my suspicions. "I smell . . . something?" He might have only been humoring me.

"I'm not a madman, I swear. It's definitely smoke . . . definitely something is burning. But where is it coming from?"

FELIPE whined, and a wave of pain washed over me. My head ached with an immediate, impersonal throbbing that made me want to close my eyes and lie down. But I *did* smell smoke. I must have staggered, because Emilio's hand was on my arm.

* * *

"Tomás, here. Sit for a moment, and I'll go find the problem. I'll get you a glass of water."

"I don't want any water."

"Stay here," he admonished anyway. "I'll go look."

"You don't believe me."

Felipe believed me. He writhed and fussed, demanding to be set loose. I would not let him. He was my only witness, and I would not let *him* leave me, too. I watched Emilio go, back into the workspace. The door swung shut behind him.

The room was growing dark. Emilio should have felt it.

Why did he leave me?

I rubbed at my eyes with one hand while struggling to contain Felipe with the other. I was very confused and I was becoming afraid. Was I having some kind of fit or delusion? Was I imagining things? Was this the sort of shell shock people talked about when they talked about the shattered men who sleep on street corners, wrapped in their own filth?

I am not like them. I am wrapped in fine tailoring, performed by my own hand. I do not drink myself to sleep on the sidewalk. The headaches come only sometimes. The smell of smoke is usually real, and not something I've conjured up in my mind.

I do not always dream of fire.

Emilio was gone and Felipe finally stopped squirming. He was either resigned to his fate or exhausted by his protests. We sat together in a chair where I give consultations and offer fabric swatches. The chair was plush but firm, with a high back.

No, the chair was hard and made of coarse-hewn wood. It had no back. It was a bench, and I was sitting upon it. I was holding Felipe, except that I was not. He was gone, and I did not know where or when or how he'd vanished. My hands were manacled in iron. The room was dark. What light came through the windows high overhead was orange, like the sky was on fire outside.

(The sky might have truly been on fire. I have seen the sky on fire. I know what color it turns.)

"Felipe," I said in a whisper so hoarse that I must have been breathing the smoke for days. I thought I could hear him whining, somewhere in the distance. He was calling me to come back, but I didn't know where I was—much less how I ought to return. "Emilio." No real answer from him, either. "Evelyn?" I tried, because there was no one else left.

"Tomás."

My name was a lightning bolt. I sat up straight; I was stunned, and I was alive. I knew that voice. I loved it. I mourned it. "Evelyn?"

There was a shape before me in the dark, shrouded with a veil (but I burned her veil). No, this was a black veil, made of thick lace. The figure approached slowly, moving like a woman moves, shaped like a woman is shaped. It wore black, and in the darkened room I saw only the edges where the light burning through the windows caught the outline and showed me a hint of a long black dress, and hands that were shrouded in gloves.

The specter shimmered and shook, and changed. In an instant, it was something else—something much larger and thicker, a looming presence with no touch of the feminine to soften it. This was a solid block of night, or something darker, something hotter. It stood above me, and its eyes flickered wetly.

"Who are you?" I did not ask it if it was Evelyn. I knew it was not. "What are you?" Maybe that was a better question.

It didn't answer that one, either.

I opened my eyes.

I'd kept them closed all this time, squinting against the headache. I do not know how I'd seen the woman, the shadow, the manacles.

(But I saw them; that's all I can say.) I lifted my lids, and I heard Felipe keening beneath my arm; I turned my head and I saw my shop as normal as it's ever been. I saw the rows of suits on hangers. I saw the counter where Silvio keeps the books if I'm busy in the back. Over there was the pedestal where I made men stand so I could pin the hems of their pants. There upon the desk, the iron and glass lamp that flipped on and off with a tug of its chain. Beside the door to the workspace, a headless mannequin torso, ready to model whichever items I required.

The door to the workspace.

The knob rattled. It turned. Emilio stepped forth, a worried look upon his face.

Behind him, the sun exploded, and the rest was light and fire and the sound of war.

I was on the floor, my head dashed against God knows what.

My ears rang. My eyes swam. My dog was barking ferociously, just loudly enough to cut through the ringing. He was pulling at my hand—his small mouth biting and tugging, his panic tempered with a fearsome and admirable determination.

I rose to one elbow. I touched my temple and felt the blood there. I saw fire on the ceiling, and I thought my clothes might burst into flames if I did not leave. I crawled, following the demands of the dog. I looked back and saw something slumped in pieces. It was not alive. It might have been Emilio. It must have been Emilio, for all I wanted it to be the mannequin. But I'd seen dead men before, men blown apart and burned, and I know what they look like, and I knew better than to crawl backward to save a single piece of him. He would never know the difference.

I followed the dog on my hands and knees, through broken glass and through smoke that came so low, so thick, that I could no longer see the blaze above me.

I let the dog lead.

One of us was in his right mind. One of us was low enough to the ground to see the way out. One of us was fighting to live.

OUTSIDE I could see the whole block was ablaze. Outside, I could breathe.

Outside, Felipe begged me to stand. Ordered me to pick him up. Commanded me to run.

I could not run, but I could shamble. I pushed past the anxious, screaming people who pointed at the stucco as it cracked, split, and splintered. I waved away anyone who wished to lend me aid. The police had not come yet. The firemen were on their way. My business was gone, and I was gone. Emilio was gone. Or the mannequin was gone. Both of them, then. Everything. All of it except for this dog, who needed someone to survive—because he could not carry on alone.

I made it home but I do not remember how.

I must have put my head down and walked like a strong, purposeful man who has business elsewhere, never mind the burned clothes and the charred hair or the bleeding head. I must have walked like the soldier I used to be, even though my head hurt so badly that the whole world moved back and forth with every step, and more than once I nearly dropped Felipe, who whispered with his tiny grunts and whines that I *must* make it home . . . I *must* pack . . . I *must* leave, before I ran out of time and lacked the strength to do so.

I must go home before home burned, too, and they put me in a sanitarium . . . and the fires would burn there, too.

There was no one on earth except for me and this dog, who watched from the mango box while I threw some clothes into a small trunk. He watched me clean myself up, and strip myself down, and tend to the cut on my head, which could have been so much worse. (It was hidden in my hair, above my right ear. Once the bleeding stopped, no one would see it at all. We would all be free to forget about it.)

I must have readied myself quickly, for I escaped the house before anyone came to question me—or even inform me of the disaster. I must have done a very good job of cleaning up; I recall that I washed my hair in the sink and combed it back.

I recall bits and pieces of everything. I recall great swaths of nothing.

Mostly, I recall Felipe watching me warily, his bulbous black eyes taking in every move, weighing every action. Not judging me, I don't think. Assessing me. Encouraging me, perhaps. Maybe he was only calculating my odds of success and survival and continued freedom. Dog is man's best friend, they say, but I barely know this one. He might have been thinking only of whom he might rely upon next. He might have been hoping that his next owner was a wealthier man.

"You can rely upon me," I swore as I attached the leash to his collar. "At least as far as Cassadaga. If I am no use to you there, I think a woman named Alice Dartle might take you in. She is a kindly sort." I had no good reason to assume it, but I said it anyway. "Or if you will give her the sniffles and make her sneeze, I will find someone else. I swear, I will not leave you alone in this world."

He stopped wriggling at the end of the leash. I took that as a sign of acquiescence.

So now we are on a train together, and I am carrying a few possessions and all the money I could pull together in such a last-minute fashion. I stopped by the bank on the way to the train station and cleaned out the business account and my personal account and even the little nest egg that Evelyn and I had been saving (except for the money I'd left for Silvio). We had been saving it in case of children, when I was to return from the war. The money would never serve its original purpose. There was no harm in taking it.

* * *

(WHY, then, did I feel like a criminal when I withdrew it? Why?)

I would say that I am carrying a small fortune, but that would overstate the case. It is a respectable sum that I could live on for months, or even a year or more—if I'm very frugal. Frugality doesn't come naturally to me, but neither does excess. In the balance, let's say this is enough to keep me for nine months. It will keep me as long as the child that Evelyn never carried.

So now.

Yes, now.

I am trying to behave like a normal man, bored upon a train. Felipe is asleep, cuddled against my thigh. I saw a smudge of soot on his head, so I licked my thumb and tried to wipe it off. He needs another bath, the poor thing. I need another bath, too. I will try to arrange one for both of us upon our arrival.

We should reach Cassadaga in another hour.

This means one more hour of neither bursting into wracking sobs nor fainting from the headache or heartache. I wish I felt numb, but I do not feel numb. Shell shock supposedly presents itself as numbness in some men, but mine is not so kind. (If that's what this is. Can things apart from war produce the same symptoms? I don't see why not.)

My mind is racing much faster than this pencil can, and my heart feels as if it's been trampled upon and then lit on fire. Emilio is gone. I know he's gone. I know I could not have saved him. (I could scarcely save myself. No, Felipe saved me. I owe my life to a dog who can fit in a mango box with room to spare for a pillow.)

I should have made the effort. Regardless of my promise to keep and save the dog, I should've remained behind with my friend, my employee, my steadfast partner in business. He deserved better than me. He always has.

Oh God, someone will have to tell Silvio. It ought to be me, but it won't be. Not now that I'm on this train, rather than sitting at home with my face in my hand, sobbing my eyes out. The train is the more dignified option, but I can scarcely hold myself together. It may not be a dignified option for much longer. I am almost out of dignity.

I envy the men on the sidewalks with their dirty blankets and empty bottles.

But Felipe helps. When I can't stand to sit still another minute, I run my fingers along his head and neck and down his back. I talk quietly to him, like *he's* the one who needs a gentle word. He sometimes looks up at me, his face full of questions.

Sometimes, he keeps his head down and sighs.

## ALICE DARTLE

Cassadaga, Florida

I WOKE UP groggy and aching. My throat hurt and my arm hurt . . . though between the two, the arm was definitely worse. Dr. Holligoss said the injury would weep, and he was not just pulling my leg: It had oozed all night, straight through the bandage and onto the sheets.

I sat up and pulled the bedding with me. I was glued to it with my own disgusting dried juices.

The pain was just *incredible*. With every turn or pull of my skin, or the bandage, or the sheet, fire ran shooting up my arm. I could not imagine simply ripping the sheet free, much less pulling off the crunchy bandage—because both were so firmly affixed by a most tender and miserable bit of my body. With this in mind, I dragged the sheet with me to the bathroom, and I held it up so as not to pull the burned skin while I turned on the taps to run a bath. I disrobed as far as I was able, but there was only so much I could do with one arm out of commission and a bedsheet attached, so when the water was high and warm (but not too warm), I climbed inside wearing my nightshirt and feeling very silly about it.

But mostly, I felt sorry for myself.

I couldn't let my arm weep alone, so I cried piteously as I dunked it slowly into the warm water, bandage and sheet and all. I thought if I soaked it all down it might peel off more easily, and I was right—for a relative value of "right" and "easy." "Easy" only meant "it was possible to remove the sheet after a few minutes of sitting half naked, stewing in water that became more vile by the moment, as the yellow stain faded and the bandage loosened."

I peeled it inch by inch, until I could throw the whole sodden mess on the floor and let the burned arm breathe. Even cool air felt like an oven on the nasty, raw wound, which still had a peculiar scrawl to it—it still made me think of someone's signature, carved right into my body.

Was that an "H" or an "F"?

Neither, obviously. It was a chance design, drawn by the random drippings of melted celluloid. There was no pattern, and it was silly to pretend otherwise.

This didn't stop me from staring at it like it could tell me something.

Eventually I pulled myself together enough to clean the wounded arm and everything else that needed cleaning, and I dressed the wound again with the ointment the doctor had given me. I stood naked in front of the sink and wrapped everything back up.

I did not do as good a job as the doctor had, but it stayed secure enough for me to finish drying off and getting dressed—and I did not want to, but I chose a long-sleeved sweater to wear over my dress. It would be too warm, but it would hold the bandage in place better than my own amateur efforts alone.

The sweater would also hide it. I hated to look at it. I couldn't exactly forget about it, not with the miserable pain, but when I didn't have to look at it, I could pretend that it wasn't as bad as all that.

I am good at pretending.

THAT'S a lie. I am a mediocre pretender, at best.

I went to breakfast with my teeth grinding together, trying to smile through the agony and act like nothing was wrong. Yes, my cough was going away, sure, I would appreciate a glass of water, no, thank you, I don't want to talk to the reporter from DeLand, of course if the police or firemen want a word with me I will make myself available. I ate alone, shooing away any offered company because I was having a hard time with all the lying. I mean pretending.

All the while, as I sat in the hotel restaurant and tried to forget that my arm was horribly burned, I thought about the letter from Ybor City. I thought about Tomás Cordero, because now the man who dreamed of fire had a name. He had a story.

And I had no doubt.

Even if the coincidence had not convinced me, all I had to do was hold that letter and listen to where it came from—listening, but not with my ears—and it was all so abundantly clear. The soldier, the fire, the loss. The dread and the fear. He wants my help. *Mine*, personally. He read about me in *The Sunflower*, and he wants to come see me.

I thought that it might not be a good idea, considering. Cassadaga has had plenty of fire already.

I'm not supposed to believe in coincidence. I don't really, now that I think about it.

OVER breakfast I mentally composed a plan. I would write back to Tomás Cordero. We would exchange a few letters, and I would see if I could help him from a distance. (I was already writing these letters in my head.) If I could not be of any use to him via the post office, then I would take the train to Tampa and visit him myself. But he probably should stay away from Cassadaga.

But the best-laid plans of mice and men . . . isn't that how the poem goes?

AFTER breakfast I took tea on the hotel porch, staring across the railroad tracks at the remains of the Calliope. I watched workmen cart away wheelbarrows full of soaked ashes and blackened rubble. I sipped from my cup while they dumped the wheelbarrows out onto a flatbed attached to a truck, in order to haul it farther away. Maybe they'd take it all the way to the ocean and dump it there.

I wasn't alone on the porch. Edella Holligoss was there, watching the grocery on the other side of the block where the Calliope used to be, and probably counting her lucky stars that the fire hadn't spread. Dolores Brigham was there, too, staring out at the wreckage, or at the houses beyond it. Honestly, it didn't look like she was staring at anything that anyone else could see. I thought about asking her if she was all right, but I couldn't find the energy.

We all three faced the blackened lot, and no one spoke until Mabel climbed up the stairs to join us, and then we were four.

She was wearing a pair of sunglasses and a dark purple dress made out of very light cotton. *Florida mourning wear,* I thought. It wasn't a very appropriate thought, and I hoped that no one else had heard it. Not least of all because no one had died. So far as anybody knew.

"How are you doing this morning, Alice?" She drew up one of the white wicker chairs beside me and sat down.

I looked down at the bandage without even meaning to. "I'll survive. I'll whine about it, but I'll survive."

She offered a weak smile and leaned back into her seat. "If you need any help with the bandage . . ."

"Thank you." I resisted the urge to scratch it. If I began, one of two things would happen: Either I'd immediately regret it, or I'd never stop scratching it again. I couldn't tell if it hurt or itched. Or which one it was doing more. To distract myself, I asked her, "Does anyone know how the fire started?"

She shook her head. "Everything went up so fast. The DeLand fire chief said that sometimes theaters just . . . they go up in smoke like that. The film catches fire so easily, and the projectors run so hot . . . it's just one of those things that happens."

"You think it was an accident?"

She lifted her sunglasses, propping them atop her forehead. "You think it wasn't?"

I didn't have a good answer. Why should I? It was a stupid question, and I never should've asked it. "I don't know what it was."

Mabel didn't let it go. "Do you think something strange has happened?"

Dolores answered before I could think of something suitable in response. "Yes, something very strange."

Now we all turned to look at her.

She didn't unfix her gaze from the Calliope. She talked in a low, steady voice, like someone who was making an effort to keep from screaming. It unsettled me down to my bones. "Something terrible and strange. Surely someone else must feel it, too. Alice." She didn't say my name like she was asking me a question. She said it like she was naming me as a witness.

I swallowed. "Yes, ma'am?"

"Is there anything you'd like to tell us?"

"Not remotely," I said, with absolute honesty. I wished I had a pair of sunglasses, because I could use something to hide behind. I cleared my throat. "But if you must know, I've been having some . . . dreams. Odd ones, full of fire."

"What do you mean?" asked Mabel. "Dreams of *setting* fires?"

"No, just . . . fires. Being in the middle of them, you know. Rather like I was . . . I mean, yesterday. But not quite."

Mabel frowned. "So . . . not a premonition?"

"No, I don't think so. I was in *a* fire, but not *that* fire. It was some other fire, on a battlefield—and I was looking for a man. When I found him, he knew my name. It wasn't the bad spirit from the reading, though," I was quick to add.

"How do you know?"

"They're connected, but different. The man on the battlefield is only a man. The bad spirit is . . ." I almost didn't tell her, but at the last moment I listened to my gut and said it anyway. "The bad spirit called himself the hammer."

She absorbed this, and I could tell she wasn't sure if she should be annoyed with me or not. "Why didn't you mention this before?"

"I meant to. I forgot to. I don't know. Please, it was an awful night, and the Calliope fire was awful, and I've just had so much on my mind."

It wasn't much of an excuse and I knew it. She knew it, too, but she didn't press. She only asked, "Did you know the other one's name? The one on the battlefield?"

I was grateful that she'd let it drop. "No, and I couldn't see his face, either. He was wearing a mask like the firemen wear. Except it wasn't exactly like that. It's hard to explain. Good Lord, but I hate having to tell people about my dreams. They always sound so silly."

"Dreams in Cassadaga are always fair game for dissection," Dolores said quietly. She went back to watching the scene across the tracks. "They very often mean more than we expect."

Edella nodded and added, "Though often we don't realize it until after the fact."

"Until it's too late?"

"If you were dreaming of the Calliope fire, then yes, your understanding came too late to prevent it." Mabel put her sunglasses back down and folded her hands across her lap. "For example."

I shouldn't have, but I said, "But I told you, I really don't think that's what it was about."

"Why not?" asked Dolores.

I shrugged. "Just a feeling. And I trust my feelings more than I trust my dreams."

I finished up my tea and left them there, because I didn't feel like pretending anymore and I didn't want them to pull the truth out of me: that I'd found a fire in my room, and that I'd been dreaming for weeks of a man who dreams of fire—and it'd only gotten worse since that open reading—and how I thought the burn on my arm looked like a signature.

It was pure madness. They'd put me away.

THERE'S also this: I cannot explain it, but I was already protective of Tomás Cordero. He was lost and confused—he was not a violent criminal or a dangerous man. He wanted help. He did not want to start trouble, or fires, either. I didn't want Mabel or Dolores or anyone else to know about his difficulties yet, on the off chance I could keep him a secret in a town full of clairvoyants.

He'd asked *me* for help, not them. I could help him; I was sure of it. I could shine some light—I could do some good in his world, and prove (to use Mr. Colby's words) that I deserved to be here.

So why did I feel this weird sense of approaching darkness?

I crossed the street and went to the bookstore, because I wanted some scenery that hadn't recently gone up in flames—and also I wanted to distract myself further. Why did I need so much distracting? My arm was a misery, yes, but that wasn't all of it. It was the fire, and the darkness. Did that make sense? Darkness and fire? You'd think it'd be brightness and fire, partnered together.

No, you wouldn't. Not when you've been in the thick of it.

When I think about the theater I think of the flames, yes. But mostly I think of the darkness, the shroud of smoke and ash, and knowing that something perilously hot was close by—but not being able to see it.

That's how I felt right then, as I wandered to the bookstore for lack of anything better to do. I felt like something dangerous was very, very near, but I couldn't see it at all. I could only fumble around and try to avoid it.

So I went to the bookstore. It's attached to the fellowship hall and the camp meeting offices. I stood before the bulletin board and read name after name of available mediums and clairvoyants, some belonging to people I'd met, some belonging to strangers. My name wasn't up there yet. It wouldn't be, not until I could take up permanent residence. Not while I was living in the hotel.

I pictured my card there, beside a little note with my address and services listed.

I pictured a rolling, boiling blackness that smelled like a charnel house.

I jerked my head up and looked around. The smell went away, and there was never any darkness to begin with.

Even so.

I quickly made for the exit, and soon I was standing on the porch in front of the bookstore—which frankly didn't look much different from the porch at the hotel. It's Florida. Everybody's got a porch. Everybody's got at least one or two rocking chairs. At the hotel, you sit there and rock and drink tea or coffee while you watch the trains come and go (or the cleanup of the theater, across the tracks); at the bookstore you sit there and rock and read whatever helpful book you were moved to purchase, or whatever pamphlet had been pressed into your hand by the visiting ministers.

But I was standing there, not rocking, not drinking or reading anything. I had stopped at the top of the steps like some kind of dummy because I was running away, and something had stopped me. I'd thought I smelled something awful, and sensed something worse. But there was nothing to smell, and nothing to flee. I felt ridiculous.

Imogene Cook appeared at my side.

Her glasses were askew, and her dark bobbed hair blew softly in the wind. I thought she looked too old to have bobbed hair, but that was none of my business. Maybe when I'm fifty I'll shave it all off and wear pants. If the suffragettes get their way (and it looks like they will), women will be voting before long—so I guess anything is possible.

"Is something wrong?" she asked me. "You've been standing there a minute."

"No, I . . . I was planning to . . . I was going to pick something up, and I forgot what it was."

"A book?" she suggested, straight-faced. "From the bookstore?"

"It might've been a book," I replied, with more shortness than was probably warranted.

"I heard you were caught up in the theater yesterday. Is that how you hurt your arm?"

"Yes."

She nodded thoughtfully. "I thought so. It's a strange wound, isn't it?"

"I beg your pardon?"

"Like the devil himself held your hand and signed his name. Or it would look like that, if the devil's name began with an 'H.'"

My breath caught in my throat. I backed away from her, one step, two steps. Until I reached the column at the edge of the steps, where the handrail goes. "Why would you say something like that? You haven't even seen it."

"I didn't say it, I only repeated it. You thought it first," she argued.

"That's . . . that isn't polite, to go around reading people's thoughts."

"I can't help it. That's what I'm here for. People always think it'd be useful to learn how to know what other folks are thinking—but I'd like to learn how *not* to do it. So hop down off your high horse, honey; you're not so special that I'm nosy about what's going on between your ears." In a huff, she turned and stomped past me, down the steps.

"Don't mind her." The voice was practically in my ear, whispered there.

I jumped half out of my skin, but it was only David—so I didn't die, but I blushed. "Oh, I don't. She's . . ."

"Quite a character, as my father likes to say." He grinned down at me with a touch of worry in his eyes. "But *you*, Miss Dartle."

"Alice."

"Alice, I know. We've done that dance already. You caught that showing of *Zorro* with the little nun."

I started to answer him, but I opened my mouth and it filled up with that smell again—burning bones and broiled skin. (No one's skin had broiled in the theater, except maybe mine. Everyone got out alive. This was something different. It came from somewhere else.) It gagged me. I put a hand to my throat and turned away from him. I coughed and coughed, and my eyes flickered with those tiny silver stars you see when you hit your head or when you can't breathe.

He said my name again. I heard it just fine, but the world was going dark, and I was gasping. "A moment," I wheezed. He thrust a handkerchief into my hands and I held it over my mouth while I coughed. "It's only the smoke," I choked out. "From yesterday."

"You breathed too much of it, I'm sure. Let me get you some water," he offered. "Here, take a seat."

A man who'd occupied the nearest rocker leaped up and offered his place, and I nodded to David like that's where I'd be when he returned with water—but the minute he ducked inside the store, I took off.

I tripped down the stairs, almost landing facedown at the bottom;

I caught myself and coughed again, and hid my face with the stolen handkerchief; I stood on the sidewalk, and then I went to the middle of the street. I stared this way and that—from one end of Stevens Street to the far side of the tracks, past the cremated remains of the Calliope and into the trees, over the rolling hills.

The Calliope. That must be the smell. The warm, lazy air currents must be carrying it back, sending it up my nostrils. "That's all it is," I told myself, or I told the handkerchief, anyway. "Just the Calliope."

I am a terrible pretender. I didn't believe myself for a second.

The clanging bell at the train crossing gonged and gonged and gonged again, warning pedestrians off the tracks. Maybe that was it: a combination of the Calliope and the train coming, both of them stinking like burned, blackened things and making such a terrible racket.

(Oh, I will hear it in my nightmares forever—the deafening roar of the fire and the sizzling ashes, and the timbers breaking and falling. Fire is a noisy feeder.)

But that sense of dread and darkness, boiled together down to some viscous sludge, it wasn't going away. Usually if I make up a good enough story, or find a good enough excuse to explain my fears away, they ease themselves off my chest. They let me breathe.

Not this one.

David would be back with the water any minute. I didn't want to talk to him. I didn't want any water. I wanted to run, as far and as fast as I could get—away from this bleak, black cloud that wasn't creeping so much as billowing. I couldn't see it (don't ask how I knew it was black) and I couldn't figure out where it was coming from, but I believed in it with all my heart.

It was coming for me, looking for me. Homing in on me like a pigeon.

Or was that too conceited? What if it was closing in on something else, something bigger than me? I tested the theory, turned it over in my head, and set it aside. It might be true, or it might be wrong. But something about it didn't fit.

The train was coming.

It rolled into town with a blast of warm air and steam, and with enough clatter to drown out every other sound (except for the crinkling pop of ashes, bursting around my face). It drew to a stop with a ferocious squeal, and finally the alarm bells at the crossing quit ringing.

David would be along any minute.

Water wouldn't help me. I didn't want to explain myself.

I darted back to the hotel, up the steps, past the rocking chairs, and into the lobby, where it was dark—much darker than it was outside, for all the windows with their gauzy curtains. I blinked to let my eyes adjust, and let the light flooding in through the windows catch up to me.

No, it wasn't that dark inside. It was never that dark inside.

The door burst open and there was David, having followed me from one woozy scene to another. "There you are!" he cried, a glass of water in hand, as promised. It sloshed over his fingers. His knuckles were very white.

"I'm sorry," I said, but I did not specify for what. "I think maybe I need to lie down."

"Let's start by having you *sit* down. Should I send for Dr. Holligoss?"

"No, don't do that."

This time, I let him put me into a tufted chaise, right there in the lobby. People were watching us and I was embarrassed, but I honestly did not think I could stand for even another moment. It was crowding me, at the edges of my vision—the smell, the pressure, like a headache swelling behind my eyes.

I coughed into the handkerchief again and I heard David tell someone, "It's the smoke. She was in the Calliope. Give her space, please. Everyone—give her room."

I accepted the glass when he pushed it into my hand, and I sipped it politely, not really tasting it or even needing it. Whatever was wrong, it could not be fixed with a bit of the yellow-smelling liquid that passed for drinking water in central Florida.

Whatever was wrong, it was very close now. It was pushing its way forward, coming right toward me, demanding to see me. It was hot and thick, and I swear to God, I think it was laughing softly—just beyond the farthest edge of my hearing.

The lobby doors opened again, admitting the new arrivals from the train.

Through gummy eyes I saw ladies in hats and men with suitcases. I saw an older couple with a porter carrying a trunk. I saw a man who was shrouded in heat and darkness. No, not shrouded in it. Haunted by it. Followed by it. Dragging it in his wake.

He looked this way and that way, around the lobby. He ought to follow the small crowd to the front desk, where he could find a room—or find directions to a room elsewhere. But he was looking for something. For someone.

For me.

I knew it was him, the same way I knew which horse to pick, and which stocks from the Saturday morning paper. I knew him like I knew my own face in the mirror, even though I hadn't expected to see him so soon.

TOMÁS Cordero wasn't carrying much—just a single small trunk and a small white dog. He was of average height and slender build, and probably about thirty years old. My momma would've called him "swarthy" but she said that about everybody with dark hair and eyes, especially if English wasn't their mother tongue. I thought he was handsome, though he was almost frail in appearance. His hands shook, and his satchel and his little dog shook, too. He wore a brown suit that might have been made for him when he was a little heavier, or a little stronger.

I sat up straight and set the glass on the round table beside the chaise. "Mr. Cordero!" I called out.

He caught my eye, and his face lit up like the Fourth of July.

He knew me, as surely as I knew him. He must have recognized me from his dreams.

# 16

## TOMÁS CORDERO

### Cassadaga, Florida

ALICE DARTLE IS a pretty woman, curvaceous and wavy haired, with kind eyes and graceful hands. She is perhaps twenty years old. I knew her immediately—the very second my eyes caught hers. I had seen her before; somehow I knew this. (I believed this.) It was déjà vu—that's what they call it. The moment I saw her, that's what it was.

She was seated on a chaise in the hotel lobby, surrounded by concerned and curious people. Someone had brought her a glass of water. She wanted them all to leave her alone; she was distracted and coughing, but they meant well and she was too polite to shoo them away.

Then she saw me.

She called my name. She knew me, too. I think she used me as an excuse to gain some breathing room, for she climbed to her feet and came to meet me. Such a sturdy little creature, never mind the cough and the bloodshot eyes. I saw strength in her, and conviction.

I saw *power*.

This was a woman who could help.

\* \* \*

THERE was a bandage on her arm, partially concealed by a sweater the shade of periwinkles. Her forehead was damp with sweat, but she was smiling. "Mr. Cordero," she said again. "It's a pleasure to meet you, but I did not know you were coming. Or . . . I thought you might come, but not right away. I was writing you a letter in return, and I'm so sorry that I haven't done it yet—I meant to finish and send it yesterday, but . . . here you are, arriving unexpected. But you're certainly not unwelcome!" she added quickly.

She spoke in a fast, rolling patter, with an accent that I couldn't quite place. She wasn't from Florida; of that I was certain.

I took her hand—the one without the bandaged arm attached—and I kissed it in greeting. "I did not intend to surprise you. Things have become . . . my situation has . . ." I faltered, unsure of where to begin or what to tell her.

"It's fine! It's all fine!" She sounded desperate to convince us both. "I'm so glad you're here."

Felipe leaned his head toward her, coming as close as he was able from my arms—in order to give her a sniff. I introduced him. "This is Felipe. He is gentle and harmless."

She let him examine her fingers, then gave him a little scratch on the head. "What a handsome little fellow." Then she looked at the hotel counter, where a smartly dressed colored man was manning the desk. "Here, let me take you to Mr. Rowe. We'll get you a room."

The hotel was nearly full, but as fortune would have it, a couple was trying to leave as I was trying to arrive. I assured Mr. Rowe that Felipe would make no messes, that I did not mind if the room had not been cleaned, and then I gave him my information and my money. I almost considered using someone else's name, in case anyone came looking for me . . . but what would be the point? I had not hurt anyone or set any fires. I did not care what happened to my house anymore, and there was nothing to be done for my business.

Or Mrs. Vasquez. Or Emilio.

With a sudden pang I thought of Silvio. I'd left a note for him at my house. I said only that I was leaving and that the house belonged to him now—if he wanted it. I left the paperwork for the fire insurance, for I had coverage on Cordero's, and I said that he should take the payout when it comes. I told him that I had done no wrong, but I would not return. I told him that I was a danger to everyone I love, and I would not put him in harm's way. I left him three months' salary in an envelope, to fill the gap until the insurance settlement.

I know, I know. It wasn't enough and I am a coward.

But what else could I do?

Miss Dartle helped me to my room, carrying Felipe so that I could manage my own trunk more easily. (There was only one bellhop, a young man named Timothy who was being run ragged in the rush of new visitors, brought by the train that had brought me, too.) She tidied the room while I unpacked. I asked her not to, but she insisted. She was nervous. She wanted something to do with her hands.

Felipe sniffed here and sniffed there, then hopped up onto the bed and curled into a ball.

"I hope you'll be comfortable here. I'm right down the hall, in room fourteen. If you need anything, all you have to do is ask, and if you can't find me, ask Mr. Rowe. He's a wonderful concierge, and he knows everything about everyone in town."

"You live here? In the hotel?"

"Temporarily. An apartment is opening up in Harmony Hall later this month, when one of the seasonal clairvoyants heads back north.

Then I can put down some proper roots. Housing is tricky in Cassadaga, with so many people coming and going all the time. But what about you? How long do you plan to stay?"

I dreaded the question, for I didn't have a good answer. I made one up on the spot. "That depends on how long it takes for me to find answers."

"About your wife."

She remembered, from my letter. I was touched. "Yes, about my wife. I brought a few things to show you . . . but I don't mean to impose. I arrived so abruptly and interrupted your day."

"No, no. It's fine. It's good. I'm sure that everything will be all right. We should meet, and we should talk—openly and honestly. I do want to tell you . . . I have some concerns . . ." She rubbed her bandaged arm with her free hand. "But it's just as well that you've come. Can I take you to lunch? It's not too late for that, is it? Supper, then, perhaps?"

I wasn't hungry, but I knew I ought to be . . . and Felipe *must* be, though he had such manners that he hadn't become snippy about it. "No, it is not too late at all."

"There's a lunch counter across the tracks, and a small grocery right beside it. You can pick up some supplies, if you need any. Some food for Felipe, maybe?"

So far, he'd been eating whatever I had on my plate—but not much of it. We would waste away if we kept up like this. "That sounds delightful, but please, allow me to pay. I have come in search of your time and expertise. It is not your job to look after me."

"You are my very first client," she fussed. "I'm not actually . . . certified yet, and my name isn't on the board, but you asked me for help, and I'm going to give it to you. I'll start with a decent welcome and some food. Are you ready?"

"Yes, of course."

Felipe seemed happy where he was, so I left him on the bed to nap—and I envied him only a little. I was exhausted but I had arrived, and I had found Alice Dartle. So far, nothing had burned down. We should get to work while we were still ahead, in whatever terrible game this turned out to be.

Outside the train was winding up, preparing to depart in a violent cacophony of noise and steam and smoke. Together, Alice and I stood on the porch to wait for it to finish leaving; when it was gone, it revealed the wreckage of a fire across the tracks. I gasped, and the sound caught in my throat.

She saw where I was staring. "Oh, that. It was a theater."

"A theater?"

"Only one screen, but the popcorn was good. *The Mark of Zorro* was playing when the film reel caught fire, and the whole building went down. Apparently it happens from time to time. The film itself is terribly flammable."

"Yes," I breathed, hardly taking my eyes off the smoldering rubble. "From time to time."

She took my arm and guided me over the tracks. "Everyone got out safely, so we thank Spirit for that."

"Thank Spirit, yes." I didn't know what the expression meant; I was only parroting her. "Were you caught inside? Is that what happened to your arm?"

She nodded but didn't offer any further information except, "It will heal. Here, look. This is Candy's."

She directed me to a small, square building with open windows and a screen door. Out front, there was a porch with a sunshade and three bistro tables—none of which were occupied. I might have considered it a bad sign, but when Alice opened the door, a warm, pleasant collection of odors wafted out: cooking plantains, toasting bread, melting cheese . . . and unless I missed it, just a hint of rum. I'm sure they use it for cooking, and I'm sure they use it for drinking. Prohibition is a silly thing when rum is as easy to buy as a soft drink.

The woman at the counter was named Candice Pearson, and when introductions were made, she offered to produce a traditional Cuban sandwich. Or two, since Alice thought the idea sounded grand. I asked how Mrs. Pearson had guessed, and she said that she hadn't, exactly. But this was a town of clairvoyants, and I should get used to having people know things without having been told.

"We don't guess so much as intuit." She winked. She handed us each a glass of water and told us to have a seat outside.

After she disappeared into the kitchen, Alice collected some napkins and led the way to one of the round tables with the pretty metalwork chairs. "She's right about everyone here knowing your business," she said. "It takes some getting used to." She pulled out her own seat before I could offer to do so.

I drew a chair for myself and sat down. "I don't mind the lack of privacy. I am here because I need the advice of those who . . . who can see more than I can see, and know more than I can know. Even if it means sharing an awkward secret or two."

Between bites of a serviceable sandwich (a little heavy on the mustard, but otherwise good), I gave Alice the barest outline of recent events. "The first fires were small nuisances, and I thought there might have been a problem with the wires in my house. Then there were more fires—bigger fires—and in the ashes left behind, I found images like these." I pulled a ruined piece of fabric from inside my jacket, where I'd kept it all this time. I unfolded it and laid it out flat on the table between us.

She set the last bites of her sandwich aside and wiped her hands (and dabbed at her mouth) with a napkin. She did not touch the fabric at that time. Instead, she used the back edge of her unused knife to turn it toward her. "Good heavens, would you look at that!"

"It's not my imagination, is it?"

"No, not at all. It's clear as day: a handprint. A left handprint, to be more precise—from someone with long, slender fingers. And"—she squinted—"a ring? A wedding ring?"

"Yes! That was how I saw it, too!"

"How did you make this image? Or how did it happen, I mean? You didn't just light it on fire; what is this, wool?"

"Yes, it's wool. I used an iron and left it too long in place."

"I see, I see." But I wondered why she did not touch. "And there are other examples?"

"I have a few others in my luggage. But the largest and most grand were on the wall of my house and inside the kitchen sink. There was a good one in the bathtub, too, but it is cast iron—and no more easily carried to Cassadaga than the house itself."

I could not read her expression as she stared down at the cloth, still prodding it with the dull end of the knife. She was thoughtful, to be certain. She was concerned, I guess. I think she might have been afraid, but I hoped not. It wouldn't do for both of us to approach this with terror.

Still, I had to tell her the truth—even if I told it gently, and in a roundabout fashion. "After these little fires, and the bigger fires, and the fires that I created in search of more images . . . there was a terrible one. My neighbor, Carmella Vasquez. Her house burned down, with her inside it. Everyone thought Felipe was inside, too, but he turned up alive and the police gave him to me. He has no one else."

"The poor little thing." She looked up from the scrap. "And his poor owner, too!"

"The fire chief said that she was smoking and fell asleep. It happens, I'm sure."

"Just like theaters burn down because of the film and the hot projectors. It happens, I'm sure."

Her tone unnerved me. It wasn't exactly thoughtful, certain, or frightened. It was the tone of a woman who has been told one thing but believes another. "You suspect foul play with regards to the theater?" I used the term the thugs do in the mystery dreadfuls.

"Something like that. I was inside the theater when the reel caught fire. I barely escaped with my life, and now you show me this fabric, with this pattern on it. You tell me about your little fires . . ." She set down the knife and hovered her hand above the wool like she wished to touch it but had some concerns about doing so.

"You can pick it up, if you wish."

"I *do* wish to pick it up, but at the same time . . . I don't. Mr. Cordero," she said my name to announce a change of subject. "What did you do during the Great War?"

"I . . . I fought."

"For that matter, how does a man from an island end up fighting thousands of miles away, on behalf of another country?"

"That is a story of another war," I said, more defensiveness in my voice than I intended. "It was fought when I was a child, and then I was brought here. *This* is my country—and when the Great War came, I left Ybor City to defend it. I fought in Germany and France, and I—"

"But *how* did you fight? What did you fight *with*?"

I might've answered her, as best as I was able. I might have tried to explain the Livens Large Gallery Flame Projector, and if I told my story well, I could have made it sound valiant and glorious. It was both of those things, when viewed from a certain angle (from hindsight, I guess). At the time, it was messy and hot and miserable.

I would have told her all of this, but we were interrupted.

Two women came over to Candy's, presumably for lunch, and they both stopped in their tracks when they saw us. Or I should say, when they saw *me*. They looked at me with widened eyes, as if I'd sprouted an extra head.

Alice called out, *"Hello,"* in a pointed fashion, the kind of fashion that says it isn't polite to stare. Though who am I to guess what is polite here, where people know one another's thoughts and sense one another's secrets?

The older of the two women was taller and lighter, with longer hair. Cautiously, she returned the greeting, and said, "Alice, I see that you have a visitor."

"Yes, this is Mr. Tomás Cordero, of Ybor City. He's come to the camp to learn about the faith and receive some counsel with regard to his departed wife. Tomás," she said. She used my first name now—implying by familiarity that they were being rude, I believe. "This is Dolores Brigham and Imogene Cook."

Both of them approached, crowding the little table. I squirmed and reached for the burned fabric swatch before they could see it for themselves. It was private, a thing between Alice and myself. It wasn't theirs to touch.

Imogene was shorter and stockier, with short, dark hair and spectacles. She wore an air of directness like a large hat that shadowed her every move. "What's that?" she asked me as I stuffed it back into my pocket. Then she asked Alice, "Is this some kind of official business? Because you really ought to conduct it on the right side of the tracks."

"This is a getting-to-know-you lunch, and it's happening over here because we wanted sandwiches," she stubbornly replied. "What's it matter to you, Imogene?"

Dolores stepped in, with more caution. "There are . . . protections within the camp's boundaries."

Alice looked as blank as could be. "Since when?"

"Since 1897," she replied.

"Well, it's news to me, and we're only eating and talking, so it doesn't matter. Besides, I don't have an office or a parlor to see clients. Where should we meet when the time for business comes?"

"In the hotel, there are rooms you can reserve for consultations. Or you can pick a time at Harmony Hall or work out of my home, if you like. Take some tea and sit on the bookstore porch—or in the fellowship hall at the rear. But stay over *there*," Dolores Brigham pleaded softly. "Stay where the best measures have been taken."

"Something's strange about this one," declared Imogene Cook. She cocked a thumb at me and frowned like I'd done her some great wrong. "It's something to do with the theater. There's something attached to him . . ." She fluttered her hands, like she was waving away a puff of smoke.

Dolores took her by the arm and said, *"Imogene . . ."*

"He only just arrived. He had nothing to do with the theater," Alice said.

"No," Imogene protested. "There's fire all around him."

"There was a fire at his house," my companion clarified. "That's all. You're seeing both that and the theater. Leave him alone."

She dug in. "No, there's something *with* him."

"He's got a little dog with him, but he left it up in the hotel to have a nap. Go away, Imogene, if you're going to be discourteous to my . . . my friend."

"So he's not a client?"

"You've never helped a friend in a professional capacity?" She didn't wait for an answer. "Stop asking questions and let us finish our lunch."

"We will." Dolores drew Imogene away from the table, her face a knot of worry all the same. "I apologize for any disturbance. It was only the fire at Mr. Cordero's house, as you said. I'm sure that's all it is. It was a pleasure to meet you," she said with a dip of her head.

I replied in kind.

They left us alone, and Alice visibly relaxed. "I do not like that woman, Imogene. She says whatever's on her mind, no matter how useless it is—and she's always so nosy. Can't mind her own business to save her life."

"Thank you for leaping to my defense."

"Think nothing of it. You gave me an excuse to send her packing."
The dear girl scowled. "She shouldn't have bothered you like that.
And what's this about protections at the campsite? No one said boo
about it until now."

"How long have you been here?"

"A few weeks, so . . . not long, in the grand scheme of things. I
know, I know—there's still plenty for me to learn—but you'd think
someone might've mentioned it sooner. Instead they talk about the
property's boundaries at the gates, like they're just as magical and
holy as things that come in threes." Now she was stewing, and it was
a joy to watch. "Well, they don't have Candy's on the other side, so
to hell with their gates."

I laughed.

She then apologized with a ferocity to match her original blasphemy. "And did you know," she went on, "that spiritualists are teetotalers? They don't drink or smoke, or anything."

"Is that so?"

"That's what they say in public, but no, not really. Candy has a
speakeasy in the back, where you can drink what you want and
smoke if you like. But a lot of them live as clean as they can, to which
I can only say, 'Good for them.' As for me, I like a nightcap without
any judgment, thank you very much. Apparently you can only get
one of those on *this* side of the tracks."

We finished our meal, and she still was anxious and irritated, so
I asked her to show me around the camp. It gave her something to
do other than fidget and swear.

We started on Stevens Street, and she took me on a loop around
the two small lakes that anchor the campgrounds. On the way, we
met a handful of the locals, and she introduced me enough times
that I will never remember anyone else's name—but perhaps some
of them may recall mine. Everyone seemed pleasant and welcoming,
though a few gave me odd looks. Not so odd as Imogene Cook

(whose name is emblazoned in my head), but I could see right away that there was something about me that worried them.

Was it my speech? My English is perfection. I've spoken it since I was eight or nine years old. I am darker than some people here, but lighter than others. I've seen a number of colored men and women— all from up north, as Alice told me—and two or three Indians. No other Cubans, or anyone else speaking Spanish so far, which I do find odd. This is Florida. I don't think I've ever been anywhere in the state without hearing my mother tongue somewhere, on some stoop or in some park.

Alice noted that most of the people in attendance (and most of the long-term residents, too) were from New England, and I probably seemed exotic to them. She said my accent is lovely, and they are only being strange to me because I am different. She said I should not judge them too harshly, for novelty makes people curious.

I know she's right, but I do not like being a spectacle—especially not when my business has burned and the newspapers or policemen may call me out, seeking to return me to Ybor City for questions. Silvio may not satisfy them with whatever answers he provides, and someone may come looking.

I wonder what newspapers this little town receives. I wonder how many people read them. I wonder how far word of my burned-up shop will spread.

Surely, not so far as this?

By evening, I was warm and tired but feeling considerably better— by virtue of the company and the calm, friendly town. I considered returning to the room to take a nap or turn in very early, and I said so to Alice. But I said it within earshot of a mustachioed, balding man with warm eyes and a wide smile, and so my plans were derailed.

He introduced himself as Oscar Fine, president of the campground organization.

"I hope you will reconsider, as we're holding our first open reading of the new meeting sessions. Have a cup of coffee from the hotel and come join us! We have a new crop of visitors, and the last crop has largely left us. My son, David, is participating for only the second time."

Alice cocked her head. "I didn't know David did . . . anything, come to think of it."

"His abilities are hit-or-miss," his father confessed. "But he's been developing them for the last year. His first open reading went fairly well, and I'm hoping for his sake that tonight's goes even better. Sometimes I fear that he's not as firmly committed to the process as he ought to be."

Alice failed to stifle a giggle. "I'm sure he'll be marvelous."

I was unclear on the concept of an open reading, but they filled me in, and it sounded intriguing—if vaguely alarming. So far as spiritualism, and speaking to the dead, and communicating with things beyond the veil went . . . this was a dive into the deepest part of the ocean.

What would I say? What would I do, if Evelyn came forward to offer me some message that did not come from a scorched bit of cloth?

In the end, my desire to hear from her—even the *possibility* of hearing from her—won out, and I asked if it would be all right to bring Felipe, who had been cooped up in the hotel room for several hours.

Mr. Fine assured me that it would be no problem for me to keep the little dog by my side so long as he was not disruptive. After the president was gone, Alice said, "Believe me, Felipe will be about the least disruptive thing in the pavilion. I did an open reading once. It went . . ."

"Yes?"

"It went . . . disruptively. At best, there was crying. At worst, there was fainting. But in the end, the people who received messages from their loved ones on the other side . . . they all seemed satisfied with the experience."

"People fainted?"

"*I* fainted. Tell me, though—are you hungry again? I'm hungry again. It's a little early for supper, but not so early that I'd like to go without."

I told her the truth: that I was content to wait another few hours for an evening meal. The sun had not yet begun to set, and Felipe was waiting for me. With that in mind, Alice walked me back to the grocery—where I picked up some meats and cheese for snacks, for both myself and the dog. He had declined the bagged dog food I'd found before we left, but I doubted he'd turn up his nose at some good salami or pepperoni.

Alice left me in the hotel lobby, and we agreed to meet again in an hour so that we could walk down to the church together for the open reading.

Felipe yawned when I opened the door, then sniffed the air with interest as I entered carrying the paper-wrapped lunch meats in a little bag. I convinced him to eat. We shared a little cheese. Then I leashed him up to take him outside, where he pissed on every corner of the garden beside the porch.

I said to him, "I think we've come to the right place. I think everything might be all right. Eventually."

He gave me a quizzical frown, but that's what he usually gives me.

"At least, our hopes are higher here than they would be anywhere else."

## 17

## ALICE DARTLE

Cassadaga, Florida

AFTER AN HOUR or so, I reunited with Tomás in the hotel lobby—where I found him seated by the front door, with his little dog, Felipe, in his lap. They both perked up when they saw me, which is a good way to make a girl feel nice. Even a girl who hasn't been wholly forthcoming.

Tomás stood up and put Felipe gently on the floor, where he remained tethered by a red leash. I didn't think he needed it, to be honest. The dog didn't seem interested in leaving his master's side, and who could blame him? After everything the poor fellow had been through . . . I'd stick close to my only friend, too.

"Are you ready?"

"Of course," said Tomás, with just a tad too much forced certainty. I didn't have to be clairvoyant to know that he was fibbing. It was only fibbing, though. He was trying to be game, not deceptive.

I wasn't exactly looking forward to this, either. I had a bad feeling about it, and I was rather annoyed with Oscar Fine for suggesting it. Tomás's dead wife was trying to reach him through warm and violent means, or so it appeared—and maybe she was trying to reach me, as well. I know *I'm* not the one who set the fire in my washroom sink, and the list of possible arson candidates is short indeed.

I know it's a leap. I know it's crazy. But I don't think it's safe to believe in coincidence anymore. Too many places are burning, and too many people are burning right along with them.

Lord Almighty. I might as well have been a witch.

WE'D strolled past the pavilion on our earlier jaunt through town, but now we walked down the gentle slope toward the lakes together more slowly, more reluctantly, though neither one of us could've said exactly why. Or maybe neither one of us would've been *willing* to say why.

That's probably closer to the truth.

All the way, Felipe trotted between us in a businesslike fashion, ears alert and eyes darting from side to side. I suppose I'd be alert, too, if I were the size of a hatbox and lived my life at ankle level. I wonder how often he gets kicked by accident or tripped over? I'm glad he's a wary little beast. He'll live longer that way.

Men occasionally tipped their hats toward us, and ladies bent double to coo baby talk at the dog, and before long we reached the open-air structure with the billowing roof made of canvas, and pews organized like they'd be in any ordinary place of worship, laid out in an angular horseshoe pattern. It was only five thirty, but the rows were already filling up with the eager, the curious, and the skeptical.

David Fine was down front, beside the pulpit, chatting with Dr. Floyd. He saw me out of the corner of his eye, winked, and nodded. He gave Tomás a more appraising look, then went back to business.

I waved to Dr. Floyd, but I don't think she saw me.

"Do you mind if we . . ." Tomás looked around uncertainly. He picked up Felipe and hugged him, and I thought of the way a child holds a doll in the dark.

"If we what?"

"Could we stay toward the back? Over here, maybe?" He sidled to a pew on the very last row and slotted himself into place before I could suggest an alternative. Not that I'd been planning to. The back row was fine with me.

I slipped in beside him and sat down. "This works." I put my hand on his arm to reassure him, and I swear, I felt him trembling. I did not know if it was hunger, exhaustion, or fear. It could have been any one of these things. I pulled my hand away quickly, before I could pick up anything private or upsetting.

I'd felt a sharp little jolt of something when I touched him. Sympathy? Pity? No, I don't think so. At the risk of suggesting something silly and inappropriate, I think it might have been admiration. Or even affection.

Ridiculous, of course. I hardly knew the man. Besides, he's a bit older than me.

Not that much older. Ten or twelve years, I think? Hardly any older at all, not that I'm thinking of him like that. (Really, I'm not.) I feel protective of him; I think that's it. I mustn't misunderstand my own feelings. Protectiveness is a good thing. That's all he needs right now, and all I'm in a position to offer him. He has been through so much, and he is trying so hard to be strong.

But oh, his arm was thin inside that sleeve. I wanted to leap up, run across the tracks, and come back with another sandwich—and make him eat it, then and there. Right in front of me.

Obviously, I did no such thing.

I sat there quietly beside him. Together, we waited for the audience to filter in and for Dr. Floyd and David to come to some agreement about how the services would be conducted and which hymns would be sung. We watched as Mabel had a word with the piano player, then went to the song boards to change out the numbers.

And then, the lights dimmed as the sun dropped behind the hills. Everything went doubly dark, in half the time you'd expect.

It was Edella Holligoss on the piano. I'm not sure why I hadn't recognized her at first, but there she was, cracking her knuckles and shuffling her feet on the pedals. She began to play quietly, signaling that the service was about to begin.

Felipe settled down on the seat between us, wedging himself in tight. I couldn't tell if he was scared or if he was just the most comfortable when he was being squeezed. I patted his head, and he didn't protest—he only shivered. But as far as I could tell, he always shivered. Tomás told me it was normal, when they're small like that. Even when the weather is warm.

I'll have to take his word for it. I don't know much about dogs.

But the service began, and Dr. Floyd gave the announcements and welcomes, and we all stood up to sing "Lord! May the Inward Grace Abound." I didn't know that one, so I didn't sing it very well. Tomás didn't sing at all, but he apologized quietly and said that in Catholic churches, they don't do such things.

He quickly added, "It's not that I disapprove; I am only unfamiliar with the ritual of it. Please, sing if it makes you happy, and if it is part of your faith."

He's such a gracious man. His wife was a lucky woman.

I'm not a bad singer, but when the hymn was finished and I'd fumbled through it badly, I whispered, "I've never heard that one before."

"You did beautifully," he whispered back, a lovely untruth.

Finally it was time for David to take his position. The pavilion went quiet, and so did we.

He closed his eyes and folded his hands, performing a tiny, silent prayer, then opened his eyes again and looked out over the crowd. He took a deep breath and let it out slowly.

"It's . . . I'm getting a young man. He had trouble with his chest—no, with his breathing. It was consumption. He died before he turned eighteen. The same week. Yes, the very same week. He's here to speak with . . . to see . . ."

A man three rows down from us sobbed out loud.

"His father?"

He nodded.

"Hello, sir, yes. He says it's you."

The reading went on in this fashion for another few minutes, when two more spirits came forward. One was a child who had been run over by a car—"The first car in the town, about five years ago . . . a big black car, and the driver just kept going"—and one was an elderly woman who wished to speak with her grandchildren. Several victims of the influenza came forward and were welcomed. Dr. Floyd had told me that there were almost always a few. It was always very sad.

But then things took a turn.

David fell silent and stared forward, toward the back of the breezy church. His eyes were wide and black, or else it was only the light. His face was pale and lean, even cadaverous, unless that was the light, too.

(I was not sure it was the light.)

"Who?" he asked. "Who," he said. "This isn't . . . you aren't . . ."

Dr. Floyd looked concerned. She exchanged a few words with Oscar Fine, who was seated beside her on the platform behind David.

Before either of them could come forward to give him any guidance or assurance, he held out one hand to point forward. "It's not you," he breathed. He swung his hand back and forth slowly, like a compass needle searching for true north. "You're not . . . you aren't . . . no. You're not who you say you are."

I had a terrible feeling that I knew which north the needle of his index finger would find, and I was right. The arm tipped toward

Tomás and me—but we were so far in the back, I could also argue that it tipped toward a dozen other people at the same time. No one singled us out as if we were the target.

But somehow I knew: He was pointing at Tomás.

"No, it isn't him," David said. His voice wobbled. "Tell me who you are."

I put my hand over my mouth to stifle a gasp.

Felipe trembled and began a low, soft, guttural growl that could not be heard more than a foot or two away. I felt it when I put one hand upon his back. He was not threatening me or anyone else. He was complaining about something. He was worried. He hunkered down deeper between the two of us on the pew.

Tomás breathed, "Me. He means me."

But David said, "It's *with* you. It's . . . it's behind you. It followed you here." He lowered his arm until it hung at his side like a stone. He went very, very pale—even paler than before, and I would've sworn it wasn't possible. He stood still, so still I couldn't tell if he was breathing. He was as immobile as a corpse.

Tomás was frozen beside me. His eyes were wide, and his mouth was slightly ajar.

"It chose you, you know." His next words were so soft, I did not quite hear them—but I could read his lips. "*He* chose you. He saw you holding the fire."

"He chose you . . . ," I echoed, and I don't know why. I didn't know what it meant, and if Tomás did, I couldn't read it on his face.

I did something rash then—while David stood there ghostlike on the stage. I reached for Tomás's bare hand (not his arm, protected by a shirt and by the sleeve of his jacket) and I grasped it hard before he had time to realize what I was doing. It surprised him. He looked at me with confusion, but he did not draw it away.

His hand was warm, almost feverish. It was dry and his fingers were thin, but strong—like a man who plays an instrument.

I closed my eyes, squinting and breathing steady, by force. I wanted to see what David saw. I wanted to hear what David heard. I wanted to know what Tomás thought. I would settle for some portion of any of those things, but I needed more information and I did not know how else to gain it.

"Alice?" he asked quietly.

"Shush," I told him.

I listened. I looked, with my eyes closed.

The pavilion was different when I looked this way. The world opened in shadow, but in light, too. There was a red tinge to everything, and I could detect outlines—crimson and gold. I saw the spirits near the stage, the old woman and the young man who had died before his birthday. I saw the influenza victims wobble and shift, withdrawing in the face of something else.

Something in front of them . . . something behind us.

I looked around, keeping my eyes shut tight, but turning my head toward the rear entrance. I could not "see" it. Something was in the way—some hulking black pit of a presence that was only roughly shaped like a human.

I recognized it. I'd seen it once before, in my own open reading: a looming shadow that had not been able to hear me. I understood now that it'd been too far away. It hadn't been senseless and mute; I'd only seen it at a very far distance, observing as it observed someone else. Now it was right here, right now. Now it could reach out and lay a hand on my shoulder.

It was watching Tomás, stationed behind him. I could've swatted it if I'd had the courage, but I didn't. I lost track of my steady breathing and snorted in the world's least graceful fashion, but I wasn't worried about being graceful anymore.

When I sat there in the shadow of this shadow, within grasping range of this horrible shape, I was worried that it *might* reach out for me and put a hand on my shoulder—and immediately, completely, without any warning, I would surely burst into flames. The thing behind us was almost unbearably hot; I believed with all my soul that if I opened my eyes I would see the air shimmering with heat, like the air you find cooking above a hot road on a summer day. My forehead was warm, my cheeks were burning, and I could feel my eyebrows sizzling right off my face.

I was still holding Tomás's hand. I'd completely forgotten, but then he put his free hand atop mine and I jumped like I'd been stung.

Down on the stage, David was still staring right at us. I was looking around again, really looking, with my eyes open like a normal, sane person who needs to see things. There was nothing standing behind me. There was no weird, radiating heat pouring off a monstrous, man-sized thing that was neither dead nor alive but knew how to hate.

The pavilion had gone utterly silent. It was so quiet I could hear my own blood pumping in my ears.

"Hate, yes. That's what it is," David breathed. "This is the scourge. This is the hammer." And then he collapsed.

His father and Dr. Floyd dashed forward, and so did half of the front row. Edella shouted for her husband, who ran down the aisle from somewhere off to our left; he reached David and rolled him onto his back, checking his breathing and pulse and beginning chest compressions that looked like they must have hurt—but nobody stopped him, and I was forced to conclude that he knew what he was doing.

I stood. I don't remember standing, but I was on my feet with my hand over my mouth.

Tomás rose beside me. Everybody rose, all around, and soon I couldn't see anything anymore. "Do you know him? The young man down there?"

"He's a friend. Oh God, what happened?" I asked, but it was nonsense and I think Tomás knew it.

"He was looking us. At me. But I think he was talking to you."

"Yes, he was. I didn't understand . . ."

Edella Holligoss was hollering her head off, demanding that all the curious and concerned onlookers back away and give her husband room to work. Dr. Floyd took up the cause, went to the podium, and called out in a booming, strong voice: "Everyone please take your leave. Dolores, where are you?"

"Here!" she called from someplace I couldn't see.

"Get to the phone! Call for the hospital in DeLand!" Dolores agreed, so Dr. Floyd continued, "Everyone else, out, please! We need breathing room! Everyone return to your tents, your rooms, or your . . . homes. Wherever, I beg you."

Slowly, the crowd oozed out the aisle and along the main thoroughfares, emptying reluctantly into the night. People chattered anxiously and gossiped wildly. No one knew what had happened. No one had seen anything except for me—and David, I assumed.

Tomás and I stood there, with Felipe still on the pew, still shivering.

I turned sideways and shuffled out, never taking my eyes off the stage. Enough people had left that I could see the doctor working, breathing down into David's mouth. I said a little prayer to the sky, and to Spirit. I said, "We should go."

"Where?"

"Anywhere but here." He was gazing down at the stage, wanting to stay. (Wanting to hear more, I believe.) But I was getting panicky. "We could go . . . we could go to the hotel, and I'll treat you to supper. The restaurant there is really quite good—or if you'd rather have a drink, we can go back to Candy's and do that, or have a smoke, or if you want we could just go down to the pier on Spirit Lake and talk. I could read your cards, or we could talk about the fires . . ."

He shuddered, just like Felipe. He collected the dog in his arms. "Why do you say that? Why talk about the fire? Do you smell it?"

"Smell what? A fire?"

"Right now, yes. Do you?" he asked.

I scanned the pavilion with a frown. I didn't smell anything except the thick night air, the azaleas, and the magnolias with their big, leathery blooms. "No, I don't." But I still felt a sting in my cheeks from the flaring warmth that had blasted me when I'd looked at the creature.

No, not a creature. Not exactly a spirit, either—or no spirit like I'd ever seen or heard of. It was real; that was all I would have sworn to. It was real, and it was hot, and it was full of hate.

Tomás followed behind me with Felipe, still asking, "Are you sure? You smell nothing at all?"

"Nothing like fire." I flashed one final look at the stage, and I could've sworn I saw David's hand open and close. I paused, then let Tomás nudge me forward again. "I'm sorry, but I don't smell anything."

We withdrew from the tent and stood on the sidewalk, joining the rest of the audience members, who mostly milled about, wondering what to do, whispering about whether David would be all right, and discussing what had happened to him. I wished I had some answers. Any answers, really. I would've settled for some hints, or even a portent or two.

I thought about following through on my threat to drag him to the hotel for food or coffee, but Tomás stopped me before I could bring it up again. He put his hands on my upper arms, compelling me to meet his eyes. "Alice, I must know: What happened when you held my hand? What did you see?"

"My . . . my eyes . . . they were shut. I didn't see anything."

"I know you were watching. Please, tell me."

So I told him, "Look, it's not as simple as 'seeing,' but I . . . I *sensed* that there was something behind us."

"Behind *me*?"

"Yes. David was trying to say that you'd brought it with you."

Tomás looked sick, like I might have punched him in the stomach. "The only thing I brought with me . . . is this dog."

"You know that isn't what he meant."

He swallowed and adjusted his grip on Felipe. "But . . . David spoke like . . . he was talking about a man. He was not speaking of a woman's spirit."

"No, he wasn't."

"Do you think what you saw . . . could it have been a woman?"

"No, I don't."

"Is it"—he looked around, over my shoulder, then over his own—"still with me?"

I shook my head. "I don't know. I can't see it anymore."

"Close your eyes."

"It doesn't always work that way."

Impatiently, he asked, "Then how *does* it work?"

"That's what I'm here to learn!" I had to plead with him now, because he was pleading with me, and I didn't know how else to respond. "But you want me to say that it's your wife, and I can only tell you that it's not. It's something else."

"Some*one*?"

"You heard me the first time."

I didn't mean to be harsh with him, but I guess I was. He withdrew, clutching that dog like a purse. He said, "I am sorry. I did not mean . . ."

"No, I'm sorry. Because I *did* mean. I think we should part company for the night. Let me go and think, and pray. I'll pull out my cards and see if Spirit is willing to guide me. You should . . ." It was a bluff. I didn't have the faintest idea what either one of us should do.

"I should see about a meal, for myself and Felipe. We ought to make an early evening of things, after such a long and difficult day. Please excuse us."

He did a little bow that broke my heart, and walked back to the hotel.

I waited for him to turn around and give me one last look, so that I could blast him with a meaningful apologetic stare, but he didn't. Only Felipe peeked his nose out from under Tomás's elbow, and that was as close to a second glance as I got.

I wasn't sure what to do with myself.

I wasn't hungry anymore, if I'd ever been hungry in the first place—when I told him we should get some supper together. I wished that my clairvoyance worked the way Tomás seemed to think it did, and all I had to do was close my eyes and see the truth.

I tried it, just in case. But all I saw was darkness, and all I got was a big surprise when Dr. Floyd tapped me on the shoulder.

"Alice?"

"Ma'am!" I jumped half out of my skin. "I'm sorry!"

"For what?"

"For yelling at you!" I barked in almost precisely the same tone. Then, more quietly, I said, "I'm just sorry in general. How's David?" I asked suddenly. "*Please* tell me he's all right."

She looked old in a way she had never looked old to me before. "He's not all right, but he might be, later on. The ambulance will be here soon."

"How soon?"

She held her hands up, bent at the wrist. "Who knows? A few minutes, and no longer—or so I hope and pray. He's breathing, so there's that much to suggest he'll survive."

"Thank Spirit for that," I said. It felt odd in my mouth. I said it again anyway. "Thank Spirit."

"Indeed." She wiped a tendril of loose hair from her eyes and folded her arms. She glanced toward the hotel, and then it was her turn to change the subject on a dime. "What happened to your friend?"

"He's very tired. It's been a long day's travel for him and the little dog, so they're turning in early for the night."

She got right to the point. She skewered me with it. "David was talking to your friend, wasn't he? What do you think he saw before he collapsed? I was watching you from where I was sitting. Your face went so red that I could see it, even in the dark."

It wouldn't accomplish anything to lie. I took a deep breath. "I think he saw something large and dark standing behind Tomás. Whatever it is, Tomás brought it here with him."

She took the next words right out of my mouth. "Well, he didn't mean to. He came here looking for help."

We both stood there, silent for a minute. Around us, the worried crowds muttered and whispered, discussing what had happened at the reading and wondering about David's condition. While we loosely huddled together, an ambulance pulled up to the campground entrance and squeezed between the pillars. Edella Holligoss ran up to it and leaned in the window to offer directions to the pavilion.

Dr. Floyd and I got out of the way and encouraged others to do likewise.

The ambulance rolled down the hill at what looked like a crawl. I willed it to move faster, but my will didn't do a damn thing. It crept and crawled down the ragged, sandy street until it came to a stop beside the church in its own good time.

I stood up on tippy-toes, trying to see if they were bringing David out, but it was too far away and too dark, and there were too many people blocking my view.

"We must have faith that he'll recover," Dr. Floyd said.

"I do. I have all the faith in the world."

"But he's the second one to fall onstage in as many weeks." She looked at me. "Let's hope this is one thing that shouldn't come in threes. Something is terribly wrong in Cassadaga these days. Don't you feel it?"

I responded as honestly as I could. "I feel a lot of things right now: worry for David, concern for my friend Tomás, pain in my arm because I need to change this stupid bandage, and yes—I think there's something strange going on."

"What do you think it looks like?"

"What? The creature with Tomás? I told you already."

She rephrased the question. "No, I'm sorry. I mean . . . there's always a shape to these things, some kind of pattern. What's the center of it? What's the thread that ties it all together?"

Before I could stop myself, I said the only thing that made any sense to me. "Fire."

"The one at the Calliope?"

"Fire in general." I looked back and forth and realized we were loud enough and other people were close enough to overhear us. "Walk with me, please? We can go sit on the hotel porch. Let's get out of this crowd."

She followed me, then drew up alongside me. I was walking at a pretty good clip. "What do you mean?"

I didn't answer until we'd taken up chairs and pulled them into a corner, away from the gaslight fixture that otherwise lit the porch and the double front doors. I leaned forward and said softly, "It isn't *just* the Calliope. I found a little fire in my room just the other day. I didn't start it—I woke up to it. It was nothing serious, except that it happened spontaneously—in my washroom sink."

"Good heavens . . . ," she said. I'd expected her to exclaim something about "Spirit," but I was disappointed. I was still figuring out how to use the expression.

"And then there's my friend Tomás—"

"Who you just met today."

"We've exchanged *letters*." I did not exactly tell the truth. It was close enough to the truth, and I didn't care if she knew I was standing on the cusp of lying. "In those letters I learned that he had also been"—I fibbed again—"experiencing fires. Small ones, and larger ones, too."

"But what does that have to do with you fainting last week?"

"I fainted because I saw something terrible and hot. It was a suffocating kind of heat," I tried to explain. "You remember how I tried to get someone's attention? Someone who wouldn't answer me? There was a spirit, and I thought it couldn't hear me. Then it did, and it answered me when I asked it a question. But it was too far away to do much more than scare me, because it was still with Tomás, in Ybor City."

"And now it's here." She didn't ask it as a question. She didn't have any more questions for me at all. "That's what you saw in the open reading. What did you ask it? What did it say?"

I told her the same thing I'd told Mabel and Dolores, how it'd called itself the hammer. "That's all it said. Honestly, I'm glad. I don't think I could have stood its presence much longer." Then I practically whispered, "Please, Dr. Floyd—Tomás wouldn't hurt anybody. He's gentle and kind, and he's afraid. We can't just send him away. Like Mr. Colby told me, if we can't do some good in the world, then we don't deserve to be here."

"I wouldn't dream of sending him away, but we have to contain this problem before someone else gets hurt. You could've been hurt. David could've been . . ." She wanted to say "killed." I know she did. I did, too, but he was on the way to the hospital and neither one of us wanted to jinx it. So she said, "Even more seriously hurt."

That was as close as she could come to admitting he might live or die, and nobody knew which.

I cleared my throat. "Lately I've been told there are . . . certain protections on this side of the tracks." I tried to keep any note of accusation out of my voice, even though I really felt like someone should've told me sooner—and I shouldn't have had to hear it from Dolores and Imogene.

"That's true, but those protections are only . . ." She bobbed her head back and forth, considering how to phrase it for me. "Well, they're more than superstition, but their usefulness is uncertain. In this case, it would seem that they're not strong enough to keep the church—or anyone in it—safe from whatever it is you saw."

"So what's the point in having them?"

"These days? I'm honestly not sure." She hesitated. "Many years ago, Mr. Colby was friends with a woman who joined the camp from eastern Kentucky. She practiced what some would call root magic, or conjure magic. Now, strictly speaking, spiritualists don't believe in magic. But we do believe in spirits and their influence, and we are prepared to accept that one man's ghost is another man's divine guide. Do you understand what I mean?"

"Just because you don't understand it, that doesn't mean it doesn't work."

She looked briefly relieved. "Correct. As much as anything, we considered the woman's efforts a case of 'can't hurt, might help.'"

"Is she still here?"

"Oh no, she crossed over ages ago—and I don't think anyone's heard from her since. Her name was Agatha Bloom. She used to travel with Mr. Colby as a secretary of sorts."

"So you don't know what she did or how she did it?" I pressed.

Drolly, Dr. Floyd said, "All we know for certain is that it didn't work." She might've said more, but a man I didn't know approached us begging our pardons, asking if Dr. Floyd could come and speak with the police—who had apparently arrived while no one was looking.

"Absolutely, I'd be happy to. Could you give me one moment, please?"

He agreed and said they'd be down at the pavilion, if she'd care to join them.

"The police?" I whispered nervously.

"They're only doing their jobs, I'm sure. They've probably come out of curiosity, or concern. This is the second time they've been summoned in as many days."

"Second time?"

"They came about the fire, remember? Cassadaga is beginning to look like a perilous place." She sat across from me, wearing a thoughtful expression and not quite looking at me so much as past me. Eventually she said, "I want to do a bit of research tonight and see what I can turn up. I'll ask my brother if he has any thoughts. I want you to do the same."

"Talk to your dead brother?" I said before I had time to soften my response.

She didn't mind, or if she did, she didn't show it. "Use whichever paths or methods work best for you, but find a way to talk to the spirits—though you must be careful which ones you listen to. They're as bad *and* as good as living people. Some will be helpful; some will not."

"I'm still learning how to tell the difference."

"Learn faster," she said, and it sounded like a warning. She rose to her feet and smoothed her skirt. "We'll talk again tomorrow."

She left me there alone, and I stayed long enough to watch the ambulance leave with David in it (and maybe his father, too). I wondered where his mother was, if she was alive or if she'd "crossed over." I'd never heard anyone mention her.

It was getting late. Not terribly late, but late enough that there wasn't anything to do except consider heading to Candy's, decide against it, hit up the hotel restaurant instead, and go to my room after I'd finished eating. I walked past Tomás's room on the way. I paused outside the door but didn't hear anything—and then I felt guilty for standing there, eavesdropping, so I hustled back to my own temporary residence.

I let myself inside, closed the door, and leaned back against it.

I sniffed the air. Nothing but the smell of the soap I'd used in the bath, and the perfume I'd left on the dresser (lilac and orange blossoms). No sign of smoke.

I remembered Tomás asking me if I smelled it, when there was nothing to smell. Was it just him? Was it just the thing that followed him?

THERE was nothing untoward to whiff in my room; of that I was reasonably sure. I locked the door behind me, turning the deadbolt wheel and drawing the chain for no real reason except that I was anxious on principle.

Something was terribly wrong in Cassadaga, and now I was not the only one who knew it.

I thought about stripping down and changing my bandage immediately, for my arm was smarting something awful; but then I remembered I still had some bourbon in my trunk, and I figured I might as well take advantage of it. I pulled the top and took a big swallow, right out of the bottle. Removing the bandage still hurt, despite my medicinal efforts. Applying the ointment hurt, too. Wrapping it up again hurt, as well. Everything hurt. But I had bourbon, so I drank some more of it.

Couldn't hurt. Might help.

The bandages stuck to the burn, and my miserable skin screamed when I pulled them off. Another swallow. I put the bottle down on the back of the sink. Another swallow, another tug, and finally my whole arm was exposed to the air. One-handed I managed the ointment jar, and one-handed I rewrapped myself like an Egyptian mummy. Another swallow. I brought the bottle with me and swirled its contents to measure them. Maybe a third was left. It was enough for one very good night's sleep, burn or no burn.

A third of a bottle and I could sleep through anything, even the searing pain of a drizzled burn that looked for all the world like a devil's initials, if his name started with an "H" and ended with a "K."

I changed into my nightdress and sat down cross-legged on my bed. I tried to think.

I had a pack of cards and some candles. Spirit(s) like warm light. (And some of them like fire.) I dragged myself off the bed again, pulled out the tapers I'd bought from the bookstore, and set them around the room. (I lit them up; I struck matches and melted enough to seal their bottoms onto coasters and plates, so they would not fall over.) I fished my cards out of my trunk, and I got back onto the bed, sitting cross-legged once more.

I took one more swallow—a smallish swallow. I had markedly less than a third of the bottle to keep me company.

I breathed deep to a count of ten, and cleared my mind as best I could. I am not good at clearing my mind, but Dolores Brigham has been helping me learn how to do it with careful breathing and meditation, so I got my mind about as clear as it was going to get. (Clearish, except for the pain, and the warm buzz of the bourbon. I know spiritualists are supposed to be teetotalers but I think that's silly. I think the bourbon helps. It definitely doesn't hurt.)

I took another long, shuddering breath and went to a ten-count one more time.

That was better. In with the coolness and calm, out with the jitters and nervousness.

The gaslamps were off, and I had nothing but the candles to set a mood.

I'd never tried to reach any specific spirit before. Usually, they come to me as they like—and none of them have ever come to share a message with me personally. In my experience, all they want is to pass along a word to someone else.

Dr. Floyd and Mabel had asked me if I'd ever sought out a spirit guide, and I'd told them no. Until I came to Cassadaga, I didn't know there was any such thing. Now, since studying here, I've gotten the impression that they're like guardian angels, and you either have one or you don't. I don't think you can just recruit one and demand its assistance.

But maybe if I just asked somebody to come on in, sit down, and have a word—with no commitment implied—I might have more luck. It was worth a try.

"Andrew Floyd," I said on my next exhalation. I thought he was as good a guide as any, and I knew that he sometimes spoke to his sister. Maybe he could lend me his ears, too. Or whatever spirits have instead of ears.

One of the candles flickered, but that might've only been a draft. I said the name again, closed my eyes again, and counted to ten again. Nothing.

Another name sprang to mind. "Agatha Bloom. How about you? You tried to protect the town. Can you help me protect it now?"

I heard a flutter of wind, and it startled me enough that I blinked my eyes open and saw my candles flutter, their flames rattling around on their wicks. The room got colder with every count. To ten. Until I could see my breath. I watched it swirl and billow like the smoke inside the Calliope. I watched the soft whiteness of it spinning and twisting, and I tried to stay calm.

"Agatha? They tell me you worked root magic." A breeze blustered against my face. It felt like it came from an icebox. "I'm not sure what root magic is, but I have an idea. I hear you were from Kentucky, and I'm not—but I'm from Virginia and I know what granny magic is. If that's what Dr. Floyd meant."

With the next breeze came a laugh, light and almost childish. It was not what I'd expected from a granny worker who traveled with a spiritualist for years. I looked left and right and watched my breath spin silk in the air.

"Hello?"

*Granny magic indeed, you sweet summer child.*

Every frosty exhale gave her a little more shape, a firmer outline, a few inches from my face. I sucked in deep and breathed out slow— giving her as much frost to work with as she felt like using. She gave me the impression of a young woman . . . or I guess that's how she felt, once she crossed over. I liked her style. If I'm ever as old as the hills and I show up as a ghost, I plan to look as young and lovely as I am right now, goddammit.

"Agatha? Is that you?"

*Truly and fully, with none other along for the ride.*

"Thank God. Spirit. Sorry. I'm still learning, but I have to ask, because you set up protections around the camp: What were they? How did they work? How can we make them stronger?"

*Oh dear, no. Those were just little charms, honey. That's all. I put them into the ground in threes.*

"What kind of little charms?"

*Bottles for good neighbors, planted at the boundaries.* Her mouth moved with my mouth, and she breathed back into me as she spoke. *Five-finger grass for keepin' out no-goods and protecting travelers. Horehound to shoo the beasts away. A little salt to seal it up, but not too much. That kind of thing.*

"Is that all?"

She nodded, and the frozen mist moved around her. *Most of the charms I know—the ones what passed down—they protect against haints and haunts. But I couldn't use those, now, could I? What if they worked?* I sensed her smile more than I could see it. I heard her girlish little laugh, though I could hardly see her lips move. The lips were all for show, I think. She did it for me, so I'd have something to look at.

I smiled shakily back. "What would I do, Miss Bloom, if I needed to protect the camp from something worse than bad? There's a very bad spirit, and it calls itself—"

She made a sharp shushing noise to cut me off. *No, don't say it. That's not his name.*

Her delicate form went loose. I could hardly make her out in the cloud I breathed over my bed. My room was so cold, my arms and legs were covered in goose bumps, mostly from the chill. But partly because Agatha was frankly a tad scary. I'm not sure I can explain why.

*Oh, darling dear. He's already inside. Good salt might bind him, but only for a minute. Not even lye would hold him out now.*

"I don't understand."

*Talk to George.*

"Warn him about . . . the spirit? The hammer?"

She made a face, and it wasn't happy. I shouldn't have called him that, but she didn't shush me a second time. All she said was, *Everyone has to go. Everyone has to get out.*

"Everyone?"

*All of you, yes. For Jesus's sake, get out before you burn. Before everything does.*

# TOMÁS CORDERO

Cassadaga, Florida

I WENT BACK to my room last night, disappointed and disheartened, with Felipe under my arm to keep me company. I do not know how I lived so long without a dog. Left to my own devices, I might have chosen a larger dog, or a different breed under different circumstances, in a different life—but this strange and shattered little thing is perfect, and I already love him beyond reason.

No wonder Mrs. Vasquez adored him so.

I split the last of the meat and cheese between us, and I sat on the bed with some of the pamphlets I'd received from the woman at the bookshop. I read through them all and forgot every word as soon as I put them down. I contemplated the book of matches in my pocket, and I wondered if the pamphlets would say anything should I burn them. But they were not important to me, or to Evelyn, either. I doubted they would produce results of any kind.

Then again, I also had a little book—a treatise on faith healing that had sounded like a good idea very suddenly, as I'd stood in the shop across from the hotel. I'd bought it on a whim, and I could burn it on a whim just as easily.

Felipe fixed at me with a disapproving glare, as if he knew exactly what I had in mind.

"It's safe here," I told him as I gathered up the book and my matches and retreated to the washroom. "It's safe, but they don't believe me when I tell them it's Evelyn trying to speak. You didn't know Evelyn," I said over my shoulder. The tub was iron, like the one I had at home. It was dry, because I hadn't used it that day. I threw everything inside it.

Behind me, I heard the soft patter of tiny feet. Felipe had followed, but he would not enter the washroom proper. He sat down right before the doorway and watched.

"I wish you could've met her before she died." I held up the matchbox and one phosphorous-tipped stick. "She would have loved you. You would have loved her, too."

I struck the match, dropped it, and let the paper curl, and blacken, and spark.

While it burned, I walked around the bathtub and opened the small window beside it to let the smoke out. I did not want the smell to fill the hall and alarm anyone. I did not want Alice Dartle to catch a hint of it and break down the door.

ALICE means well. I *know* she means well.

I believe that if I can make her understand, she will be able to help us. Evelyn needs help communicating with me, and she must have something deeply important to say—for she has gone to all this trouble. She needs a medium. Alice is just such a medium. I don't know why she is so afraid. All I am asking is for her to perform her job, a job she advertised in a magazine. In a roundabout fashion. She should not be afraid.

I am not afraid. Not anymore.

Or . . . I am not afraid of the same *things* as I was before. Now I am afraid that no one will believe me when I try to explain that it is only my wife and not some holy terror. Any oversized sense of darkness, fire, or a masculine presence these sensitive folks in Cassadaga may sense around me . . . it's only the war. It's only the charred, melted baggage that I brought back with me. At worst, they sense perhaps a faint and lonely soldier or two, rendered ghostly by the great Livens machine. Maybe that.

Nothing darker, or worse. Nothing I can't live with. Nothing I didn't create myself.

So why did I long for reassurance?

I know my wife's face, her hands, and her script. I watched the paper burn in the bathtub and I asked aloud, very softly, so no one in the next room (or outside) might hear me: "Have I done the right thing? Have I come to the right place, my love?"

The first edge of the flame ran out of fuel and fizzled out. The rest was shortly behind it, though the book smoldered a minute longer.

I got down on my knees, leaned over, and blew gently on the ashes to scatter them—and see what might be left behind. Of course, she did not disappoint me. She never did. She never could. There in the ashes I saw two little letters, in that familiar handwriting.

*Sí.*

*Sí,* I replied, a promise and a prayer. *Sí,* of course. *Sí.*

## ALICE DARTLE

Cassadaga, Florida

SOMETHING IS TERRIBLY wrong in Cassadaga, and growing wronger by the day.

By the hour, even. I am at a loss. I am grieving.

I am confused and afraid. By everything. Of everything.

As hard as I tried to obey Agatha Bloom and visit Mr. Colby, he was resting under Dr. Holligoss's care and I was denied entrance. I considered making a fuss, but I settled instead for passing along the message that I'd spoken to Agatha and that she wanted me to speak to him. The doctor promised to share it when the old man awakened.

"I really think it's quite urgent," I tried one last time.

He lowered his voice and replied, "So is Mr. Colby's condition, Miss Dartle. He's had a spell, and now he's resting. I'm sure he'll be glad to know that you came by, and intrigued by the thought that you've spoken to Agatha. She doesn't talk to just anyone."

"But she did. She spoke to me. She said it was critical—that we're all in danger, and we should pack up and go. She says that the awful spirit can't be kept out!"

"Forgive me, Miss Dartle, but we know this much already. Dr. Floyd and Mr. Colby spoke earlier, and she told him she had an idea—but she needed some time to research. Between us, Mr. Colby left that meeting looking quite pale and weak, and when he became light-headed I was frankly afraid. He is upset and he's been put to bed. While he sleeps, the rest of us are rousing the rest of the . . . of the council members, or elders, or whatever you'd like to call us."

"And then what?"

"Then . . ." His expression was set and determined, if not altogether confident. "I strongly suspect that we will choose not to run. We will figure out a way to fight instead. So unless Agatha gave you any hints or suggestions, there's little of her message that cannot wait. Go back to the hotel, Alice." He sounded so weary when he called me by my first name. He made me feel weary in return. "Take some food, have a nip of whatever you've brought, and try to get some rest."

I did my best to obey. I didn't feel like eating, but boy, did I feel like nipping. I finished the rest of my bottle and fell into bed.

I dreamed of fire.

SHORTLY before dawn I woke up smelling smoke, and as if I was already prepared for this eventuality, I threw myself out of bed. I wasn't at all alert; I didn't even feel the sting of my burned arm ripping free of the sheets. Not then. I had my feet on the floor before I had any real chance to take stock of my surroundings.

My heart pounded. Shaking, I crammed my feet into my slippers.

The lights were off, but the window was open to let the cooler night air inside, and on the far side of the nearest hill, dawn was brightening the sky to a shade of lavender touched with pink.

"Where is it?" I asked, not that there was anyone present to answer me. "What's going on?" I continued, in case Agatha Bloom or anybody else was hanging around and felt like being helpful. Nobody was. Nobody did.

I pressed the switch to turn on the light, then turned in a circle—looking at every corner and sniffing with my nose in the air like Felipe does upon catching wind of a sausage. The smoke was not close. Not in my room. It was somewhere outside, I was sure, blowing in with the rising warmth of the morning sun.

I checked the washroom to be safe, and it was safe enough to make me feel silly. No smoldering ruins in the sink. No awful ashes in the tub. The fire was nowhere near me, and I was secure.

Not everyone was so lucky.

I went to the window and hung my head out, looking over the little town and still trying to pinpoint that smell. Yes, it was riding on the breeze. Yes, it was coming from outside. Yes, something out there was on fire.

"Fire!" shouted someone below. "Fire! Help, there's a fire!"

It wasn't just me. I couldn't decide if I was relieved to be vindicated or appalled to be correct. I didn't know where the danger might be, but I hollered out the window, "Call the firemen! Somebody call the firemen!"

The cry was taken up in short order, and Cassadaga rallied to answer it. People came bursting from the hotel, from Harmony Hall, and from the Brigham house—where I knew that several people were boarding besides the Brighams themselves. People poured out of every door, trailing onto the sidewalks and into the street without knowing where to look.

I hollered down, "Where is it?" in case anyone could answer me.

Was it the hotel itself? How was I to tell? If I could not see the fire, it could be anywhere. It could be right under my feet.

A fire bell began to ring, and between that clanging noise and the men running to and fro with buckets, everybody understood right away that there was great peril and that everyone needed to move. Never mind the hour. Never mind the uncertainty.

Never mind that my eyes were still full of dream grit. Never mind how useless I would be in case of an emergency—I could not stand there in the relative safety of my room (still assuming that this blaze was not in some distant wing of the hotel itself) and let the town go down in ashes without making some kind of effort in its favor.

I grabbed my housecoat, my small travel purse (it had my money in it), and my carpetbag (it had some clothes in it). Then I flung myself into the hotel hallway armed with these necessities (in case I was wrong, and it *was* the hotel ablaze).

I didn't see or smell any smoke in the corridor, but maybe it hadn't reached the second floor yet. People were running past me, heading outside through the stairs at one end, which led to the lobby, and the stairs at the other end, leading to the porch. I started to run, too— then I thought of Tomás and Felipe, and I doubled back to their room, temporarily abandoning the nearest route of escape.

I pounded on the door and it opened on my third round of knocking.

Tomás stood there on the far side of the door, wild-eyed, his hair askew and his pants rumpled. I'd caught him in the process of hastily dressing. Felipe barked when he saw me and ran to my ankles, darting in a figure eight around and between our feet. "There's a fire!" Tomás said, with the sudden alertness of someone who's been yanked from sleep. Lord help me, I knew the feeling.

"That's what I'm trying to tell you!"

"Is it here? In the hotel?"

"I don't know!" I replied, but someone dashing past us answered more precisely.

It was a man, and he said over his shoulder as he ran, "No—it's on the next street over! A house is on fire!" Whoever he was, he was gone in a moment, his footsteps thundering down the steps and out into the night.

"Whose house?" I asked, as if Tomás would have the faintest idea. I was supposed to be the clairvoyant one. If anybody ought to randomly know whose house was on fire, it ought to be me. But I didn't. So I asked my customary stupid question instead.

"I . . . I . . ."

"Stay here," I commanded. I'm not sure why. Because I wanted him out of harm's way? Because I didn't want Felipe underfoot? Because I feared the pair of them might exacerbate the problem? Tomás might make things worse, or the darkly shadowed thing that kept him company might do it for him. I was already half afraid that his monstrous companion had something to do with the newest fire, but I couldn't say that out loud. I couldn't accuse him. There was no *reason* to accuse him. None of this was his fault.

(I looked for the smoldering man, but I did not see it standing behind him. I didn't know if that was good or bad. It may have let him alone at last. It may have gone wandering, starting fires outside his immediate vicinity. Its absence might be a boon, or it might not mean anything at all.)

"I will absolutely not stay here." He was already wearing shoes— real shoes, not slippers—though one was only half tied. He used his foot to nudge Felipe inside the room, and then he shut the door to keep him there. "I'm coming with you."

I wasn't accustomed to running around in a nightdress and a housecoat, much less to running in slippers that kept sliding loosely on my toes, but I tripped down the main staircase anyway—into the lobby, out to the porch, and down the steps, with Tomás staying close in my wake.

Out on the sidewalk, people ran past us, and toward us, and in front of us. They were shouting and crying; someone new was screaming to call the firemen—and I had the hysterical thought that the department in DeLand ought to just leave a truck parked by the front gates to save time in the future. We might as well keep one at the ready.

I looked up and down the road but still didn't see the blaze. Oh, but I could smell it. It was the scent of war and death, and summer in hell. The ashy soot overpowered the tropical flowers. It dimmed the gaslamps along the streets and left everything looking foggy.

I squinted, stared, and found it.

It was farther down on Stevens Street, not the next street over, but at least it was not the hotel. At least little Felipe was safe, shut up in Tomás's room. There were so many false rumors, and there was so much uncertainty—but I was certain that I could see the fire now, flames licking high past a roof, and pearl gray smoke wafting out the topmost windows.

"Oh God," I said, once again having completely forgotten to mention Spirit.

I broke into a run, my slippers flopping, sliding, and almost going flying with every step.

One by one the streetlights popped off, in almost perfect time as I passed them—or as Tomás passed them, for he was hot on my heels. One of us had some terrible timing, or perfect timing. I don't know which.

The sun was coming up, and Dr. Floyd's house was coming down. It was only a block or two away, and it was all downhill, but my lungs were screaming from trying to run in the sand and keep my slippers on at the same time and still make it to the good pastor's front yard.

A bucket brigade was doing its damnedest, since Spirit Lake was only a few dozen yards away. One by one the buckets were passed from person to person, to the last man up front—who threw the little splash of water into the flames, through one of the front windows. They would've made about the same headway if they were using coffee cups.

"Where's Dr. Floyd?" I asked anyone, everyone. "Has anyone seen her?"

Behind me, someone sobbed, "She's still inside! Somebody help her!"

But how? Who would go willingly? No one in their right mind. Where were the firemen? Not here yet, for the drive from DeLand took a few minutes more.

When I turned around, I had another question—one that shook me almost as much as all the others: *Where was Tomás?* He'd been right behind me, following in my footsteps as the streetlights had popped off, one-two-three. He'd been almost beside me by the time we reached Stevens Street, and now he was nowhere to be seen. I scanned the bucket line, wondering if he'd joined while I wasn't looking. I looked around the crowd, from face to face. I saw the helpless, the horrified, and the lost.

He wasn't there with them, either.

Oh God.

# 20

# TOMÁS CORDERO

Cassadaga, Florida

A FIRE BELL began to ring. It was the one at Harmony Hall, I think.

I am not afraid of fire anymore. I have commanded it and been commanded by it. I have killed with it and nearly died from it. It holds no more horror for me.

It held no more terror when I stared at that house in flames. I thought of the battlefield, yes. I thought of the flame projector, of course. I remembered the screams and the headaches and the incessant percussion of artillery.

But this excess of memory—this compression of my own time and history, taking up too much space in my brain—it could not control me, not now. Not anymore.

It certainly could not stop me, not when I saw the two-story house on Stevens Street.

By the time Alice and I arrived, the house was a funeral pyre with windows broken and curtains flaming. Someone was inside—a doctor, they said. A woman, I heard. The minister, I gathered. Could anyone still be alive in there? Everyone wondered, except for me. I knew it was possible, just as I knew it was not very likely. But yes, anything was possible. Fire is strange, and it moves in strange ways—carving out pockets of hot air between the walls of flame and the clouds of smoke.

It happens. Not often, but it happens. Everyone who'd come out to look . . . every man and woman with hands on mouths in disbelief . . . every child, gazing wide-eyed in astonishment . . . every single person in Cassadaga, was clinging to that very slim hope.

I did not search the scene for a qualified fireman. If one had been present, I would've heard the trucks. More bells would've been ringing over the sound of the house coming down. The trucks would've been rumbling.

I was the nearest thing to a fireman for at least a mile. My credentials were slim, but they were better than no credentials at all.

A woman standing on the other side of Alice had wrapped herself in a blanket, for modesty or warmth. "Pardon me, ma'am?" I said to her. I did not wait for an answer. I swept the blanket off her shoulders and threw it over my head. It was rude, but it was necessary. It might allow me to save their beloved minister. Or it might not, but what could I do except try?

Now protected, however slightly . . . into the house I ran.

The front door was already open. It might have blasted open from the heat, or some more timid soul might have tried it and found the path too perilous to proceed.

I was not timid. I was a soldier. I was not afraid of fire.

Alice screamed. I know it was Alice. She has a powerful voice that carries easily and cuts through a crowd like a sword. She was screaming at me, or for me. She was calling my name again and again, furious and fearful—but she would not follow me. She *could* not follow me; two women had seized her and were holding her restrained while she struggled against them and still screamed, still called.

That's all I gleaned from a single backward glance. After a moment, I could not hear her.

In another moment more, I was inside the house, inside the fire.

It crawled along the walls and pooled on the ceiling, so the house was not long for the world and no number of ready and loaded fire trucks could save it now, even if they arrived in the blink of an eye. The heat was intense, but I had felt such heat before. The air was thick, but I kept myself low. The darkness was profound, but I have spent much time in darkness, and I could work past it.

"Doctor?" I cried out, and heard nothing in reply. I said it again, as loud as I could—for all that the crackling flames and the groaning, failing structure were as noisy as hell around me. I could hardly hear myself. I tried again anyway, a third time.

The third time is always the charm—isn't that what they say?

I got a response, but not the one I expected. I'd expected a cough or a plea for help, something living but dying, calling out with dwindling breath. I was wrong on all possible counts.

*Este camino.*

Two words. A woman's voice, but not the voice of the minister. I knew, because I knew the voice. I recognized the woman from two words, breathed so sweetly through the flames.

"Evelyn, *ayúdame . . .*"

*Por aquí.*

There was a corridor, a dining room—a very long table filled most of it. Beyond, a library. The shelves were an inferno; the books were burning and dead. On the floor was a body, a woman. Burned and not quite dead. Her foot twitched when I touched her. Her eyes fluttered when I rolled her over. Her lips moved when I picked her up and slung the blanket over both of us, and in a crouch I dragged us both back through the dining room while the cinders fell and burned holes in the blanket, holes in my shirt. An ember burned through the back of one pant leg, and it surprised me—I teetered and nearly dropped the woman, but I recovered and I held her firmly.

Back down the corridor and to the parlor I carried her in a crouch; I held her as low as I was able, so that one of us might breathe, at least. If she was still breathing at all. If she was even alive.

We missed a collapsing corner of the ceiling by the breadth of a hair. A fresh blast of heat bloomed up in its wake, searing my shoulder and the back of my neck. I felt the skin of my right ear boiling against my scalp. I smelled the ash of my own hair.

The door was just ahead.

It was a black hole with glimmering lights on the other side—the light of the rising sun, and the light of lanterns, and lights coming on in nearby windows. It all swirled as my vision swam from the heat and exhaustion, from the thick and poisoned air. It was a universe of constellations spinning, framed in that narrow rectangle.

I reached it, hauling the woman in a graceless, staggering hold. I was hurting her. I hoped I was hurting her—it would mean she was still alive, even now, and I was not bringing her out a corpse.

Out the door we tumbled together as the whole house creaked and strained, and finally I quit stealing air from the space near the floor—where it was only as hot as an oven, but not ruined with the smoke of burning wood and books and flesh. The air on the other side reeked of smoke, and my own seared skin, and the ends of my hair that were burned away, but it was clean enough to make me gasp and suck it down.

I was saved from drowning.

I was tiring from the heat and aching from the burden.

I stumbled down the short porch steps, and a man caught me—while another man caught the doctor as she fell from my grasp. Another blanket was tossed over my head, and I felt a dozen pairs of hands patting away, snuffing out all the little sparks I'd brought along with me.

The woman was pulled in one direction and I was pulled in another, but when I extricated myself from the blankets I saw her laid out in the middle of the sandy street—away from the house, which would surely come down at any moment. The bucket brigade had surrendered to the inevitable, and now those townspeople who were not attending the doctor were watching her home go up in smoke.

Alice was at her side. (I did not know the woman's name. I only knew her titles.) I joined my friend, staggering and breathing too hard, clutching my chest, still catching up on all the air I'd lost when I'd gone inside.

"Tomás!" she said to me. She did not look at me. She could not take her eyes off the woman on the ground, with her hair burned mostly away, and her hands cooked down to the stringy red and black sinews and bone. "Tomás, you went inside!"

"I am not afraid of fire." I wheezed. I coughed. I bent over and let my head hang while I caught my breath. I would catch my breath. I would throw these clothes away and wear new ones. My hair would grow back and my ear would heal.

This was all the silver lining that I could muster in my exhaustion and pain—for it had been for nothing. I am not afraid of fire, but I know what it can do. I know what it *does*. I had not rescued a corpse, only by moments. Well, she could pass in peace, in the cool sand of the street where the sun hadn't baked it yet. She could die among friends instead of among flames.

She was not gone yet, but she would leave us soon. Her eyelashes were lost, and her clothes were scorched tatters, but she lived long enough to gaze right at me, and right past me. Her chapped, blistered lips moved, and Alice leaned close. "Dr. Floyd, you hold on. You rest up, and the ambulance is on the way."

The woman spoke, a cracked, jagged sound like wind over coals. "It isn't *her* . . . ," she said, and she said it to *me*. Her head rolled to the side, so she could see Alice. "It's him. He's here. He's free."

Her eyes did not close. They only went blank.

She stopped breathing, and no one dared to push on her chest like they did for David. No one imagined for a moment that it would help. Her skin would slide off in their hands. Her ribs would snap like sticks. She was gone.

Alice exploded into tears. I tried to comfort her but she pulled away from me—she pulled away from everyone and stumbled off toward the hotel. Then she changed her mind and went off in another direction, crying into the sleeve of her housecoat all the way. I watched her stumble, tripping over shoes that weren't meant to see the outside. She caught herself, found the sidewalk to the hotel, and disappeared around the corner. I assumed she went inside.

She was safe. Then all was not lost.

I looked to the burning house and watched as the roof fell inward, sending up a great shower of sparks and ash. People on the sidewalk gasped. The flames were very bright against the dim sky, going from navy blue to something lighter. The fire made everything gold and black, all blinding light and absolute shadow. The southern wall toppled to the ground and flames went shooting out from that side, too. The front porch awning dropped and fell to burning pieces.

The fire bell across the way had stopped ringing, but it began again as the truck arrived, both of them present in time to do nothing of any real value. No other houses were close enough to be threatened, and there was nothing left inside to be saved—human or otherwise.

I looked back at the woman I'd pulled from the house. One of the ash-stained blankets had been draped lovingly across her face and torso. A weeping woman tugged the hem down to cover the victim's gruesome hands, which had curled up toward her chest like fists anticipating a fight. I knew that stance. I'd seen it happen before, on soldiers who'd been doused in fire—or those who had simply come too close to it. They call that petrified pose a "pugilist's stance," after the way a boxer holds himself in the ring.

\* \* \*

To think, I used to enjoy watching the occasional fight. Now all I can see is the curled-up wrists and balled-up hands, held close up against chests. It doesn't matter that it's a defensive pose one way and a death pose another.

Everything contracts away from the flames. *Everything.* That's all I see anymore.

My eyes were stinging. I had nothing clean to wipe them with, so I didn't. I knew better. I only blinked, and only wiped my nose with the back of my dilapidated sleeve. I left behind a smudge of charcoal and snot on the Egyptian cotton, but it was ruined anyway. No laundering would save it, not in a thousand years.

"It isn't her," I repeated the woman's last words. Some of them. I turned them over in my head. I knew what she meant, but she was wrong, of course. It *was* Evelyn's voice I heard in the burning house, guiding me to Dr. Floyd. (That's what Alice had called her.) It *was* Evelyn answering my questions in the charred books that I still needed to clean out of the hotel bathtub. It *was* Evelyn, bringing brimstone to Cassadaga.

No. That wasn't right.

Maybe that's what the doctor meant: It isn't *her*; it isn't *Evelyn* setting all these fires in Florida.

Yes, that must have been what she intended. There must be some-one else setting these terrible fires. Something else. But not—and *never*—my Evelyn.

It was a great relief to reach this conclusion, even as I watched the last walls of the dead woman's house tumble into the center, bringing the second story with them. Evelyn was with me, and these fires were not her doing (not that I ever honestly thought they might be). My kind, gentle, beautiful wife would never harm another soul. She would help, yes—she would guide me through the inferno, for the chance to save another. She would lend me her advice and her aid.

Beside me, a woman asked loudly, "What on earth is *wrong* with you?" It was Imogene, whom Alice does not much care for. I turned to face her and see what she wanted. Was she talking to me? "Yes, I'm talking to you."

Flustered, tired, and mildly injured, I replied, "I only wished to help. I am not afraid of fire."

"You're an idiot, but that isn't what I meant. You're smiling. You're standing there, watching the house fall down into ashes, and you're just . . . you're *smiling*." Disgusted with me, she glared and hugged herself, rubbing her arms against the faint chill of early morning.

"I am thinking of happier times," I said. I did not need to explain myself, but I supposed it did look strange. I wiped the smile from my face and hoped I now appeared serious enough for her satisfaction— and everyone else's. "I was remembering my wife."

"Did she die in a fire or something?"

"No," I told the insufferably blunt woman. "She died of the flu, but I heard her, just now. Inside the house, she spoke to me. She told me where to find the doctor." I could not prevent a glance at the blanketed form in the unpaved street. "She told me what to do."

Imogene frowned, but she always frowns, I think. She narrowed her eyes and looked past me, over my shoulder.

"I'm sorry, what are you looking at?" I asked, since bluntness may call for bluntness.

"Nothing. That's the strange part. Every time I've seen you," she began. She stopped and lowered her voice. "Every time I've seen you, there's been a . . . a big, dark cloud, casting a shadow from behind you."

"Nothing is behind me, madam."

"That's what I'm trying to tell you: Whatever it is, you've lost it.

I'm not sure which is more frightening, really—the thought that you had it in the first place, or the thought that it's wandered off alone." She shook her head and rubbed at her arms more vigorously, despite the radiant heat from the doctor's house. It warmed everything, even this far away. Still she rubbed and rubbed. "I don't like it, either way."

"I . . . I'm not sure what I should say in response to that."

Her frown hardened. It became a frown of fear. "It used you."

"I have no idea what you're talking about."

She backed away from me, still clutching herself and shaking her head. "It *used* you," she said again, with emphasis. "Now it's *free*." Then she turned her back and ran—fumbling awkwardly through the sandy thoroughfare in stocking feet, as far and fast away from me as she could get.

## ALICE DARTLE

### Cassadaga, Florida

I went to the hotel, but I did not go inside. I changed my mind on the front steps, before I reached the porch. I turned around, seeking some course of action apart from "run away and hide."

But I wasn't thinking straight. I was breathless, crying so hard that I couldn't see.

I couldn't imagine it—I couldn't understand it or make any sense of it! How could Dr. Floyd be dead? She was practically the heart and soul of Cassadaga! Or . . . she was *one* of the hearts and souls, if a place can have more than one. There's Mr. Colby, of course, but he is elderly and infirm, and he might have founded the place but he could no longer lead it.

Dr. Floyd was a leader, the very sort that the town so desperately needs. Dr. Floyd was a leader, and so is Oscar Fine, who was probably at the hospital with his son—or he might've been. I didn't see him anywhere. I just hoped and prayed he hadn't been inside the pastor's house, now crashing into coals and ashes on Stevens Street.

Who was left? Cassadaga was running low on figureheads. Dolores Brigham was respected, but not terribly keen on taking charge, so far as I could tell. Mabel was too quietly guarded and fragile to assume such a role. Dr. Holligoss? In a pinch, I supposed.

I stopped staggering around blindly for a moment, for in considering Dr. Holligoss, I remembered what Agatha Bloom had told me: *Talk to George.*

But I'd already tried, and the doctor had rebuffed me. Well, now the doctor was busy with other business, and maybe Mr. Colby was awake and ready to hear the concerns of his former secretary. I sure hoped so. I hoped, and I thought, and I prayed for anything at all to hold in my mind—anything but Dr. J. A. Floyd. Her skin seared and split, her hair burned away, and her eyes red, bulging, with no lashes or brows. Her skin pink and stretched. Below the skin, all the rest exposed. Red and wet. Her hands, held up like a fighter ready to throw a punch, or block one.

I shook my head and held my hands over my ears, not that it did anything. It hardly muffled the clanging bell or the shouts of the campground members. It did not keep the waves of heat from washing over me. I felt them all the way down the street when the walls fell in and the roof fell down, sending sparks and outrageous warmth pulsing across the road.

The sun was coming up, and I did not give a damn. The sun couldn't tell me anything. Dr. Floyd was dead and I was going to scream or vomit, or maybe both. But I couldn't just stand there with my hands over my ears. I had to do something productive, something useful. I had to do something good and helpful. If I couldn't do any good, then I didn't deserve to be there.

I had to try one more time to warn George Colby, wherever he was. It was the only instruction I'd received, and delivering this message was the one task I clung to in the midst of this awful dawn. Maybe I didn't really expect him to tell the town to pack it in; maybe

I only wanted to see him, to hear his voice and know that he was alive.

I needed to see him. I needed to know that there was something left, someone left. Somebody in charge, standing between us and the flames.

The sun was rising and nobody cared. It was already hot and bright outside. It was already a new day and I hated it.

I doubled back toward the main road and ran into Dolores, just as I was digging my feet in and out of the floury white sand and trudging down the road. I'd lost one slipper, and I didn't know where. I kicked the other one off. It landed on the curb. For one preposterous instant I felt like a litterbug. I almost bent down to pick it up out of some lingering sense of civic duty, but somehow I lacked the energy.

Dolores stood on the edge of the sidewalk where she'd been since the firemen arrived, her hand over her mouth like it was glued there. Her hair was unwound, and it spilled down her shoulders and back. I'd never before seen it down, and I hadn't realized how long it was. It fell past her waist, brown and streaked with gray.

I seized her by the shoulders, like I meant to shake her awake. I barely got her to look away from the fire and meet my eyes. "Where's Mr. Colby? Is he still upstairs in your house?"

She shuddered and lowered her hand to her chin, dragging her lower lip with it. The lip slipped back into place. She swallowed dryly and pointed loosely toward her own house, across the street. "Yes . . . yes, he's there. He wanted to come outside to help, but I talked him out of it. I . . . I put him back into his bed. He's—"

I'd lost interest already. I let go of her and ran across her yard, picking up sand, grass, and at least one awful little spur. I paused on the porch, hopped on one foot until I'd dislodged it, and shoved her front door open. It wasn't locked. It wasn't even closed all the way, it was just swinging on the hinge like she'd run outside and forgotten about it. Probably that's how it'd happened.

"Mr. Colby?" I called. The staircase wasn't in the usual spot, but I found it around a corner. I paused at the bottom with a hand on the rail. "Mr. Colby? Are you up there? Are you all right?" I didn't wait for an answer. I just started climbing the steps, guided by intuition and impatience. I'd never actually been upstairs in Dolores's house. There were three stories to it, including the attic rooms, but I stopped on the second landing and got lucky. I looked left, looked right, and saw a door that hung ajar. A light was on inside the room, and I heard the rustle of someone sitting up in bed.

"Mr. Colby?" I nudged the door the rest of the way open.

He was upright, busily stuffing a second pillow behind himself. His hands were so spindly that his bones might have been matchsticks, his hair was ferociously white—almost the silver-white of Dr. Floyd's, and just like that, I teared up all over again—and his knees were doorknobs on twigs beneath the blanket across his lap and legs.

"Alice, dear."

I went to the bedside and dropped to my own much-better-padded knees; he smiled sadly and gestured toward a chair right behind me. I felt like an idiot. I stood up again, drew the chair forward, and shakily sat down. "Mr. Colby, it's Dr. Floyd . . . she's—"

"I know."

"You heard from her . . . already?"

He swung his head smoothly back and forth. "No, dear. My eyes have failed me a bit, and my joints have rebelled. But my ears are still good." He waved toward the window, which was open; whispers of the chaos outside rose and crept inside, teasing the light cotton curtains that hung from the rod above it. "I've caught it in bits and pieces. I've gathered the worst."

I was crying again, silently this time—except for the drip of my nose and the subsequent sniffles. "Sir, I have to warn you."

"Warn me? Oh, I think we're well past warnings."

"Yes, but last night . . . or earlier tonight . . . God, I don't know what time it is. Mr. Colby, I spoke to Agatha Bloom."

His eyes widened, and his brows crept up his forehead. "Agatha? I haven't heard from her in years. She reached out to you?"

"Something like that. I mean, I reached out for her. She was kind enough to answer."

"I've tried . . . many times. I wonder why she . . ." The eyebrows drooped again. "It doesn't matter. What did she say? It must've been important."

"She said I needed to warn you. I asked her how to keep this awful spirit out of the town, and she said I couldn't. She said he's already here."

"I think it's safe to assume that she's right. What else did she say?"

"Something about good salt, and that it might bind him—but not for long. She said not even the lye could've kept him out. Please, sir—what does that mean? I know that salt is good for circles, for summonings and holdings, but I don't know what you're supposed to do with lye, or what good it is for protection."

"It . . . Well." He adjusted his thin spectacles with their light round lenses. "Lye, she said? She's speaking of an old charm, a bit of granny magic. You spread lye at all four corners of the property and say your prayers—it's a powerful ward to repel enemies and foes and any other visitors with ill intent."

I nodded vigorously. "And if it won't work, that's bad, isn't it?"

"It isn't good." A wail outside the window gave us both pause. I couldn't tell what was being said, but Mr. Colby told me, "Dr. Floyd will be dearly missed. Tomorrow night, I'll try to speak with her and find out what happened."

"Why? Why can't we . . . dial her up now?" I knew it didn't really work like a telephone, but I had to ask in case I was wrong. Now would be an *excellent* time to be wrong.

He shrugged. "Very few people come through right away, though once in a while someone will straddle the line between the worlds. It may sound odd, but I've known of people who received spiritual visits from the living."

I was boggled by the idea. "Living people? Who can . . . project themselves that way?"

He mustered a feeble smile. "You're learning the language. You're a good student, despite what Mabel says about you."

I resisted the urge to demand to know precisely what she'd told him, because I could guess. I bet she told him I'd been hanging around Candy's. I bet she exaggerated how many seminars and workshops I'd missed over the weeks, and I'm sure she didn't tell him that I'd attended at *least* half of the ones I'd been assigned to.

I did not seethe. I said, "Thank you, sir. I am doing my best."

"You came here to learn. It's your goal, and your job to pursue it. No one here will compel you to do anything." Good heavens, but this old man knew plenty. If the situation had been any different, he might have winked at me.

"I came here to learn, and I have learned quite a lot. But I have not learned how to handle anything like this. Even if I'd spent all week, every week, sitting and listening and taking notes, I doubt I'd have any better idea what's going on here."

He nodded unhappily and sagged against the pillows. I heard the sound of a truck and the crank of a fire hose unspooling. I wished to God that I didn't recognize that sound well enough to identify it, but I did, and that's what it was.

He said, "I don't know what to do either, not with all my years of experience—but if Aggie thought the lye wouldn't hold out the wickedness, then we truly have trouble in our midst. Does this have something to do with your visitor from Tampa?"

"How did you know I had a visitor? Or is that a silly question? And he's not from Tampa."

"From somewhere near the bay, then." His feeble smile went softer. "Even if no one in Cassadaga was a clairvoyant, we would still have our gossip, and gossip never sleeps. A Cuban fellow, I hear? Very well dressed, says everyone."

"He's an American. Fought in the Great War, even."

George gracefully ceded the point. "Then he's also a patriot and a hero."

"His name is Tomás Cordero, and he ran inside Dr. Floyd's house to save her. He ran right through the door with a blanket over his head—like he wasn't afraid at all. Like he'd seen it before . . ." I thought of the dream, when he was only the man in the mask who knew my name. "I know he worked with fire in the war. He must've gotten used to it."

George was watching me thoughtfully. I wonder if he could see my dreams, or if his spirit guide could tell him my memories. He asked, "What did Mr. Cordero do in the war?"

"He worked with a machine that threw fire at the enemy. It was some kind of . . . it was like the opposite of a water hose. It was a hose that held fire and sprayed it out on the battlefield. But when he used the machine, he wore protective gear—and he looked very much like a firefighter. I suppose that was the point, wasn't it? To protect him from the heat and flames."

"How long has he been here in town?"

"Oh, no time at all!" I was quick to defend him. "He didn't arrive until after the Calliope fire, if that's what you mean. He isn't afraid of fire, but he doesn't love it enough to . . ." I almost said, "create it," but I knew it wasn't true. He'd told me it wasn't true. George might know it wasn't true if I said it out loud. "Look, he's not some kind of violent arsonist," I said instead. "He would never hurt anyone."

"Not on purpose. But men bring things home," he said slowly. "When they go off to war, it's not just the memories they carry back from the front."

"He would never hurt anyone," I said again.

"No, but . . ." He folded his hands in his lap and stared thoughtfully toward the open window. "He *did* hurt people, once. He killed them. He was a soldier."

"That's different."

"Very different, I agree."

"Then why would you bring it up?"

He didn't answer that one. He asked another question instead. "Where did he fight, do you know?"

"Germany and France, I think."

He made a dismissive little noise that said I hadn't told him anything of value. "I wonder if you could narrow it down. You said he had a machine that shoots fire? I've never heard of such a thing."

"I hadn't either, until he told me about it." It wasn't really true. He hadn't told me; I'd seen it, and that's how I knew it was true.

He mused, "It was something new, made by the military. Something unprecedented. Everyone everywhere, dead or alive, notices when something unprecedented appears. Who might have seen that exceptional weapon . . . and wanted to use it? Who would want to turn the power of the flames against your friend Mr. Cordero? Who would use it against people like us?"

I thought of the angry, black-robed men who used to burn witches. A flame projector would've been more efficient than stakes and straw. Think of how many would burn, and how fast. That's what I thought.

That's not what I said.

"MANY people die in the process of war," I said. "Who knows which one of them noticed? Who can tell which one might've followed him home?"

"You should ask Mr. Cordero," he said. "Ask if he had any friends who died by his machine. He may have turned it on the enemy, but accidents happen. Did some unfortunate American cook to death on the front? Did another soldier carry a grudge?"

"I'd carry a grudge if I cooked to death *any*place," I said from the bottom of my heart.

"Perhaps it's something like that." He yawned, though he covered it with the back of his hand. "Or perhaps it's something altogether unrelated. I apologize. I am old, and it's very early—despite the awful excitement."

My stomach fell again at the mere mention of it. "Yes . . . the awful excitement. I'm sorry to bother you, sir. Please get some rest."

I wanted to stay where I was, right there in his room, and not leave for a while. I did not want to go outside and watch the sun rise over Dr. Floyd's body, and listen to the crumbling, burning ruins of her house. But I patted the old man's hand, thanked him for his time, and that's exactly what I did.

Back outside, I kept my eyes straight ahead and tried not to look at anything but the way forward, back to the hotel. I kept my feet one in front of the other, sinking in the sand, slapping on the sidewalks.

By the time I reached the lobby, they were as gray as ashes.

# 22

# TOMÁS CORDERO

## Cassadaga, Florida

I WAS EXHAUSTED, but after all the excitement that morning, I could not possibly return to bed. I opted instead to rise and make a half-hearted effort to begin the day. My ear hurt from where the fire caught it, and my throat hurt—my chest hurt, too—from breathing in too much smoke. I could not magically compel it to become an ordinary day, but I could drink some water, patch myself up, and ready myself for whatever was yet to come.

I took Felipe downstairs to the restaurant, to see about breakfast. He spent the meal on my lap, accepting scraps and peeking out from under the tablecloth to see if any of the nearby ladies wished to pet him. Or feed him a bit of scrambled egg. Or biscuit. Or ham. No, thank you, the greens give him gas. Even if he makes that face. Try a bit of cheese instead. That gives him the winds, too, but he won't vomit later.

At last, he was almost behaving like a normal dog, and not a terrified mouse.

I was pleased to see it, though the improvement was small (and might well have been imagined). I was just thinking how a few days of relative quiet and comfort might turn him around, when Alice stomped up to join us at the breakfast table. I could not tell if she was angry or frightened, but she was definitely tired and dirty; she still wore a smudge of soot across her forehead, as if it were Ash Wednesday and this was a Sunday at Padre Valero's church—not a hotel full of people who spoke to the dead.

Those two things aren't as far apart as they sound.

"Tomás, you just *left*. How could you leave me? How could you leave . . . ?" Her question petered out. I do not know what else, or who else, I should not have left. The dead woman?

I sighed and suggested that she pull up a chair—a useless thing to say, since she'd already done just that. "Clearly, I did not go far. Sit with us. Have some food."

"Us?"

Upon hearing a familiar voice, Felipe poked his head above the table line. "Yes, us. And what should I have done? There was nothing else . . . ," I said vaguely, not wishing to be insensitive. "I retrieved your friend, but I could not help her. I am very sorry, Alice. I wish I could have done more, but I was a soldier, not a doctor."

I was trying my best to calm her, but still I managed to fluster her. "Yes, you . . . you did bring her out—and that was amazing, it really was. You scared me to death," she said, and immediately reconsidered her choice of words. "You scared me silly, I mean—running into that house like that. It was so brave . . . I wasn't trying to say that you should've done *more*, or that you hadn't done *enough*. I'm only . . . I wanted to see you, to talk to you, to ask you what had happened in there. But when I came back from Mr. Colby's, you were gone."

WHICH reminded me: *She* left the scene first. I have no idea why she was upset with me. I must assume that she wasn't. She was angry with herself but needed someone else to share it with.

*   *   *

STILL, I tried to be reasonable. "It was not brave; it was sensible. I was the best-qualified person to make the attempt, until the firemen arrived. I stayed with the doctor until the ambulance came to take her away, but she was gone by then. You know that." Her eyes filled up, and her nose and cheeks went pink. "After that, I returned to the hotel to see about Felipe. He'd been indoors for hours, and I feared for the hotel rugs. I did not intend to abandon you in your hour of need. I apologize."

"No, no, don't apologize. You're right." She sniffed. She collected a cloth napkin from an unused place setting on the next table over and used it to dab her eyes and wipe her nose. "I'm sorry, it was ridiculous of me to think you'd still be there, standing in the street. I was only confused—I'm *still* very confused, about everything—and I guess I must have been worried."

"Did you think I'd gone back inside the house a second time?"

"No. Maybe? The house collapsed, and you weren't there, Tomás. You could've been anywhere. I knocked on your door, but you didn't answer."

"I must not have heard; I took a bath to wash off the smell of the fire. I had to change clothes and shave and make myself presentable. I was not trying to hide from you. See? You've found me now. Here I am, at your service, and I am so very sorry about your friend. She was the church's minister, is that right?"

The poor girl was openly weeping now, trying to muffle the little sobs and hide herself behind the coral-colored napkin. When the hostess came over, I asked for a cup of coffee for myself and a glass of water for my companion. Alice came up for air long enough to add, "And some oatmeal and fruit, if you could be so kind. And some orange juice. And some toast, with jam." After the woman had gone, she said, "It's been a difficult day already, and it's hardly eight o'clock. I deserve toast."

When the coffee and juice arrived, I told her to go ahead—ask me any questions she liked, though I did not know what she wanted to hear, or what she thought I could tell her. I could not have possibly predicted her line of inquiry.

"I wanted to ask you about the war."

I was frankly surprised. Almost too surprised to reply. "What on earth for?"

"Because fire is the thread that ties everything together: the fire you used in the war, your difficulties at home, and our difficulties here. *Your* fires came first. Not the ones at your shop or at Felipe's house . . . but on the front. I saw the machine—you know I did. You saw me when I saw you."

Oh yes. The dream, where the young woman appeared in a night-dress on the battlefield, her hair long and wild, her eyes big and wet.

"You saw the Livens device. They called it a flame projector." I did not want to talk about the war, and I'd certainly had enough of fire for a lifetime. But I'd come here for help, and to be free of the flames. It would do me no good to avoid the subject. I could not hide from it any better than I could hide from the unrelenting Alice. (Had I been trying.) "I had a knack for it, as they say, so I was assigned to the British unit that employed it . . . temporarily. Mostly, I assisted with its maintenance." The flame projector's basic mechanics were not wildly different from those of an industrial steam iron. Not in general principle.

"Are you making a long story short?"

I recalled the gloves, the masks, and the screams. "As short as I can, yes. It was a fearsome thing, and that was the point, I think. The projector was destructive, of course, but more than that—it was terrifying. Imagine being on a battlefield . . ." I tried not to imagine, only to remember. I didn't succeed particularly well. I continued anyway. "Imagine you're on one side of a fight, and on the other, there is a machine that hurls liquid fire a hundred feet or more, in a brilliant golden arc. It took hundreds of men to tote the thing around, and a crew of . . . well, there were eight or ten of us required to deploy it." I laughed, small and rueful. "It was a huge waste of manpower, for all its magnificence."

"Why would you say that?"

"Because it only ran for a few minutes at a time. All that work, all that money spent on fuel and machinery, and looking back now I can say for certain: It was mostly for the sake of theatrics."

"But it *killed* people. It terrorized them."

"Excessively, yes."

The hostess brought the oatmeal and fruit and promised Alice toast and jam to come. She thanked her and said, "Then the flame projector did its job, didn't it?"

"Yes, but at what cost? If the eight or ten of us had been given Gatling guns we could've done more damage to the enemy. Although . . ." I slipped a bite of ham under the tablecloth. Felipe slurped it down. "Fear is a weapon, too, as I know better than anyone. And it was . . . my God, it was a frightful thing to behold."

"There you go, then." Her tears now mostly dried, Alice reluctantly withdrew from the subject and less reluctantly saw to her breakfast.

I saw to my coffee.

We both finished up, but when it was time to leave the table for someone else's breakfast and coffee needs, Alice was not quite finished with me. She braced herself as if she were preparing to propose something unthinkable. She took a deep breath, released it, and said in a dramatic fashion: "Tomás, I want to read you."

"Read me?"

"Yes, like when I held your hand in the service—but in a more controlled fashion. I've asked Dolores Brigham for use of the fellowship hall this morning. No one else needs it for anything, so we can have a little room, and a little peace and quiet."

"What do you hope to see, when you 'read' me?"

"It's more about what *you* hope to find. You want to reach your wife, don't you? You came here for help? Isn't that what this is all about?"

I set Felipe on the floor and took the end of his little red leash in my hand. "You know I want to reach her—more than anything in the world. But no one seems to think that it's Evelyn communicating with me. Have you changed your mind?"

"Yes and no."

"I must tell you, I heard her speaking inside the doctor's house. She told me where to find your minister and how to bring her out. That was not the work of some terrible flaming shadow; I know it for a fact."

"How can you be so sure?"

I tried to keep from sounding annoyed. "I've never been more certain of anything in my life. That voice came from the Evelyn I always knew and loved—helpful and kind. Lover of animals and children and buyer of bouquets for the Sunday table. Helper of persons in need."

"And most definitely not an arsonist."

"No, not an arsonist. You heard the doctor's last words; she said as plain as day, to me—she said, 'It isn't her.' It isn't Evelyn, setting the fires. That's what she meant, I would swear it on my life—and on the life of anyone in this town."

"Good God, don't say such a thing. Even if that *is* what she meant." Alice sounded dubious, but her uncertainty was honest. It meant she was open to the possibility of Evelyn's presence. It would have to suffice. "Please, come with me. This will be odd and awkward, but I think it's important."

"Very well. Read me, Alice Dartle. Tell me what you find, and tell me if it matters. Tell me how to stop the fires."

"Let's not get ahead of ourselves," she muttered. "I've missed a lot of classes."

She led the way out through the hotel, across the street, up the porch, and into the bookstore. On the far side of the bookstore was a fellowship hall lined with wood paneling and filled with long tables for potlucks and other social events. It was a large room—far too large for two people alone, but this was the place where Alice wanted to read, so that's where we would sit together.

I don't know why I felt so reluctant. Was it her lack of confidence? A fear of what she might find? This was why I'd come to Cassadaga. Literally, I had traveled all this way for this exact moment. Why did I want to run from the room? What was I so afraid of?

Was it all the sunflowers?

They were on the tablecloths and in vases. I should've taken it as a good sign. I don't know why I didn't.

"I'VE been learning some things, from the classes I've actually attended and the seminars I've listened to," Alice informed me. "I'm a good student, I swear." She pulled out a paper bag and used its contents to draw a large white circle on the floor. Before I could ask, she explained, "This is salt, and it helps protect a space. We use it to keep bad things out when we're trying to talk to the other side."

"Why?" I asked.

"To be real honest with you, I couldn't say. As far as I can tell, a lot of this kind of thing boils down to one of two things: either because that's how it's always been done, or because it can't hurt and might help. Right now, I'll take all the help I can get," she added under her breath. "Now, come on, have a seat with me here, inside the circle."

I stepped over the thick white line and Felipe tried to follow me. Alice picked him up before he could scatter any salt, and she gave him a hug.

"Can he come, too?" I asked. "I want him to be safe, inside the circle."

She handed him over. "I don't see why not."

I sat cross-legged on the hardwood floor, and he curled up in my lap. She sat down across from me, so close that I was almost uncomfortable. Our knees brushed one another when we shifted. It was an awkward thing, but a reading must be personal, mustn't it? It must be invasive and close. One must open a book before one can know its contents.

I should not have been concerned. Evelyn had spoken to me without the ashes this time. Evelyn was there beside me, and she was good, and now Alice would see that for herself. So why did I fidget and fret? Why did I anxiously pet Felipe's head and hope that this all went quickly?

THE lamps were all off, but light trailed in through the windows so the scene was hardly dark, and only a little dim. Still we felt hidden, there on the floor between two large tables, sitting in our salt circle. On the other side of the wall we could hear chatter in the bookshop and the chime of a cash register. Out on the sidewalks, people walked by muttering about the fires, all the fires, so many fires.

I knew of only two in Cassadaga, but it's a small place. Two must feel like a thousand.

Alice took a deep breath, and then she took my hands. "Tomás Cordero, are you a praying man?"

"I have been known to pray in the past. I do not pray very often anymore."

"Now's as good a time as any to try it again, don't you think? Say a short one, to whatever God you believe in—even if you don't believe very much that anyone is listening. Even if you only hope there is a God to hear you. Say hello to Him, and ask Him to watch over us."

"Why?"

"Can't hurt, might help."

I pretended to indulge her, closing my eyes and muttering a quick Our Father in Spanish. I trusted she wouldn't understand or recognize it, and I hoped it wasn't rude, but I didn't mind if it was.

I don't pray on command; that's all.

When I was finished pretending, she closed her eyes and began speaking so quietly that someone on the other side of the salt could not have heard her. "I've already seen the battlefield, and I've seen you in your gear, with the machine that takes eight men to fire. I've seen the flames and smelled the smells, and now I wish to see past them. I wish to see the source. I've seen the flames . . . from something altogether unprecedented. A new thing, under the sun. Who else . . ." She was hardly even whispering anymore. She was moving her lips, and a small bit of air was coming out. "Who else saw the flames? Someone else . . ."

"Evelyn?"

Her tight-shut eyes crinkled with irritation, then relaxed. "No, not Evelyn. She had no idea what you were doing over there. You left it out of your letters. You didn't want to scare her or make her worry."

"That's . . . true. But is she here? Is she with me?"

Silence. Then a little tilt of her head. "Evelyn?" she asked. Silence. A shake of her head. "If she's here, she isn't coming forward. You're alone. Nothing is following you; nothing is attached to you. It's strange . . . there *was* something with you, when you first arrived."

"That's what everyone says," I complained.

She didn't open her eyes. "That's because it's true. You wore it like a rucksack full of bricks. Whatever it was, it wasn't your wife. There was nothing ladylike about it. It was big and manly, and it had a gaping . . . hunger," she tried, then changed her mind. "No, a bottomless hatred. It had a hungry hatred that wanted to swallow up everything, everyone. But who was it?" she asked. I do not think she was asking me. "Such a noise the war made. Such a roar the fire made. Nothing like it, ever before on earth. A sound to wake the dead. A ruckus like a thousand witches burning at once."

She adjusted her grip on my hands and turned mine over so the palms faced down—and hers were underneath.

"I saw him, before you got here," she said. Eyes still closed. Hands still warm and a little damp. "I was giving an open reading, like the one you saw where David collapsed. After the regular spirits came and went, there was someone else waiting in the wings. He stank of fire. I started calling him 'the smoldering man,' when I had to call him anything . . ."

Her voice faded out.

Her voice faded in.

"He saw you there, with the fire machine. It woke him up. It reminded him of something. It called to him, or he called to it. Then when the war ended, he came home with you. He was along for the ride, watching and wondering what you'd done with the machine. He wanted to see it again. There was so much left to burn. And then you began starting fires."

I almost pulled my hands away. She sensed it and gripped mine more tightly than I liked.

"I didn't take the machine back home. I couldn't have. Not if I wanted to."

"He didn't know that. He is much too old to understand what he saw. And you . . . you were setting your fires, looking for Evelyn. She couldn't hear you, but *he* could. He wanted a way in, and all he had to do was pretend."

"No one pretended. Evelyn sent me those messages, with the soot and ash."

She shook her head. "No, she *didn't*. She isn't here, Tomás." She opened her eyes and fixed me with a clear, commanding stare. "Dr. Floyd was right, but not the way you want. Your ghost isn't Evelyn. It's never been her."

"You're *wrong*."

"You're *lost*, Tomás. And this thing . . . this spirit that came from the old world . . . he stayed with you because you invited him to. When you set those fires, you set out a welcome mat."

"I invited *Evelyn*," I insisted. I was ready to toss Felipe from the circle and follow immediately after him, but Alice clutched my wrists and held them in her fierce little talons.

"When you open a door, you don't always get to pick who comes through it."

"Let go of me."

"Not yet. Please," she added, when I began to pull away from her. "He's gone now. He left you, and I don't know why, but it's important."

"Imogene said he was free."

"And Agatha practically said he was unstoppable. God help us if they're right." She squeezed and released my wrists, then took my fingers and opened them. I didn't realize I'd clenched them. "God, or Spirit, or whoever. There's nothing left of him with you, except the smell of smoke and a bad impression of hate . . . hungry hate . . ." She used those words again. "I keep feeling the fire . . . smelling the fire. Fire is hungry, too. Isn't it? It consumes everything, if you let it."

"Usually. Eventually."

"Lord Almighty, the *smell* of it . . . you know?" She wrinkled her nose. "Like it's right here, in the room with us."

Now that she mentioned it, yes. "Wait. Alice? Alice, open your eyes. I smell it, too."

"It's only in the reading."

"No, I don't think it is."

I yanked my hands away, and this time she let me. I got to my feet and wobbled, for I was very tired and the smoke was getting stronger. I couldn't see it, but I could smell it. Felipe was prancing and whining. And I could smell smoke. Real smoke, not dream smoke or reading smoke. I knew it in the pit of my stomach.

Alice scrambled to her feet, too, scraping up the salt circle as she went. "Where is it coming from?"

"I don't know."

We both went for the fellowship hall door. I reached it first. I pulled it open with a jerk and saw only a startled bookstore clerk and two surprised customers looking at me like I'd gone mad. "Does anyone else smell smoke?"

The clerk sniffed the air. "It's just Dr. Floyd's house. We'll be smelling it for days."

"No," Alice argued. "It's something else. It's something new."

Out we dashed, to the porch, into the street. Alice froze and seized my arm. She pointed at a trail of smoke rising above a house not terribly far from the wreckage of Dr. Floyd's. It wasn't coming from a chimney; it was coming from a room on the second floor, a gray-white puff, curling and coiling out toward the sky.

"That's Mr. Colby's room!" she squeaked. "We have to get him out of there!"

But behind us, an old man cleared his throat. "That's true, but don't raise the alarm. It's all right, Alice. Everyone is out, and I've just rung the fire department."

She whirled around, appraised the old fellow, and seized him in an embrace that nearly knocked him over. She hugged him so hard I thought she might break him. "You're not inside? You're safe! You're even out of bed! Oh, Mr. Colby . . . what's happening?"

"An electrical problem, I think. Some books caught fire, but I threw them into the bathtub, and all will be well. I've warned Dolores, but please, don't make a show of it. People will begin to worry. Everyone is so very anxious right now."

Even as he said this, someone shrieked about the smoke, and people began to cry, and the word "fire" made the rounds up and down the street. Shout by shout, panic spread like the influenza. People ran and people hollered. The well-intended ruse was ruined.

He sighed. "Well, I did try, didn't I?"

"Yes, Mr. Colby. You surely did." She looked back at me, stricken and confused, as if I had any answers for her. I didn't even have answers for myself.

Mr. Colby patted her hand. He stared straight ahead, at the house with the curl of smoke twisting out the window. He whispered to her, as quietly as she'd whispered to me not five minutes earlier: "In the ashes, in the bathtub—and on the floor, where I'd dropped them. There was a message, and I think we must call the council together."

She turned her wide and horrified eyes to him. "A message?"

He turned to me and kept his voice just loud enough to be heard over the fresh commotion. "Let's call it a threat. You've brought us something awful, Mr. Cordero." I had never been introduced to him, but Alice (or anyone else) could have told him my name. "Whatever it is, it's happy here. It has found what it was looking for, and it wants to stay."

"What does it want?" Alice asked. He did not answer or look at her yet. He looked back at the second story of Dolores Brigham's house. "Mr. Colby, what does it want?"

He steeled himself, and steadied his stare, then his voice. "It wants for us to burn."

## ALICE DARTLE

Cassadaga, Florida

THEY BROUGHT DR. Floyd's body back to us right away.

I'm not sure why they ever took her to the hospital in the first place. She was obviously dead, and there wasn't anything that any doctor was going to do for her. So I don't know why they took her, and I don't know who got them to give her back so quickly—but her body was returned this morning, and by this afternoon there was a hole dug in the little plot up at Lake Helen. It's not half a mile away and it's an easy walk, so everybody went up there to pay their respects when Mr. Colby offered to say a few words while the gravediggers put her into the ground.

Lake Helen's cemetery is a small thing, just a handful of acres a little ways past the loose hills of Cassadaga's camp. It's mostly flat and empty, and what few graves are already there generally belong to people from Lake Helen or DeLand. I thought it was odd, until Mabel told me that most spiritualists would rather be cremated than buried.

"Our bodies are merely the clothes we cast off when we cross over. We don't need them anymore. There's no sense in preserving them or keeping them around." She'd explained this as we walked together, up the sandy road on the far side of the tracks. Tomás had walked beside me, with Felipe trotting along, too, at the end of his leash.

We arrived, and we milled about with the other folks from the camp meeting—waiting for Mr. Colby to arrive.

Tomás asked quietly, "Then why do we bury Dr. Floyd? If your dead are usually burned?"

Mabel sighed sadly. "For one thing, her brother is buried here. For another, the nearest crematory is in Jacksonville, and since she never specified one way or another . . . we all thought it'd be better just to . . . I don't know." She stared down at her shoes. They were black, like everything else she was wearing, despite the faint sear of weird midwinter heat. "We wanted to put this all behind us, put her mortal remains to rest. We don't really believe she's gone, exactly," she explained. "She's gone somewhere else, but she hasn't ceased to exist. If we're very fortunate, she'll return and offer her advice and . . . and guidance." She cleared her throat. It sounded thick, and un-happy. "We shouldn't be sad. But it's all right to be sad, if we are."

"Good," I said. I could barely get the word out; I had to shove it out, past the lump in my throat. "Because I'm just miserable about it. I hardly got a chance to know her, but she was so welcoming. She made me think there was a place for me in this world, all evidence to the contrary. The first night I came here . . . and she fed me supper. We talked about witches . . ."

The memory jogged against something else in my head, so I stopped talking and tried to figure out what my brain was trying to tell me.

Tomás asked me what was wrong.

"Nothing," I said. "I'm just thinking."

The trees were tall and scraggly, and the shade was spotty there in the cemetery—but we took what we could get. It was too hot when the sun was out, and just fine when it wandered behind the thin, high clouds that waved back and forth. The grass was spotty, and it was hard to walk in the naked sand—where small brown spurs hid, and snuck into shoes, and made a funeral even more wretched than it was already bound to be.

The whole camp meeting had emptied out for this, even people who had arrived only a few days before on the train, like Tomás. Dr. Floyd was known well beyond this corner of Florida, so people may not have met her, but they'd heard of her. Folks came out from DeLand, too, and I heard there was someone present who came from as far away as Longboat Key, wherever that is.

All told, there were maybe three hundred people present. The crowd managed to make even this small, vacant cemetery feel . . . well . . . crowded. Elbows and shoulders knocked up against me from all sides, as everyone crowded as close to the rectangular hole in the ground as they could get.

I thought about how hard it must be to dig a hole in the sand. It must take forever. It must be hopeless work—for every shovelful out, half a shovelful topples back in.

I thought about all kinds of things, rather than the red and bubbling body of Dr. Floyd, not quite dead, still trying to speak. Lying in the middle of Stevens Street, her hands burned to the bone and coiled up in fists.

All right, fine. I thought about that, too.

Mr. Colby arrived in a car driven by Oscar Fine. Oscar came back from the hospital in DeLand this morning, saying that David was doing much better and would be released either today or tomorrow—but he wasn't quite strong enough to make the funeral. David had sent his apologies. He said he'd be home soon. That's what Mr. Fine told everyone after he'd parked and helped Mr. Colby up to the grave site. He made a few little announcements like that, and then he stepped aside to let the founder speak.

He looked so frail and so small. His suit was loose and his hands shook.

"Thank you so much for being here, everyone. I appreciate your presence, and I know that Dr. Janice Alicia Floyd appreciates it, too. Hers has always been a brilliant mind, and we have been very fortunate to have her company for these last twenty years. In that time, she has always graced Cassadaga with her keen wit, her wise advice, and her diplomatic flair for organization."

A few people chuckled. I did not. It might have been an inside joke, and that was swell—but I was leaking tears again, clutching a fresh handkerchief to my face.

"She has been a teacher and a mentor, and an upstanding citizen—of our town, and of the world. Now she is an upstanding citizen elsewhere, undoubtedly improving her new location with the practical charm and friendliness for which she has always been known.

"Today, we release her physical remains to the earth, so that they may return to whence they came. Today we remember our friend and colleague, and we reaffirm our commitment to continuing the great work she pursued throughout the last decades of her life.

"Like the sunflower, she turned her face to the light and followed wherever it led her. Now those petals have closed, and they will not open again. Now she has joined the light, and we shall see her every time we lift our eyes to the sky and ask for Spirit's warmth and guidance."

THERE was more, and it was lovely—every word, every condolence, all of it—but at the end, people began throwing sunflowers into the hole in the ground and I simply couldn't stand it anymore. This new faith of mine was too new to sustain me, too fresh to grant me the calm acceptance of these other people, who commune more easily and frequently with the dead than I do.

I wanted to run to her house (but it was gone) and knock on the door, and ask if she had any cucumber sandwiches, and then we could talk about witches (and how they so often burn). I wanted to cry into her shoulder (but that was gone, too). I wanted to run, even though I never want to run. All the way back to Cassadaga, with a spur in my shoe that I couldn't dig out with my fingernails if my life depended on it, and a snag in my stocking, and my heels sinking into the sand with every stupid step.

But I just walked.

Tomás was largely silent beside me. He carried Felipe, who had decided he wasn't interested in walking anymore (and that might have been because of the spurs, so I could hardly blame him).

As we neared the gates of the camp, the sun was just beginning to take on that orange hue that says it's getting late. The sky wouldn't start getting dark for one more hour, but it would be very dark in two. I looked for sunflowers and saw a few planted up against the side of the bookstore—growing tall enough to touch the eaves. I'd never noticed them before, but they were tilting on their stems, leaning to the west.

As we crossed the train tracks, Tomás finally said, "That was a lovely service, don't you think?" But he sounded like he wasn't too sure about the whole thing. It must've been wildly different from your average Catholic funeral. (I think he used to be a Catholic.) Lord knows it was wildly different from any Methodist funeral I'd ever attended, too, but that didn't mean it was bad or wrong.

It was just different.

"Lovely," I agreed. I dabbed at my nose with the handkerchief, which was hardly any more helpful than a wet washcloth at that point. "I've never seen anything like it, have you?"

He shook his head. I thought for a moment that he'd say something else on the subject, but he looked up and brightened. "Alice, isn't that your friend from the church?" He pointed at a man who was walking toward us, up the road, between the hotel and the bookstore.

"David!" I exclaimed. "I thought you weren't coming!"

There was David Fine, thin and wobbly, but he was upright and very alert. His eyes were wide and positively twitchy. His dark hair was ruffled by the breeze, and one of his shoes was untied. The laces straggled behind him in the powdery white sand. He did not look well, but apart from his rumpled state, I could not have said what exactly was wrong. But something was wrong.

He did not look at me when I said his name. He was looking at Tomás.

"David?" Edella Holligoss emerged from the bookstore. "David, you're back!" she happily observed, then paused, one hand on the nearest porch column. He didn't look right to her, either.

"*He* did this," David said, one arm hanging at his side. (The other arm was folded, his hand grasping his forearm, holding it steady.) He stalked steadily toward us—yes, that's what he was doing. He was stalking. Toward Tomás. And me.

He wasn't blinking.

I stepped in front of Tomás. I did it on instinct. "David, I guess they must have released you from the hospital, but are you feeling quite well? You don't appear . . ." I held out my hands and walked toward him, hoping to intercept him.

He still stared ahead, past me, at Tomás. I was surely blocking most of the view.

That didn't stop him. "He did this. He brought it here. He has to take it away."

David lifted his hand. It'd been hiding in his pocket. His fingers were wrapped around a gun. I didn't know what kind of gun, because even when Daddy tried to teach me, I'd never cared anything about guns. All I knew was that they killed. It was the only thing they were good for.

And now David was holding one. Now he was lifting it and pointing it.

I shrieked his name, but I couldn't stop there. "What are you *doing*!"

He reached me and he pushed me—he shoved me aside—and he fired: One, two, three shots. All in a row. My ears were ringing. People were shouting, but I could barely hear them. I could barely hear anything.

I clapped my hands over my ears and looked around, scanning the scene for help. Someone must know what to do, because Spirit knew that I didn't have the faintest idea. I saw Mabel—slender, waifish Mabel—leap from the hotel's porch and into the street. She tackled David head-on, knocking him to the ground. She flattened him but didn't stop him. It took Edella and Sidney to do that when they joined in and kicked the gun away.

I flailed for Tomás. He was hunkered over, facing away from me. His arms were wrapped around Felipe, protecting him. His left shoulder was bleeding; the wound spurted and blood spread down the arm of his jacket and I couldn't see if he'd been hit anyplace else.

I trudged toward him, tripping over myself in the sand. I grabbed him by the arm—I know, I shouldn't have! I know, it hurt him!— and pulled him around. I tried to draw him away from the street, where this wasn't a showdown, this wasn't the O.K. Corral, and it wasn't a duel, and I didn't understand what was happening.

David writhed beneath a small crowd of people who meant to hold him there, and his gun was unattended on the sidewalk, out of his reach. I kicked it even farther away.

Tomás was bleeding, and David was screeching, and none of this made any sense. The blood. The words. The reasonable, funny, brilliant friend of mine, who was covered in sand and wriggling like he might bury himself in it, beneath the weight of well-meaning others. Then there was his father, who arrived a moment later—and helped haul him off to Harmony Hall, only a few feet away.

Dr. Holligoss abandoned them all and ran to Tomás, who hadn't moved. He was frozen in a standing crouch, holding the little dog away from harm.

"Give him to me," I said. "Tomás, give me Felipe; let me hold him."

Dr. Holligoss said, "Over here, sit down. You must sit down." He led him to the curb.

I took Felipe. Tomás did not protest, and neither did the dog—who did not wiggle or squirm. He only shook, like he might vibrate himself into pieces and escape this terrible life. I tried to comfort him, petting him desperately enough that I'm sure I made his terror even worse, but what could I do? What do I know of dogs? They're adorable and they bark, and they are faithful. What happens when they need reassurance? When you need to lie to them and tell them everything's all right?

Maybe you can't lie to a dog. Maybe they always know the truth.

"OFF with this," said the doctor, yanking on Tomás's jacket.

He was glassy-eyed and blank; he was shocked—yes, maybe it was shell shock, coming back to him now. Or maybe David had just surprised the shit out of him.

He'd surprised the shit out of *me*, just about.

I could still hear David yelling his head off in Harmony Hall—they'd taken him to Mabel's office, since that was the room right there down front, on the corner. He was writhing and fighting and spouting off nonsense. The only part I caught with any clarity was the phrase "He'll need three of them! He'll need three!" But three of whom, what, or which, no one managed to drag out of him.

Tomás sat like a stone while the doctor dropped his bloody jacket to the ground and unbuttoned his shirt, peeling that halfway off him, too. It was indecent, a little, but this was a battlefield and I told myself there was no such thing as indecency when somebody might bleed to death.

The bullet had entered from behind; Tomás had turned just in time, shielding the dog with his body. I want to say that I couldn't imagine such a thing, taking a bullet for a dog—but right then and there I was holding Felipe like I could save him, or like he could save me, and I completely understood why Tomás did it.

"The shot didn't go through. Mr. Cordero? Mr. Cordero?"

Tomás finally heard him. He swiveled his head to look at the doctor. "Yes?"

"I need to get you to my house. I have a medical office there. We need to fish this out and stop this bleeding."

"I'm bleeding?"

"Oh, Tomás . . ." I was crying again, this time with fear and confusion. He didn't even know he was bleeding or how serious this was. It must've been the shell shock—he must not have understood; that's what I thought.

But then he held up his hand and weakly waved it, like he would shush a nervous child. "No, no. It's only a scratch, and he only hit me once. I've been hurt worse and fared just fine. Did he harm anyone else?"

Vigorously I shook my head, but since I hadn't thought to look until he asked, I checked over my shoulder. I didn't see any signs of anyone else in trouble, except for Candice Pearson standing on her porch across the tracks, surveying the broken glass from the window that David had shot out with one of the bullets that had otherwise missed their target.

"He broke a window," I snuffled. "And he shot a hole in you."

"If that is the sum total, then we should count our blessings," he said graciously. He held very still while Dr. Holligoss pressed his own handkerchief to the wound, blotting it to see it better.

"Alice, help me get him to his feet."

"I don't need help . . . ," he said, then swooned when he was halfway upright.

I swooped in and ducked under his good arm, with Felipe tucked under mine. "I've got him," I confirmed. "Show us where to go."

Ladies gasped as we went by, and Tomás staggered so badly that other men offered help—but it was only twenty yards to the doctor's house and the bleeding had slowed. I hardly had any blood at all on my sleeve; most of it was absorbed by the bandage I was wearing, and I might save the shawl with cold water and soap.

Not that I really cared about either of those things. I'm not even sure why I'm writing that part. Of all the things on earth that simply don't matter . . .

I helped him onto a narrow table and did my best to console the dog while the doctor got to work.

It took twenty minutes to remove the bullet and provide Tomás with stitches to close the hole, but it felt like hours. He was getting cleaned up when Mabel arrived, bearing his bloody jacket. (We'd left it on the sidewalk. I'd forgotten about it. She was using it for an excuse to stop inside and talk to us; I could tell that much immediately.)

Tomás was leaned over a padded bar, positioned so the doctor could see his wound better. He hardly looked up when he said, "Thank you for returning the jacket, but it is ruined now. It is a pity. It was a good piece."

"That's not entirely why I'm here," Mabel said, confirming my suspicions and fidgeting her fingers into knots. "The police have been summoned. They haven't arrived yet, but when they do, they'll want to talk to you."

"How is the young man?" Tomás asked with a wince. Dr. Holligoss was tying the bullet hole shut, and I was too fascinated to look away—for all that it hurt to watch. The needle rose and fell, and all he did was flinch. I couldn't have stood it with half so much calmness myself. I probably would have passed out cold . . . except I'd done all right with the burn on my arm, hadn't I? I might be made of tougher stuff than I thought.

I should give myself more credit.

"David is . . . the same." Dr. Holligoss answered Tomás's question. "Edella gave him a sedative and a shot of rum, and he's calmer now, but he isn't himself. He tried to *murder* you, Mr. Cordero. In cold blood, on the street, in broad daylight. Something is terribly wrong— he isn't himself. I want you to know that."

Tomás let his head droop while the last stitches were pulled firm and tied off. "He is precisely himself," he said softly. "He only said what you all have told me—what even Alice has told me: I have brought something awful to Cassadaga, and he wants me to take it away again."

"Sir, that's not—"

"It's the meat of the matter," he interrupted. "It's the *truth* of the matter. He's right. I've been selfish and impulsive, and I have endangered you all. This was never my intent, but it was naïve of me to think that it would not come to this. I always believed . . . I still believe . . . that my Evelyn was with me. But apparently"—he shook his head slowly, sadly—"she was not alone. And now, for better or for worse . . . I am."

"You came here for help," I said, not to remind him, but to assure the doctor and Mabel by saying it out loud, insisting upon it. "We *will* find a way to help."

"Maybe there is no help to be found for me—not here, or anywhere else. I should not have come to Cassadaga, and I apologize for doing so. I should leave. If I leave, maybe the danger will follow me once again. Perhaps I can lure it somewhere else."

Mabel didn't agree. "Where would you take it, even if you're able? Better that you stay here with us and leave this thing with us—for at least we might prepare some defense against it. Besides, it's loose now, whatever it is. *Who*ever it is. It had to be somebody, once upon a time."

I remembered what Mr. Colby had said the day before. "It's found what it wants, right here. It wants for us to burn. Tomás, you won't help that by leaving. Whatever you've brought will remain behind, as likely as not."

"Staying won't help, either. I have wasted everyone's time, and worse. Thank you, Doctor," he said as the bandage was taped into place. "I regret the necessity of asking, but could I trouble you for a clean shirt? Something to wear back to the hotel. I'll have it laundered and returned to you as soon as I'm able."

"Of course. I'll go find one and get you some pills for the pain. Something to help you rest."

"I don't need—"

"Yes, you do."

The doctor left, but Mabel and I stared down at Tomás, who sat up straight, then slipped into a hunched-over posture like he was exhausted beyond words. From his spot at the foot of the examination table, his feet did not touch the ground. He swung them slowly, like a bored and sleepy child.

"You can't leave," I informed him.

"Not yet," Mabel agreed. "Stay and give us some time. We need to confer . . . and do some research . . . and . . . and talk to David, too. What's done will not be undone so easily, should you take the next train out of town—and it might be for the best. We understand what it is. We have resources to address it. Not everyplace you might hide can say the same."

"Very well," he relented, or he pretended to. I don't know which. He looked to me, or rather, he looked at Felipe, sitting in my arms—as quiet as a church mouse. "I am glad that he's taken to you. If something were to happen to me, I would hope that you'd keep him and care for him."

"Nothing is going to happen to you," I told him.

"Oh, Alice," he replied. He filled my name with such surrender, such tragic certainty. I hated the sound of it. "Don't you know by now? Something happens to everyone, eventually."

# 24

## TOMÁS CORDERO

Cassadaga, Florida

My shoulder was stiff and sore, but it was by no means the worst pain I'd experienced in my life, so I wore the injury like I wore the borrowed shirt: because I had little choice in the matter. I only had to take care that I did no damage to either my injury or the white button-up, which was a satisfactory piece from a good department store. It would suffice for the very short journey back to the hotel, where I had every intention of packing my things, sending off the borrowed shirt to be laundered, and sending myself off to parts unknown—or as yet undecided.

I had already decided to leave Felipe with Alice. Not because I wanted to, but because I was a danger to everyone and everything, and I would continue to be, so long as I lived. I would not endanger the little dog. Like so few of us who walk this earth . . . he deserves better.

It was as David declared, before he took measures to murder me: *I brought this here, and I must take it away again.* I regret to admit that no one here knows how to attempt any such thing, least of all me. I can only imagine that if I were gone—truly gone, *dead* and gone—then the thing might accompany me into the afterlife. Or if not, from the other side I might be some better use to this community (as opposed to presenting an incontrovertible danger, while I remain here in its midst).

I had made up my mind.

But every little thing conspired to thwart me. The painkiller that the doctor had provided left me woozy, or else the loss of blood did, and I was in no shape to sneak away. Then, of course, Alice was at my side every ridiculous moment, even when the police politely requested a word with me—and theirs was the kind of polite request that would not be delayed for any sake, even that of suicide.

I talked to them, I told them the truth, and I took my leave. That was all.

They wanted me to press charges against David, who sat sullenly in the back of their car while we chatted. I declined to do so. I said only that it was a private matter, and a misunderstanding. The young man is correct, and I won't see him punished for it. Or I won't see him punished any further, with any encouragement of mine.

The authorities took him away, regardless of my protests.

I don't know what they intend to do with him.

It was quite dark by the time I finally returned to the hotel.

Alice insisted that I keep Felipe with me, a four-footed chaperone, and I agreed. I promised that I would not pack my things and disappear, and I promised that I would change my clothes—and have Mr. Rowe launder the borrowed shirt and return it to Dr. Holligoss. I told her that I needed to lie down.

That last part, at least, was true.

It didn't matter what was and wasn't true otherwise. None of those other things would come to pass, all promises to the contrary.

Outside the window of my room, I could see people standing on the street and pointing at the curb, the sidewalk. They were pointing at my blood, which had not yet been cleaned away. Even in the freshly fallen dark, it was easily spotted. The streetlamps pointed it out, shining a spotlight upon the scene.

Someone kicked sand around, hiding the gore on the unpaved street.

That was the extent of it.

I was so very tired that I could almost imagine lying down and going to sleep right then and there, and never awakening, never rising. What a pleasant option, I thought. If only I had some useful poison to send myself off . . . what a delight it would have been. No more fires, except the fires of hell.

If indeed there is any such thing.

(The spiritualists tell me that there is not.)

But I had no poison—not even the doctor's pills, for he'd given me only enough to help, not hurt. I had only exhaustion and pain. And a gun. And some promises I would not fulfill, but might delay. I lay down on the bed, and Felipe jumped up beside me. He curled up in the crook of my arm and began to snore.

I will miss him when I'm dead.

## ALICE DARTLE

### Cassadaga, Florida

I SAW TOMÁS and Felipe to their room and took all Tomás's promises
to be gospel—knowing that they probably weren't. He was up to
something. He was hurt and sad, and he was surrendering in some
way. Or he was trying to.

Well, I wasn't going to let him.

I talked Mr. Rowe into keeping half an eye on him, and then I
talked Mabel into lurking about in the room next door. The walls
are as thin as paper, and if he were to try anything—whether it be
sneaking out of town, harming himself, or whatever else (I didn't
know what to expect from him) . . . she could intervene. She could
send for me or someone else. She could do *something*.

"Go talk to Dolores," she urged me before I left her. "When we
were trying to calm David down, she came into the office looking
for you. She said she wanted a word with you."

"About Tomás?" We were whispering, because it's as I said: The
walls might as well have been made of the daily news.

"I assume, but maybe not. Go find out. I'll stay here and keep watch . . . or keep listen, as the case may be."

I left the room with the utmost stealth. The knob scarcely clicked when I shut the door behind me, and I tiptoed down the hall like my life depended on total silence. I felt silly for being so sneaky, but I also suspected that it was necessary. Tomás was being peculiar, and I was deeply afraid that I knew what he was up to—but I didn't dare speculate. I refused to let myself. I opted instead to devote my attention to protecting him, to saving him.

I was here to help, and one way or another, I was going to help the living daylights out of him.

By the time I left, it was very, very dark outside. I daresay it was proper nighttime, and not that dull late afternoon with the rosy glow at the edges of a dark blue sky. No, the sidewalk lamps were already blazing, and all the windows were lit up yellow from the gaslights within.

It was chilly, too. Not cold, but cool enough that everyone but me was sporting a sweater of some kind. I still had my bloody shawl and my bloody bandages to keep me warm.

To be fair, they weren't *that* bloody. You had to really look if you wanted to see any blood, and the odds were good that if you did find some—you'd assume it was mine.

I'd forgotten to stop by my own room and change clothes. I had a lot on my mind.

I stepped down the curb where Tomás had bled all over the place, unable to tell if the dark swatches there were shadows or stains, and unsure if I cared (if *anybody* cared). The next good rain would wash it off, or else someone from the hotel would get it—probably poor Mr. Rowe, who got roped into just about every odd job that presented itself. Why not blood removal? It couldn't just stay there. It couldn't be a very good advertisement for tourists.

I shook a little sand out of my shoe and went across the street to

Harmony Hall, where I knocked on Dolores Brigham's door and fidgeted nervously until she said, "Come in, Alice."

"It's me," I said belatedly, and stupidly. "I'm here, I mean. Mabel said you wanted a word?"

"Yes, I do. Have a look at this."

I made a noise that sounded perilously close to *eew*, and did my best not to turn up my nose. For there sat Dolores Brigham at her desk, guarded by a fortress of filthy, stinking books assembled around her. Some of the books were blackened and smelling of soot. Many were swollen with damp.

"These came from the rubble of Dr. Floyd's house. They were in her library," she explained before I could ask, like she always does. I still can't decide if it's reassuring or upsetting.

I sat down opposite her. Gingerly, reluctantly, I poked at the nearest waterlogged tome. It squished at the slightest pressure, and the dents created by my fingerprints stayed right where they were. It appeared quite thoroughly destroyed. "Someone managed to pull these out of the rubble?"

"Yes, and don't make that face. They're dirty, but they aren't garbage. Yes, they smell terrible, but there's nothing to be done about that." She pushed one toward me, across her desk. It left a trail of paper peelings and slime. "Look at this one: *The Art and Mystery of Pyrographia*."

"Is that what it says? I can hardly tell."

"Here's another: *Banishment, in Lore and Practice*." She pulled down one more from the seeping pile. "*Send It Away: To Call upon the Saints*."

"Do . . . do we believe in saints?"

"Certainly we believe in people who've manifested extraordinary abilities throughout the ages. If they honed their skills through religion, we are prepared to respect their expertise. Who are we to say which path to grace is correct? How can we even know how many paths exist?"

"I never thought about it that way. What about that one?" I asked, pointing at a very large volume, which Dolores had left open in front of her. The ink had run, but much of it was still readable. There were notes in the margins, but I couldn't make them out; from where I was sitting, they were half washed-out and upside down.

"After having a word with Dr. Floyd's brother, I believe that this is the book she was reading when she was interrupted by the fire. She threw it under the table—in hopes of protecting and preserving it."

She turned it around for me. It left another smear of soggy paper streaks behind itself.

Across the top of the page, the book's title had been printed in very small type. "*The Burning Times: Witches, Women, and Punishment in Fifteenth-Century Europe*," I read. "Mr. Colby said that the dark spirit wanted us to burn. Wait—where *is* Mr. Colby?"

"He's resting in one of the extra rooms upstairs. He's quite old, but the last few days have made him"—she paused—"even older. At any rate, his fire-damaged space is all cleared out now." She shook her head unhappily, and I don't blame her. Her house had almost gone up, too, just like Dr. Floyd's. So much the worse if the founder had been inside.

"I'm afraid for him," I confessed. "I don't know how much longer he can go on like this."

"I'm afraid for him, too. The crossing comes for all of us, in time, but the world will be a darker place when his day arrives."

"Dolores, what are we going to do?" I cringed to hear myself sounding so pitiful, but there it was. "How do we stop the fires?"

"You once told Dr. Floyd that fire is the thread that ties all our troubles together. Fire is only the weapon—it isn't the source of our difficulties." She chose a page that was badly stuck to several others, and carefully, slowly peeled it free. While she worked the fragile sheets apart, she said, "*Three* are the threads, as is so often the case. Fire, and witches, and hammers. Alice, could you remove the bandage, please? George said I should take a look at your arm."

"My arm?"

"Before he went to sleep, he said that your burn is a knot in the thread, and I must pull it loose. Would you mind unwinding your bandage?"

Just thinking about my injury made it hurt again, but I could hardly tell her no. "Sure, just give me a minute. The wrap is filthy, and I need to change it anyway." I picked at the edge of the wrap.

While I worked at the gauze, she kept reading and searching in the tome at hand. "Ah, here's the passage I was looking for." She tapped a large paragraph in the middle, and since it was upside down to her, she told me to read it for myself.

I did. I read it in silence, trying to keep my lips from moving.

*While the pursuit and prosecution of witchcraft were prevalent through the continent off and on for decades, even centuries, the zeal with which the accused were hounded and tried was given a significant boost in 1487—with the publication of* The Malleus Maleficarum *(*The Hammer of Witches, *in English;* Der Hexenhammer, *in German). This treatise was both a paranoid screed and a handbook, detailing the symptoms of witchcraft, the likely perpetrators of witchcraft (who were almost exclusively women), and the best means for eradicating the practice—which involved a goodly number of stakes and matches. Compiled by a Dominican clergyman (Kramer, with additional—and possibly minor— assistance from fellow Dominican Sprenger), this new weapon against the devil spread far and wide, with the advent of the printing press, well beyond the borders of Speyer, Germany, where it first appeared.*

My head jerked up. I'm sure my eyes were as wild as a lunatic's when I blubbered, "The . . . the hammer? Of witches?"

Dolores looked up from the page. "A hammer to be used upon

them. A weapon of God, forged against evil—or that's how Mr. Kramer thought of himself, I'm sure. Wicked men rarely know what villains they truly are, and they even more rarely care. Alice, do you know if Tomás fought anywhere near Speyer?"

"I haven't the faintest idea. But . . . maybe?" I'd stopped unwinding the bandage to stare down at the book. It was calling me, drawing me. Or something was. Maybe it was Dr. Floyd, whose first name was Janice, and I'd only just learned that much after she'd passed.

I reached for the book, and closed my eyes, and laid my hand on the disgusting wet pages.

THE world flashed bright, then dark.

I saw Dr. Floyd holding the book open in her arms. She reached for a pencil to take notes. (I was always told that you shouldn't write in books, but then again, I always thought that was a silly admonition.) She scribbled something in the margin. She heard a noise. She looked up. A hulking, shadowy figure loomed behind her. She saw it in the mirror that hung along the library wall. She opened her mouth to say something, to call its name; she *knew* its name. I could see it on her face. She called its name. I couldn't hear it. I don't know what she called him.

I know he called himself the hammer.

He grabbed her by the throat and lifted her; he pulled her up, he pushed her against the ceiling, and every place he touched began to burn.

DR. Floyd was standing in the library, holding the book, scrawling a note with the pencil.

She looked into the mirror, and the angle was such that she was looking right at me.

* * *

MY eyes jerked open. "She wrote something," I breathed.

"There are some pencil marks, yes, but I'm not sure what they mean."

"She drew a line, and a circle—around those names, Kramer and Sprenger. And there, in the margin she wrote . . ."

*"See appendix,"* Dolores filled in. "But the appendix at the back of the book is nothing but wet pulp."

I traced the ever-so-faint pencil lines with my fingertip, back and forth between the circled words and the margins, to the shadow-light impression of another piece of scrawl. "This bit is very short, just a couple of letters. It's just . . ." I froze.

"Alice? What is it?"

"I know what she wrote, under the bit about seeing the notes."

"How? You can barely see it. I'm not even sure what it says, and I've been examining it with a magnifying glass."

"Well, *I'm* sure," I said, with more certainty than I'd ever felt about anything in my life. The last twists of the fabric bandage came free from my arm, and fresh air hit the burn like a slap. I displayed the gruesome injury and pushed the book around to face her once more, so she could see them both at once. "Look, don't you see? It's as plain as the nose on your face."

Dr. Floyd had written down the initials "H" and "K."

Mr. Kramer, who called himself "the hammer," had written down those same initials, right there on my skin.

Dolores gasped slowly, and through her nose. "Let's not leap to any conclusions—"

"I don't believe in coincidences anymore." I rose from the chair and paced in a circle. I tried not to look at my arm, and I tried to think.

"Alice . . . ," she said, like she was trying to slow me down. She didn't try very hard. She was poring over the book's passage, dragging her finger lightly along the text.

I kept talking, because of course I did. "It was *unprecedented*; that's what Mr. Colby said. The flame projector that Tomás used on the battlefield was unprecedented, and even the dead might take notice. *This man*"—I jabbed a finger down at the book—"this man noticed. He came along for the ride. He came here for us. Tell me, do you know what . . . what . . ." I looked at the book again. "Kramer. What his first name was? I bet you it started with an 'H.'"

"It was Heinrich," she said. His name was barely a whimper. "Heinrich Kramer. If . . ." She stood up and held up her hands. She sounded stronger when she said, "If that's the spirit attached to Tomás—or the spirit who *was* attached to Tomás—then we have a name for this hammer, and we can take some action."

"We can?"

"Names matter, Alice. They mean things. That's why God named Adam, and Adam named the animals. It's all about establishing a hierarchy." She turned around and went rummaging through her own books, a much smaller collection than the one that had burned at Dr. Floyd's house. "I wish that Janice's book on banishments wasn't such a wreck, but there are other resources on the same subject. I'll need to do a little reading . . ."

"David said that Tomás would need *three*, but he didn't say three of what. I guess he meant three things to send the spirit away?"

She paused. "Three is a holy number. It goes all the way back to the Trinity and to the three angels' message of Revelation."

"So . . . three angels, maybe?" I said, thinking it unlikely. "Agatha said something about using salt to bind it, but not for long."

"Angels—or, more likely, three kind spirits . . . but we'd need to amplify their energy. We should scare up some bells, and yes, some salt. We'll give it everything we've got, including his true name, not the one he picked for himself."

My arm hurt. The air was somehow both hot and cold around it, and I couldn't look at it. I didn't want to see those initials. I asked her, "Will it work? Can we send him away?"

"Let's hope so."

"With just . . . spirits and salt and bells? We'd need the Liberty Bell to send off a man this bad."

"We don't *have* the Liberty Bell," she said, almost crossly. "But we have access to three other very large, very loud ones. It can't hurt anything but our ears to try them out. I'll call the fire department and ask them to bring over a truck. There's a bell on the truck and a fire bell in the hotel. We have one here in Harmony Hall, too. Right near the telephone. I'll see if Edella can bring over a big bag of salt. I'll see if both of them can."

"But *which* three spirits do we need? And how do we ask them to come and help us?"

Dolores chose another book, opened it to the end, and scanned the index columns she found there. She chose some other page near the front. "I don't know which three; we'll have to figure that out as we go. They'll be close to us . . . close to one of us." She ran her finger down the text. "If no one shows up, we'll petition the Highest Good. If you can't wrap your head around the idea of that, try praying to the Father, Son, and Holy Ghost. Some people find the comparison helpful."

"What about Spirit?"

"What do you think a Holy Ghost is? We seek the very Highest Good, to the best of our understanding—and we trust Him to honor our intent. Or Her. Or some combination of the two, or neither one. It's impossible to guess the gender of the universe." She was reading while she was talking, doing a half job of both. "Generally speaking, the rest of any solid summoning involves elevating yourself and brightening your own light to confront the darkness."

"How the hell do I do that?"

"Without swearing, for starters. Begin with *love*," she implored me. "Alice, reach for your love for others, for yourself, for the world at large. Listen, I want you to go and get your friend Tomás—and explain this to him, as best you're able on short notice. I'm sure he's resting, and I'm sure he's in pain, but let's get him to the fellowship hall. David kept rambling on about how Tomás would need to send the spirit away, since he's the one who brought it here. That might mean that he's the one who calls the appropriate good spirits, so go rouse him and bring him over. Explain this to him as best you're able. I'll get George up, and I'll grab Oscar, too. Where's Mabel?"

"She's at the hotel, watching Tomás."

"Good idea. I'm glad you were thinking ahead. He was planning to leave us tonight, one way or another."

"I know." I didn't know. (I'd only feared. I'd refused to consider it.) I was only agreeing with her.

Now she was muttering to herself. "We'll need everybody. All the guides, all the speakers, all the people praying."

Perhaps she meant spirit guides, but as for speakers and praying people, that sounded like a crowd. "Will all those folks fit in here?"

"Just *go!*"

I almost fell over myself, running out of her office. I forgot I left the bloody bandage behind, but she could throw it away herself. I forgot to run back to Dr. Holligoss's office for a fresh round of ointment and rags, but I needed to get to Tomás, so I let my ugly arm go naked, and I felt the air stinging on the burn with every step. But I could live with it.

WE had a name. We had the sketchy outlines of a plan.

We had a town to save.

We had *ourselves* to save.

I had Tomás to save. He'd asked me for help, and I was gonna deliver the hell out of it.

* * *

ALL the way to the hotel (which was hardly any way at all, to be honest) I pumped my arms and tried to ignore my burn. It was awfully itchy, but itchy was not the end of the world, I thought. Until I kicked up a little sand and then I was silly enough to scratch it, and then it hurt all over again and my skin was screaming.

But I could ignore that, too. If Tomás could stay upright and moving with a bullet in his shoulder, I could run a hundred yards from Harmony Hall to the Cassadaga Hotel.

I stopped before I made it all the way.

I made it only to the sidewalk.

From there, I could see a weird orange glow behind some windows on the third floor. Not the glow of gaslamps, and not the gleam of candles, but something bigger, slower, and hotter. I could see movement and flow, shadows and brightness.

But it wasn't a fire. It couldn't be. No one was making a sound. No one was screaming and calling for the trucks. Obviously, I was seeing things. Obviously, nothing was wrong. People walked back and forth on the sidewalks, and on the far side of the railroad tracks I heard music coming from Candy's place—where people were probably drinking and playing cards in the back room.

It was a peculiar moment, a quiet moment.

A moment that no one noticed at all, except for me while I stood there, staring up at that beautiful white hotel with its pretty porches and rocking chairs, its potted tropical plants and trays for coffee or tea.

I noticed the sweet smells of night-blooming flowers—of sunflowers closed for the evening, and jasmine, and azaleas, and magnolias, all tangled in the breeze. I noticed the thin white clouds that shuffled back and forth across the sky, broken up with the big, ragged leaves of palm trees swaying back and forth.

I noticed the idle chatter coming and going behind me. It was mostly about the gunshots, and did you hear that a man was nearly murdered, right there on the street in front of the hotel? It was a Mexican man; that's what I heard. From Mexico? Yes. Or some-place like that. Well, he didn't die, though, did he? Not so far as I heard. Is it a bloodstain? That must be it. But he didn't die? I don't think so. I hope he doesn't die. I wish I had a picture. Do you have a camera? No. Yes, but I didn't bring it with me to Florida. Next time I will.

I noticed the current of fear that darted along the lights, electric and gas. I wanted the sun to come back. I wanted the flowers to open.

I did not want to notice a warm orange glow the color of juice spreading on the third floor, but I did. Selfishly, I thought of my trunks in the room with a big brass "14" on the door—but then I thought of Tomás, a few rooms down the hall, and Mabel, next door, and I had a moment where I wondered whether I wasn't being com-pletely ridiculous.

No, it was not ridiculous. That's why I ran inside.

(DOLORES was already calling for a fire truck because we needed a bell. I told myself this, and I tried to take some comfort from it. There was a fire truck on the way, and it was bringing water and trained men with the right equipment to wage war. Not that it would ever be enough.)

MR. Rowe was at the desk. He smiled at me, the clean, professional smile of a man who does this all day, every day, but he is a kind man and I think that most of the time, he probably means it. I don't think he smiles to lie; that's what I'm trying to say.

"Mr. Rowe—something is wrong on the third floor!" I said in one long string as I ran past him and to the wide stairs with the brass rail along the wall. "You must sound the alarm!"

"Miss Dartle?"

"Sound the alarm!" I shouted back, for I was halfway up the first flight by then, taking the stairs two at a time.

"The fire alarm?" he asked in response, but I didn't answer. "Dear Spirit, please, no . . ."

By the second-floor landing my knees and thighs were aching, but I kept going. Heat rises, yes? Fire must rise. I hoped fire rose, because maybe it would just keep going up and take the roof—and then stop there. Could it be that easy? No, surely not.

I kept climbing anyway—as fast as I could, as far as the middle of the stairs on the way to the third floor. That's when the heat hit me. It smacked me in the face, and I started screaming. "Fire! Fire! Everybody out, there's a fire!"

At that moment or a split second later, Mr. Rowe found the fire bell and set it to ringing—and ring it did. It rang like it was calling down the Second Coming, clanging its head off into high heaven. I didn't know if anyone was on the third floor or not, but I knew it wasn't likely to be empty; everyplace in town was full up for another couple of weeks. But then again, it was early in the evening. People might not have turned in. There was a late worship service going on down at the church pavilion, and a sale in the bookstore—which didn't close until nine.

I didn't hear anyone up there. No one answered my summons when I hollered, "Everybody out! Everybody, get out! Keep your heads down and get out! The hotel is on fire!"

Surely if anyone was up there, they felt the heat, and they were way ahead of me—long gone, out the door, and down the stairs at the other end of the hall. I hoped and prayed it, even as I thought that surely they would've sounded the alarm on the way out. If there'd been anyone. If anyone was alive and had escaped.

It was too hot there for me, too much a wall of hot wind with a billowing crown of smoke. I wasn't Tomás, with his brave familiarity and confidence. I was only me, and I had a bad burn on my arm, and it warmed to the fire like they were reaching for each other, and I couldn't stand the thought of it.

So I ducked back down to the second floor, where you could only just smell the smoke—but it was safe to breathe. (Smoke goes up, too. Just like heat. Just like fire, I bet.)

I pounded on the door where Mabel was hiding out, and then I pounded on the door where Tomás had damn well better be safe and sound. He didn't immediately answer, and I thought I had a moment before things got impossibly bad, so I ran to my own room a few doors down. I practically kicked the door open, and I stood there perplexed—for a second or two, at least—unsure of what to save and what to leave. What was important enough to risk life and limb for? What could I sacrifice and leave behind?

I grabbed my purse with my money and my carpetbag with the essentials. These seemed like logical choices. Logic was in short supply, but this was the best I could do. I slung both across my chest, like a pirate loaded up with his blunderbuss, and I went back into the hall.

The first tendrils of smoke were crawling along the ceiling, but I had time. I had room. This was not life-or-death, not yet. It couldn't be. We would only lose the hotel. We wouldn't lose anybody in it. (Not unless there was someone on the third floor. The third floor was lost.)

"Tomás!" I screamed as I freshly pounded on the door. *"Tomás!"*

"Alice?" he mumbled from within.

Oh God, I'd completely forgotten: Dr. Holligoss had given him pills. "Tomás!" I pounded both fists on the door and tried the knob. It wasn't locked. I shoved the door open, but it stopped on the chain, leaving just enough room for Felipe to poke his head out and bark like crazy.

I dropped to a crouch and let him lick my hands. "Tomás!" I shouted over his head, through the crack in the door. "Get up! The hotel is on fire! You have to get out!"

Mabel opened her door with a bang. "Alice!"

"Mabel!" I stood up straight. "The hotel is on fire!"

She was wild-eyed and fuzzy haired. She must've been napping, or I'll give her credit—she accidentally fell asleep while listening to Tomás fall asleep. I'm sure it was as boring as can be. Heaven knows I might've nodded off myself. "We have to get out! *Everyone* has to get out! Help me!"

She didn't reply; she just rallied and started running down the halls, beating on doors, because apparently the persistent clang of the hotel's fire bell wasn't enough to stir everybody. Not everybody had been around for the Calliope fire and Dr. Floyd's fire both, so not everyone understood.

Mabel made them understand.

Tomás was slow to rally, despite the efforts of the bell, the pounding of my fists, and the shouts of Mabel—who was working the hall like she meant to bang it down. "I'm . . . I'm here. I need to get . . . give me a moment, *por favor*."

"You don't *have* a moment!"

Felipe was losing his mind, so I told him—like I expected him to understand me—"Felipe! Go back! Move out of the way!" Tomás clearly wasn't "up and at 'em," like my daddy always used to insist, "boots on the floor, little lady," so it was time to quit making noise and start breaking things. To no one's amazement more than mine, Felipe obeyed—clearing the doorway. "Here goes," I said to myself, or to Felipe, in case he was clairvoyant, too.

(Or maybe I have some kind of animal ken, if that's even a thing. Maybe that's why I knew the horses—they were listening to me and talking to me. And I was listening back.)

I retreated as far as I could. It wasn't very far. The hall was maybe ten feet wide.

I ran forward, my good arm and shoulder in the lead.

I am small, but I am stout. That's what polite people say, instead of fat. They either say that, or they call me "curvaceous" if they want something. The fact is, I am strong. I am close to the ground, because I am not very tall. I have mass, as an old science teacher once told me.

I flung all of my mass at the door. I smashed into it at full speed, or as much speed as I could muster from a ten-foot lead. Something splintered, but it wasn't enough. I'd have to try again.

The smoke was coming lower, lower, and lower. Down from the ceiling, to tousle the top of my head. I had to duck to keep away from it. I didn't have time for many more charges at Tomás's door, but I mounted another one. I backed up again, took a deep breath from the good air that was just below my chin level, and threw myself forward again.

This time the chain broke. Or the wood that the chain was screwed to—that's what broke. The door flew open. Felipe was on the bed, guarding his master and yapping madly. Tomás was not quite awake.

But I was there. I could help.

"Felipe, you have to follow me! You have to stay with me! You understand?" He did not nod, but I had to have some faith in something, somewhere, so I had faith in that little dog. I believed with all my heart that he would stick close to his master, if not to me. If I could move Tomás, I could move Felipe.

I scooped Tomás off the bed despite his protests, and I slung one of his arms over my unburned one. I got him onto his feet. More or less. I got him walking, except for how each foot dragged behind the one before it.

"Tomás, wake *up*. We *have* to get out."

People were running past us down the hall now, coughing and covering their faces. We needed to join them. I looked down at the dog, who would be all right for a while. He was low enough down there on the floor that he had better air than the rest of us did.

"Stay close, little fellow," I told him. Then to Tomás I yelled, "Wake up!" really loud, and right into his ear.

He said, "Ow. No, please don't."

"Then get your feet in gear, and come along!"

"Where's . . . ," he began, the last letter dragging out for a few seconds. "Felllll . . ."

"He's right here. He's with us. Come on, before the hotel comes down around our ears."

"What did the doctor . . . ?" The last letter of that one ran long, too. "Give me . . ."

"Something for the pain, for your shoulder. You need to work through it. You need to get yourself together, Tomás. Do it for me. Do it for Felipe. We have to . . ." I dodged out of the way as a man ran past us to the stairwell. "We must elevate ourselves with love."

"Everyone I love is gone," he informed me with a slur. "Everyone except for you, and him." His head lolled down toward the dog. "If this is love. I hardly know you. I hardly know . . . Felipe. It's . . . different. But it's . . . love . . ."

"Then it'll do—because you're going to need all that love, and all those dead people."

"What . . . ?"

"Three spirits . . . we need three spirits. I'll explain"—I coughed—"later."

I hauled him bodily toward the stairs, Felipe on my heels—expertly navigating everyone's ankles and toes and miraculously not getting stepped upon. Mabel had gone on ahead, ushering everyone out in advance of us and running back in to grab any stragglers—and Mr. Rowe met us near the bottom of the steps. "Is there anyone else?" he asked through a rag held over his mouth and nose.

"Mabel's checking!"

Another bell joined the chime of the hotel bell as the fire truck pulled up to the scene. "Out," he urged. "I'll see to Mabel, and you get *him* to safety."

I nodded and caught Tomás when he slid down the last step to the lobby. It was mostly clear in there. Everything looked fine, except for how there was no one sitting on the chaise by the tearoom, and there was no one in the restaurant, and there was nobody getting coffee for the porch. Everyone was outside, and some of those people had been lucky enough to grab a few belongings before escaping. I had my purse and my carpetbag hanging across my torso and around my neck, and I had Tomás hanging across my shoulder. That was all I could carry.

My muscles strained, but I am strong. I am stout. And Tomás was now upright and a little more alert than before. His feet were working again, but they were working slowly.

"Faster," I urged him.

"There's no fire down here . . ."

I don't think we heard each other. It was hard to hear anything over the bells.

(WE would need one more bell if we were going to do all this in threes. One was left in Harmony Hall; isn't that what Dolores said?)

MABEL and Mr. Rowe came swooping up behind us, encouraging us forward. "The second floor is lost," Mabel said.

Mr. Rowe added, "It's all coming down, sooner rather than later!"

With their help, I got Tomás the rest of the way outside and down the porch—where we could feel the heat from the fires above, and hear them even with the din of the bells. There was a crackling, fizzing sound that ran through the background; there were flickers of spark and ash as the cinders came out from the broken windows and blew out into the night.

Tomás muttered into my neck and along my shoulder, "Not real fire. Not a normal fire. They don't . . . they don't move like this . . ."

The rest of what he mumbled was in Spanish, so I didn't understand it.

"Come along, Tomás. You can do this. We're almost there."

We lured him down the sidewalk and into the street, like we'd taken Dr. Floyd. It was far enough away to be safe, and we were all gasping for air, coughing, needing to rest. All of us, even the people who'd been inside, who now stared openmouthed in horror at the hotel—as it blossomed into something unearthly and bright.

One by one the last windows shattered, and the flaming curtains billowed outward. One by one the rooms collapsed, and the hotel shuddered to its knees. First the south corner, then the north. The other two followed.

The fire truck had arrived, and no one cared, except the people with homes nearby. There was nothing to be done for the hotel, so the firemen concentrated on keeping the rest of the town wet—spraying water on rooftops so the traveling cinders had no place to catch, and soaking down the grass, the porches, and the trees.

Dolores called for everyone's attention, loudly enough to be heard over the confusion. I hadn't realized her voice was so powerful. I'd never heard her speak above an ordinary voice, but when she shouted . . . my God, the whole world heard her.

"Everyone, please—into the bookstore and the fellowship hall. Everyone!" She received a collection of confused stares in return, so she hollered it again and I took up the cause.

"Everyone!" I added my less impressive voice to the mix, and I helped Tomás to his feet. He was holding Felipe again, so it was more awkward this time, but I got him to hand the dog off to Mabel so I could walk him over to the bookstore, up the steps, and inside, where the lights were low, but they weren't on fire. "We will need every last one of you!"

Gradually, people turned away from the burning hotel. Reluctantly, they left it.

Believe me, I understood. The inferno was a spectacle to behold, but there were still plenty of buildings left to burn, and it was time to put a stop to it. *All* of it.

"Tomás?"

He looked at me with dull, tired confusion. "Alice?"

"We're going to fix this. We're going to fix it right now."

He wanted to believe me, but he didn't. Not quite. It was written all over his face. "Now? Are you sure?"

"Absolutely," I lied. "We know what to do. All we have to do now . . . is do it." It came out sounding silly, but I couldn't think of a better way to say it, and he got the gist.

He leaned on me heavily, but he put his own two feet—one in front of the other—all the way into the fellowship hall, where paintings of sunflowers decorated the walls, and Mr. Colby was seated at the front of the room. A cane rested atop his knees. His hands were as spindly as twigs on a winter-dead tree. His hair was as white as the halos of the saints. But he was there, and he was ready.

More ready than the rest of us, thank Spirit.

Somebody had to be.

# TOMÁS CORDERO

## Cassadaga, Florida

THE FELLOWSHIP HALL's lights were turned down low, like usual—or like the last time I'd been there, when Alice read me, and frightened me, and confused me. Now it was not only dark but also very crowded. There was scarcely room to stand, and barely room for the anxious people to pace in small circles or fret back and forth, from foot to foot. They grasped one another and whispered and cried. They prayed, and they called upon their spirit guides and helpers. They'd been staying at the hotel, or they had loved the hotel. As I understand it, the place been the center of the town for decades, and now it is gone. One way or another, that is my fault.

Either no one knew that I was the source of their difficulties, or everyone was too kind to make any accusations. I didn't know most of them. I hardly knew the people I recognized, for I'd been in town only a few short days (though it seemed like a lifetime); but I saw a few faces from the train, and a few from my introductions around town. I was among strangers, but they were not unfriendly strangers. They were only frightened.

I did not see David Fine. The police had taken him away, and I wished they hadn't. He ought to have been there with everyone else. He belonged there more than I did. He certainly understood the danger of my presence better than anyone else. But he was absent and this, too, is my fault.

I reclaimed Felipe from Mabel, who was holding him like a casserole dish fresh from the oven. I'm sure she is a good and loving woman, but heaven bless her—she had no idea what to do with a dog. He cuddled into my good arm, attached to my strong shoulder, which was unpunctured by bullets. I patted him with the other hand, and I whispered to him in Spanish. I think he likes it when I do that. It is probably a simple matter, and the language is more familiar to him than English.

He sighed and buried his head in my shirt.

THIS shirt was one of my own. The last one I owned, for the moment, though thank God or Spirit or whoever that my wallet was in the pocket of my jacket. I could buy more clothes or buy the material to make my own. I distracted myself by thinking of what I would do if my shop in Ybor City had not burned to the ground. What cuts would I use? What would Silvio recommend? I've always appreciated his opinion. What would Emilio . . .

I quit daydreaming.

It would only make me cry, and Felipe needed someone strong. I could not be strong for Cassadaga, but I could be strong for him.

ALICE is strong. She's not very tall, but she's as sturdy as a boulder. She carried me from the hotel or she dragged me, however you choose to look at it. I could not have made the short journey across the street without her. Without her, I would lie in the middle of the hotel's flaming coals and shattered timbers. Without her, I would be lost.

She stood beside me, protective as always, trying to give me breathing room that the crowded space could not easily provide. It was growing quite warm in the hall. The air outside was cool enough, for Florida's winter, but the fire across the street was cooking the whole block, and the frightened press of people clustering together. Their breath, their fear, their whispers. All so warm, and all so close.

Dr. Holligoss appeared and seemed vaguely appalled that I was out of bed—then he swiftly shook his head and was quick to say, "I'm so glad you aren't in the hotel. I remembered the pills I gave you, and I was afraid . . . but I'm glad you made it out."

"Did everyone?" asked a woman behind me.

Mr. Rowe replied, "I believe so, but I cannot say for certain. So many people were at the prayer meeting. So many people were down at the lake."

"How did the fire begin?"

"Where did the fire begin?"

"What will we do? Everything we had was inside . . ."

THROUGH the window we could all see the glow of the hotel—truly an apocalypse, by now—even though we were across the street and on the far side of the building in which we cowered. The light from the enormous fire was brighter than the moon by far, and harsher than the gaslights and lanterns that were scattered throughout the hall.

Behind all of this claustrophobic terror, the bells were ringing.

Such awful bells they were, not Sunday church bells or tinkling wedding bells, but fire bells—metal beating on metal to no tune, no rhythm except the incessant, mind-numbing gong, again and again and again, so hard and so fast, and so loud.

It was strange, then, how we all were able to hear the feeble Mr. Colby when he rose from his chair, leaned on his cane, and declared to the room at large: "Thank you all for being here. We need you all—each and every one. We need elevation and prayers, and we need"—he coughed weakly into the back of his hand—"our community."

Everyone fell silent, except for the bells. Everyone listened, even me. Especially me.

"We have an intruder," said Mr. Colby. "He came uninvited, attached to a visitor who came here seeking assistance. Although this visitor is welcome and blameless, the intruder he carried is a dangerous spirit, bent on our destruction."

Dolores Brigham stepped onto the low stage to stand beside him. Her voice was much stronger, and it carried better past the clanging bells and the hushed, horrified chatter that rolled around the room. "We have reason to believe that he is the revenant of a German cleric, a notorious inquisitor who literally wrote the book on identifying, prosecuting, and punishing witches."

"But how can we know that's right?" I muttered.

"Oh, we're right," Alice muttered back.

"How can you be certain?"

She shuffled through the press of the crowd to face me, then held up her arm for me to see the injury she'd kept hidden thus far. It was a nasty burn, a sprawling thing that went from wrist to elbow, coiling from the underside of her arm to the top. It looked too deliberate to be random.

It looked like . . .

"Because," she hissed. "He signed his name on the mess he's made. He left me the 'H' for 'Heinrich,' or for 'hammer.' That's what he calls himself: the hammer."

It was hard to argue with her, in part because yes—it looked like a signature. And in part because I could not read it and did not know what it said. She was as likely to be correct as she was to be wrong. It was too much to hope, really.

Any hope was too much. I instinctively distrusted it.

Dolores Brigham continued. "This man believed in trials by fire, and he believes he's found a nest of witchcraft. He means to burn this place to the ground, building by building. He means to kill us all if he can."

"He believes that he's doing God's work," Mr. Colby said gently.

ALWAYS so gentle, that one. More gentle than Valero, I think. Even in the face of unfathomable darkness and fiery extinction, he looks for grace. *This* man should be numbered among the saints. What would his symbols be? Who would pray for him?

A pentacle. A cup. A wand.

The accused. The bedeviled. The lost.

MY new friend is not so gentle, but there are saints for that, too. Peter was a notorious brawler. Longinus had his spear. The French girl, Joan, who led an army before she died in the same flames that would take us, too.

Alice would do them proud, I think.

SHE cried out, "No!" and stomped up to the platform, rejecting the forgiving spirit of Mr. Colby. She took her place by his side, where everyone could see her. "No, no, this monster doesn't think he's doing God's will—he's doing his own will, chasing and torturing and killing innocent people, just like he did when he was alive. Maybe he used to hide behind God, and act with a church's authority. But I think he was a maniac. He's even worse now that he's dead, and we shouldn't feel any great sympathy for him. He'll destroy us if we let him."

"But we won't. We won't let him," Dolores said, placing a hand on Alice's shoulder.

"How will we stop him?" asked a young woman—so young I am tempted to call her a girl. She was shivering, hugging herself with a shawl. She had escaped the fire in her nightdress. She was barefoot, and her feet were covered in soot and sand.

"We are going to banish this thing, using the best weapons in our spiritual arsenal. We will call upon the help of three spirits." As Mr. Colby said this, the bell over at Harmony Hall began to ring, joining the other two and raising the din even higher, louder. It was miserable, and I could not imagine how it could help. "And three bells."

Dolores Brigham said, "We *do* have a plan. We *must* not panic."

"We will all sit together," he said. "We will pray, and concentrate, and call upon every good guide we've ever known. We must elevate ourselves with love."

The girl raised her voice again. "Is that how we'll find the three spirits?"

Dolores, Alice, and Mr. Colby looked back and forth at one another, and my stomach sank. It might have been ungenerous of me, and it might've been a ridiculous pessimism on my part—but I knew on the spot that they had no idea how to go about finding these spirits, or any confidence that their efforts would work at all. But I had to be strong for Felipe, who was shaking again. I patted him and wrapped him in my arms, even though my shoulder was as stiff as a rod and scarcely wanted to move.

I was still groggy; that might've been it. There were pills, and they were making me slow and sad, and hopeless.

"Mediums, please gather over here." Dolores indicated one of the long banquet tables. "Clairvoyants, here—and here." There were more clairvoyants than mediums, apparently. "Other assorted talents, over here. Interested devotees who lack higher abilities . . . I want you all to gather and proceed single file to the pavilion."

Protests rattled around the room, but she waved them down.

"We need you at the church for two reasons: One, we need your prayers and your positive energy—every last bit of it. Two, there's nothing at the pavilion to burn. Only the canvas sheets and the columns, and the pews, I suppose. It's the closest thing to a safe place we can offer, and from there, you can lend us your energy. Do we have any meditation guides who are willing to lead?"

Several hands were raised, and with a little negotiating, about half the people in the fellowship hall were able to leave in a quiet, orderly procession. The rest of us could breathe again. Everyone spread out and moved wherever Dolores directed.

I was surprised at how well it had worked. It almost gave me hope.

(But not really. Not quite.)

Now there were three groups, and much more room. I joined the group on the platform stage, where Mr. Colby had returned to his seat. I asked, "How can I help?"

"Join our circle," the old man said. "Sit with us and help us raise energy."

"What about these three spirits?"

"This is how we reach them." Dolores Brigham took my hand and directed me to sit cross-legged on the floor. "By meeting them on their plane, by reaching their level and showing our intentions. This is how we seek their grace."

So while the people at the medium table sought out spirits to guide them, and the clairvoyants at their tables meditated toward solutions, I took Alice's hand with my sore arm and Mr. Colby's hand with the one that didn't hurt. (Felipe climbed into my lap and curled up there.) Dolores closed the circle by taking a seat across from me and clasping the remaining hands of Alice and Mr. Colby.

Around us the bells rang, and the people bargained or conspired with the dead. Beyond the doors of the fellowship hall the hotel burned to the ground, and a hundred people sang songs down by the lake, praying for angels.

"It's something to do with the water," said Dolores to me.

"I beg your pardon?"

"You were wondering about the lake, and why they should pray there. The lake itself is no more sacred than any other body of water, but it does something . . . It"—she hunted for a word—"*amplifies* something, like a phonograph's horn or a radio's antenna."

Mr. Colby added, "We don't know why, or what the mechanism is. Only that it matters. Now. In this circle, Mr. Cordero, *you* are the phonograph's horn, the radio's antenna. You were the focus of this man's attention. He tricked you, and he lured you here. He may hear you more clearly than he hears us."

"Should I . . . call to him?"

"Yes," he said firmly.

At the exact same moment, Alice said, "No."

The old man smiled at her. "If we bring him close, we keep him away from those at the church. If we bring him close and accept the danger ourselves, the spirits may be more likely to hear our calls—for our peril will be the greatest."

"You want to bring him here so we look the most desperate?" she asked incredulously. Her hand was sweaty in mine.

"I want to bring him here because we'll be more focused. We are better prepared to handle him than anyone else."

I strongly doubted it, but here we were. I had no better ideas and no theories to propose.

Dolores looked like she had something to add. Like me, she kept it to herself. "George," she said instead. "Call upon your guide. Everyone, close your eyes and appeal to the Highest Good. Tomás, see if you can find the smoldering man."

"The . . . ?" I began to ask.

"That's what Alice calls him. But his given name is Heinrich Kramer."

"If we're right," Alice was quick to say, somewhat undoing her previous confidence on the subject.

"We *are* right," Mr. Colby assured her. "Now, let your own instincts be your guide. As often as not, these instincts are provoked by higher guides who can communicate no clearer. Listen to them, as you are able. Respond to them, as you feel moved to do so."

I closed my eyes as instructed. I had no idea who was right, who was deluded, and who else was going to burn before the night was out. "Very good, then. I will try."

I did not know what I was doing.

I listened to the bells, the murmurs, the prayers. I felt the sticky salt fingers of Alice clenching my hand on one side, and Mr. Colby holding lightly to the other. With my eyes closed, I heard more—individual conversations, personal entreaties to spirit friends and angel guides. Appeals to saints and calls to heaven. I fancied that I could even hear music rising above the fire bells, rising from the pavilion down by the lake. Sounds and energy and the best of intentions amplified by the water, or by the goodwill that flooded this tiny town full of kind, thoughtful people, who had never tried to send me away—even though they should have, immediately upon my arrival. Even though they knew all along that I was a danger. They never tried to reject me.

Except for David.

David might have been the wisest of them all, if not the kindest. Unless he was only trying to spare the rest—and therein was his kindness, of a roundabout sort. But that's a tangle for another time.

*Heinrich Kramer.* I turned the syllables over in my head and in my mouth.

A solid German name, all hard consonants and sharp vowels. An angry-sounding language, even in romance—that's what I'd learned on the front. Nothing soft or welcoming about it. Nothing soft or welcoming about its landscape of brutal forests with fearsome wolves, or its heavy food, or its messy warfare.

Though I might be biased on that point.

*Heinrich Kramer,* I thought.

The hammer, you've called yourself. The smoldering man, that's what Alice calls you. You've frightened her to the very edge of her wits. You've harmed her. You scrawled your name on her, as if to claim her for your own. But she is not yours, and neither is this town. Neither are these people, who have embraced me in spite of you.

(I spoke to him without opening my eyes, or my lips, either.)

*Heinrich Kramer*, you son of a bitch.

You've burned down my shop, and you've murdered my friends. You destroyed my neighbor's house and left this dog an orphan. I led you here, to a quiet place filled with gentle people. You burned the theater before I even arrived. Now you've taken the hotel, and who knows who might have been left inside it. You won't stop there, though.

I know better than that. God knows better than that.

GOD . . . *knows.*

I heard the words like the creaking of a furnace door opening for a shovelful of coal. They grated together and sizzled. English words, or I heard them in English. Surely Heinrich Kramer must have spoken no Spanish, and I never learned more than a few words of German. So this was our meeting ground, a language that belonged to neither one of us. Neutral territory, of a sort. If there was any such thing.

My eyes were shut tight, glued that way by terror and determination.

I saw him anyway.

He stood impossibly tall, impossibly black, and very featureless, every inch of him—from the swirl of his wild hair to the points of the boots that clomped when he stepped, he was a beastly dark thing that moved like it weighed a thousand pounds. Slow but unstoppable. He was a creature burdened by its own size but strong beyond belief.

He (I must think of him as a man, though he does not look like a man anymore) was walking down a dirt path—no, a dirt road. The road outside the fellowship hall. No, a path through a field.

No, he was walking along a trench.

He wore some tremendous coat or cloak; I couldn't see the details of it, but it flapped around him as he moved. Everything flapped around him—birds, grass, the tangles of razor wire and pikes. Everything shuddered and shimmered as he passed, as if his very existence disturbed the fabric of the universe.

(And it did. Oh God, it *did*.)

He moved with the momentum and straightforward certainty of a locomotive on a track, smoke and fire pouring from his footsteps, filling his wake with ashes. He was moving toward me, staying in the trench, pushing past the men who did not know he was there and never had known, because this man had been dead for hundreds of years before they died, right there, in those trenches. In those fields.

He was coming for me, or coming for the machine.

It was in my hands—my hands, and the hands of seven other men. The thing was a brute, an impossible brute. It could scarcely be managed even with our team of soldiers. It could hardly be aimed, much less controlled.

This dark spirit did not care. It wanted to burn the whole world down, and the Livens projector would suffice to see it done.

GOD . . . *knows* . . .

I gasped and squeezed my hands to feel the other hands inside them. I was not in France, not on the front. I was not in a trench in gear that made me feel like a potato being baked in an oven. I was sitting on a low stage in a fellowship hall filled with wood paneling and praying spiritualists. Not woods. Not trees. Paneling made from trees. There were long tables for meals. Not stretchers for corpses. Not bodies laid out on the ground where they fell. Tables.

No soldiers, just feverish prayers. No dead bodies, just ghosts.

*You join them. You can burn with them.*

LIGHT flared up behind him, casting him in a shadow darker and deeper than the bottom of the earth. Light flared up behind me in the fellowship hall. In the doorway with a bookstore on the other side. I looked over my shoulder, eyes still shut. I saw only *him*, standing at the threshold, staying there. I saw a line at his feet, pure white and glowing—but somehow casting no light on his features.

"Salt," mumbled Dolores. Then she said, *"Oscar,"* in a whisper the man couldn't have possibly heard.

But there was Oscar Fine, rearing up behind the wrathful being. He held a bowl in his hands. (I could see it. I could see everything and nothing, but I could see the bowl full of salt.) I watched the salt fall in a semicircle, trapping the cleric's shade in the doorway— neither in nor out.

In between life and death. Past and present. Hither and yon.

Mr. Colby sighed so hard I thought it must be his last breath, his whole soul escaping all at once. But he said, "We've got him, but the circle won't hold for long. Now we need help. Now we call upon the angels of our better nature. We call upon the guides. We appeal to the Highest Good."

I turned my face back to the circle, my eyes still shut. (They couldn't shut everything out, no matter how hard I tried to make them.) What was this "Highest Good"? Was it God? I didn't really believe in God. Should I appeal to wisdom? What had that ever gotten me? To hope? I no longer believed in that, either. Not as great or useful, much less the very height of anything.

To love?

I should elevate myself with love; that's what I heard—but I've heard a lot of things I don't believe and don't understand, and I've been given a number of directions that I don't know how to follow.

I could appeal to love. I could love, and I could hold it in my heart and send it out to rise with the energy from the hymns at the pavilion and the prayers at the tables behind me.

I heard a whimper from my lap, and I almost disengaged my hands to pet Felipe, whom I so dearly loved, counter to all expectations. But the other hands held mine firmly, so I only whispered down to the dog, "It will be all right, very soon."

I loved Felipe as I had never expected to love anything inhuman.

It was irrational, for he was no child and he could not speak. He could not offer advice or any real contribution to my home or my work. But he contributed to my life. He is a stalwart thing, faithful and clever, and he has taken up a position by my side.

I took that love, for this one preposterous little dog that looked like a rat crossed with a greyhound, and offered it up to whatever great good might hear it, or feel it, or accept it in the spirit I intended. I felt it warm in my chest, and I fed it. I nurtured it. I felt it grow.

A light flared in the circle of hands.

I opened my eyes without meaning to, and the light remained, so purely white that it must have been the light of the saints, the light of heaven. And when I closed my eyes again, I could see it even more clearly. It had the shape of a woman, tall and wide, her hair done up in a bun with a comb. She wore a long skirt and sharp-toed shoes, and a shawl across her shoulders. Her arms were folded beneath her breasts, across her waist.

*I have heard you, and I have come.*

"Who is this?" asked Mr. Colby, as serenely as a monk.

I forced her name past the clog in my throat. "This is Carmella Vasquez."

Felipe saw her, too. He gazed at the light, and I felt the slow thump of his tail wagging against my leg.

"She is the first. Who are the other two?" Alice asked. "We need two more."

The spirit in the doorway roared, and for an instant all the bells went silent. For an instant, all the prayers stopped. After this gasp, everything began again—but when I looked back, I saw that the salt was smudged. Heinrich Kramer was shouting it away.

He howled again and threw himself at the barrier, and the salt slipped further.

The boundary failed a grain at a time.

BUT I could elevate myself with love.

My suit was covered in soot, and I was wearing my night slippers. Everything else was lost, except the wallet in this jacket, which was too warm for the Florida evening—or that must have only been the spirit, for I remembered now: The night was cool. The air was almost brisk when the hotel caught fire and burned. My feet were cold when I stumbled across the grass and across the street.

This second angel, or spirit, or ghost, or whatever it was . . . it was as hot as an oven.

I thought of Cordero's and all the fine cloth stacked up in beautiful bolts. All gone. Even the presses and scissors would have melted. Even the wool could be reduced to ashes. So could we all. So had Emilio, dressed so fine and speaking so smartly, so smoothly, so reassuringly to all my customers.

A second light sparked beside the first and stood next to Mrs. Vasquez.

THIS one was smaller and lean, with slick dark hair brushed back and a suit that cost more to make than he'd earned in a month—but he wore it so beautifully, as he wore everything. His hands were long and slim, and his smile was more than I ever deserved, at any moment, in my whole life.

*I have heard you, and I have come.*

Tears leaked down my face, and I shook my head. "I left you. I left you, and yet you have come here. You have answered me."

*I was already lost, but you saved yourself. I would have saved you if I could. So really, you did exactly what I would've done, and I always do the right thing.* He winked. The spirit *winked.* Of course it did. It was Emilio.

"Who is angel number two?" Dolores asked.

"This is Emilio Casales," I choked. "I already owe him more than I can ever repay. I cannot ask more of him."

"Well, that's love, isn't it?" Alice clamped her hand around mine like a vise. She was crying. I wished to God that I properly loved her, but I hardly knew her. I respected her, and I appreciated her immensely—I would not have survived so long without her. She was beautiful, and she was confident and brilliant and strange. Another week without her, and I would have surely been lost.

In another lifetime, perhaps. In another lifetime, it could be different.

Did these people believe in such things? Other lives, other times, other chances?

In this life, I'd already had such a love. A very different woman, a little older than Alice and leaner, with a narrow face and full lips, and wide eyes. Her hair was the envy of the islands and the glory of heaven. Her smile and her heart had won me in an instant and kept me forever.

"Evelyn . . . ," I breathed her name.

Everyone said that she was not there, that she would not come. The spiritualists had insisted from the start—even my dear Alice had insisted—that Evelyn was gone and that she had never been with me in the first place.

I did not believe it. It did not make any sense to me. Even if she had *not* been the one to crawl through the fires, and leave her hand-prints in the ashes, and gift me with kisses in the soot . . . even if these were only the cruel tricks of a cruel man, long dead and vin-dictive still . . . this did not mean that she had left me alone. If that was true—if it had ever been true, even a single part of it—then I had nothing to live for anyway, and nothing to fear from death.

"*Evelyn . . . ,*" I said again, more urgently.

THE threshold was failing. The salt was scattering.

Wood splintered and the paneling cracked around it, where the thrashing monster flung itself from side to side. I did not know how long the doorway barrier would hold. Not more than another min-ute, surely. I could already see the floorboards through the salt.

In another minute, this spirit would be loose.

In another minute, he would have a roomful of witches to burn. And me, because I'd joined them.

Then what? Then where? The rest of the world, I suppose.

A third light sparked, smaller and brighter than the other two—then it flared, caught, and burned. This light spelled out the shape of a woman, one I knew well. One I had married, in the very dress she was wearing now, or some memory of it—long and ivory, covered in lace, with a veil that belonged to her mother and fell to her shoulders.

She was barefoot and holding flowers, but they weren't the flow-ers from our wedding. They were the sunflowers from the kitchen window, no longer dead and brittle but living and vivid—a shock of golden yellow in the center of the circle.

I gasped and sobbed, and only the small weight of Felipe kept me from leaping to my feet. (That, and Alice. She has a grip like a vise.) *"Evelyn!"*

*I have heard you. I have always heard you. Now I have come.*

HEINRICH Kramer screamed at the sight of them and opened his arms wide enough to shatter the doorframe. It cracked and buckled, and the salt blew into the fellowship hall, scattering into nothing helpful at all.

BUT three bells were chiming, and I thought that the hotel bell *must* have stopped by now—*must* have melted into a painted puddle of molten steel—but somehow I could hear it anyway, as clear as day; and I heard the fire truck bell, and the one at Harmony Hall. They clanged some strange harmony, and if this was the music of the spheres, then I welcomed it.

Three spirits shimmered before us, summoned and elevated to angels.

They rose as one, and they lost their shapes a little—fading back into the loose figures of light as they'd first appeared in the circle. I could not take my eyes off Evelyn, though.

(I knew which one was her. I knew that she'd always been with me.)

They wound themselves up in a circle over our heads, faster and faster until they were a perfect, seamless ribbon of light, spinning as fast as a hurricane. The ribbon was blinding, even with my eyes closed. It was simply pure—too pure for this world. Too pure for these eyes, and I thought that it must've been what Moses felt when he glimpsed the back of God.

We all sat there, hands held in the little mortal circle that held up this greater golden circle, and the wind tore at our hair, but it wasn't wind and we loved the feel of it—we lifted our faces, and I said, from the bottom of my heart, to the golden whirlwind above, *"I love you."*

Heinrich Kramer charged toward us.

The light leaped and caught him. It clutched him and swallowed him. It extinguished him like a campfire.

SOMETHING exploded, and someone screamed, and no one could see anything at all—eyes open or eyes closed. We were all blinded, for all of us had gazed into the sun (no, but something greater, much greater).

Felipe whined and butted me with his head, licking my hand to get my attention. Alice was babbling something, but I couldn't hear very well, either.

When my vision crept back, it accompanied a ringing in my ears much higher pitched than the fire bells, but the fire bells were dying out. The hotel bell was quiet, and the fire truck bell had stopped. Even the bell at Harmony Hall was clanging more slowly, winding down like a clock.

Alice was talking, she was excited and frightened, and she had let go of my hand.

Mr. Colby had let go, too—he was standing with the help of his cane, surveying the room.

There were fifty or sixty of us, many on the ground, many rubbing our eyes or shaking our heads, trying to chase away the sound and shake the sense back into ourselves. The tables were upended. The door was shattered, and half the wall had come down with it.

But in the center of the room, the site of the explosion (or whatever it was), an enormous black stain was burned into the floor. At the center of the stain were three small gifts, left behind.

A dog collar. A silk pocket-handkerchief. A bouquet.

## ALICE DARTLE

Cassadaga, Florida

FEBRUARY 1, 1920

THE HOTEL IS gone, and the great trucks have come to clear away its remains. Men with shovels are dumping load after load into enormous containers, shifting the rubble from here to there, and soon they'll take it away to someplace else. A landfill, I guess. There's certainly no use for any of it now.

Oscar Fine and George Colby already have plans to rebuild. They're talking about selling bonds to raise money—because Cassadaga can't go without a hotel, not for very long. Too many people come to visit for the services and to learn about the faith. We can't house them all in these few scant blocks—not if we turned out every bedroom, porch, and patio. Not if they all brought tents and all camped down by the lakes that are already filling up with the promise of spring's mosquitoes.

The next hotel will not be a wood one—that's what I hear.

An architect from New Jersey said that we should build the next one from stone or stucco. He drew up some loose sketches, saying we should do it in the mission style—since this is Florida. A pretty peach stucco; that's what he recommended.

He also recommended fire doors.

As a safety measure, I'm sure they'll be incorporated. Even though there's no Heinrich Kramer anymore, to hate us all and try to burn us down. Fires happen from other things, too. Electrical problems and lightning, carelessness and accidents. This is a town that loves its candles and leaves them burning.

Stucco it is.

FOR now, everyone gathers at the bookshop and the fellowship hall— where Imogene Cook and Dolores Brigham have pooled their resources to open a little café. There's tea and coffee, and sometimes cookies or sandwiches. Mostly the food comes from Candice Pearson, who wants very badly to show that there's only a set of railroad tracks between her business and theirs. It's not a canyon.

As for me, I've moved into my new room with what few belongings I managed to save. I've bought a few things since the hotel burned, when I went to DeLand for a shopping trip with Imogene. She isn't really that bad. She just says what she thinks, and there's no drawbridge between her brain and her mouth. No canyon there, either.

You get used to it.

David Fine is still in jail, but we're working on it. Tomás still refuses to press any charges against him. He has every right to. No one would think less of him if he did.

But he won't.

THIS morning I went to the fellowship hall to see about breakfast, and I found Tomás there. As he spoke with two men, Felipe snored on his lap.

One of the men was a police officer, and the other was an extraordinarily handsome man about my own age, wearing a small pair of wire-rimmed glasses and the nicest suit I've ever seen. I thought they must be talking about David, and maybe the good-looking fellow was a lawyer.

At first I kept my distance because I didn't want to interfere, but then Tomás called me over and said it was all right. He wanted me to meet his friend.

He introduced me to the officer, whose name I forget, and to Silvio Casales, whose name I will always remember. (Lord, what Momma wouldn't do if I brought a Spanish man home and called him mine.)

"There was a fire at Mr. Cordero's shop," the policeman said. "And then Mr. Cordero . . . he disappeared. We had some concerns, but then the fire marshal discovered the corroded gas pipes. The lines were a hazard in the walls, and no one knew until it was too late."

"The place simply . . . Well. It was as if someone threw a stick of dynamite in the window," said Silvio in an accent that made me want to melt. It was just like Tomás's, so I don't know why it made me giddy. It's not like I'd never heard it before. "My brother was inside," he added. "He lost his life in the fire."

Oh. That took the edge off my giddiness. "That's terrible—I'm so sorry to hear that." I looked at Tomás like he might explain.

He did, but only a little. "I was inside, too. I escaped without being harmed too badly, but I hit my head and I was very confused. I went home and left a note for Silvio, and I came here. I scarcely remember the preparation or the journey. It is all a blur." Something about the way he said it . . . I didn't believe it at all, but the look on his face said that it was important that either Silvio or the policeman (or maybe both of them) needed to believe it. "Then I came here, and you saved me."

I blushed to the roots of my hair and the tips of my toes. "You saved us in return, if I recall correctly." But then I thought we'd better not explain all that in front of these friendly outsiders. Not all at once. It'd be an awful lot to take in.

Tomás gave me a discreet wink to show that we were thinking the same thing. Then he said, "You're being too modest. You've been such a help to me—I couldn't have . . . have found my way without you."

"I'm so glad I could help, you have no idea. It's all I've ever wanted to do, and when you first arrived"—I put on my most earnest face for the policeman—"you were so very addled, and I was so very worried."

Silvio sighed. "It's a miracle you arrived at all! Much less in one piece, and with Felipe in tow. I feared that you'd lost your senses!"

"War strain," said the officer, with a tone that said he knew all about it. "Prompted by the fire and the explosion, I should think. My own brother came back with a hard case of it. Sometimes he gets confused, too. And sometimes he wanders off. Eventually we had to put him someplace . . ." He cleared his throat. "Just for a few weeks, until he could get his head together. And it looks as if you've found yourself again. A trip to Cassadaga was all you required, so count your blessings, I say."

"I count them daily. Hourly, even, and high among them is this good man here—for Silvio has been taking care of my affairs in my absence. It was not fair of me to ask it of him, and I regret having left him behind. But I . . ." He turned to me. "Alice, you know better than anyone: I did not know what to do."

Silvio scoffed. "Bah. It was nothing, a trifle! Someone had to take care of the insurance men, and I know your books better than anyone. The house only needed a man to lock the doors and mail the mortgage to the bank. I'm just so impossibly glad to find you here, and to know that you've been safe."

I snorted, then immediately went as pink as a strawberry cake. "Oh, excuse me. I'm sorry. Yes, Tomás has been quite safe. This is a quiet, peaceful little community. Positively dull. Not a bit of danger to be found."

"It's a tad . . . odd . . . ," said the policeman. "But everyone seems very nice."

"That's Cassadaga in a nutshell!" I said cheerfully. Too cheerfully. I laughed because I couldn't stop myself, and that only made me even pinker.

On this note, the officer excused himself, saying that he'd gotten everything he came for and wishing us all a good day. Tomás invited me to take the empty seat he'd left behind. I dropped my bottom into it so fast that he didn't have time to finish the offer.

"What will you do now?" I asked him. "Will you go back to Ybor City or stay here?"

"Silvio and I have been discussing that. I am not sure what the future holds, but there is a bit of insurance money from my shop."

"Fire insurance," Silvio clarified. "The fire department loves him. He makes them the most wonderful suits."

"I made a suit for one of them. One man's father, to be precise."

"It was the *right* man. The payout is swift, and it's enough to re-build . . . if that's what you want to do," he said to Tomás, with a gaze that was one part adoring child and one part concerned parent.

"I came here to speak with Evelyn, and I have done so." He fiddled with his cup of coffee, swirling the contents to stir them. "Whether you believe me or not," he added to Silvio. He already knew that *I* believed him. "She and I were interrupted, you know. She died while I was away at war. We . . . we had such plans. There might be some chance that we . . . that we could talk again."

I was torn.

I wanted to tell him that it wasn't likely. She'd done what we'd asked of her: She'd given us light, and love, and help. Now she was really and truly gone—passed to the other side, for good, or that's what my heart believed. But I'd been wrong before, now, hadn't I? And the heart is deceitful above all things; I know that much is true. The Methodists taught me that in Sunday school.

I also wanted to tell him that Evelyn might wish for him to move on. After all, he was still young. There was still time for him to find another wife and even start a family. He was handsome and kind. Since she truly loved him—and I *know* that she did—she might suggest it.

He might not want to hear it. He might ignore that message, even if he did receive it from her.

Or you never know. He might not.

SILVIO smiled, and it lit up the room. Or just me. Who cares? He's stunning, even with the cute little glasses, and I can appreciate a stunning man. He might like a soft woman, and he might like books.

Or you never know. He might not.

But no, I bet he does.

I tried to keep from grinning. I gave up on that, just like I'd given up on blushing.

SILVIO was still graciously, lovingly trying to steer Tomás back into some semblance of normal life, and I adored him for it.

"But the insurance money will not last forever. You *should* rebuild before it runs out, and then we're both out of luck. You could even rebuild here, if you like it so much—and if you want a fresh start. I could help you . . . ," he said, a long, lingering hint in his tone. "There is much to recommend the place, and I have no other family to keep me in Ybor. I could use a fresh start, too, I think."

"But here?" Tomás asked.

"Why not? Look around you. So many visitors, passing through each season . . . visitors who probably have not considered the weather, and plan to stay for weeks at a time. They will wish they had not brought so much winter wool. They will need new clothes. They will not want to find a car to take them to the nearest town with the shops they need."

"Best of all, they have money," I said to bolster the case. "Some of them have quite a lot. They come a thousand miles and stay for ages. It isn't a cheap trip. You could perform a valuable service to the community!"

"I . . . Well, I could think about it. I would not wish to do it alone, and I cannot ask Silvio to pick up his home and move here. He has no more family, but he has a house—"

"Which I rent."

"And a girlfriend."

"Not for weeks."

"Really?"

They lapsed into Spanish, and I didn't follow it. I'd already caught the most important part: He did not have a girlfriend. The naked finger on his left hand said he had not traded her in for a wife. This was excellent news.

Then they switched back to English, and Tomás laughed. "I am sorry. I was only surprised. I will think about it, all right? Will that make you both happy?"

Silvio said, "For as long as you are thinking about it, unless you decide to leave. I really *do* hope you'll decide to stay here." He did not take his eyes off me.

Tomás noticed and smiled. "Very well, then. For the two of you, I will consider it."

"For the two of us?" Silvio asked, his forehead attractively furrowed.

"Yes, for the two of you. And for Felipe, who seems to like it here." He waved one hand, like there was a much bigger picture we were missing. "I'll think about it, and I'll probably do it, for the only good reason on earth."

"And what's that?" Silvio asked.

Tomás stroked the back of the sleeping dog's head. I know he was thinking of Evelyn, but I hope a tiny part of him was thinking of Silvio and me when he said, "My old friend, I will do it for *love*."

# ACKNOWLEDGMENTS

I've said before (and will no doubt say again) that I hate writing acknowledgments because I'm always afraid I'm going to leave somebody out. The usual suspects always get first billing: my editor, Anne Sowards, for taking a chance on this weird little love story; my wonder agent, Jennifer Jackson, for all the heavy lifting; my husband, Aric Annear, for listening to me whine a whole lot.

Also, in particular for this book, I have to thank my cousin Jacqueline Chamberlain, the hostess with the mostess! Thanks a million to her for putting up with me for a research trip to Cassadaga, where we took the tours, followed the walking trails, and kicked around in the bookshop buying all sorts of fun (and useful) things. I very much appreciated her company and hospitality.

Likewise, many thanks to the kind folks at Cassadaga, who were patient and lovely at every turn. Thank you for the readings, the conversation, and the willingness to share the history and lore of this marvelous little community.

I hope I've done it justice.

## ABOUT THE AUTHOR

**Cherie Priest** is the author of more than a dozen novels, including the award-winning Clockwork Century series (*Boneshaker, Dreadnought, Clementine*), the Cheshire Red books (*Bloodshot, Hellbent*), and the Borden Dispatches (*Maplecroft, Chapelwood*).

### CONNECT ONLINE

cheriepriest.com
facebook.com/cmpriest
twitter.com/cmpriest

## ALSO BY CHERIE PRIEST

### THE BORDEN DISPATCHES

*Maplecroft*

*Chapelwood*